THE PRICE OF SAFETY

MICHAEL C. BLAND

This is a work of fiction. Names, characters, places, and incidents are products of the author's imagination or are used fictitiously and are not to be construed as real. Any resemblance to actual events, locations, organizations, or persons, living or dead, is entirely coincidental.

World Castle Publishing, LLC
Pensacola, Florida
Copyright © Michael C. Bland 2019
Hardback ISBN: 9781950890798
Paperback ISBN: 9781950890804
eBook ISBN: 9781950890811
First Edition World Castle Publishing, LLC, April 6, 2020
http://www.worldcastlepublishing.com

DEDICATION

To Mom. This would've been your favorite.

Chapter One

Igniting a miniature sun was the riskiest thing we'd ever attempted, yet we were doing it in front of the entire planet.

While Nikolai bragged about our innovations to the cameras, reporters, and two hundred VIPs assembled, I stood sixty feet away, facing the control panel of our unlit sustained-fusion reactor, searching for any indication our creation would explode. The seven-foot-long, concave control panel displayed the time remaining until ignition. Forty-five seconds.

I didn't use the control panel to conduct my search. Instead, I projected our schematics and stress tolerance estimates onto the lenses in my eyes, the data hovering before me like a clear computer screen stretched across my vision. Hidden from everyone.

"...each pod contains the highest concentration of dark matter ever collected," said Nikolai, the CEO of our company, who'd been my friend once. "Eighteen months' worth of space harvesting efforts."

We'd designed not only the pods but the entire ten-acre complex: the energy grid, the fifty-yard-wide containment chamber where we'd try to light the "sun" that would power our reactor, the domed observation room with celestial images on the ceiling and a massive window that revealed the chamber, and Nikolai's temporary stage in front of the window. We'd also devised the safety protocols, power regulators, and energy-capture systems. The biggest risk was the medicine-ball-sized metal core we hoped to ignite. A single flaw could doom everyone here.

If we succeeded, though, our reactor would provide mankind with cheap, reliable energy—and us a spot in the history books. Nikolai would become richer than ever, with countries begging for our reactor. I'd see my creation come to life, which would tangibly better mankind, fulfilling a promise I'd made.

My personal cell phone buzzed in my pocket, a number I didn't recognize flashing in the corner of my augmented sight. I ignored the call and reluctantly stopped my search as the countdown neared zero. Years of planning, of calculations and simulations and more money than I cared to contemplate, came down to this moment.

Beside me, Amarjit, my bushy-eyebrowed director of robotics, took a deep breath as I activated the reactor. Four titanium-geared positioning robots, each twenty feet tall, stepped forward in unison inside the solar-cell-lined, circular containment chamber, and lifted the dark matter containment pods to precise spots around the core. Reinforced metal rods moved two additional pods into position, one rod descending from the ceiling and the other rising from the floor.

"Dark matter is the key to our efforts," Nikolai continued, his sharp chin pointing at the crowd. He wore his graying hair short, his thin frame coated in a pale suit. He also wore his datarings, which was odd, as my team and I were handling the sequence. "This unique substance causes regular matter to draw on itself. The resulting compression, which will occur at the molecular level throughout the core, is what we're confident will create the fusion spark."

The robots locked their joints into place.

I hadn't wanted anyone here but was outvoted by our board, my simulations used against me. But the simulations were distorted with assumptions. I wasn't sure the core had the right mix of elements, wasn't sure about the pressure needed. Wasn't sure about a lot of it.

I took a breath myself — aware of the lives at risk, the stakeholders and VIPs and broadcasting cameras — and powered up the dark matter.

The robots' hands and the two cradles glowed as they released energy into the pods, activating the matter. Combined reverse-gravitational pressure enveloped the core to five hundred million newtons per square meter, squeezing it from all sides.

There was supposed to be light, the purest imaginable, maybe preceded by a flash.

But nothing happened.

Our readouts measured the core's compression, but showed nothing that indicated an ignition: no fusing of molecular fuels, no sign of liquefaction.

As anxiety crawled up my spine, I increased pressure, but nothing changed other than rising stress levels in the robots' joints. I maxed the energy to the pods, compressing the core to pressure levels found under the Earth's crust.

Amarjit shot me a look, his caterpillar-sized eyebrows squeezing together.

I knew the danger.

The pods were made of aluminum, the only metal that could contain energized dark matter without interfering with its reverse-gravitational force. But the dark matter became more volatile the more we assaulted it with energy, and the pods had limits to what they could hold. With the forces we were manipulating, it felt like depending on a balloon to contain a shotgun blast. If one ruptured, our entire complex would be decimated, along with a portion of Los Angeles. The city south and west of here should be protected from the blast by the mountainside we'd carved into, but maybe not. The amount of destruction would depend on the energy levels when everything went to shit.

The readouts on my lenses flashed red. We'd reached our thresholds, yet the core remained unchanged.

My personal cell phone buzzed again, the same unknown number.

Ignoring the call, I told Amarjit, "We're aborting." I touched the control panel to kill the power to the pods, but the system didn't respond. "What the hell?"

I waved Nikolai over, but he wasn't looking at me; he faced the chamber instead, his determined expression one I'd seen countless times. His hands hung at his sides, but his fingers were moving, entering commands. His silver datarings flashed as he typed on his legs, the rings registering his fingers' movements as keystrokes — tracking where each finger moved as if he was typing on a keyboard — and sending his commands to his neural net, which I realized was now the only access point to the fusion reactor.

Behind him, the crowd became restless.

"Boss," Amarjit said.

I followed his gaze. Inside the chamber, the robots extended their arms, moving the dark matter closer to the core. First two inches. Then four. Then six.

"I'm not doing it," he said.

"It's Nikolai." I slapped at the digitally-projected controls, but they didn't react. "He fucking cut us off."

WARNING flashed red in my vision as alarms sounded.

7

The faceplate of one of the robots buckled from the reverse-gravitational forces emanating from its pod. The knee joint of another started to twist.

"Dray," Amarjit said.

"I see it." My hands skittered across the control panel as I tried to reboot the system but failed, my brow damp with sweat.

A strained sound reverberated inside the chamber, followed by a pop, and a crack stretched across the curved window before us. The air surrounding the robots shimmered like asphalt on a summer day.

I brought up the master settings to search for a power override. "Can you take command of the robots remotely?"

"No," he said as he jabbed at the panel. "They can only be controlled from here."

Robot Number Two—with the twisted knee—contorted further as the pressure from the dark matter mounted, sparks flying from its wrists. None of our simulations had covered this, but I knew what would happen. A few more degrees and its joint would shatter. It'd be thrown against the wall, the pod ripped open. We'd be obliterated in the explosion.

I needed to cut Nikolai's signal.

The control panel rested on a bioplastic-enclosed base connected to a hollow metal railing. The dataring receiver had to be in the base. I hadn't included one in the panel's design, but it would've been easy for him to add. I wondered what else the self-serving bastard had done.

"You bring any tools?" I asked Amarjit, who shook his head. "Get everyone out of here."

"There's no time."

He was right. "Then save yourself. Go."

As he hurried away, I squatted below the panel, took my metal ID badge from around my neck, jammed it into the cover's seam, and tore away the bioplastic to expose the motherboards, quantum cubes, and fiberwires that connected to the panel. I spotted the receiver immediately, an inch-long, fan-shaped device, and ripped it out, severing Nikolai's connection.

I stood and hit the sequence to reestablish a link to the robots.

As systems came online, I wondered why the core hadn't sparked. The reaction sequence should've initiated, especially with so much pressure. That's when I noticed the liquefaction gauge. A section of tritium had liquified but was stunted, limited to the second quadrant. Closest to Robot Number Two.

Where the pressure was angled.

I'd approached this wrong. I'd directed pressure uniformly around the core.

Regaining control, I linked with the robots to pull them back, but first shifted Robot Number Three—the least-damaged one—to the right, angling the pressure from its pod—

The core ignited.

Throughout the tritium veins that threaded the core, protons added to atoms in a domino effect, the veins turning into contained plasma, and brilliant light burst forth, painting the chamber. No explosion threatened us, no pressure, unlike the destructive effect of nuclear fission. Instead, warmth from the molten metal reached me through the glass, the chain reaction spreading over the core's surface to begin consuming the denser, solid metals that would feed it for the next twenty years.

The warnings in my lenses, thrown in stark relief by the star we'd created, turned green as I pulled the robots back to reduce the pressure to acceptable levels, though one regarding the robots' structural integrity remained red.

The chamber's window tinted, returning our vision to us.

Nikolai threw up his arms to the crowd. "As promised, nuclear fusion! The first of many Gen Omega plants we'll build across the country to address America's energy needs."

Applause washed over us.

"Bastard," I murmured, shaking with adrenaline.

I reduced the dark matter's energy to the minimum amount needed to keep our newborn sun suspended in position, while Amarjit, who'd rushed back to help, ran diagnostics on his robots, two of which no longer stood straight.

A phone number flashed on my lenses, the same one as before. This time it was calling my work cell. Possibly one of my employees. "Dray here."

"Dad, I need help," my nineteen-year-old daughter said.

I was caught off-guard, not only because it was Raven's voice, but because of the fear in it. I'd never heard her so afraid.

Concerned, I moved away from Amarjit. "What happened?"

"You've got to come."

"Are you hurt?"

"Not me. It's...." Someone else. Trever Hoyt, her boyfriend, who Raven had gone out with tonight. He was a decent kid, though opinionated and a little snobbish. I had hoped she wouldn't get serious with him, but they'd dated for almost a year. "Do you remember the time in New Trabuco when I hit that rock? It's worse than that."

She meant there was a lot of blood. His blood, presumably. "You need to call the po—"

"I would, except it's me."

I didn't understand, then did. She'd caused the bleeding.

I started to ask if they'd been in an accident, but she was being cagey for a reason. Normally talkative and bright, she was avoiding saying certain words, aware that spiders patrolled the airwaves.

Watching what she said. Trever bleeding. The way she was acting, it could only mean one thing: she'd done something illegal, as hard as it was to believe.

Though I was still sweating, I felt a chill. No one got away with a crime. Not in 2047.

The people around me, the media and VIPs and shining fusion core, Nikolai waving at me to join him on stage as he said my name and proclaimed this was the start of "more wonders to come." None of it mattered now.

I squeezed my finger-thin phone. "Where are you?"

"His parents' place. Their work. There's a spot we made where you can get in. I'm in a small building just past a maintenance road."

My concern increased. She meant Trever's parents' facility. I'd never been there and didn't know what they did, but I'd heard visitors required a security clearance due to the sensitive nature of government contracts the Hoyts had. It was a place she never should've been.

"On my way."

* * *

I exited the 605 at Beverly and raced through Whittier, passing countless neighborhoods, most of which were dark this time of night. I closed my data streams to reduce my digital trail, and tried to avoid the surveillance that existed even in this sleepy part of Los Angeles, the cameras and traffic scanners and microphones that monitored most of the country. I wanted to take side streets to further reduce my history, but needed to get to Raven. She wasn't the type to ask for help. Strong and resourceful, she helped others, cared about the neglected and abused — otters, immigrants, the homeless — and debated fiercely, but never with a mean spirit. She would become a force as an adult — though with the way she'd sounded, I worried for her future.

My thoughts flickered to my son Adem, who'd died before he learned to talk. Even with how safe I'd helped make our world, I couldn't protect him. Couldn't save him. I feared I wouldn't be able to save Raven, either.

I passed the guarded entrance to Hoyt Enterprises and followed the fortified, ten-foot-high wall for blocks until I located Trever's red-and-black McLaren. I tried to tamp down my fear as I parked my Chrysler E-650 sedan beside the metal wall. I had to be levelheaded and calm, though I didn't feel either.

Spotting the hole Trever and Raven had created, two of the vertical panels pried apart, I went to it. I'd maintained my weight over the years, but I'd always been thick. As a result, I had to squeeze my way through the gap.

Multi-story buildings occupied most of the compound's interior — production, office, warehouse — though they stood back from the wall, the structures dark, the only light in the complex coming from the entrance far to my left. Closer to me, one-story storage structures stretched in long rows, the nearest five yards away. Straight ahead was an empty space followed by an asphalt road and a cluster of residence-type buildings barely visible in the darkness. To my right, a flat-topped building sat on top of an unlit hill adjacent to the facility. The property was fenced, and the two parcels shared a wall.

I started toward the residence-type buildings, sticking close to the nearest storage structure, followed the structure to the far end, and found a security camera staring at me. I froze, but my image had already been captured.

My apprehension growing, I continued forward and crossed the road.

The buildings were old, possibly the property's original development. Three could have been homes, another a garage, a fifth some kind of lab. I hesitated, unsure which one she might be in, heard a sound to my left, and cautiously proceeded toward the residence in that direction.

"Raven?"

She appeared in the shadowed doorway, pulled me inside, and hugged me, trembling.

"What are you doing here?" I asked.

"It was Trever's idea. Dad, he attacked me. He tried to rape me."

I stepped back.

She was an attractive young woman, my wife Mina's mostly-Mediterranean genes and my mutt DNA combining to give her tanned skin, jade eyes, and a smile I'd known would be trouble. But as my eyes adjusted to the darkness, I saw the swelling in her face, her bloody lip. Her shirt was torn.

A primal rage began to grow. "Did he...?"

"No." Her composure, thin as it was, cracked. "I didn't mean to hurt him."

Her words tempered my anger and fear, though not by much. "Whatever you did was self-defense. You were justified. The police will see the truth."

"I can't."

"They'll listen."

She grabbed my arm. "His implant. I ripped it out."

His neural net, the implanted technology that linked our brains to the web, work, and every other digital source. Federal law required that every citizen have one, and tampering with them was punishable by death, regardless of the circumstances. There had been complaints about the law's extremity, even demonstrations, but nothing had changed, and most people didn't care, too enamored with the access their implants granted.

My lips felt numb. "Is he alive?"

"I don't think so."

She led me to the next room, where Trever lay in a pool of blood, his body contorted, his implant nearby.

I'd never seen an implant outside of a person's head. The part that was usually visible, the silver-dollar-sized reflective end, stuck out no more than a quarter-inch from a person's temple. However, the entire implant was over an inch and a half long, with two curved leads that jutted deeper into the brain: one about two inches long and the other about five inches.

"He grabbed me and tore at my clothes," she said. "I tried to crawl away, but when he grabbed me, I kicked him as hard as I could, and he rolled off. That's when I saw the pipe."

She indicated a rusted drainage pipe, one end curled back where it had broken off.

I squatted beside it, careful not to touch it. "You hit him with this?"

She nodded.

"How many times?"

"Just once. When I swung, the pipe caught the edge of his implant. I didn't mean to."

Trever wasn't the first corpse I'd seen, but he was the first born of violence, which made me unsettled. His right temple was caved in where his implant had been. The metal ring that had secured his implant in place was missing, along with a chunk of his skull. Raven's years of playing softball had saved her from a heinous act — but at a terrible price.

A fierce protectiveness rose inside me, joining my fear. The police would be methodical. I had to anticipate what they'd find.

The building we were in was being renovated. The floor had been reduced to a concrete slab and the walls gutted, with spools of wire stacked in a corner and construction supplies strewn about. A nearby wall had blood splattered in an arc.

Nothing contradicted her story, though doubt nagged at me. "Ripping out his implant was a fluke," I told her. "It was self-defense. A jury won't convict you."

"He didn't rape me. I stopped him. If people could've seen his face, how he lunged at me, what he said, they would understand, but there aren't cameras in here. No one will believe me."

A prosecutor could claim her injuries were self-inflicted. Say she'd torn her own clothes. Without hard evidence, she was in danger.

She didn't have to add that Trever's parents were politically well-connected. Mina frequently interacted with them as chief of staff for the mayor of Los Angeles. Jesus, Mina. She was going to be horrified.

"What do we do?" Raven asked.

"I don't know. Who knows how many cameras I passed getting here, not to mention the GPS in my car?"

When I left the reactor, I'd shielded my face from the cameras I knew about, but dozens of others had probably nailed me, including the one inside the facility. Hell, our phone call could be used against us.

My work cell had a built-in scrambler, so the cops would only get one side of our conversation, but with the other evidence, it'd be enough.

She didn't plead, didn't back away. "I'll turn myself in."

I started for her, careful not to step on Trever's implant, but paused. The implant.

If she hadn't ripped it out, hadn't killed him, I would've wanted her to confess to the police. But if she did, she would pay the ultimate price.

She couldn't just leave. Not only had she been caught on camera, she was leaving DNA: blood, hair, dead skin. I was, too.

We had to do this a different way and hope it worked, because I couldn't lose her. She and her sister were my world.

"I have an idea. You're not going to like it," I told her. "I've heard rumors about people stealing implants. Cops don't want to admit it happens, because it's one of the only crimes they struggle to solve."

"Why would people steal...? Oh. To become someone else."

I nodded. "Each has a unique code cops can use to identify us if they get a warrant. A criminal who wants to hide from authorities can't unless they obtain a new code, which means a new implant — one that's been stolen, wiped, and recoded."

"You want to blame Trever's death on implant thieves."

"To do that, I'll have to take yours."

Her eyes grew big. *"What?"*

"If yours isn't stolen, the authorities won't believe you." I held out my hands. "I'll take it out straight, minimal damage. You can tell the police you two were here hiding out or whatever when men jumped you. Trever tried to defend you, but they overwhelmed him and ripped out his implant. They were easier on you, as you didn't fight, using the same pipe — "

"The same pipe? Dad, I don't want to die." She looked panicked.

I took her in my arms. "You won't. I promise. Tell the cops the men were masked and didn't say anything."

When I let go, she wiped her cheeks. "How do the police find me?"

"As soon as I take your implant, I'll call 911."

She paled further, eyes darting, but nodded.

I had her lay near Trever, yet far enough away that she didn't touch his blood.

"I'm scared," she said.

I wasn't a father. I was a monster for suggesting this. But I had to keep her safe.

I touched her cheek. "I'll make it as clean as possible. With the right amount of force, it'll pop out." I had the strength. I'd manhandled the robots we'd used in the reactor. "This is the only way."

As she rolled onto her side, I picked up the pipe. I placed my hand on her head, my calloused fingers nearly palming it. "I love you."

I gently slid the hooked lip of the pipe under the edge of her implant, wincing when the pipe touched her skin. After seeing Trever's neural net, I knew Raven's had been implanted straight into her skull. If I pulled up, like removing a nail, it'd minimize the damage. I didn't want to do this, and would probably never forgive myself, but it needed to look like a criminal stole her neural net.

I had an image of her in prison garb, curled on a metal cot. Another of her strapped to a gurney, getting a lethal injection.

I couldn't let that happen, whatever the cost.

I held her in place with my free hand and pulled on the pipe, at first gently and then as hard as I could. For the briefest of moments, the ring held — she screamed — then gave way with a wet sound. The implant tumbled to the ground as I fell back, the pipe nearly flying from my hand.

She started to shake and gasp. Sparks flickered in her eyes, and blood welled up in the hole I'd opened in the side of her head.

A panic unlike anything I'd ever felt seized me.

What had I done?

CHAPTER TWO

I grabbed Raven's shoulder as she twitched on the concrete floor and called her name, my panic constricting my throat, but she didn't respond. Not only had her implant come out, the ring holding it in place had as well. Blood trickled down her face, thin and glistening.

I hadn't expected this, had thought the removal would be clean with nothing more than a drop or two of blood. I'd injured her, caused who knew what kind of damage to my daughter, who meant the world to me.

Fighting my emotions, I pulled out my phone. I'd planned to step outside and wait a minute before calling to add a time buffer for when the police recreated the scene. But she was dying.

The call connected.

At first, I couldn't speak—whether due to my panic or hesitation about the timing, I didn't know. The dispatch's questions grew urgent. They'd trace the number, send someone. It's what they did, which was why it had been wrong not to put my faith in them.

Raven stopped jerking, which laced my panic with terror.

"My daughter's been attacked," I forced out. "She's bleeding. Please hurry."

"Where are you?" the woman asked.

"Hoyt Enterprises. Crash the gate if you have to."

"What's your name, sir?"

I dropped the phone and stood.

Raven's implant rested a few feet away, gleaming in the faint light. I needed to hide hers and Trever's before the cops came. First, I needed to break them. They emitted unique ID codes I had to stop.

I picked hers up—it was still warm. My fingertips tingled as I plucked Trever's implant from its bloody spot, aware I'd just tampered with a crime scene, and went outside.

I searched for a weapon in the moonlight but came up empty. I hurried back inside, grabbed the rusty pipe—not letting myself look at her—dashed back out, and lined the implants together on the hard-packed earth, breathing hard.

She couldn't die. She couldn't.

I gripped the pipe with both hands and brought it down.

Clang.

Sirens wailed in the distance. If I was caught, Raven and I would be executed. My vision grew blurry as I tried again.

Clang.

The sirens grew, and lights from police cruisers reflected off the hills in the distance.

Rage blasted through me. The implants were keeping me from her. I wanted to throw them into the darkness, but the cops would comb every inch of this place.

I lifted the pipe and brought it down as hard as I could.

Crack.

Discarding the pipe, I split the broken casings the rest of the way to reveal their federally-classified secrets: a sub-terahertz transmitter, what looked like two kinds of memory sticks—which surprised me—a cube processor, and a bio battery. There wasn't a GPS transmitter, which I'd wondered about in another lifetime when my daughter wasn't horribly wounded, though people could be tracked in other ways.

I forced my fingers into the cluster of wires, separated the leads to the tiny, perpetual battery, and yanked them out, killing the signal. A yank with the other implant finished the job.

The sirens were loud now. The police were at the gate.

I didn't want to touch the remains more than I already had. They were fashioned out of rare metals, a couple of which hadn't been discovered until thirty years ago. Scanners could pick up one or two parts per billion.

Other than my wallet, phones, and ID badge, my pockets were empty.

Not knowing what else to do, I removed one of my shoes and pulled off my sock, scooped the implant remains into it, and tied the end. Then I stood, jammed my sockless foot into my shoe, and ran for the perimeter wall, dashing across the road and between two of the

17

long storage structures to avoid the camera I knew about. Spotting the gap in the wall, as the ambient light was marginally brighter on this side, I angled toward it and shoved my way through.

Flashing red and blue light painted the street.

I froze.

A cop car shot past.

As the noise from the vehicle faded, I caught the buzz of drones approaching.

I ran to my car, which unlocked as I neared, shoved my sock underneath the front seat, and slammed the door. Cringing from the sound, I locked the car and ran back to the wall, hoping I'd find the gap immediately —

The complex turned bright as day. They'd turned on every light inside.

Security lights outside the complex also turned on, one bulb after another, the string increasing in speed toward me.

I scrambled toward Trever's hole, which was backlit from the new illumination, and ducked through moments before the spotlights nearest me turned on, but was revealed by the harsh light inside the complex.

I kicked up scrub grass as I ran back to Raven, racing between two of the storage structures. When I reached the end, I dashed into the road as an ambulance approached, the emergency vehicle following the curve in the road toward me. In seconds, the paramedics would spot me.

Without slowing, I dove toward the closest building, the small lab, and just made it before the ambulance's headlights painted the area. I ran to the end of the lab, raced past the garage, and ran toward Raven's building, nearing as tires slid and doors opened. Two paramedics exited the ambulance. Further back, a police car approached, lights flashing.

Drones settled overhead. I didn't know if they filmed my return, what direction they came from.

"She's over here," I yelled, pointing to the building to my left.

They must have heard my desperation, for they followed me inside.

Curled on her side, Raven's limbs were off kilter, as if she'd tried to curl into the fetal position but failed, one hand twisted away from her, her skin chalky.

Seeing her so injured and unresponsive was like a physical blow.

The paramedics dropped beside her, checked her injuries, and grabbed devices from their bags, but all I saw was her. Blood streaked her face in disjointed lines like retinal images of lightning bolts, the hole in her head black in the faint light.

The two men covered her hole with a medicated disc — proof she wasn't the first with this kind of injury, a detail my brain desperately grabbed onto — and rolled her onto a hand-held stretcher. I stepped forward to help lift her, but a monitor bracelet they'd attached to her wrist began to beep. The medics scrambled; one started chest compressions while the other placed a bag valve mask over her face. My heart clenched as I watched, my skilled hands useless.

A cop spoke beside me. "What happened here?"

My story seemed pointless at the moment. Still, I pushed out, "I found her like this."

The medics lifted her. They must've gotten her heart started again. The bracelet had quieted.

I followed them outside, vaguely aware of the cop following, asking my name, the facility's bright lights casting harsh shadows everywhere.

The medics laid her in the ambulance.

I climbed in, ignoring the cop's questions, and sat as the medics closed the doors, one administering to her while the other drove. I felt conflicted about the second medic driving instead of helping her, but he drove faster than any auto system would've dared.

His partner hooked Raven to more machines and inserted an IV line. According to a monitor, her heartrate was inconsistent, her blood pressure in the 60/40 range and dropping.

I shouldn't have left, should've answered the policeman's questions, but I couldn't leave Raven's side.

After we arrived at the Whittier Medical Center, I followed the medics as they wheeled her into the hospital and past the waiting area, where footage of my fusion reactor turned their wallscreens white when the core ignited.

Multiple hospital cameras watched us, cataloging us, as the medics steered her into an orange-tinged trauma room where a team of four nurses waited. The nurses rushed into action after the medics moved Raven to the hospital bed, throwing out phrases like "V-fib", "use the quantal array", and "push 10 cc's of epi-thono". The computer system heard the instructions and loaded the requested medicine into a syringe-gun via an attached tube, which one of the nurses administered to Raven.

The door opened, and a thin woman with blue scrubs and blonde hair entered. Most people were genetic mutts nowadays. Not her. She looked Norwegian — slender neck, almost translucent skin. She forced her way through the group to take a position by Raven's head. A doctor — no, a surgeon. I hoped she was the best one on the planet. I didn't want to distract her — though I wanted to plead with her to save my daughter — or get in the way, so I pressed against the wall near the doors.

A pear-shaped nurse with spiked hair approached. "Please follow me. We'll talk outside."

"I'm not leaving."

"Sir, it's policy."

"I don't care."

The surgeon spoke up. "He's fine so long as he doesn't interfere." Her eyes were commanding, a lighter shade of blue than her scrubs. She shifted her focus back to Raven and turned on the internal-organ hologram, which hovered above Raven's body like a dying ghost.

The nurse frowned. "Your name?"

A monitoring device of some kind hung on the wall behind her. I suspected they hung in every room of the hospital.

I hesitated, not wanting to create a trail but unable to avoid it. "Dray Quintero."

"Address and date of birth?" When I gave both, she nodded. "I've accessed your information. Same insurance?"

"Yes."

"You have the credit rating. Do you accept fiscal responsibility for your daughter's treatment?" After I consented by staring at an agreement-of-service prompt that appeared on my lenses, she eyed me. "You're one of the founders of that big science company."

I nodded, though notoriety wasn't what I wanted, especially right now.

The surgeon expanded the three-dimensional hologram to focus on Raven's head and torso. "There's damage to the patient's heart, lungs, and central nervous system," she announced. "Her skull is cracked in three places, with multiple bone fragments."

My work phone buzzed in my pocket. Nikolai. I'd kept my hands hidden, but when I pulled out my phone to turn it off, the nurse looked down at my palms, which were marred with rust and dirt. I jammed my hands in my pockets and ignored the call.

Alarms beeped. "There's cranial bleeding," an older nurse said. I saw it on the hologram: I'd torn the sack that protected Raven's brain. Blood was mixing with the sack's fluid.

Fear gripped me.

"We need an O.R.," the surgeon said. "Now."

* * *

What seemed like seconds later but was more like an hour, I gazed down from the upper-level observation room as they operated on Raven. I should've called Mina—she'd texted four times, once to congratulate me and three asking where I was—but couldn't face her. This would resurface memories of Adem, not that either of us could forget him.

There was also the political side of this nightmare. With Trever's parents' connections, every politician in the state would hound the police to find his killer. Mina would need all the rest she could get to deal with the coming fallout—and I needed to face what I'd done to our daughter.

The O.R.'s hologram was more detailed, the resolution so high I would've appreciated its clarity if the view wasn't of the damage I'd inflicted. The surgeon expanded the image to such a degree the cracks in Raven's skull stretched across the room, a floating topography of broken chasms.

I watched, my hands clenched, as the surgeon extracted the last of the blood from Raven's cranial fluid—the edges of Raven's skin clamped to the hole in her temple—then sewed the tear in the brain sack. Once the surgeon finished, there was a discussion about setting a new ring into place.

I looked for an intercom. I didn't care about the ring or anything except Raven's survival. There was no intercom, though, so when the surgeon held out her hand for the new ring, I pounded on the glass. She looked up but, even though her eyes were compassionate, set the new ring, using the hologram as a guide to secure it to the unbroken portions of Raven's skull.

After she finished, she began to mend the major cracks in Raven's skull. Ninety minutes had passed now, maybe more, I didn't know for sure —

Machines began to beep.

"She's arresting," the surgeon said. "Charge to two hundred."

The head nurse primed a charging station while one of her subordinates filled a syringe. Another nurse turned off the hologram, probably to give the surgeon a clear view but granting me the same horrible gift.

The head nurse handed paddles to the surgeon. With a whap, the charge jerked Raven's torso, but the beeping continued.

I pressed my fists against the glass.

"Charge again."

The anesthesiologist looked up at me, pressed a button, and the glass darkened to block my view.

Alone for the first time since the paramedics arrived at Hoyt Enterprises, I covered my face as the anguish I'd suppressed overwhelmed me.

* * *

It was only hours earlier that everything had been normal. More than normal, in fact, as our family had been together.

Mina had wanted to throw a dinner to celebrate my reactor. It was premature, but it was the first desire she'd expressed to me in months, so there was no way I would've refused.

I was checking out the table she'd prepared — candles burning, the fifth place-setting in memory of the son we'd lost — when Raven arrived. "You made it," I said, hugging her. Since starting at UCLA last year, I hadn't seen her as often as I'd liked.

"I wouldn't have missed this."

Talia, my twelve-year-old daughter, came up, which earned a hug from Raven as well.

As Talia fought to escape, Mina set a plate of flank steak on the table to join the chimichurri sauce, rice pilaf, and real corn she'd made. "Perfect timing."

When we toasted to my hoped-for success, she paused before drinking, her glass hovering beside the empty place-setting. I'd come to resent that setting, as it symbolized more than Adem's passing to me; it symbolized the happiness Mina and I had lost.

I saw Raven notice Mina's pause. In what I suspected was an effort to keep the mood upbeat, she said, "You've gotta be excited, Dad. Lots of articles say your reactor is the next step in energy."

"This is more important," I said. "My family, all together."

Talia waved her hand. "Shmaltzy. Let's talk specs."

"Eat," Mina told her, not unkindly.

Talia lifted her fork. "Can I go to the lighting? No one will know I'm there."

"As if," Raven said with a smile.

"I can help," Talia told me, her auburn eyes wide. "I've scoped your designs. You made the reactor core out of deuterium, tritium, and a lotta other 'ums'."

"How...?" I started. Only three people on the planet knew the core's makeup. "Did you hack into our servers?"

"You never wanna gab about secret stuff."

I knew she was good, but the security I'd built was quantum-based. Unbreachable.

Raven appeared amused and Mina displeased. "You keep hacking, you'll end up in jail," Raven told her.

"If I do, you'll Greenpeace me."

"You'll *hope* I Greenpeace you."

"You'll probably be too busy slobbering with Trever," Talia said with an eyeroll.

"How are things going with him?" Mina asked Raven, lighting up at Trever's name.

Raven got a gleam in her eye I didn't recognize. "Fine. He and I are going out tonight."

"You are?"

I shared Mina's confusion. Instead of her usual college attire, Raven was dressed like she was going hiking, with a dark shirt and tan shorts.

"We're going indoor rock climbing," Raven said. She lifted her fists, her golden-brown hair glinting in the candlelight. "Don't worry. You raised me tough."

* * *

The memory gutted me, the observation room's blacked-out glass hiding her fate.

The pear-shaped nurse appeared to collect me. "The next few hours will be crucial. If she hangs on, she'll have a chance."

I had no concept of time, not how long I'd been in that room or how long we walked through monitored corridor after monitored corridor.

The nurse ushered me to Intensive Care, where Raven had been placed.

My daughter didn't look tough. She looked broken. Tubes and tape covered her, a web of life-support I'd cast her into. Her chest rose and fell, but that was the only movement. A thick, cottonlike substance hid the upper half of her head. I had the strange urge to touch it.

Two nurses checked their instruments and made notations via their datarings. From their gazes, I knew real-time data was projected above Raven's bed. I couldn't see any of it, as I wasn't part of the staff. The information I could see — heartrate, blood pressure, and temperature — was for my benefit, shown on an old-style monitor hung on the wall. All appeared stable, albeit low.

Besides the bed and monitor, the room contained a recliner, chair, and tiny bathroom. The only window was imbedded in the door.

One of the nurses spoke to me. "You should get some sleep."

I was too wrecked by what I'd done. I moved the chair as close to Raven's bed as possible to watch over her.

The nurses left, others came back, and Raven breathed.

Family first. It's what guided me. But I'd done this, forcing my elder daughter to fight for her life.

Society had accepted the implants and cameras — embraced them, in fact. The implants granted us a competitive edge, while our comprehensive, multi-layered surveillance protected us. Yet the laws that had given rise to both had forced me to harm the one who'd changed me. When Mina gave birth to Raven, and later Talia, I discovered meaning to my life. Purpose. And Raven had grown into a clever, big-hearted, vexing young woman who reminded me of myself.

If the police figured out her crime, they would execute her.

I remembered the day she'd alluded to in her call.

We'd lived in New Trabuco Canyon, the driveways angled sharply down on either side of the narrow gorge. They were too steep for anyone to bike down, especially a seven-year-old. Yet Raven did that day, until the angle stole her ability to control her bike. Careening down our driveway, she hit a rock, sailed over her handlebars, landed on the concrete, and slid almost to the street.

I ran after her, nearly tripping in my rush.

A car zipped past her as she stood, the car seemingly inches from her, but she didn't flinch, though I did when I saw the blood bathing her chin, neck, and shirt. Nor did she cry — not then, not when the E.R. doctor stitched up her chin, his gentle banter falling on deaf ears. I was proud of her strength even as Mina and I chastised her that night, telling her our rules were to keep her safe.

I stayed beside her bed that night, stroking her hair well after she fell asleep, until it was my turn to feed Talia, who was four months old at the time.

I'd wondered if Raven had done it for attention. Or maybe her adventurousness had already manifested.

When I left for work the next morning, I caught movement through the opened garage door. It was Raven, leaning over her handlebars as she flew down the driveway again. She stayed upright this time, down the driveway, across the street, and up the neighbor's driveway. When she turned her bike around, she saw me and smiled. She'd wedged a strip of padding I'd set aside for one of my projects between her chin and the strap of her helmet to protect her stitches.

My exasperated pride hitched as she leaned forward to come back. I threw out my hands to stop her — but she didn't.

From my chair in the ICU, the scar under her jaw was visible, though faint after so many years.

She gave a tremor as if remembering that day as well.

I reached for her hand but noticed my own, marred by rust, dirt, and bits of dried blood, which I'd been too distracted to wash.

I'd hurt her more than anyone she'd ever met.

I was disturbed when she received her first implant. It was the law, but still, three months was too young. I felt the same way when Talia received hers. Seeing Raven get her youth net replaced by the adult version when she turned sixteen wasn't any easier. I was torn between satisfaction of the wonders she could access and the sense she'd been marked.

The door opened, and I hid my hands.

Raven's surgeon entered the room. She carried a tray with four prefilled syringes; two contained liquid that shimmered, while the other two held a milky-white substance. A shortrange medical transmitter sat nestled between the two iridescent-material syringes.

As the door closed, she set the tray beside the bed. "Mr. Quintero,

I'm Dr. Nystrom."

"Doctor, please, how is she?"

She gazed above the bed, though I suspected she'd had Raven's vitals streaming to her lenses since the surgery. "It's sooner than I would like, but I need to take the next step." She began to uncap the syringes' needles.

I stood. "I don't like the sound of that."

"I'm going to inject nanobots to the damaged area. They'll not only heal her skull, they'll strengthen the bio-cement I used to secure her new implant ring to her frontal and temporal bones. The nanobots will create a lattice that'll be strong enough to handle the same pressure as the rest of her skull. It'll protect her as her bone grows back. She'll heal faster."

"Why is it sooner than you'd like?"

Her enthusiasm faded. "I'd prefer her vitals were better. But the nanites will adhere to any bone fragments I missed and pull them from her bloodstream. They'll also dissolve blood clots that might break free."

She seemed to be holding back. "What's the risk?"

"We don't know what kind of condition she'll be in when she wakes." If she wakes, she didn't add. "Not only was her skull damaged, so was her dura mater—the sack that surrounds her brain. Since our neural nets are first implanted at three months, they don't penetrate the dura mater except for two leads that run from the implant to behind each eye socket. And because the neural nets are installed when we're so young, our brain develops around them, as does the dura mater.

"When your daughter's net was stolen, her attacker tore that sack, which allowed blood to seep into her brain. I extracted the blood and repaired the damage, but these nanobots will continue her healing."

"What aren't you telling me?"

She picked up one of the syringes as if to delay her answer. "If she codes again, and we have to shock her heart, the nanobots will be affected."

They'd be fried. They'd float free, becoming as dangerous as loose blood clots. "Don't."

"Having a neural net is the law. Besides, she'll want a new one as soon as possible."

"Not if she's braindead."

"Please, you need to understand, Mr. Quintero—her attackers stole a part of her. Everything she's stored is gone: passwords and texts, pictures and videos she's downloaded, the multitude of settings that oversee the gateway to her digital world. It'll take her a long time to recover, even if she wakes up with a new net already implanted. She's not even going to have that, not for a week or two. The sooner I start this, the sooner she'll feel normal.

"The next few hours will be key," Nystrom added. "Every minute her heart beats without help, her chances improve."

I sat, overwhelmed by the enormity of my actions.

"The surgery went well," she said. "Her skull is holding up, and I replaced both lenses, which shorted out when her implant was stolen. She's lucky to be alive. Few survive this type of attack."

I rubbed my head. Unbidden, the image of the two implants smashed open flashed in my mind.

The doc said something else, but I didn't catch it.

I glanced away to refocus and noticed a man in a pinstriped suit, tailored but out of style, at the nurse's station. His dark hair was short, his features faintly Asian. From my experiences as a youth, I identified him: a detective. Waiting for me. Or both of us.

He probably already knew. Hell, I only wore one sock. That right there warranted scrutiny.

Nystrom explained what she was doing as she cut away the bandages and injected the nanobots into Raven's bloodstream, then the milky, liquid-carbon material the 'bots would use to strengthen Raven's skull.

I couldn't concentrate on the surgeon's words, though. I had no idea what to do about the detective.

My face must've shown my fear, for Nystrom tried to distract me. "Raven. That's a pretty name."

"It was my mom's middle name. She thought we were American Indian, but we're not."

"She must've adored Raven."

"She died before she was born. Yesling's Disease." It was a respiratory illness that had become prevalent the last few years, claiming thousands, adding to the deaths caused by the viruses that periodically swept the globe. "Doctors told me living in the Central Valley was why she got it. I think it was the opposite. I think this city killed her."

"I'm sorry." Nystrom continued to work. "What about her other grandparents?"

"She never met my father's side." I hadn't, either. Or him.

She applied new bandages. "You OK? You keep glancing at the door."

"The man out there, at the nurses' station...."

"The detective? I though the nurses told you. He wants to talk to you about Raven's assault. Go ahead. My team and I are monitoring her condition."

I'd learned to trust the police when I was a teen, but now I wanted to avoid them.

"Could you enforce some sort of hospital policy? Tell him to come back later?" I asked.

Her expression turned cold.

"They'll be desperate to find who did this," I said. "So I am, but I'm too focused on Raven to be any help."

The surgeon picked up her tray of empty syringes and went to the door. I couldn't read her, our bonding nothing but memory. She was part of the network—a witness, a strand of society's web—that was now against me.

CHAPTER THREE

A shadow passed Raven's door.

I tensed every time someone neared. The detective was going to enter any second, question me, maybe arrest me. I couldn't stop him. The door didn't lock.

I'd switched to the other side of Raven's bed so I wouldn't be visible, as if by moving out of sight, he'd forget about me. Foolish, but it was all I could do.

There were other people scattered about the hallway, including a guy in a green barn jacket with a baseball cap that hid his face, but none would stop the detective. I suspected the only reason he hadn't come in yet was out of respect for Raven's condition, though that wouldn't last.

I would've gone to him and held out my wrists if it would reverse what I had done to her.

I'd always believed in law enforcement. If I hadn't met Nikolai freshmen year at UC-Berkeley, I might've joined the force. Yet the moment Raven committed a crime, I chose a path I'd promised to avoid.

One of her monitors beeped twice. I straightened, fearing the monitor's alarm would sound. If her heart stopped again, the staff would risk destroying her to save her.

Seconds slipped by, but the monitor remained silent.

The door opened behind me.

"Dray," Mina said, entering the room with Talia.

Their outfits confirmed they'd been ready to leave for work and school when I texted. Mina wore a charcoal-grey power suit and her jade pendant necklace, an expensive impulse purchase she'd justified by virtually visiting the orphans who'd made it. Talia wore yellow shorts and a "Betcha" T-shirt, her hair in a ponytail. She hugged me like an afterthought, then squeezed tight before approaching Raven's bed.

29

I saw the fear in Mina's brown eyes. "Why didn't you call sooner?" She kept her tone neutral, though I knew better. Hospital rooms evoked painful memories for both of us.

"She's alive, that's what matters."

She fingered her pendant as if it were a cross. "What have the police told you?"

The detective was still out there, talking to the pear-shaped nurse.

I glanced to see if Talia was listening. She leaned against her sister and took a selfie with her phone, which looked like a four-inch, coated wire with nobs on either end. "You better not post that."

"It's just blackmail," Talia said.

"If she finds out—"

"I won't blat. Least, not 'til she's home."

Mina touched my arm. "The police? Your text said she was attacked."

Trying to speak low enough so only she could hear, our bodies almost making contact, I told her what happened, starting with Raven's call.

When I finished, she pulled away. She had to know there was no other choice.

"Don't say anything. To anyone," she said. Her eyes darted to Raven and lingered there, as if memorizing her face.

"That'll make me a suspect."

Talia stared at the monitors, one hand on Raven's leg.

"I'll ask Mayor Gein for help," Mina said.

I shook my head. "We can't tell anyone."

"I'm not saying he can make this go away, but he can give us some guidance."

"He could turn us in."

She dropped her gaze, working through the angles. It'd be risky to confide in him. Then I remembered the doctor. I hesitated to tell Mina, who lifted her eyes and scanned my face as if memorizing it, too.

"I have to try," she said.

* * *

I woke up at a weird angle, my head lying on an expanse of white.

I'd fallen asleep by Raven's side, my head on her bed, my body succumbing after being awake for who knew how many hours straight. I blinked to clear my vision and found Talia in the recliner, more than likely checking out her favorite websites—or hacking the hospital's system. No one else was here, but the detective stood in the hallway; he had the look of a man who was readying himself to break the rules.

"There was a big-o fight earlier," Talia said. "Stiff in the suit and the blonde doc. He wanted in, but she said it'd 'endanger' Raven. Would it?"

Maybe the surgeon had helped after all. Raven's condition hadn't changed from what I could tell.

"Where's your mom?"

"Went to snaggle food. Do I have to school it tomorrow? It's too late to expect it."

I checked the time. 9:18 p.m. I'd been at the hospital almost twenty-four hours.

The longer I avoided the detective, the guiltier I looked. They would investigate the Hoyt grounds, including my car—if they hadn't already, a thought that shot fear through my spine. I needed to distract the man, needed to dump the evidence and rehearse Raven's story with her. It was our only chance to avoid arrest.

But first I needed to know she was OK.

Mina entered with a sack of In-N-Out. She still wore the same outfit. "Any change?"

"Not that I can tell."

Talia grabbed the sack. "Vitals are better, and the lattice is mostly done. I wasn't sure what a 'lattice' was, so the doc described it. So wicked." She unwrapped a cheeseburger and took a bite.

Mina joined me by Raven's bed. "I met with Gein and his attorney," she said in a low voice. "It wasn't easy getting their buy-in without giving any details."

"And?"

"We need to see how bad it is before we can respond."

"That's all they said?" I asked in frustration as Talia ate noisily.

"I pushed as far as I could. Trever's parents are demanding the death penalty. We have to be ready for the worst."

I hoped her mouth would quirk with one of her sarcastic observations, but it didn't. She didn't.

The charge nurse came in. "Good news. We're going to move Raven to a regular room."

Talia spoke before I could. "She hasn't woken up yet."

"She's getting better," the nurse said as she unhooked Raven from the monitor. "The nanobots have completed their task. The lattice in her frontal lobe has been completed, and her vitals are much stronger."

"Are those robots gonna stay in her?"

"No. Now that they're done, they'll travel to her kidneys so she can pass them naturally."

Talia smiled. "Gross."

Dr. Nystrom came in. She stopped beside me and spoke quietly. "We kept Raven too long. The fact she's still here, even though she's no longer critical, has drawn attention—as has your refusal to leave." Looking at the monitor instead of me, she continued in a normal voice. "Her swelling is down, which is a good sign, although it's too early to tell whether she's suffered any long-term damage. Once she wakes, we'll send her home."

I wanted to object, but couldn't with Talia and the nurse there.

"If you'll step outside, we need to detach her from the machines before we move her," the nurse said.

"I have to wash my hands," I said. I'd washed them a half-dozen times already, but they didn't feel clean.

When I stepped out of the bathroom, the detective was waiting for me. "Mr. Quintero, I'm Detective Sanchen. We need to talk." He held a scanning device of some kind, which looked like a flattened ice cream scoop with a readout on the handle.

"Sir, if you could give us a few minutes," Nystrom said.

"Your patient's being moved, so your rules no longer apply. I was respectful by not getting a warrant, but if you delay me any further, it'll be obstruction."

I'd pushed it too far. The man looked anxious. I nodded to the surgeon. "Thanks for your help."

She handed me her card. "I'd like to be the one who implants her neural net."

Sanchen stepped between us. "Now."

My mouth was dry as we left Raven's room. Mina and Talia, who stood near the nurses' station, gave me quizzical looks, but I shook my head to keep them from coming over. Everyone else seemed oblivious, except for the barn jacket guy, who wasn't looking at me, his face obscured by his cap, yet he seemed tense. I wanted to run but followed the detective into an empty patient room.

32

As he lifted the scooped device, I heard a muffled beeping. A light in his eyes flashed in time with the sound. He shifted his focus, and the alarm silenced. For a moment he looked lost, then he grabbed my arm and pulled me toward the door.

CHAPTER FOUR

Hours later, I sat in an interrogation room deep in the precinct's police station, the room lined with recording devices of every kind.

The detective had taken my phones and warned me not to access my implant. He'd also searched for an audial system, an optional upgrade to neural nets that consisted of speakers surgically placed in the ears and a microphone under the jaw that took the place of cell phones and headphones. I didn't have one—nor did Mina or the girls, to the girls' disappointment—as I didn't like the idea of having an imbedded microphone that could be tapped into by any government employee with the right clearance, laws and Washington spokespeople's assurances notwithstanding. Besides, if the girls had them, I'd never know if they were listening to me.

I didn't think Sanchen knew Mina had already contacted me.

It was when I was in the backseat of his car, not cuffed but feeling like it.

Where are you? she'd texted, the words appearing before me.

With as little movement as possible, I slipped my datarings onto my middle fingers. *Taken for questioning,* I typed on my thighs.

Where? By who?

Sanchen. L.A. County detective. This was risky, as anything we texted was admissible.

The detective drove into the lot of a drab, blocky building.

Norwalk facility, I added before disabling all communications and removing my datarings. Norwalk was a separate city from Los Angeles, so Mina's pull would be minimal.

Sanchen didn't tell me they'd proven my crime—didn't tell me anything. But the longer I stared at myself in the tinted mirror that covered the far wall of the interrogation room, the more I knew. Forensics would prove my guilt, or a camera I hadn't noticed. Or they'd found the implants in my car.

I tried to control my breathing. People were watching me from behind the mirror. I was a concerned father, I told myself. Nothing more.

I wasn't sure how long I waited for Sanchen, but it felt like days. When he finally entered, I expected him to demand I confess. I feared I would.

He sat down, his movements startlingly loud. "Why did you avoid me at the hospital?" He wanted to make me defensive.

"I was focused on Raven," I said. "She's in bad shape."

"You left the scene of a crime."

"I left with my daughter — who's the victim here."

"The crime committed against her and Trever Hoyt is akin to treason, yet you left the scene and avoided me." He paused to see if I rose to his bait, then continued. "Your actions are concerning, as you may have vital information that could've enabled us to catch their attackers quickly. You saw me at the hospital, yet you hid in your daughter's room."

"I wasn't hiding. She was fighting for her life. I lost one child years ago. I can't lose another."

He searched my face. After a moment, he said in a less-hostile tone, "Describe the events of the other night."

I dropped my gaze. Ever since I was fourteen, cops had been my guardians. Heroes. Now I had to lie to them. "I got a call from Raven. She told me she was at her boyfriend's parents' facility and someone was after them. She told me how to find her, so I did. When I got there, she was on the ground." I curled my fists as I remembered her shaking, sparks flickering in her eyes.

"What about Trever?"

"He was...." I found myself hesitating. "Not moving. There was a lot of blood."

"Why were they there?"

"Wanted time alone, I guess."

"They both live on campus. If they wanted time alone, they could've kicked out a roommate. Or Trever could've paid for a hotel room." An entire hotel, he didn't have to add.

"I don't know."

"That's not a believable answer."

35

"It's the truth."

"Why didn't you call 911 sooner?"

"I didn't know what happened until I got there." I almost added I was a big fan of the police, but it would've added to my hypocrisy.

"Why didn't she call us?"

I shrugged.

"Tell me something you do know: where were you when she called?"

"The Gen Omega fusion reactor."

I suspected Sanchen's team had found the implants, and he was waiting for me to perjure myself. He had to have noticed my missing sock.

"What did you say, exactly, when she called?"

"I asked where she was," I started, then stopped. "I don't remember every word. I haven't gotten much sleep."

In the ensuing silence, the mirror loomed large. Whoever was on the other side could monitor my temperature, heartrate, M-wave readings, Tach levels, and other biometrics. I'd watched a show that detailed some of the tech they used; it had been a reality show, as crime dramas weren't broadcast anymore.

"What did Raven say they were doing that night?"

"Why are you focusing on them? She and Trever are innocent."

"Because they were up to something. The facility's cameras were disabled from the perimeter where they broke in all the way across the compound. Whatever they were up to was premeditated."

I was relieved they didn't have me on video—especially hiding the implants—but the detective was right. This wasn't a date gone wrong. "That had to be Trever. He must've been involved in something he shouldn't have been. Whatever it was, Raven suffered for it."

"What was the incident with a rock she referred to?"

The police had her side of our phone call, and might succeed in decoding mine, given enough time. "When she was young, she was riding bikes with a friend when a man tried to kidnap them. They swerved to get away, but Raven hit a rock and fell. Her friend stopped to help her but was grabbed. Raven hid in the forest until I got there." It was a horrible story, and a boldfaced lie, one they could pin on me if they unscrambled my half of the call.

"Why was she so cryptic on the phone?"

"She was being cautious. Things can be misconstrued."

"What things?"

I remembered my breathing. I was probably lighting up their gauges. "I've told you what I know."

His frown deepened. "Raven and Trever were pretty far inside the facility. How did their attackers know where they were?"

"Once my daughter gets better, I'm sure she'll tell you."

"This isn't your first time in a police station, is it, Mr. Quintero?"

"No, it isn't. When I was a teenager, my mother's boyfriend beat her. She couldn't protect herself, so I did."

"You broke the law."

"Look, I respect cops. They helped me back then. One even dated my mom for a couple of years."

Sanchen stared at me, then stood and began to pace.

A bead of sweat crept from my hairline, but I resisted wiping it off. He was probably communicating with whoever was behind the mirror. He could be reading the notes from my case, checking the recording of Raven's call. Hell, my bio-readouts could be scrolling across his vision.

I tried not to squirm. Or look at my hands. No matter how hard I'd scrubbed, I still felt the rust.

The detective stilled. "What were you doing *outside* the building when the ambulance arrived at Hoyt Enterprises?"

"I was looking for them," I said, aware my actions were suspicious. "I didn't want the paramedics wasting time trying to find us."

"Did you see anyone other than the first responders?"

His question surprised me. "No. Why?"

"We found tracks near the building with minute traces of her and Trever's blood. We've confirmed they weren't made by you, the paramedics, or the officers on the scene. So far, we can't determine if the tracks occurred before you arrived or after Raven was taken to the hospital."

I was so stunned I didn't say anything. Someone had been there. Did they see me smash the implants? Hide them in my car?

Sanchen leaned forward. "What aren't you telling me?"

His revelation destabilized my resolve. I felt like I couldn't catch my breath. My story was about to unravel.

A tiny spot in his eyes flashed.

He went to the door, paused, then left the room, leaving me to my doubt and confusion.

Less than a minute later, a pudgy man entered and held out a business card. "Mr. Quintero, my name's Winstin Ozawa. I'm your attorney. Your wife hired me."

I could barely lift my head to look at him, my neck was so stiff. "Can I go?"

He nodded.

Sanchen was in the hallway. "You don't want to do this," he told me. "The more you cooperate, the better for you and your family."

I started to respond, but Ozawa propelled me down the hall.

"We'll find who did this," Sanchen said. "No one gets away with a crime. Not these days."

* * *

After collecting my phones at the desk, I exited the building to find the sun had set.

"If they contact you in any way, call me," Ozawa said. "And be careful. With a crime like this, due process goes out the window real quick."

Sanchen hadn't believed me. His tone at the end, the veiled threat, made it clear I was his prime suspect. It was only a matter of time before he charged me.

Who else had been at the Hoyts' facility? I needed to talk to Raven—and get rid of the implants. Fast.

I thanked Ozawa and opened my neural net's communications software. Messages from Mina scrolled across my vision that a lawyer was coming, that I should stay quiet. The ones after that surprised me: Raven had been released. While she had only woken for a few moments, it'd been enough.

I couldn't believe it. Sanchen had kept me so long Raven had been discharged and brought home. Did Sanchen know the truth? Was he going to follow me to see what I did? I could lose my mind from this.

I brought up my car's link. It was still at Hoyt Enterprises—maybe another trap. I instructed it to come to the station, then reconsidered and directed it to stop two blocks away. When it arrived, I made sure no one was near, got in, and shut the door—but didn't sigh with relief. My problems were far from over.

As I headed for home, I wanted to reach under the seat for Raven and Trever's implants, unsure if they'd been found, but couldn't risk it.

38

Instead, I searched the console, sides, roof, and corners for cameras or listening devices as I drove.

When I turned into my subdivision, the streets appeared empty.

Unable to wait any longer, I flipped the Chrysler to autodrive and reached under the seat. I tried to keep my head up to mask what I was doing, but as my contemporary-style house came into view, the garage door starting to rise, I ducked my head and jammed my hand under the seat. I touched nothing but carpet as I dragged my fingers back and forth.

The car glided onto the driveway.

I contorted my body and shoved my hand further, my fingers grazing the edge of something. My sock. Relieved, I grasped it, pulled it toward me —

The car stopped abruptly, causing me to smack my head on the dash.

The rear of my oversized, two-car garage held my latest project, the best thing I'd ever conceived. It was big, too, ten feet wide and eighteen feet long. Yet there was enough room to park both mine and Mina's cars.

Even though things looked normal, something had triggered my car's anti-collision sensor. I was only halfway in the garage.

As I scanned the windows, I shoved the sock in my pocket, then drove my car the rest of the way in and closed the garage door. The broken implants rested heavily against my thigh as I got out.

My project appeared undisturbed underneath its sloping tarp. A couple of tools on my workbench had been moved, though.

"Talia?"

A long heartbeat later, my younger daughter popped up from behind my project. "This is hipcool, but I can't figure it."

I exhaled. "What part of 'off-limits' didn't you understand?"

"It's all slick like a glider, but you stuck a weirdo engine in its belly. At least I think it's an engine. No exhaust, though. And the battery pack's dinky."

"Did you take off the engine cover?" She would've had to remove six screws to do it.

She put her hands on her hips, giving me a fleeting glimpse of the woman she would become. "If you didn't want me to snoops, you shouldn't have said don't touch."

"You shouldn't be looking at things that aren't yours. This is secret, and none of your — "

"You hid it in the garage."

"How about I put it in your room? You can sleep out here."

She giggled. "You'd never do that. So, what is it?" She began to slide the tarp off, revealing the white, carbon-fiber body and some of the red pinstriping I'd added to simulate speed. I put my hand on the tarp to keep it in place, but she tugged harder, and the material slid off the bubble cockpit I'd picked out of nostalgia.

"It's something that could ensure your and your sister's future." I'd worked on it for months, outside of the office. "How is she?"

"Sleeping." She gave a mischievous grin. "Can I fly it?"

"Don't you have homework?"

"I've wrapped it except for Creative Writing. My teacher wants me to pick a 'spirit animal'." She squinted her nose.

I smiled. Touchy-feely stuff wasn't her strong suit. "Then you shouldn't be out here."

"I wanna scope your contraption."

"Go inside, or you're grounded."

"Wow, straight to that. You should start smaller. Hey, why was that detective so snarly?"

"You need to go to bed."

"I'm not tired."

Ordinarily, this was cute. Not tonight.

I needed to ditch Raven and Trever's implants. Sanchen wouldn't stop until he found their attacker. The less evidence I left, the better, which meant I couldn't leave the implants here. I wanted to dump them tonight, but a camera somewhere would spot me driving around so late. Besides, Sanchen could have a drone assigned to me.

Talia took advantage of my distraction to crawl under the glider. "What a weirdo engine."

I signaled my robot assistant to come over and hold up the glider. The garbage-can-sized, purple-striped 'bot did, tilting the prototype sideways to reveal Talia and the glider's underbelly. She had the engine cover off and was focused on the prototype's heart, the color-coded wires, rotatable force generator, regulator, and accentuator that were wrapped around a softball-sized sphere I'd fashioned out of a double wall of aluminum.

"I don't get it," she said.

"It's what makes this fly," I said, warring between my need and her scientific curiosity. "The ball contains condensed dark matter. We used something similar the other night at the fusion reactor, only less concentrated."

"So, it's some sort of fuel?"

"Not like you'd think. When the right force is applied, the dark matter activates and affects things around it."

"Like how-so?"

"You're looking at a propulsion system, the first of its kind."

I couldn't hide the implants in the glider. It would be the first thing they'd inspect. Confiscate. Take apart. Hold long past the time we were gone.

I couldn't hide the implants in the house, either. If the cops searched the place, the traces of rare metals would seal our fate...unless I could mask the metals, hide the implants where they'd never look.

I nearly told Talia to go inside, but she was so riveted with the glider I suspected she'd raise a storm, which might draw Mina out here. "I need your help. I need to hide my research."

She sat up. "Why?"

"I'm not ready to show anybody. I have to make sure my design and research are safe."

"Is that why Raven was jumped?"

Lying about what I did wasn't getting easier. I unhooked the dark matter sphere, causing it to tumble out. Talia caught it before it hit the ground and looked at me. I went to my workbench and unplugged the cube drive, then closed the shade over the window. The garage became darker, lit only by a single bulb.

"Dad?"

I held out the semi-opaque cube. "Hide this and the sphere up there." The ceiling's garage was taller than average, nearly two stories. It was lower than the roofline, though, due to a storage space I'd built.

I accessed the ladder via my implant. At my command, it descended, unfolding like a DNA helix.

"Seriously?" she asked, her face hard to read in the darkness.

Before I could assure her, she grabbed the cube and went to the curved ladder. As she climbed, cradling the sphere and cube in one arm, I slid to the sink.

41

She noticed I'd moved and stopped.

"I'm watching you," I assured her.

She continued up, though she glanced back every few rungs.

Facing her, I leaned against the sink, reached behind me, and twisted the cover off the drain, coughing once when it squeaked to mask the sound. Then I took the implants, palming them in case she looked again—she'd reached the top—and slid my hand into the sink. As she pushed open the hatch to the storage area, I blindly dropped the sock into the drain. The p-trap would hold the implants until I moved them; the water in the trap would shield the rare metals from the cops' sensors.

Still facing her, I twisted the cover back into place as she slid down the ladder.

I would've chastised her for descending like that except I didn't want her to become curious about my actions.

The sink was a weak hiding place, but it was temporary. I'd move them tomorrow.

"Bed. Now."

When we entered the house, I looked around; the table where we'd toasted my hoped-for success, and where years earlier, Raven had begged we install a windmill on our roof. The wall Talia had damaged when she snuck a chemical compound from school and forgot it in her backpack, which became unstable and blew. The corner where our Christmas tree stood every December, with the opening of presents always chaotic and too brief.

I could lose all this.

My family.

Our home.

I steered Talia to her room, then went to Raven's. I needed to make sure she was OK, talk to her, practice our stories so the cops couldn't poke holes in them.

She was asleep, as was Mina, who still wore her gray suit, an arm curled around Raven's waist. Raven had more bandages, her face puffy.

Her room was unchanged from when she'd moved out, with memorabilia from her younger days scattered about: a softball trophy topped with a hologram player, a doll she'd "toughened up" by shaving half its head and carving a heart tattoo on its arm, and empty picture frames. The frames would light up when she woke, the frames linked to an app that gauged when and where the frames appeared in her vision and projecting pictures she'd loaded over the years: high school moments, vacations, best friends — images she wouldn't see anymore, as they'd resided in her implant.

I went around the bed and took down the frames.

Chapter Five

A flickering light in my lenses woke me, followed by an image: Mina, Raven, and Talia collapsed against each other in laughter, shadowed Half Dome behind them. The trip, taken three years ago, had been a reward for Raven's teeth alignment, a thirty-minute procedure that had inflicted a week of recovery. The image was the first time she'd smiled since the alignment, nearly a month later.

Eyes still closed, I shifted my vision, the image remaining stationary as I looked toward a red dot in the upper left corner. My lenses registered the movements my eye-muscles made, that I'd "looked" toward the dot, and the alarm stopped.

I flicked my eyes to the right.

Readouts and texts scrawled across my vision while icons appeared in their pre-set spots. I pulled up our security system — which was dumb since the police had the tech to break in unnoticed — and read the report that no one had entered the house during the night.

When the cops failed to find Raven's fictitious attacker, they would come here. I had a couple of days, max.

Mina's voice came from down the hall. I found her in Raven's room, our daughter asleep behind her.

"Who are you talking to?" I whispered.

"Myself. When did you get in?"

Her response was odd, but I had other concerns. "I need to wake her."

"Her sleep's induced. The nurses said she'll heal quicker."

A cream-colored device was attached to Raven's wrist, the size of a deck of cards, with a tube injected into her hand. It disturbed me — more proof of the pain I'd caused.

"I know the doctor is monitoring her remotely, but what if something happens?" Mina asked. "The hospital's an hour away."

I leaned over our daughter. Bandages covered Raven's temple, although the dressings weren't as thick as the ones in the ICU. Her skull didn't look deformed — my fist clenched at the thought — but there was a bump where her implant had been. "I didn't think they'd install a new net until she healed."

"It's a placeholder, to cover the hole." Mina's voice caught for the first time. "They said it's like a plug, so her body doesn't fill in the space."

I saw the worry in her eyes, her heart-shaped face pale. "Stay home today. Call me the moment she wakes up."

I got ready for work. Before I reached the garage, Talia joined me. "Mom said you'd shuttle me to school."

"There's a new invention you can take. It's called a bus."

"Missed it."

I couldn't retrieve the implants with her around. Maybe if I programmed the car to drive her and then come back for me…. But that would be out of the ordinary. Arouse suspicion.

"We going?" she asked.

* * *

An hour later, I pulled into the Angeles Commuter Train Station, Talia at school, me empty-handed, pretending this was any other day.

I drove past the memorial for the 2031 Irling Riots, now a favored spot for the homeless and lost, and into the seven-level garage. It was nearly full, so I was forced to park on the roof. That wasn't out of the ordinary.

I had a permit to drive the commute to downtown but rarely did. Even with the city's extreme measures to restrict the number of cars, traffic remained a slow-crawling torture.

I passed through the station's scanner, avoiding the guards' gazes, and went to the platform. No one reacted to me. Even though I'd been featured in articles and programs over the years, it was rare for someone to recognize me. I hoped it stayed that way, though the fusion reactor had generated a lot of coverage.

I entered the next train heading downtown and scanned the car for a place to dump the implants. But the car, illuminated via strips of lighting streaked with grime, didn't offer any hiding spots other than possibly the bathroom, though that was too obvious. There were no storage areas, no gaps in the seats.

45

A man slipped onto the train before the doors closed. Athletically built with an angled jaw, he wore a well-made synth jacket and a baseball cap that covered his hair.

He gave me a sidelong glance as he leaned against the doors.

I wanted to hide but couldn't—and didn't want him to know he'd rattled me.

My back rigid, I sat near the middle of the car as the train moved forward. Other than the man who'd followed me, I felt surrounded by mannequins. No one talked. No one moved other than some who typed with their datarings, faces expressionless. It was eerie, a level of disassociation I'd never noticed so keenly before. Their eyes flickered as content played on their lenses. Many had headphones; others likely had audial implants. The ones typing appeared to be working, hooked into their employers' systems to finish a report, answer their email—too wrapped up or stacked up to notice anyone.

I didn't look at the man in the baseball cap, couldn't relax.

The woman next to me was oblivious to my struggle, her bag open at her feet. If I'd had the implants with me, I could've dropped them inside. She never would've known. But cameras would've caught me. Three hung overhead, spaced throughout the car.

When the train stopped at the next station, I stood and walked toward the bathroom at the far end as if I needed to use it. Instead, as more passengers got on, I went to the door that led to the next car and peered through the window, hoping to find a place to ditch the implants. There was a gap between my car and the next, the concrete channel the train hovered in visible between them, but cameras on both cars guarded the open space.

If I was going to try dumping them here, I'd need a diversion, something subtle but big enough to shield my actions. I didn't know how to pull that off.

The train started forward again, the car trembling as it glided over cracks in the channel.

The man in the baseball cap had pushed away from the door. He seemed to ignore me, but that was an act. He'd moved to see what I was doing.

As we approached downtown, I tried to estimate how many cameras we passed, not just near the tracks but attached to the skyscrapers—both the gleaming and the pitted—the billboards, electronic guides, security stations, and other locations. Many were privately-owned, used for security or to sell person-specific content, but every device watched and recorded, their files accessible to the police at the drop of a warrant, all linked via the communications system I devised.

A woman in her twenties suddenly laughed, which made her neighbor flinch. She didn't seem to notice, intent on whatever content played on her lenses. There was so much crap out there, no one ever had to watch the same thing twice. There had to be a way to use the distraction of trillions of bytes of streaming data to hide my crime.

Actually, there wasn't. Nothing distracted the cameras.

I glanced at the man. Everyone else was plugged in, oblivious to the world around them due to work or amusement, but not him. He was looking at me.

When we arrived downtown, the train gliding to a stop in one of the terminal's forty or so tracks, I stepped out of the car and scanned the underground area for a place to hide my crime. Paint-chipped trash cans, the channel under the train, the concrete-block-encased restrooms, all looked viable if not for the cameras.

The man exited the train right behind me. I didn't run. He would see wherever I went.

* * *

I entered our company's headquarters, walking past holograms of our milestone robotic designs and under the depiction of our first dark matter harvest, which we achieved just outside the asteroid belt, the depiction arched across the bulbous, three-story lobby.

Scanned, identified, and assessed before my third step, I walked toward the bank of elevators expecting not to be harassed. I should've known better.

A well-built security guard bisected my path. "Hey, Mr. Quintero."

I stopped grudgingly. "Hi, Canton."

"He wants to see you."

Canton directed me to Nikolai's private elevator, pushed the top of three buttons — the destination of the middle one unknown to everyone except Nikolai, one of his fucking games — and sent me to the 92nd floor. The ride was swift; the doors opened to the penthouse seconds after closing.

I'd been here countless times, but the view still impressed. Nikolai's suite took the entire floor, with a 360-degree view of Los

Angeles: mountains to the east, ocean to the west, humankind's efforts in between. Sunlight bathed the genetically-modified cherrywood floor, the informal seating area he never used, and the drink cart I suspected he used a lot.

Whether out of nostalgia or obligation, he kept our picture on the wall. The "Gang of Five" who'd started our company, the other four geniuses in their respective specialties and me the engineer who turned their ideas into reality. The picture had been taken after we'd finished college, months after we started Gen Omega believing we would be different. I was in peak shape from playing running back for the Golden Bears, able to take all those nights of Budweiser and supreme pizza while we argued and worked, rarely getting home to Mina's apartment before midnight.

We looked young. We looked like friends.

Nikolai's voice cut through my thoughts. "Where the hell have you been?"

I turned as he appeared from his bathroom. "I had a family emergency."

"Couldn't think of a better excuse?"

I bit back my response to keep this brief. "You wanted to speak to me?"

He sat behind his wood-and-glass desk. "What's this shit about not moving the reactor robots?"

"They're damaged. You move them, they could collapse, taking the core with them."

"They're impacting our results. Output is thirty percent lower than projected. If buyers learn about this—"

"Imagine the output if the core's lying on the ground." We'd buried twenty feet of the most flame-resistant material known to man in the chamber floor, though I didn't know how it would hold up to our blazing sun.

"You need to solve this."

My annoyance sharpened my tone. "You solve it. Do you realize what would've happened if one of the robots collapsed?"

"They should've been designed to handle the pressure."

"We agreed on those tolerances months ago. Want to see the email?"

"I want you to care. If you'd showed this much passion the other night, we wouldn't be having this argument."

"Our controls were in place for a reason," I said. "If a robot collapsed—"

"They didn't. They held, the core lit, and now we have orders for eighteen more plants, seven of those outside the States. We've become giants."

"That's all you care about." I was damned if I was going to tell him about angling the pressure.

"I gave you the limelight, called you on stage, but you left. Do you realize how that looked? Where have you been, anyway?"

I didn't want to say. I'd given him enough over the years—but it might seem odd to the police if I didn't tell him. "At the hospital. Raven was attacked. Her implant was ripped out."

He fell silent, his face revealing his shock. "Oh god, how is she?"

I shifted my gaze. From where I stood, skyscrapers stretched in clusters down the coast like the broken spine of some massive, long-dead monster. "Healing."

"Hey, Dray, I'm sorry. Take some time off. Go be with her."

He said the right things, but I didn't trust his altruism. Besides, I needed the cover of my daily commute to dump the broken implants. "I'll think about it."

"You're distracted, which means you're no good to me or anyone else."

"Stop acting like my boss. We're partners, remember?"

"Make the right choice, Dray. Take the time."

* * *

The lights turned on, and my sound system launched "Seven Nation Army" from The White Stripes as I stepped into the three-room suite that made up my office. I'd created the playlist to pump myself up for the reactor lighting, but now it seemed in bad taste. Raven and Talia made fun of my oldies music, but it was way better than the "thump-guitar" noise they liked, which sounded like the classic R&Ber Prince if he'd sucked.

"Music off," I said.

I didn't like our company anymore. Not that it was mine. Nikolai had succeeded in fracturing the five of us until I was the only one left to fight him.

Sketches, prototypes, parts, and other items covered my desk, couch, and distressed-metal coffee table in the main room. My worktable in the second room had a motor I'd fixed for one of my subordinates, and next-gen dark matter containers, which I'd planned to use in future reactors.

I had meetings lined up. Reports to read. All were secondary concerns now. Nothing that helped me get rid of the implants.

I canceled the meetings and left to search the building, taking the grapefruit-sized motor as cover.

My office suite was the nexus of the company's design/development division. I passed scaled mockups of the latest dark matter collector we launched into space, and other projects in various stages of concept. Past the models, one of which was seventeen feet long, rows of work spaces held my engineers and designers. The opposite side of the floor contained testing rooms, support areas, and overused coffee stations.

The elevator banks were a calming blue, as if our decorators feared someone would fly into a caffeine-infused rage if they waited too long for an elevator. The color didn't help my mood.

The storage floors—our building's warehouse area—offered a rarely-visited maze of nooks and crannies in which to hide Raven and Trever's implants. But I had to be aware of my actions, which were continually tracked by the building's system, so I went to the robotics manufacturing department.

Their design-build area was a fraction of the size of our large-output facility in Arizona, just three floors in scope, but it did have an assembly room, raw materials storage, testing area, and most importantly, a metal melting furnace.

I skirted the mini-production line, past stacks of metal arms, processor-spines, and kinetic drivers, and approached the opening in the floor, which was lit with an orange glow. A cauldron of liquid metals swirled below, the heat beating my face and hands: tungsten and steel and titanium, with a separate reservoir of Inconel nearby.

There were safeguards to prevent anything from contaminating the glowing metals, but I knew how to turn them off. Once I dropped the implants—and the damn sock—inside, they'd be obliterated. Unrecoverable.

I realized it wouldn't work.

The safeguards could be turned off, but the finished metal would be checked for impurities. The implant's rare metals would be discovered, and the police would be called. Even though they'd never be able to recover the data on Raven and Trever's drives, they'd work out where the implants came from.

Amarjit approached. "Boss, we need to talk about the reactor."

"You're upset about your robots," I said, half-distracted from trying to come up with a solution for the implants.

"I was never told they'd be subjected to that kind of pressure —"

"We miscalculated."

"We have to redesign them."

I didn't have time for this. "Let me know what you come up with."

I barely made it past the production line when he caught up to me. "You're disappointed. Let me show you something that will cheer you up."

I wanted to decline, but could tell he felt he'd failed me.

He led me out of the production area and down a wide hallway. "My team has been working on this for months. They're still prototypes, but they're ready for you to see."

We walked into the presentation room—which was designed for clients, with mood lighting and Peruvian granite—where five robots stood in a line. The three identical robots in the middle were nearly eight feet tall, with wide shoulders, flattened faces, and sunken, glowing eyes. They had a lower center of gravity, short legs, and long arms, which made them gorilla-like. Their hands were huge, their fingers consisting of large blades, each over a foot long, that flattened out and widened as the blade approached the wrist.

"I present our line of earth movers," Amarjit said. "The big guys are our diggers, and the other two clean up behind them."

The two on either end were much shorter. Built on all-terrain frames with balloon tires, the "clean-up" robots had two arm-like appendages with wide scoops on the end. I realized the scoops locked together to create one long scoop.

"Who are these for?" I asked.

"Anybody who needs something dug. What do you think?"

I was disturbed we were angling to take away even ditch-digger jobs.

"Here, try one," he said. "Where are your datarings?"

I retrieved them from my pocket and put them on.

He showed me how to link up with the 'bots. "OK, you're in."

The interface was our standard software design, modified for the type of work these robots would perform. At my command, the center one straightened and stepped forward. Another gesture, and the robot raised a razor-clawed hand.

Amarjit said, "They can destroy anything that stands in their path, and only need charging twice a year."

I could feel the robot's strength from the way it moved. I found myself staring at its clawed hands, which were designed to shred dirt and rock.

"Aren't they majestic?" he asked, grinning like a proud father.

I had an idea how to solve my problem.

CHAPTER SIX

My lenses tinted to protect my retinas from the strong, Southern California sun as I exited my car at City Park.

It had taken San Gabriel years to clean up what had been a contaminated site, transplanting trees, bushes, and over a hundred tons of fresh dirt to convert the location into a community green space — dirt I could use to hide the implants. If I was right, my scramble to the train station, the train to my car, and my drive here, would be worth it.

People wandered about the park, families and teens and dogwalkers and joggers, enjoying the weather or possibly looking to hide their own crimes. I avoided eye contact as I traversed one of the trails, which became elevated in spots to arch over creeks and wetland areas. If I failed to find a place to bury the implants without being seen, I could use one of the raised spots to toss the implants into the murky water that drifted under the floorboards.

I paused at an elevated spot in the middle of a meticulously-designed valley. A quick check confirmed there were no cameras. Amarjit's robots had made me remember this place, which Mina and I visited before Raven was born. I'd noticed it didn't have cameras back then, and it still didn't.

I'd found a place in L.A. that wasn't constantly watched. My relief was immense — and short-lived.

Someone stopped beside me. "Peace and quiet is rare, don't you think?"

It was the man from the train.

He wasn't wearing a hat this time, but it was him. He was a couple of inches taller than me, just over six feet, with silver hair — not white or gray. Silver. It wasn't natural, nor was his presence here. He stuck out among the parkgoers, conservatively dressed in a white Oxford and gray slacks.

"Come here all the time," I said cautiously.

"You're in a tough position. I can help. I admire your work, by the way," he said with a warm smile.

I had the urge to run but didn't, not sure if I could get away — or if running would make it worse. "Who are you?"

"The name's Kieran. Have you had a heart-to-heart with your daughter? Ask what she was really doing at the Hoyt plant. Who she was meeting."

Even though I stood in a field bright with sunshine and Kieran's smile remained warm, I felt threatened.

"If we work together, we could turn what happened into a positive," he said. "I can protect you and her, shield you both from prosecution."

"You work for the police?"

"I'm with The Agency." I could hear the capitals. He leaned toward me. "We used to be the NSA, but we evolved."

He had a dot on either side of his head, what I first took as moles, except they were symmetrical — infrared scanners woven into his brow. Then I saw the other implants. I'd only ever encountered people with one neural net implanted in their head, two max. Kieran had a half dozen, maybe more, dotting his skull and blending with his silver hair. What the hell was he hooked into?

"I can be a good friend," he said. "It wasn't an accident Raven was at the Hoyts' that night. If I'd known what was going to happen, I would've stopped it. That's one of the reasons why I'd like to help you. Make amends."

"What do you want?"

"Find the truth. She did an admirable job trying to cover her actions, but…well, you need to have that heart-to-heart. Give her a chance to come clean."

He raised an eyebrow at me. I realized he was reading my heartrate, which had accelerated. Probably my temperature, too. He was a walking lie detector. "She was a victim," I said. "They both were."

"Don't lie," he said. "And don't hide things in your garage."

I opened my mouth, then closed it, even though I wanted to deny his statement.

He nodded as if in approval. "I can help you out of this mess. But first, you two should talk."

"She hasn't done anything wrong."

"We're past that."

I'd never felt so trapped. "Can I go?"

"I'm on your side. Trever stole money from his parents, so if Detective Sanchen tries to hardline Raven, you can fight back with that. And speaking of stealing, you need to be more aware of what your company is doing. Look into their newest product line: hoverbikes."

"I haven't heard of any 'bike' project."

"You're not supposed to. Check them out. Now, you're going to want to answer that call."

"What—?" I started, when my phone rang. I didn't recognize the number. My eyes didn't leave his face as I fished out my phone and answered. "Hello?"

"Mr. Quintero, it's Detective Sanchen. I need to talk to Raven."

"She's sedated—"

"I was informed her auto-inject sedative is ending, so she should be awake by now. I'm a few blocks from your house."

* * *

I broke every speed limit in my mad dash home.

When I got there, Sanchen's car was already in the driveway. I parked behind it and hurried inside, my anxiety level spiking. I'd considered calling Ozawa but didn't, as I feared we would look guilty.

Mina stood in the hallway, two dozen steps from Raven's room. I could see our daughter sitting on her bed, hair mussed. Sanchen sat in her desk chair, his back to us.

"Why aren't you in there?" I whispered to Mina.

"If I act overprotective, we look suspicious."

"Shit." I couldn't believe Raven was alone with the detective, unaware of what I'd told him and probably groggy from the sedatives.

"Language," Mina said, even though Talia wasn't around.

I went to Raven's room and shook Sanchen's hand, unnerved that he'd already started asking her questions. For all I knew, our story had already unraveled.

"Raven was explaining what happened the night of the attack," Sanchen said. He refocused on her. "Please continue."

She pressed her pillow against her stomach. "Like I said, it wasn't my idea to go there. It was Trever's."

"His parents' factory is an odd place for a date."

She glanced at me before answering. "He wanted to show off."

"You look tired," I said, sitting beside her to get her attention. "How about we continue this later?"

"I insist," Sanchen said. He crossed one leg atop the other as if he had all day.

Her eyes flickered to me. "I was a little scared to be there." I could hear the lie in her voice. He was going to find out the truth — it was what cops did. "We were only inside for a few minutes when we heard footsteps, then a guy in a mask attacked us. Trever fought him, and I ran off. When I went back to see if Trever was OK, he was on the floor, bleeding. The guy in the mask grabbed me, held me down, and ripped out my implant." Her eyes flickered to me again. "It's all I remember."

"When did you call your father?"

I wanted to stop her. I worried she would screw up, that he already knew the truth.

"After I hid. When the guy attacked Trever. I've never been so afraid."

"Where did the pipe come in?"

She shifted, whether out of guilt or to give herself time to think, I couldn't tell. "When I came back, it was on the floor. I picked it up in case the guy in the mask was still there. He wasn't, so I went to Trever. I wanted to help him but didn't know what to do. He even clawed at me and tore my shirt before collapsing. Then his attacker came back. I swung at him, but he knocked the pipe out of my hand."

"You fought him, even though he had a gun?" Sanchen asked.

I exchanged a glance with Mina, who stood in the doorway. Raven wasn't being consistent.

"I saw what happened to Trever," she said, her voice wavering. "I had to fight."

"So, you only planned to be at the facility for a few hours? Then what?"

"Go home. I had class the next day."

I tensed, waiting for him to bring up the phone call and ask what childhood story she'd alluded to. I put my arm around her as she squeezed her pillow.

"Did you help with the cameras?" he asked. "They were blacked out."

Her voice was weaker. "What cameras?"

"The ones monitoring the facility."

"They were? Trever must've done that. He said we wouldn't get caught. I guess that's why."

"They're blacked out across the entire compound, following a series of covered walkways. You could go all the way to the forest at the far side without being tracked by camera or satellite, and disappear."

"I guess."

Sanchen uncrossed his leg and leaned forward. "You're lying to me, Ms. Quintero. Your roommate told me you and Trever were running away."

I looked at her, stunned.

She scooted out from under my arm, her eyes starting to glisten. "It was just for a weekend."

"That's a lot of money for one weekend."

"What money?" Mina asked, looking as alarmed as I felt.

"We found your backpacks filled with weeks' worth of clothing and five hundred thousand dollars. You weren't going away for a weekend. Where were you headed?"

Raven looked at me, her face pained and defiant. "We wanted a life together, just the two of us."

I couldn't absorb her words.

She dropped her head. Past her, the hologram softball player swung its bat.

"If you were running away, why go through the factory?" Sanchen asked. "You've changed your story twice now. Want to tell me again about the attack?"

She looked at him with a fierce expression. "I don't know what Trever planned to do."

"But you were going to run off with him."

"I only lied about running away because it'd upset them," she said, nodding toward Mina and me.

"Then explain so I understand. Why did you block the cameras? What were you doing there?"

She threw aside her pillow. "I'm going to be sick." She ran down the hall to the bathroom. Seconds later, she retched.

I stood as Mina checked on her. "I think you should go," I told Sanchen.

"I need answers."

"Don't you think she's been through enough?"

The detective stood slowly. "Is this what you want, to not cooperate?"

"If I hadn't wanted to cooperate, I would've forbidden you from talking to her. You can continue your questions another time."

* * *

I led Sanchen outside to make sure he left. When we reached his car, I remotely started mine and had it park in the street so he could leave.

He pulled his hand out of his pocket and patted me on the back, resting his hand there for a second. "She's been lying to you for a while."

I forced myself not to flinch at his touch. "Trever must have influenced her."

"She has one chance to come clean, Mr. Quintero."

"I'll talk to her."

He stepped away, offering a glimpse of the mag pistol in his shoulder holster. "You found her within seconds of her implant getting ripped out. How?"

"I got lucky." My words tasted bitter.

"I'm surprised you didn't see her attackers."

"I wish I had."

He opened his door but paused. "I don't believe either of you."

I had to give him something. Make him think his skepticism was wrong. "I was approached by someone. A guy with silver hair named Kieran."

Sanchen's jaw flexed. "You don't want Agents around."

"They're the old NSA?"

"They're much more than that, augmented after the '36 terrorist attacks. Personally, I think they're more powerful than the FBI." He seemed to reconsider. "I can try to protect you, but you need to come clean."

I frowned as he drove off, not sure why he'd left. It wasn't due to my bravado or Raven getting sick. Then I realized the reason. I could still feel his pat on my back, remembered him sitting in Raven's room with his arm casually hanging down.

I reached over my shoulder and searched where he'd patted me, then plucked it off my shirt. It was a millimeter-sized microphone.

I remembered Ozawa's warning. For this kind of crime, virtually every law was discarded.

Dozens of these could be scattered about Raven's room, the hallway, anywhere he'd been. We'd never find them.

I ran for the house.

CHAPTER SEVEN

After I warned Raven and Mina about Sanchen's microphones, my thoughts circled to Kieran. He had a reason for telling me to search my company.

Frustrated that I couldn't grill Raven for fear Sanchen would hear us, I took the train to the office to check the R&D labs. Even though I was doing Kieran's bidding, it was better than staying home where I couldn't demand answers.

I searched the labs for an hour but came up empty.

I thought about Nikolai's private elevator. I was convinced his elevator's middle button led to one of our storage areas. We had six entire floors, 45 to 51, dedicated to storage, four of which had restricted access. Whatever I was supposed to find was on one of those floors.

The storage areas contained hundreds of storage pens, some stacked on top of others, a sprawling labyrinth of steel-and-wire containers of various sizes, each biometrically coded. Still, searching for a mysterious "bike" was better than waiting to be arrested — or thinking about Raven's plan to run away.

I started on the 51st floor and worked my way down. As I went, I kept an eye on the notifications along the edge of my vision for any indication I'd tripped an alarm. I rarely came to these floors, more focused on our latest project than searching the past.

The 50th and 48th floors were twice the height of a regular floor, which allowed for taller storage pens. Even so, I didn't find Kieran's mysterious project in the 50th floor or the adjoining levels.

When I stepped onto the 48th floor, I proceeded down the central corridor, which stretched away in the muted light with smaller branches splintering off to either side in a haphazard fashion. The layout on this level was different, the maze dictated by the size and placement of the cages it held.

I looked in each enclosure as I walked down the main pathway, passing next-gen laser cutters, electromagnetic engines, and other prototypes, their creation teaching us important things as we toiled to make our ideas real. I'd been through the process countless times over the years. I still was, working on my latest design outside of the company.

As I thought about my glider, I grimaced. I'd hidden it from Nikolai. He'd think turnabout was fair play — and that he had a right to my creation.

I quickened my pace, ignoring the smaller cages. He'd need at least a ten-by-twenty, maybe larger. It took a few minutes to find it: a back cage, set in the corner of one of the offshoots, away from the central corridor.

A sinking feeling ran through me as I approached.

Two large objects that looked like black Wave Runners occupied the cage, one an eight-foot-long two-seater, the other a longer three-seater. But they weren't Wave Runners. Jet engines jutted out from behind the raised seats, and instead of the body curving up like a Wave Runner on either side where the rider's feet rested, it remained flat. I couldn't tell why the bodies had been designed that way, but I knew what the objects were: the "bikes" Kieran had warned me about.

The enclosure also held a fuel container and two crates, possibly auxiliary parts.

I had to get inside.

I stepped to the bioscanner to unlock the cage. It scanned my iris and flashed red. I frowned. As a founding member of our company and Head of Engineering, Design, and R&D, I had access to the entire damn building.

Nikolai.

I closed my eyes and used my implant to connect to the mainframe. As gigabytes of data layered across my lenses, I traversed the stream down multiple sublevels to Building Operations, then slipped inside an unmarked path that led to the security server. I entered my passwords using my datarings, searched for my employee ID, and found my multiple, multi-stringed identifiers. The identifiers were the digitization of my iris, each multi-string a securitized digital snapshot taken at a slightly different angle. I knew because I'd designed the system.

I copied my identifiers, found Nikolai's file, and pasted my strings into his folder, adding to the data already there. Normally when the system scanned an iris, it searched the entire database for a match, but since he'd keyed this lock to just himself and maybe a trusted assistant, it would limit its search to just their files.

I logged out, opened my eyes, and tried the scanner again. This time, the cage unlocked.

When I approached the nearest bike, my wariness turned to confusion. Each flared section, which jutted out to either side of the bike in the front and rear, had a circle through its center, each circle lined with tiny jet nozzles. Clearly the four circles were supposed to provide lift, but the nozzles were too small for the size and weight of the machine, even with the body being fiberglass.

The jets sticking out of the back were big, though. Unlike my glider, this thing would go *fast*.

To prove my point, the bike had leg clamps that secured the rider's calves — obviously so whoever flew the machine would stay on.

I wanted to experience it, sneak the smaller hoverbike down the freight elevator and through the docks on the first floor to some secluded spot, where I could launch it and fly out of the city, past the desalination plants that dotted the coastline and out over the ocean — but I didn't want Nikolai to know I'd found his secret. Besides, this was an untested device I knew nothing about. Untested, but fully developed, which meant it had been hidden from me for some time. I needed to know why.

I climbed on and activated the machine.

The jet nozzles lit, sky-blue flames ringing the insides of the circles. As I stared at them, the bike rose. It didn't make sense that they actually lifted the bike, especially with me on it. I pushed down on the handlebars to land, the bike wobbling, and turned it off.

Grabbing a multi-tool, I slid under the vehicle, removed the screws, pulled off the panel — and found a dark matter sphere like the one I'd manufactured for my glider. It was nestled inside the cradle I'd designed to hold the softball-sized sphere, though the low-level force generators, which would manipulate the dark matter to propel the vehicle, weren't clustered to one side as mine were, but surrounded the sphere instead.

I was right. This was a smaller, streamlined version of my project. Nikolai had discovered it — and stolen it. My hope of starting a business to provide for Raven and Talia many times over, something that couldn't be corrupted by old friends, was being taken from me.

I flashed back to when I'd manipulated the propulsive aspect of dark matter while I prepared it for the fusion reactor to see what else it could do. When I hooked a small sphere of concentrated dark matter to a low-voltage, tightly-modulating current, it lifted into the air. I grabbed it with both hands as it rose, the sphere lifting me off my feet as it pushed away from the earth—before the cord, stretched to the limit, detached from the modulator, and I dropped to the floor.

It was why the bike stayed aloft, not because of the circular jets.

Nikolai had altered my idea, setting the force generators all the way around the dark matter to negate gravity altogether, instead of using it as a combined source for thrust and lift. Following a set of wires to the bike's seat, I discovered that when someone sat on the bike, the seat activated the dark matter, the power level sent to the sphere dictated by the weight of the rider.

Nikolai—or his team—had used my design to create a gravity-defying machine. The jet circles, while acting as a way to steer, hid the true source of the bike's ability, for dark matter not only negated gravity but could push against it.

The design was ingenious. But it was based on my idea.

What else did my company know?

* * *

By the time I reached the parking garage at my train stop, I was exhausted from searching the storage levels' video feeds and erasing my images. It'd taken hours, and I nearly missed my train, the last one of the night.

The garage's elevator doors opened and I got in. A man in a green barn jacket, his face hidden by a hat, entered as well and pushed the button for the sixth floor before stepping behind me. I pushed the button for the seventh floor—and felt a gun jam into my back.

"Don't turn 'round."

My heartrate accelerated as the doors closed and the elevator rose.

"We only got seconds." His voice had an odd cadence with a touch of Creole. "Don't say nothin' you don't want cops knowin', and act as if there are cameras always on you. *Always*. You have no clue the access they have."

My worry became tinged with anger. "Who?" I asked, though I

suspected I knew.

I tried to look back at him, but he jammed his gun to stop me. "Don't. You're bein' watched twenty-four-seven, Dray, more than you know. I knocked out the camera in here, but others are everywhere — and listenin' in ways you can't believe."

Knocking out cameras. I made the connection. "You were at Hoyts' facility."

"I didn't know there was a problem, or I would've helped her. You took their implants. Don't move 'em. Don't go near 'em."

"Why are you telling me this?"

"To warn you. You're gonna need to run—"

"You were at the hospital. I remember your jacket."

"We can help, but you need to get away 'fore it's too late."

"Away from whom?"

"Cops. Silvers. You won't last long." The doors opened onto the sixth floor. "Don't look back."

He shoved me hard.

I tumbled out of the elevator and fell to the floor. By the time I got up, the doors had closed.

Incensed that the guy had threatened me, that he didn't save Raven from Trever, I ran to the stairs, took them two at a time, and leapt out at the seventh floor.

The doors were already closing, the area empty.

CHAPTER EIGHT

The next afternoon, Mina's manicured nails threatened to break my skin.

We sat in one of the pews of the First Congregational Church, Raven beside us, as the mayor talked from the podium.

"Trever was gifted in everything he did." Gein's voice boomed through the cavernous chamber, while hologrammed, sorrowful angels hovered beneath the arched, stone ceilings overhead. "To have him taken is a mother's worst nightmare. Our nightmare."

It had been Mina's idea to be here. I understood why, but still, the funeral brought back unwanted memories. The church was different, but the words were similar. My suit was the same. The casket was wrong, though. It was too big.

She continued to squeeze my hand, gripping so hard my fingers went numb. I wiggled them to try to get circulation, but she didn't let up as she stared at the back of the person in front of her.

At least Talia had been spared, left at our neighbor's house instead of dragged here.

Gein's surrender of the podium two minutes later signaled the end of the public sentiments. Raven stood, but Mina and I were slow to rise with the rest of the mourners. When we did, I followed Mina out of the emptied aisle and took her in my arms. Her body vibrated like a high-rev engine.

"You OK?" I asked.

She didn't answer. But she didn't crack, either.

I let go. "Where's Raven?" But I knew.

I led Mina through the sea of black clothes toward the Hoyts.

Trever's mother's voice rose as we squeezed through the last layer of people, who had backed away to give them room like this was a schoolyard brawl. "I want to know what you did to my son."

Raven stood before the Hoyts, spine straight but shoulders slumped, as the crowd watched in silent judgment.

I stepped between her and them and faced Mrs. Hoyt as Mina pulled Raven away. "I'm sorry for your—"

"She must answer my questions," Mrs. Hoyt told me. Beside her, her husband's gaze was weighed with accusation and grief.

"This isn't the time or place."

"Your daughter's the reason he's dead."

"Raven loved him."

She leaned forward. "She will tell me. And I will have justice."

I joined Mina and Raven in the parking lot, my body vibrating as well. Minutes later, we were on the road.

As I drove, Mina turned to Raven. "I know you're upset, but we have to talk before we get home."

Raven remained silent.

Mina had more patience than me, but a bite crept into her voice. "We're running out of options. Mayor Gein called in favors, but the police aren't backing down. You need to tell them the truth—all of it, including what you haven't told us."

I turned onto our street but slowed to give Raven time to respond.

"Trever's parents won't stop," Mina pushed. "You heard them."

"Shit," I said. Kieran stood in front of our house, a black Tesla parked at the curb.

When we got out of our car, his smile wasn't as warm as before. "You must be Mrs. Quintero. And you're Raven. You get your looks from your mother."

"I don't believe we've met," Mina said.

"No, though you should know who I work for." He looked back at Raven. "Still being rebellious, I see."

"If this is about her neural net, we see the surgeon tomorrow," I said.

"Good, but that's not what I'm referring to. Is it, Raven?" he asked her before facing me. "I'm trying to clear your vision. There's a reason she was at Hoyt Enterprises that night."

Raven said, "I told them everything."

"You were going to run away and join the Army of the Founding Fathers."

"That's nuts. Dad, that's nuts."

66

I heard the panic in her voice but couldn't make sense of Kieran's claim. The Army of the Founding Fathers was a domestic terrorist group, one of a handful that existed along the West Coast and in the Rocky Mountains, occasionally making the news with unsubstantiated warnings and random attacks on government facilities.

"I've been watching you," Kieran told her. "I know more about you than anybody: your GPA, the websites you look at, where you marched in your first rally. You know all about the Fathers, don't you? You met them a couple of times—"

"This doesn't make sense," Mina said, visibly as stunned as I was.

"Trever fell in with them first, but you became just as committed. You even met one of the rebels without him, at that consignment shop, among the recycled clothes and outdated readers. You'd covered your tracks, using UCLA's computers anonymously and triple-encoding your communications, but your meeting exposed you." He ran a finger along the edge of her jaw. "That's why you turned on Trever, isn't it? Because of that rebel."

"Back off," I said as Raven trembled.

He dropped his hand. "I went to your dorm the night you and Trever ran away. I was going to follow you, have you lead me to those rebellious criminals, but you'd already left. Then you killed Trever, ruining my chance."

I said, "She didn't kill him."

"You and I are past telling lies."

"It's not a lie," Mina said. "Raven didn't hurt him."

Kieran, who'd talked in a maddeningly reasonable voice, started to sound less so. "Yes, she did, and he would've been just the first. She wants to join a group of murderers and incite civil war."

Mina stared at Raven, who didn't deny it. "There must be a mistake...."

Before, I was stunned. Now, I felt betrayed. Raven wanted to become an enemy of the state, to take down the society I'd strived for years to improve.

Talia walked across the lawn from the neighbor's, her yellow shirt and orange shorts a sharp contrast to our funeral clothes. "Hey! What'd I miss?"

"Go inside," I said.

"Don't bite my face off."

"What do you want?" Mina asked Kieran as Talia went to the front door.

"Raven needs to tell me every interaction she's had with them: who she met, where, what was said, everything. Dray, I have a role for you as well. Help me, and I'll end the police investigation."

"What 'role'?" My voice was strained.

His look softened. "I don't like doing this. I want to protect all of you." He paused. "Come with me. I want to show you something — away from prying ears."

Talia, who had entered the house, closed the door the rest of the way.

I passed Raven as I followed him to his car. I couldn't bring myself to look at her.

* * *

As Kieran drove, I stayed silent. I understood what he'd revealed. I just couldn't believe it.

He could've taken advantage during the drive. I probably would've admitted everything. He seemed to know it all already. But he didn't speak the entire ride.

He drove north toward the San Fernando Valley, then west past Van Nuys. When he finally stopped, it was in front of a heavily-fortified gate that protected an unmarked office building. The guard scanned our faces and IDs, then let us pass. Kieran parked, and we got out.

After passing door security, we walked down a hallway to a door with a biometrics scanner, where he paused. "I want us to become partners. No matter why we met, I think we'd make a good team. The best way to start is to show our hands. I can trust you, can't I?"

I nodded guardedly. I didn't trust him at all.

He used the scanner to unlock the door and ushered me inside.

Inside the large, dimly-lit room, a scale model of ten city blocks rested atop a grand conference table, the tallest building roughly twenty mini-stories high. The buildings had enough detail to reveal what they were supposed to be — apartments, a hospital, office space, with interior rooms visible behind plastic windows.

"If you're concerned your tax dollars are being used to play house, don't be," he said. "We built this to demonstrate our latest creation."

He approached a cluster of computer servers. When he turned them on, tiny, hovering lights filled the miniature city in a three-dimensional grid, while the building walls disappeared to reveal the people inside. "Traditional surveillance relies on cameras installed throughout a coverage area, augmented by satellites and patrol drones. But the system is flawed. Hoyt Enterprises is a perfect example. It has covered walkways, covered parking, and with their cameras knocked out, no record of what happened the night Raven was attacked. With this new system, we'll never be blind again." He held up an object no bigger than a dime. "These are the key."

He placed a tiny drone in my hand, smaller than I'd ever seen. An array of cameras and sensors stuck out of the top and bottom.

"These will be cast throughout the city. L.A. will probably be first, but we'll quickly expand up and down the Coast. Each drone can remain stationary for months at a time. The best part is the sensors, and how we've linked them. Our software processes every image and sound they capture in real time and cross-references the data with facial recognition software, audial recordings, pattern behavior, employment and residential records, known associates, everything. They have penetrating radar, able to see through brick, stone, and concrete in 10K detail, yet are small enough no one will notice them. And they're whisper quiet."

I was astonished—and wary. The country already had a near-inescapable surveillance network. I'd developed it. My software linked the tens of thousands of cameras that watched everyone. I was nowhere near Talia's level, but I could program and had worked out the logic that the system needed, which my company created in a joint effort with the government. Our design connected every public and private camera, which utilized a hundred different operating systems, in a way that not only provided a single point of access to every one of them—with a court order, of course—but provided near-instantaneous coverage, seamlessly transitioning from one camera to another anywhere in the country when a suspect was targeted.

Yet this was another level. The current system wasn't woven with government or private records, biometrics data, or the other identifier systems he'd listed. It also didn't have cameras that provided that level of penetration. In fact, Kieran's system far exceeded every other current surveillance network.

It would strip the country bare.

The exposed people reflected this, mimicking what the drones would see. I could tell what each one was doing, from watching TV to having sex to building bombs in their basement.

I fought to keep my voice level. "Who'll have access?"

"The Agency. We'll help the police on occasion, but really, it's for us. We're like guardian angels, protecting you in ways you aren't aware of — though with better funding." His bemused expression from his lame joke faded. "We need order. I was a kid when the foreign attacks got bad. We have to do better."

"This isn't order. It's intrusion."

"If we'd had this tech in place, we would've known where Raven and Trever went. Would've protected them. I can get his parents' lawsuit dismissed," he went on. "The detective will be tougher, but I can make him back off. This system will enable us to find every terrorist group in the country and stop them before they hurt anyone."

"You'll be able to monitor everyone." Control them, I didn't say.

"We already can ninety-five percent of the time. This is for that last five percent, the rebels — the 'freedom fighters' — who know how to avoid our existing technology. We're at war, Dray. We need to win."

Watching the projected people, what they symbolized, I no longer felt wary. I felt afraid.

Kieran asked, "Did you find your company's dirty secret?"

I held up the tiny drone. "Is this how you discovered it?"

"No. There were easier ways."

"They stole my idea."

Kieran nodded. "I told you that to prove I'm on your side. I want the technology you developed. It'll help us respond faster, get to threats quicker. Your company wants to use your creation for profit, selling bikes to the rich — unless you steal it back. We can help. We'll be partners. You and your family will be set for life."

All of our problems would go away. I'd keep Raven safe, my family safe.

Yet my fear remained.

"You'll have license to create anything you want: dependable energy, better ways to transport, communicate, anything you can dream of — and your bikes," he said.

My eyes wandered back to the tiny figures inside their homes. Living their lives, oblivious, while others conspired.

"The future is coming, Dray. Don't get swept aside."

* * *

I found Raven in her bedroom when I got home, reading or planning an uprising, I didn't know anymore. Before she could say a word, I pulled her down the hallway and into the bathroom, where I turned on the shower full blast.

"What're you doing?" she asked.

I turned on the sink, both faucets, then drug her into the shower. She fought to get away, but I pushed her under the spray. "I can't breathe," she cried.

I pulled her out to take a breath then shoved her back under. After I was sure she was covered, I tilted the showerhead to spray me, blasting every inch of my black suit. When I was satisfied, I angled the showerhead to spray the curtain, increasing the level of white noise in the room. "Why were you at Hoyts' factory?"

"I told you."

"No more lies, dammit."

"Let me go," she said. She tried to get out, but I stopped her.

"Was Kieran right? Were you going to become a terrorist?"

She sagged. Nodded. Her hair was plastered, her makeup running, but all I saw was my little girl.

"Remember when that guy Kyle Berenskey was murdered?" she asked.

"The terrorist? He shot three people in a convenience store."

"He didn't hurt anybody. He was a hacker. He was going to warn us."

"I saw the footage—"

"It was fake. Agents used it to justify his death. They create videos, stories, even people to make anyone they want look guilty. Homeland Security has an entire division. Initially it was to counter foreign propaganda, but now they use it on us. The government's trying to control us. The rebels are fighting back."

"Don't trust them. They're criminals."

"That's what the feds want you to believe," she said. "I met the owner of that store. He admitted none of it happened."

"What about the victims?"

"There weren't any. The Agency made them up. Kyle had evidence that the government watches everyone, using the cameras that are everywhere to track us—"

"They're there for a reason. You don't remember the terrorist attacks, how terrible they were. The surveillance ended all that."

"At what price? If we're so safe now, why haven't they taken everything down? They want to keep us in line."

I let go of her. The cameras were a good thing. They just monitored threats. Didn't they?

The shower noise filled the silence.

"You taught me not to rely on technology, so I stopped," she said. "That's what led me to the truth. The government is hiding something. I don't know what—the rebels were going to show me when I joined—but the government's killed to keep it secret. People need to know."

The feds could do it, making photorealistic movies from their keyboards, creating fictional citizens in their databanks—and making others disappear. It'd explain the occasional news stories that seemed to contradict each other. But I didn't believe her. It was too massive of a conspiracy—as was the solution. It wouldn't be as simple as telling a reporter or posting something online. It'd take overthrowing the government.

Kieran's employer.

He was right. There was a war—and she was his enemy.

"Dad, they're lying to us. The rebels can show you," she said. "I wasn't running away from you or Mom—"

"Those terrorists won't look out for you. They'll get you killed."

"They're not terrorists. They're trying to expose the truth."

"What about Trever? Did he 'not want to rely on anything' either?"

"He wanted to stick it to his parents. That's why we met at his factory. They have some federal contract." She leaned against the wall.

"What happened between you two?"

She avoided my gaze. "I told him I had feelings for Jex."

"Who?"

"Our contact."

"You cheated on him?"

"No! I wanted to break up with Trever first, but when I told him, he became furious. Joining the rebels, running away, was his idea, all of it except me falling for Jex." She teared up. "I didn't mean to hurt him." She slid down the wall and hugged her knees.

My body grew numb. Whether she'd acted out of passion or a misguided desire to help people, the result was the same. Our family

had been ripped apart.
We just hadn't been separated yet.

CHAPTER NINE

I don't remember sleeping that night. Every idea I came up with was a dead end — and I was angry at Raven. She'd lied to me — about Trever's death, about why they'd been there. The dinner Mina held the night of the reactor, Raven hadn't come to wish me luck. She'd come to say goodbye.

I wondered if I was the reason she'd wanted to join a terrorist group. Maybe I still struggled with Adem's death. Maybe I was absent at times, and she'd felt abandoned. Whatever the reason, I'd failed her.

I pushed my thoughts aside as best I could. I needed to figure out a way out of the mess she'd put us in. I wanted to talk to Mina but couldn't, not unless I pulled her into the shower. I thought to use her morning routine, joining her under the spray to reveal what I'd learned and hopefully figure a way out of this, but my body betrayed me. I fell asleep before her alarm went off. When I woke, she'd left for the day.

An hour later, I knocked on Raven's door. "It's time." I didn't wait for a response before I went to the car and pulled out of the garage. I'd taken the day off for this. After we got back, I would move the broken implants, while Mina was at work and Talia at school. Toss them in a different park, a ditch if I had to.

When Raven exited the house, her hair was pulled back, her bandage visible.

After she got in, I headed for the highway, driving manually to give me something to do. I didn't understand how she thought becoming a terrorist was at all acceptable. Nor could I understand myself. I'd broken the law, something I'd never thought I would do.

What did that say about me?

I turned on the radio, stations appearing along the bottom of my vision: my oldies station, renewed jazz, news stations. I selected news, tuning in as they reported on a manhunt in the mountains outside of

Reno. By Raven's reaction, I could tell she suspected they'd found a rebel hideout.

A police cruiser appeared behind us. Following us. The cops were being blatant now. I wondered how much longer I had. When I pulled into the medical building's parking lot, the cruiser pulled in as well.

The building was white, a contrast to the rest of the city. Dr. Nystrom's office had color though, greens and yellows that I supposed were meant to uplift.

In a blonde swirl of efficiency, Nystrom ushered us into an examination room, situated Raven in a dentist-like chair, and removed the bandages. "You're healing well," she said, her gaze alternating between Raven's head and the projection of her skull on the far wall. "The lattice hasn't shifted and bone has filled in, so there won't be any problems implanting a new 'net. Have you had any discomfort?"

Raven sat up. "You're putting one in?"

"Of course."

"I don't want it."

"What?" I asked.

The doctor seemed equally stunned. "You need a neural net."

Raven said, "I don't want it."

"You'll limit your future. You have to be able to sync with an employer's systems. If you don't have a net, you won't qualify for most jobs."

"I'll manage."

"It's the law," I said. We have enough problems, I didn't add.

Nystrom asked, "How's your eyesight?"

Raven responded thoughtfully. "There's a haze to things. Up close, everything's fine, but distance is murky."

"That's probably your natural vision. You don't have the implant telling your lenses to correct for distance. There's a link—"

"I can see. Things are just hazy."

The doctor leaned in. "That might be a byproduct of the new lenses I installed. Your iris has healed well, though."

"Just seal up the hole where my 'net was and let me be natural."

"That's not an option."

"Then give me a fake implant," Raven said.

"There aren't 'fake' ones. They're all real, each one monitored and sealed. The neural net I have for you has already been registered in your name."

"Fine. I'll keep using the plug—unless you want me walking around with my hole exposed."

"Haven't you missed your classes, your connections, your friends? The web-wide events like that free concert The Flock did for their new album?"

I struggled to keep my cool. "Don't you remember your friends' reaction at the funeral when they saw your implant missing?"

"They're being lied to as well," Raven said. "I need to help them, fight for them."

I was mortified, not only by what she was doing, but that it was in front of someone else, making Nystrom a future witness—more proof Sanchen could use against us.

"You don't do this, you'll be hunted down and arrested," I told Raven.

"It's my life."

* * *

We argued during the drive home. Nothing I said made a damn bit of difference. "The rebels could turn on you. Did you think of that?" I asked.

Silence.

"My only chance is to bargain with Kieran, give him what he wants to keep you out of jail."

"You can't trust him. He's part of the system," she snapped.

"You need to tell him everything you know."

"I'll die first," she said as I pulled into the driveway. She opened the door, forcing me to stop the car abruptly, and stormed into the house.

I hesitated to take the implants, afraid she'd run away while I was gone, but I was almost out of time.

When I opened the garage door, I saw Mina's car, which meant she and Talia were home.

I entered the house, considering whether to move the implants even with them here, and found Mina in the kitchen wearing a tailored work dress.

"How'd it go?" she asked.

I turned on the faucet and told her what happened.

She paled.

"Have you made any progress with your contacts?" I asked.

"I'm pulling every string I have."

Talia came in. "Sweet, you're home," she said to me. "I wanna show you something."

Mina said, "I'll talk to Raven."

I followed Talia to her room, which had a desk, dresser, a simboard covered with diagrams of her computer's software system, and a plastic tub with sensor boards, mothercubes, and one of my old motors near the foot of her bed.

She sat at her desk and started to type, her datarings capturing her fingers' movements as she tapped on the clear desktop and sending her commands to the Saunder portable datapad I'd gotten her last year. Roughly the size of a dinnerplate, the datapad's mechanics allowed it to collapse into the palm of her hand, yet was more powerful than most people's computers, a fact that had made Mina nervous and Talia giddy.

She'd linked it to her flatscreen, which took up a third of one wall.

"When was the last time you saw one of your friends in person? Outside of school?" I asked.

She shot me a frown. "I have friends."

I feared her generation would be even more disconnected than mine. The proliferation of robots replacing workers stacked the deck against her. And after the bird flues and animal virus mutations of the last twenty years that had wiped out thousands, people seemed more interested in using holographic feeds to experience things instead of interacting with each other.

"Check this." Talia nodded at her flatscreen.

She had a browser open. Along the top were the words LOS ANGELES POLICE DEPARTMENT, and under that was "Case File 204708051041: Hoyt – Quintero".

"Did you hack into their database? Jesus, Talia—"

"I had to do something! No one's blabbing. It's like everyone's been taken over by aliens."

"It's for your protection," I said as I scanned the folders listed: Evidence, Records, Witnesses, Surveillance. I glanced out the window. Jesus, the cop who had followed me earlier was parked across the street. I quickly closed the blinds.

"We need to scope what they're planning. Here, squat."

She got up, but I didn't take the chair. "How did you do this?"

"I used fake gene-codes. It wasn't hard. Well, not too hard."

I was good with computers, but nothing like her. I would've been proud if this didn't scare the shit out of me. "Shut this down."

"You gotta look." She pulled up a subfolder with a list of videos. "That detective's scanned these. The tops are the ones he's watched the most times."

I sat and opened the first one. The clip lasted only a few seconds, taken the night of the attack. It was of my hands marred with rust, dirt, and blood when I revealed them to the pear-shaped nurse. The E.R. room had been crowded, so the clip hadn't come from the camera on the wall; instead, it came from overhead, the view close. Had there been a camera directly over us?

Shit.

The footage had a flicker that seemed familiar, although I couldn't place why, not that it diminished the view.

My heartrate quickened as I pulled up more videos. There were images of me in the ambulance, outside the police station, on the train. One video was jerky, like someone filmed while they ran, of me at the reactor as I hurried to my car and drove off.

Mina entered the room. "What are you watching?" She inhaled sharply. "God, Talia, what have you done?"

"I'm trying to help."

I replayed the last video and pointed at the screen. "This was after Raven called me. I didn't know anyone was filming, didn't even know anyone was outside."

I pulled up another where I drove past the frame, slowing as I approached the hole in Hoyts' wall, the timestamp of my arrival visible in one corner. Another video showed the pipe I'd used, the view zooming in on a set of smeared prints. I suspected they were mine.

I looked at Mina. "You know what this means."

She left the bedroom, waving for me to join her. I followed her to the kitchen. "We can't run," she said. "There are other ways."

"Name one."

"Ozawa is a great lawyer. He helped a family that...." She paused. I heard it too: a noise in the hallway. Talia could be listening.

Mina stepped close, her nearness almost foreign. "He's the best defense attorney in the state. I'd trust him with your life."

I looked in her eyes, then moved closer, relishing the contact. "What about Raven's? If the police figure out the truth, they'll convict her, too. She'll die."

Mina slumped. I put an arm around her, but she pulled away, turned on me. "Take the fall. Tell them you killed Trever."

"If I change my story, do you think Detective Sanchen will believe anything I tell him?"

The anger in her eyes faltered.

"We can't stop this," I said. "Our only chance is to flee the country, but we have to go now. All of us."

"And the police outside?" she asked, her voice strained.

"I'll come up with something."

* * *

We packed quickly: changes of clothes, datapacks, multivitamins. I didn't have much cash, less than five hundred. We'd need more. Mina selected jewelry we could pawn.

Before she and the girls finished, I went to the garage. My bin of leftover parts contained a motorized hinge, pieces of plexiglass, sensors, and gyroscopes. Under my worktable were hardier pieces, including a Luken titanium landing strut. The strut made me think of those security ramps that could stop a tank.

I checked the motorized hinge. It could be calibrated.

I welded the strut to the hinge, along with scraps of steel for rear brackets, then attached the sensor to the still-cooling construct. I scored the strut so it'd look discarded and amped up the hinge's motor. Finished, I wiped my prints off the construct. They'd know it was me, but I didn't want to make it easy for them.

I considered taking my datacube and dark matter sphere from where Talia had stashed them, but didn't. They wouldn't do us any good, and I didn't want to delay any longer.

As I stepped back into the house, Raven exited her bedroom, her face a range of emotions. She shouldered her backpack, then lowered it as if the cop parked outside could see it.

Talia appeared as well. Nervous but grinning.

I was nervous, too.

Mina couldn't seem to concentrate, whispering under her breath as she stuffed clothes into her purse. It reminded me of how she'd acted months after our son's death. Like then, the path of our lives had been altered. I worried how she'd cope this time.

We climbed into my car, Raven and Talia in the back like in the trips we used to take when they were little.

The policeman outside our house followed us, as I'd anticipated, which was why I had Mina drive. "Head to the Oasis."

She gave me a questioning look, then nearly floored it as she drove east out of our neighborhood, maintaining control but distracted. I put my hand on her arm, but it didn't calm her, so I stared at the police cruiser via my side mirror. Even though Mina exceeded the speed limit, he didn't pull us over. Raven and Talia added to my nervousness as they fidgeted.

The Oasis appeared, a retail complex wedged into what had been a four-block manufacturing complex, the access roads and shops an urban maze. A string of stoplights hung before us, waiting to catch us.

Mina slowed as we approached the first light, having deduced what I wanted, with the cop two cars back. Before she reached the intersection, the stoplight turned yellow. She floored it and we shot under the light, leaving the cop pinned behind the other cars. The next two lights began to turn in sequence. We made it through both. "Turn here," I said.

She turned right, drove deeper into the complex, then at my direction took an access road that cut behind a row of shops to an alley that angled through a cluster of warehouses.

She pulled over and I jumped out, my construct tight against my stomach to shield it from whatever might be watching. Stepping behind our car, I placed the device strut-side up in the middle of the pavement, near a crack that stretched across the deserted access road, and turned on its sensor.

I ran back to the car. "Go."

Mina drove past the warehouses. "I see him," she said, watching through the rearview mirror.

There was a loud pop, followed by the scrape of metal. The cruiser had triggered the sensor as the cop drove over it and the hinge snapped open, driving one end of the strut into the cruiser's undercarriage — and lifting the passenger-side wheels off the road.

Mina took off.

As we headed toward the interstate, I snaked under the steering wheel, careful not to interfere with her driving, and ripped the power from the car's GPS system. When I sat up, we were already on the 10, which turned into the Pacific Coast Highway. I scanned the skies but didn't see any drones.

We passed seaside homes and a scattering of restaurants scrunched between the road and ocean as we headed north, waves crashing to our left. Past Malibu traffic dropped off, and we had the road to ourselves. Mina sped up to add distance from the police that were surely searching for us.

The highway constricted to two lanes as we followed the coast toward Oxnard. We rounded a corner—and a car blocked the road. Kieran stood in front of it, hands in his pockets, silver hair gleaming in the sunlight.

He'd tracked us. I wasn't sure how—drones, satellite, or some other method—but it didn't matter. With the Pacific to our left and mountains to our right, we were pinned.

Mina stopped the car.

I couldn't overpower him, couldn't hurt him. His car was heavier than ours; even if we hit his at an angle, we wouldn't have the kind of speed to get past, and my car would suffer too much damage. I only had one option.

Hoping to bullshit my way out of this, I got out.

"I'm trying to be a nice guy, Dray," he said.

"This isn't what you think."

Mina, Raven, and Talia got out as well, though I wished they hadn't.

"I'm risking my job to help you," he said. "I can't help, though, if Raven refuses to have a neural net."

"I'm not afraid of you," Raven said.

"Let's calm down," I said as Kieran approached.

He ignored me. "You refused the implant. That's a law I can prove you broke." He grabbed her, nearly too fast to see, and pushed her onto the hood of my car.

I hooked his arm to get him to let go. I was strong, having worked on machinery my whole life, yet I couldn't budge him. He was enhanced— whether via gene-coding or surgery augmentation, I couldn't tell.

He shoved me so hard I went flying; I hit the ground over a car-length away, the asphalt scraping my jeans.

"You have no right," Mina shouted.

"I know you looked into me. You should know the power I wield," he said.

"I don't know anything. You and your Agency are ghosts."

I got to my feet and charged. As I approached, Raven slipped from his grasp and tried to run. He snatched her ponytail with one hand and turned back to me as I leapt, caught me in midair, and threw me to the pavement.

It took a second for my eyes to focus. My ears rang.

Mina was yelling, Raven was clawing at Kieran's face, and Talia swung at his legs with a stick she'd found. Seemingly unfazed, he gripped the side of Raven's head and pinned her against the car's hood. With his other hand, he set a small box beside her and opened it. From the government-coded sticker on the lid, I knew what was inside.

He tore off her bandage, pulled the cover from the hole where her implant had been, and tossed it over his shoulder, where it landed in the dirt.

I got to my feet again, jumped on his back, and desperately hooked his arm with all of my strength, but I had no leverage. I reached for the bumper with my foot, hoping to hook it to create a fulcrum.

Kieran pulled a neural net out of the box, the two leads extending and locking into place.

I strained to stop him, Raven struggled to get away, and Talia hit him again, but he didn't slow. He centered the neural net over the hole in her temple — I yanked on his arm as hard as I could to stop him, to not hurt my child — and rammed the device into her head.

He then jerked his arm back, slamming his elbow into me. I landed on the road.

Kieran stood over me as Mina ran to Raven, who cupped the side of her head and screamed.

I felt sick, furious, and heartbroken. "How dare you," I roared at him.

"Do what I want, get me the tech, and we'll be friends again, Dray. You need friends."

CHAPTER TEN

I led Raven, Mina, and Talia into Whittier Medical Center's E.R. forty-five minutes later. There had been closer E.R.s, but the team here had saved Raven the night of the attack. They knew what she'd gone through.

She continued to cup her head, half-leaning against Mina, who kept an arm around Raven's waist. Talia followed close behind.

I waved down the first nurse I could find, who hurried over with a wheelchair and helped Raven into it. We followed him down the examination-room-lined hallway, Talia asking if she could push Raven, but I was stopped by the pear-shaped nurse who'd interrogated me the last time. I wanted to yell at her, furious with Kieran and tormented about Raven, but answered her questions as my family disappeared into one of the rooms.

As she accessed my information, I glanced at the entrance. Our new police tail, which had arrived after Kieran left, pulled into view.

"I want to interview your daughter alone," the nurse said.

Her statement snapped my attention back. "Why?"

She took in my clenched fists. "We have to determine our patients' safety."

"You think *I* did this?"

Before she could respond, Mina and Talia appeared. "The doctor needs your help," Mina told her.

Without a word, the nurse disappeared into the room. Mina hugged me, squeezing hard. "I want to hurt him."

I squeezed back, our shared anger and grief bonding us greater than I'd felt in years. "Did the doc really ask for the nurse?"

She shook her head, which made me smile. She pulled away. "We need to call Ozawa."

"I want Kieran locked up too, but The Agency will protect him."

"I'm not talking about that. We can't run from this."

"We don't have a choice."

"How, Dray? Both the police and Agency were watching us."

"We'll be smarter next time. We'll make it seem innocent to get a head start."

"It won't work."

"We can't rely on your political connections," I said, not unkindly. "They won't get involved, especially once charges are filed. We'll leave as soon as Raven is discharged and stick to the interstates so we can't be grabbed without witnesses."

Talia chimed in. "I can help drive. What? I'll use the nav system. I won't touch the wheel."

The nurse emerged from Raven's room, frowning at Mina before walking away. We went in.

"...it's not legal," Dr. Nystrom was saying. "I could lose my license."

"He invaded my body. I want it out," Raven said. The area around her temple was bruised, her eyes red.

"Even if I wanted to remove the implant, your skull is too fragile. The entire side could fracture. You understand what would happen, don't you?"

Mina curled her arm around Raven's shoulders as she visibly tried not to cry.

Nystrom looked upset as well. "If it's any consolation, the leads went into the existing channels in your frontal lobe, so there's no tissue damage. Any problems accessing the 'net?"

"I haven't tried," Raven said softly. "I just want it out."

"Is there any way to remove it?" I asked.

Nystrom shook her head.

I wondered if there was a tracker in the new implant. Kieran wanted the rebels. After what he'd done, he probably assumed Raven would try even harder to join them.

She looked like a shell of her former self. "Will you give me more nanobots to heal?"

"Do you promise to leave your implant alone?" Nystrom asked.

Raven didn't respond, which the surgeon appeared to take as consent.

As Nystrom injected a new set of 'bots, Raven asked, "Did you get in trouble for not implanting my neural net?"

"A little."

Mina asked, "How long will it take for her to heal?"

"The next twenty-four hours are critical. After that, the nanobots should have the new lattice in place, but it'll take two or three additional days for the artificial bone to set."

Under my breath, I said to Mina, "We may not have that long."

Talia hugged Raven, who curled into her.

Nystrom said, "Why don't I replace your lens again? It's a quick procedure. Maybe it'll help with your hazy vision." She indicated Talia. "It's pretty squeamish."

As Nystrom retrieved a small, coded box from a locked cabinet, Mina gently pulled Talia toward the door. "We'll wait outside. Come on, nugget."

"I wanna stay," Talia said to no avail.

Raven took my hand. "Will you?"

Nystrom said, "I'm not supposed to let anyone see them." She took in Raven's despair. "Fine. But this stays between us."

From the box, she removed two clear bowls approximately three inches in diameter. Each contained a lens floating in saline. I understood the procedure, using medicine's decades of cataract surgery expertise to replace people's lenses, but I was curious. I leaned closer. Processors, receivers, and a kinetic battery encircled the synthetic lenses, the components along the outer rim, and a curved rod extended from the edge of each lens, thin as a human hair, with a miniscule bulb at the end.

"What's that?" I asked, pointing at the bulb. I suspected I knew, but it couldn't be.

"It's a calibrator that makes sure the lens is always focused correctly. The sensor rests in our natural blind spot, where the retina folds into the optic nerve, so it doesn't interfere with our vision."

"Are these in everyone's lenses?" I heard the alarm in my voice.

"Of course. It's how we all have perfect vision."

I remembered the video Talia had hacked. I glanced down at my hands, my heart accelerating. "They're not just to correct our vision—and the implants aren't to help us. They're to control us."

CHAPTER ELEVEN

Dr. Nystrom and Raven looked confused by my pronouncement. "The lenses don't control us," Nystrom said. "We're free to access anything we want. There's federal oversight to make sure we never have restrictions."

"Those 'calibrators' are cameras — which means every person is a walking security feed. The police can tap into them anytime, record what we see, and use it against us."

"Mr. Quintero, you've been under a lot of strain — "

"I saw it. A video, taken at this hospital. It was footage of my hands, captured from the eyes of your nurse. The video even caught her blinking." That's what the strange yet familiar flicker had been.

Nystrom said something, but I was too floored to catch it. My own eyes betrayed me. How the hell could we run if the authorities saw where we looked? I had to warn Mina and Talia, but how without alerting the police or Kieran that we knew their secret? Whoever was probably watching through my eyes would see their reaction.

"...times of stress, things aren't always what you think," the surgeon was saying.

"Remember how the implants were revealed to us?" I asked her. "They'd been controversial until their makers showed they couldn't be tampered with, so Congress passed them into law. We all got swept up in the promise of what they could do. But we got it wrong. We shouldn't have worried about our information being hacked. We should've worried about our lives getting hacked."

America had fallen behind in so many areas: business, innovation, wealth, technology. If it wasn't for our military, we would've become a second-rate country. China, India, Russia, and most of Europe had been more innovative and more competitive, leaving us behind.

The implants had enabled us to reclaim our worldwide status.

Synched with employers' private systems, and with mankind's collective knowledge at our fingertips, we'd tripled our productivity, magnified our ingenuity, and recaptured our global dominance.

"That can't be true," Nystrom said, though she sounded less sure. "The calibrators aren't supposed to record anything, just gauge the clarity of our vision."

"Which they do by streaming what we see to our lenses, which adjust to sharpen the image — but the data is also broadcast to our implants and out to whoever can access it." We'd been told our implants registered eye-muscle movements to track where we "looked" within our lenses' interfaces. But our implants actually saw our change in focus. Saw everything.

"That's how the government is able to tell their lies," Raven said. "They can see what anyone's doing — oh god, or did."

I knew what she was thinking. "They wouldn't be able to record everyone's broadcast all the time. The sheer volume of data, twenty-four-hour feeds from over eight hundred million people, would be like trying to drink from a firehose the size of our house. They probably just watch those who are suspected of breaking the law."

"If they weren't before, they're watching me now — and you and Mom and Talia, along with who knows how many others. Don't you see? They want to control us, *all* of us, to stay in power. They're lying to us like the Founding Fathers said."

I faced Nystrom. "I want my implant out. Both of ours. The whole family's."

"Mr. Quintero, please calm down — "

"I'll pay whatever you want."

"What you're asking is akin to treason. Besides, it'd be taking a piece of you, the repository of all your settings, uploaded files — "

"This isn't my implant. It's empty," Raven said.

"We'll take the risk," I said. "We have to."

Nystrom looked upset. "I can't."

* * *

Trying not to look anxious — hell, borderline, full-on panicked — I ushered Mina and Talia down the hallway and into an unoccupied room.

"Don't look at my lips," I told them. "You won't believe me, but what I'm about to say is true."

"Now I can't stop looking at your lips," Talia said.

I covered my mouth and told them what I'd learned.

"Whoa, Dray, how hard did Kieran hit you?" Mina asked with a smile, which faded as I continued. When I was done, they looked stunned, confused, and frightened — so I averted my gaze.

"It can't be," Mina said.

"We've seen it: the police video we watched of my hands," I said. "Remember the strange flicker? It was the nurse blinking."

"Oh, knarl," Talia said.

Mina said, "You're sounding as paranoid as Raven."

"Are they watching right now?" Talia asked. "Can you tell?"

I risked looking at Mina. "Why do you think our lenses and first implant are installed when we're so young? It's so they can monitor everyone — and no one resisted! No one even thought about it."

Raven entered the room. "I wondered where you were. Dad, keep your voice down."

Mina helped her sit on the empty bed before turning to me. "What you're suggesting is wrong."

"The question isn't whether it can be done, but would someone use the access to retain power? The cameras are there, so it becomes a moral question. That's the problem. They watch everything we do, which means they know our secrets. They can control us."

As I said the words, I understood Raven's need to run. Maybe she'd known deep down that something was wrong. It didn't excuse her betrayal, or alleviate my hurt, but we had bigger problems.

Talia gasped. "They saw me hack into the police's server, didn't they?"

"You did *what*?" Raven asked.

"Not only that, they have proof your mother and I were accomplices," I said. "We have to watch what we do. No more hacking, no more anything illegal."

Mina's eyes were fixated on a spot across the room. "Are you communicating with someone?" I asked.

"Of course not. Dray, this isn't possible. There's monitoring, oversight, not to mention civil rights issues. The world's too complicated for something of this magnitude."

"The ones who would've protected us are the ones who are doing it."

"The government's not your enemy."

"Are you sure, Mom?" Raven asked. "If Dad's right, no one would ever be able to conspire against them. They'd stay in power forever."

Talia asked me, "Why haven't the coppers busted me for hacking them?"

"Kieran is playing a game. He wants us to lead him to the rebels." Sanchen had a different goal—a guilty verdict—so he was gathering as much evidence as he could.

Talia crossed her arms. "I don't believe you about the lenses."

"Neither do I," Mina said.

I suddenly remembered Trever and Raven's implants. Did I look at them when I hid them in the sink? No. If I had, the cops would've taken them by now.

"Dad?" Raven asked. "If you're right, how do we get away?"

A weight pressed against my shoulders. "I don't know."

* * *

The next morning, I walked guardedly through the train station. There were more people than last time, two dozen or so, drinking coffee, buying tickets, each one unknowingly filming everything they saw.

Capturing images of me.

I tried to act normal, though I didn't feel that way. Not anymore. I'd known cameras and digital footprints could be tracked—as could a person's neural net if the government really wanted—but this was a level of monitoring more intimate and invasive than I ever could've fathomed.

The sensation of being watched stayed with me on the train. Zoned out or not, passengers' eyes still filmed unless content covered their vision. Even if so, mine were filming, revealing everything I saw.

Union Station's main terminal was worse; sensors and cameras and people layered every square inch of the place, a web of inescapable views that could track us. Convict us.

This would drive me insane.

As I forced myself down the escalator and through the terminal, random people giggled or frowned or said something out loud, each captivated by their implants. I'd barely noticed in the past, as it was as normal as someone sneezing. Now I tensed. I wondered if Raven was right, if her terrorist friends actually were fighting for the right reasons—not that I condoned their actions.

Entering my office building didn't ease my tension.

Although I'd come here to hide in the motions of the ordinary, I didn't feel safe, not even when I reached my office suite. Our security and technology, and the products we made, seemed ominous, especially as we'd indirectly participated by advancing processing power and global communications systems, both of which were now used against everyone.

I wanted to rip the cameras out of my eyes. I imagined I could feel them, resting against my retina, swiveling as I shifted my gaze, but it would take medical expertise and specialized equipment to reach them. I had to focus on my neural net instead, to neutralize it somehow.

I scanned the sonicors, motherboards, connectors, and robotic parts scattered across my desk, searching for ideas—and realized I'd just shown whoever was watching everything I had at my disposal. I couldn't just sit at my desk, though, and stare at a blank wall.

Neural nets broadcasted across a wide spectrum, but any signal could be blocked with the right materials. I reached for a datapad to enter some notes, but froze. Not only would my intentions be seen, but if I succeeded in cutting off my feed, I'd reveal to the cops—who had to be actively watching me—that I knew the truth, blowing the one advantage I had.

At least I didn't feel guilty about lying to Sanchen anymore.

I had a flashback from childhood—the night I'd taken down Mom's boyfriend, and the look of understanding on the police officers' faces when they found us, my fists bloodied, one of my arrows jutting out of her boyfriend's leg. The officers had made sure he was alive, attended to the wounds he'd inflicted on Mom, and then covered up my crime.

Neural nets were just starting to be implanted around that time, a fantastic gateway to seemingly unlimited knowledge that lawmakers had embraced. Everyone had.

I felt more protective of my family than ever. We couldn't rely on the cops. Not like back then.

Scanning my desk again, I got to work.

Hours later, as Silversun Pickups' hits thumped in my ears, I slid the lipstick-sized, cylindrical cover over the components and locked it in place. The pulsor was done. When Raven pressed the bottom, the device would trigger a pulse of electroenergy strong enough to pulverize a car door. I used my ion blade to cut the tiny capacitator's guide so it would fit in the casing I'd made, then slipped the knife into my pocket. While I was taking a chance by looking at what I was doing, only a pulsegun manufacturer would know what I'd made.

I slid the casing onto a second pulsor, not sure if Mina would use it but making one just the same. I considered making one for Talia but didn't, as she'd "accidentally" try it on someone as soon as she could. I'd made an electrorod for me, which was similar to what the police wielded. It wasn't as powerful as the pulsors, but it still packed a punch.

I wasn't sure what else to make. Every idea I came up with was lethal.

It didn't help that I kept thinking about the implants hidden in my garage. I needed to dump them. Today. But how, with the cops watching through my eyes? Even if I went somewhere without cameras or people, their software could pinpoint my location with a single landmark.

Which meant I couldn't give it one.

The hoverbike was the answer—fly to the middle of the Pacific where there was nothing but water in every direction. I'd attract attention rocketing across the city, so I needed to grab the implants first. Getting them to the office would be risky. I suspected the police had deployed sensors that could detect the rare metals used by the implants—the pegastrium, fermium, and other metals used in both the implants' i929 processing cubes and their sub-terrahertz-spectrum transmitters. Luckily for me, I worked at a place that had the kind of sealable container I needed.

After I hid the pulsors and electrorod in my desk, I raided the R&D lab's supply closet for disposable gloves and a triple-seal material container. If I loaded the broken implants into the container correctly, I could move them without tipping off the police.

A calendar reminder appeared in my field of vision. It was my day to pick up Talia from school. I texted Mina, but she responded she couldn't get Talia, as she was working on "angles", whatever that meant.

* * *

The multi-level Union Station was packed with the first wave of commuters heading home for the evening. Many, I suspected, were like me, needing to pick up kids from schools—kids whose eyes tracked them without their knowledge.

To reach my train, I needed to go up a three-story escalator, through the promenade, and then down the correct stairs. I'd already looked up my train on the way over, so I knew which track was mine.

I stepped onto the escalator.

"Don't turn 'round."

I recognized the Creole voice as a gun pressed into my back.

"You understand now?" the guy asked. "You look at me, it's a death sentence."

"I'm not the only eyes they're looking through. They see us talking, they'll arrest both of us."

"Not 'less you react." Which meant he was shielding his face. "They don't look through everyone's—too many to track—but they're lookin' through yours. Once you become a suspect, you're watched constantly 'til you screw up. Which you will."

Hearing him substantiate my assumptions didn't calm my paranoia. "What do you want?"

"Ta help. Memorize this number." He recited ten digits. "When you're ready, call for instructions."

"Why should I trust you?"

"We have more to lose than you. What you did to protect Raven is what we look for. You should join us. Make a difference."

Did you let Raven get attacked, I wanted to ask, but didn't.

"You've been lucky, but you won't last," he said. "That night at the hospital, I was gonna distract the detective. If he'd gotten his hands on you sooner, you would've been toast."

"Why does it matter when he talked to me?"

"Each net's got two memory sticks: a main one, and another that holds a twenty-four-hour loop recordin' of everything you see. That way, if you're killed—"

"It records who did it."

"Yep. Stops recordin' when your heart stops. You prevented the detective from downloadin' your video 'fore it was recorded over."

I remembered Sanchen's alarm beeping. "That's why he became more anxious the longer I stalled."

"Ai-yeah."

"Raven's implant, and Trever's, would show what really happened." The cops had the tech to retrieve the memory sticks' data, even though I'd submerged them in water.

"Where are they?" the rebel asked. "We can move 'em."

The top of the escalator approached. Shadows moved about the floor above us, but people weren't visible yet.

"You didn't help Raven. You haven't even asked how she's doing."

"I'm shredded 'bout what happened. She and Trever didn't come to the meet-up point, stoppin' way before it. I didn't find 'em 'til after you did. It kills me I didn't protect her."

The top neared. Five steps. Four. "I'll handle things my way," I said.

"You're in over your head."

The top arrived.

"Is Raven OK?" he asked as I stepped off.

"Little late to ask."

CHAPTER TWELVE

I pulled into the parking lot of Talia's middle school, the red, Spanish-style roofs a contrast to the gray walls of the complex. Thirty or so students stood in an arc in the parking lot, their backs to the campus, and typed with their datarings, their fingers like spiders twirling around captured flies.

I parked and walked past them to the entrance. As I approached the nearest building, the door opened and Kieran walked out. My hands clenched. I wanted to make the coldhearted brute suffer like he'd made Raven suffer.

He actually smiled. "I hope I didn't hurt you too much."

I struggled to reign in my anger, aware of where we were. The power he wielded. "You could've killed Raven."

"I knew what I was doing. I want us to be friends, Dray. I understand you have trust issues. Dad knocked up your mom but didn't want to leave his wife. I can give you proof that'll force him to recognize you as his son."

"That's none of your goddamn business."

"I'm trying to help. Speaking of which, tell Raven not to stress about the days she's missed. We'll adjust her grades at the end of the semester."

I'd underestimated him. Unlike Sanchen, Kieran wasn't bound by laws — or rules.

"You're still upset about what happened," he said. "You know how important it is she has an implant. It's for her betterment."

I wanted to punch him so badly my muscles ached.

He looked over his shoulder as Talia appeared behind him. "Congrats on that test today. You've got a good head on those shoulders."

She stopped at the edge of the walkway and picked up a large rock. Holding it high, she started toward him until I intercepted her.

"No," she said as I pried the rock loose.

"I like you," he told her.

"What do you want?" I asked, holding her as she struggled to get to him.

"You. Your data, your glider, and the bikes your company created. Do that, and we'll forget Raven's transgression."

"Don't do it," Talia said.

"I'm sure you can access my company's data without me," I said.

"Everything's locked away on the 48th floor of your building," he said. "Bring them and join me."

"Why do you need me? Take the bikes yourself."

"I want the man who conceived them."

"You're asking me to steal."

He dropped his friendly act. "The police are coming. Sanchen is convinced you've hidden Raven and Trever's implants in your house. You don't want his men snooping around there, do you?"

"I don't know what you're talking about."

He smiled. He'd heard how forced my statement was. "I can protect you, but only if you give me what I want."

A kid hurried past and joined the other students in the outward-bowing arc.

I realized Kieran had intercepted me here so we could talk without anyone eavesdropping. That's why the kids were in the parking lot. It's where the school's interference of their neural nets ended. Schools blocked uplinks to prevent students from cheating or getting distracted—which meant he was probably telling the truth.

"Sanchen is talking to a judge right now," Kieran said. "He's getting a search warrant. If they find the implants, you'll be arrested for murder."

"You really think I hurt my own child?" I asked as Talia pressed against me.

"I don't care if you did. Get me what I want."

* * *

I was so rattled I barely remembered the drive home. I had to ditch the implants now. If Kieran was right, I had minutes at most.

I ushered Talia into the house. "Go do your homework." Without waiting for a reply, I dove into the basement to find something to use as a hook. It didn't have to be long, but it had to be strong enough.

It took almost five minutes to find what I needed, time I didn't have. With my hooked wire in hand, I ran upstairs and entered the garage. I noticed the water immediately, two drops on the ground near the sink.

I ran my hand inside the bowl. There were a few more drops, as if something had been pulled out of the drain. "Talia," I yelled. I felt the drain cover, jerking my eyes away before I touched it. The cover was loose. She'd taken them. How stupid was I to think she hadn't seen me hide them? Her hands must've been small enough to grab them.

Shit.

As I searched the house, I remembered she'd been quiet on the way home. That hadn't been like her.

I went out back.

Our backyard was mostly natural, with trees and a patch of turf planted years ago. Few of the neighbors had fences, which meant she could've gone anywhere, weaving between houses and cutting north toward the Roosevelt Golf Course, southwest toward her school, or east toward the freeway.

I called Mina. "Have you talked to Talia?"

"No. Why?"

Someone rang our doorbell, which triggered an alert in my vision. "You need to come home right away."

I hung up and answered the door. Sanchen was there, eight uniformed cops behind him. "Mr. Quintero, we have a warrant to search your house."

"I need to call my lawyer first."

"No. Now, Mr. Quintero."

I reluctantly stepped aside. "What's the reason for this?" I asked as they entered, hoping to stall the inevitable.

He directed his team to spread out. "I'm not going to discuss our investigation, but I do have some questions. We found rust from the murder weapon at the hospital, rust that came from you. Care to explain?"

Hating that I couldn't go after Talia, I said, "When I found Raven, I heard something. I feared her attacker was coming back, so I picked up the pipe and looked around," mentally cringing that I'd left it where I'd broken open their implants.

"You didn't mention that before."

"I didn't think it was important."

"Your daughter was seriously wounded, but you left her to 'look around'?"

A cop passed by with a scanner, the open end collecting god knew what. Actually, I feared I knew: Talia had moved the implants. She would've left a trail.

I needed to get the cops out of my house, needed to find her. "Am I being charged with something?"

"You have one last chance to confess. If you do, I'll try to minimize the ramifications for Raven. Trever's parents won't stop until they find his killer. They might even understand you protecting your daughter... but I don't think you protected her, did you? Trever's body was bruised. Did you see him hit her, rip out her implant, so you did the same only not as gently?"

I could use Sanchen's suspicion, warp it to clear Raven and me, but didn't have time to work out how — and couldn't let him get his hands on their implants. "I didn't touch him."

Sanchen eyed me for a second, then joined his men.

I had to find Talia before they did.

I remembered her hacking into their system. She was terrible about closing out of things.

Sanchen's men had spread throughout the house. At least two were in the basement, and someone was in the garage. The rest were focused on our bedrooms. Three were in Raven's room, two in the master. One was in Talia's, opening drawers. The movement caused her screen to turn on. I stepped into the room as it did, the LAPD's subfolders appearing on the wall behind the young police officer. Not wanting him to turn around and see it, I said, "The detective's looking for you."

The officer frowned at me but left.

I sat at Talia's desk and grabbed her datapad. Typing quickly, I used the department's server to access the national surveillance system and logged into the encrypted network via my backdoor credentials — which I'd left as a little rebellion, not that I'd ever expected to use it. I pulled up the facial recognition program and targeted L.A., then accessed Talia's pictures on her datapad and uploaded a rare, face-forward, serious-expressioned shot of her. I filed her image under a false name and instructed the program to ignore all other requests until it located her.

"What are you doing?" Mina whispered, nearly making me leap out of Talia's chair. I hadn't heard her come in.

I unhooked the datapad, collapsed it, and put it in my pocket. "Do you know where Talia went?"

"No."

Sanchen called my name. Mina and I found him by our back door. "Where's your younger daughter?" he asked.

I glanced at Mina. "She might've gone to a friend's."

"With a houseful of cops? No, she left for a reason." He led us to a spot near the rear property line and pointed to a leaf. "We found metal residue. The implants were here."

A faint ring marred the leaf: a dried waterdrop. The water must've interfered with their airborne sensors, but as soon as it evaporated, they'd found the residue, a few parts per billion in the back of our yard.

"Where is she?" he asked.

"We don't know," Mina said.

Sanchen keyed his commlink. "Dispatch, initiate a citywide search for Talia Quintero. Inspection team, box up everything, including the spaceship in the garage." He dropped his hand and looked at me. "You should call that lawyer."

Mina touched my arm as he walked away. "I'll call the D.A.'s office, see if I can slow them down."

"OK, but stay here," I said, my voice as quiet as hers.

"Where are you going?"

"To level the field."

CHAPTER THIRTEEN

Ignoring my car's computer-operated autodrive, I wove through traffic toward downtown, the engine whining as I pushed the speedometer toward ninety. As I drove, I checked Talia's datapad, but the police software hadn't found her yet.

I searched through my phone contacts, the numbers scrolling along the left side of my vision, found the one I needed, and sent it to my car's system. "Amarjit," I said when he answered, "I need you to get something for me. It's urgent. "

"What's wrong? You sound distressed."

"No time. Listen closely." I jammed the accelerator and gave him exact instructions.

When I finished, he asked, "Are you shitting me?"

"Don't tell Nikolai. Don't tell anyone."

When I exited the highway downtown, the heavy traffic forced me to slash my speed, so I selected my work address, put the car in autodrive, and expanded the datapad. No results yet. I fished an audiolink out of my glovebox and linked it to the 'pad, which enabled me to hear the cops' chatter as they searched for Talia.

I was two blocks from my office when the screen flashed and a beep sounded in my ear, followed by the words I'd feared. "Suspect's been spotted, Griffith Park, south of the boy's camp." The facial program reflected her image, which had been captured by a camera at the camp's entrance. She'd gone over a mile in undeveloped terrain.

As soon as the program found her, it alerted me as I'd instructed, then proceeded to the next scan on its list, which was also for Talia, and alerted the police.

I called Amarjit. "You in position?"

"Dock B. Should I bring it out?"

"No, I'm almost there." Taking control of my car again, I cut through a back street toward the rear of my office building, across our lot, and into the warehouse-sized loading area to Dock B.

Amarjit waited anxiously by the service elevator. "I didn't know where to hide it," he said as I exited my car. He pushed the elevator button, and the doors opened to reveal the hoverbike hidden under a tarp. "I had to cut through the lock like you said. It felt wrong."

"You did good." I yanked off the tarp and made sure the bike wasn't bolted down.

"You want it on one of the semis?"

"No." I climbed on and felt the seat depress. "Stand back."

When he did, I activated the prototype. The circular jets ignited, casting the dented elevator cab in blue light as I rose, the back jets coming on a moment later. I shoved the handles forward—

And with a *whump* shot out of the elevator, across the loading dock, and out of the building, rising as I flew across the parking lot, between two high-rises—reflected in their windows, visible to thousands of people, along with the cameras and sensors I'd triggered—and across the city. I struggled to maintain control, to remain upright, to fight my vertigo. Realizing I'd slowed slightly, I pushed harder on the handlebars. The bike responded, my legs pushing against the couplings that wrapped around my calves.

The wind nearly drowned out the audiolink. "Suspect went into the ravine. I'm sending two officers after her. Be alert. She may try to ditch the evidence."

Any acknowledgement was buried under reports of my flight.

As I angled northwest, the HOLLYWOOD sign swung into view and settled to my left. It grew larger as I approached, the various neighborhoods gliding under me as I flew past the sign and toward the mountains my daughter was trying to hide in.

A police helicopter appeared in the distance, headed toward me. I suspected it wasn't the only one.

"Suspect in sight. Thirty yards away," came a voice over the audiolink.

The hills that contained my house slid under me.

I leaned over the handlebars and angled down, my desire to get to Talia trumping my vertigo. Squinting from the wind, I dropped within two hundred feet of the ground but didn't know which ravine was the right one. I searched for the telltale blue of my adversaries.

I spotted the boys' camp but not until I was on top of it, a smattering of tents and a one-story wood structure that nearly blended into the rising hillside. I wrenched the handlebars, turning tightly in the air, and oriented to the southwest.

More reports came over the audiolink. "I lost sight of her." "We're forty yards from your position." "Found her."

I couldn't locate the ravine. Trees spread out in every direction, their canopies masking much of the terrain.

"I see her. Closing in."

Past a clump of brush, the vegetation dropped away into multiple ravines to the left, the fauna following the landscape. I angled toward them and spotted three cops clustered at the top of the nearest one. I flew into the ravine, which looked deserted, and descended.

Movement caught my eye to the right. Two cops in blue were halfway down the side, their body language telling me where Talia was. I dropped quickly, jet-blue circles of flame bright around me. My earpiece erupted as the cops warned each other of my arrival. The chatter was so loud I almost missed her cry.

"Daddy!"

She waved as she stepped into a miniscule glade below me. Past her, a female cop ran toward her, dodging sagebrush as she hurried down the sloped landscape.

I dropped farther, kicked out, and then swung toward Talia, the glade just big enough to get within a few feet. "*Get on.*"

She took three steps, leapt, and landed on the bike's ledge.

I hooked my arm around her waist and planted her on the seat in front of me. "Hold on."

She grabbed the handlebars, the cop shouted at us, and I tilted the bike, using its underbelly as a shield in case the officer was desperate enough to shoot.

Before she could, I triggered the back jets. Talia and I rocketed so fast I struggled to keep straight. We flew over the roads, freeway, houses and buildings and lives of those beneath us.

In the pulsing wind, Talia screamed.

A police helicopter approached from the south, a different one than the first chopper I'd spotted.

I slowed to regain control. "You have them?" I shouted.

She held up a fist. The top of my sock was visible, squiggling in the wind. "I didn't look at them, not once." Her scream hadn't been from fright but excitement.

I glanced at the helicopters. They'd follow our every move, as would every person on the ground and every camera hooked into the Internet. There was only one choice. "Give them to me. And hang on."

Neither of us looked as I took the implants from her.

Talia pushed her body against me and gripped the handlebars with both hands. I tightened my own grip — the implants' broken pieces jabbing my palm — angled the bike up, and, with the helicopters closing in, triggered the jets again.

Full blast.

The helicopters dropped away as we rose — so did the mountains, the city, the coastline. In seconds we passed the clouds, the sun the only thing above us.

As the wind slammed my face, I debated where to go. I wanted to throw the implants so high they'd burn up like meteorites when they fell. The heat, and the impact when they struck land, should pulverize them — but the cops could find them. Hitting water would preserve them, but they'd be hidden by the vastness of the Pacific Ocean, and the saltwater would eventually corrode them.

I turned toward the ocean and angled higher.

The bike didn't have an altimeter, so I didn't know how high we flew, but the air became frigid, and the sky turned more white than blue, the earth's curvature visible. Seconds later, the white began to fade.

"Daddy?" Talia asked, her voice barely audible.

I found it hard to breathe. "Almost there. Then we'll go back." The fuel gauge was fuzzy, but I thought we had enough gas.

The sky darkened further. Half gray now. Good enough. "I'm going to throw them," I said. "Don't look."

Was my voice always this hollow?

My movements sluggish, I slowed and leveled the bike — no way was I letting go of the handlebars going so fast — hooked my arm back, threw the implants as hard as I could —

And Talia, who'd stopped pushing against me, fell off the bike.

With a surge of adrenaline, I lunged and caught her foot at the last second.

My fear gave me a moment of clarity: we'd suffered from a lack of oxygen and numbness from the cold, her smaller body succumbing first. But I'd lunged too far. The bike rotated sideways, pulled by our momentum, and although the clamps held my calves in place, my butt lifted from the seat, turning off the bike's gravity-nullifying effects.

We plummeted.

As we fell, I grabbed Talia's ankle as tight as I could, the bike falling with us, though it caught the wind and swung above us. The clamps kept me attached to it, but it turned me upside down.

Talia regained consciousness and screamed. Beneath her was nothing but the Pacific miles below, the coastline in the distance. The wind tore at us, trying to snatch her away. As we fell, I pulled her to me, gripping her calf, then thigh, squeezing so tight I probably bruised her. She struggled to reach me but almost slipped from my grasp. We started to spin—her, me, and the bike. Nausea competed with my adrenaline. I caught her waist and pulled her close.

We wrapped our arms around each other, her legs clasped tight around me. I closed my eyes, but only for a second. "Hang on," I yelled.

The bike rotated above us. It seemed unreachable.

I pulled with my legs to draw us up and tried to sit on the bike upside down. As soon as I pressed on the seat, the antigravity force kicked in—and turned us from a heavy falling object into a weightless falling object. With our speed and angle, the abrupt change spun us, throwing me off the seat—returning gravity to us—and flipping us end over end, the bike's weight wrenching my legs. Talia screamed, and I struggled to hold onto her.

Gravity and the wind slowed our spin as we fell, settling us after a minute with the bike once more above us.

I had to try again—and hurry. Not only were we closer to land, but one of the leg-clamps was loose.

I lunged for the bike, one hand pressed against Talia's shoulders as I reached for the handlebars with the other. I managed to catch it, yelled at her to hold tight, and let go of her. I caught the other hand-grip, my back to the ocean, and sat down.

Once again weightless, the bike spun and twisted, the coastline—larger and closer than before—swinging into view, then disappearing. I managed to hold on but was disoriented, the world flipping around me, and the loose clamp became wobbly.

I triggered the back jets, but that made the spin worse. I cut them, then pushed forward on the handlebars and tried quick bursts to cut into our momentum. After a few more bursts, I stopped our spin, but we were pointed straight down. I triggered the jets again, longer this time, arching down and outwards until we were parallel with the ocean, then slowed. Seconds later, we were nearly stationary.

Talia shook. So did I. I held her.

The coastline was below us. We'd made it back over land, the implants hidden somewhere in the ocean.

"You OK?" I asked.

She nodded.

"I'll go slow. You can just look at the sky."

"No, wait." She loosened her grip and turned in the seat. With my help, she settled in front of me, gripped the handlebars, and pressed her shoulders into my chest. "OK, go." Her tremors faded after a minute. "Go faster."

I did, but it wasn't enough. After some urging, I pushed the jets to the max.

When we dropped low enough to get reception, I called Mina, who hooked in Raven. "I have her. We're on our way home."

"Thank God," Raven said, which Mina echoed. "I'll meet you there."

After I hung up, I had Talia hold out her hand so the wind could scour her skin. "Did you ever put the…sock in your pocket?"

"No, just held it."

L.A. grew in definition, highways becoming visible. "How long did you know I'd hidden something in the sink?"

"You're not that clever, Dad."

* * *

Reports filled my ear as the police sighted us, their voices sharp over the audiolink. As helicopters closed in to intercept us, I slipped Talia's datapad into her hand, decreasing our angle so she didn't have to hang on so tight. "Wipe the whole thing."

"Alls of it?"

"They're going to take it as evidence. Don't look at it."

"I won't." She kept one hand on the handlebars as she cleared the datapad's memory.

The helicopters surrounded us and followed us to the treetops. Police cruisers approached the house, joining the ones already there as we dropped between the trees, arriving the same time we did.

Mina ran up as we stepped off the bike, but Sanchen barked at her. "Stay back." He shoved me against the bike and angrily patted me down. When he came up empty, he scanned me, then Talia, then Mina. He had one officer seal the datapad, another scrape our hands for residue, and instructed others to search the bike.

Mina put an arm around Talia.

"Don't move," he snapped, then turned on me. "You interfered."

"She's a little girl—"

"Who stole evidence."

He swiveled toward the bike. His men didn't find anything, although they did discover two storage compartments I didn't know existed. Damn thing seemed ready for production. "Where'd you get the jet?"

The helicopters hovered overhead while much farther away, forced to keep their distance to avoid tangling with the helicopters, reporter-drones circled.

"It's a concept vehicle," I said. "Like the one in the garage."

Past him, Raven parked and exited her car.

"It's evidence now." Sanchen signaled his men. "Confiscate it."

"You can't. It's my company's."

Raven ran past us, fell to her knees, and hugged Talia. "I was so worried. You OK?"

Sanchen interrupted. "Raven Quintero, you're under arrest for colluding with known enemies of the state."

Mina and Talia argued her innocence. "I haven't colluded with anyone," Raven said.

"We found the calls you made the night Trever died, the one to your father and the one to a burner phone. Burners aren't registered, but they leave a trace, and we found the receiving end. The person you talked to walked past an ATM at precisely 8:42 p.m. that night. He's a domestic terrorist. We found the conversation, too. You weren't attacked by thieves. You were trying to join the terrorist's group. I bet you planned all along to kill Trever."

"My daughter's not a murderer or any of the things you claim," I said.

"She tried to join them again yesterday. Didn't you, Ms. Quintero? You called the same man."

She gasped, and I stepped between them. "That's enough."

As a cop approached to cuff her, she whispered something in Mina's ear. The cop separated them before Mina could reply and secured Raven's arms behind her back.

"I'll get you out," I told her.

Sanchen faced me. "You're under arrest as well, for interfering with a police investigation."

"I was only —"

"My men had Talia surrounded, but you interfered, and I think more. There were traces of rare metals in your garage —"

"I use a lot of metals in my research."

He leaned close. "Whatever you did up there, I'll find out."

CHAPTER FOURTEEN

The next twenty-four hours—twenty-eight, thirty, however many it was—were excruciating. Sanchen and another detective interrogated me repeatedly, baiting me to respond, to defend myself, threatening my daughters' futures, and when I didn't respond, threw me in a jail cell.

I aged in that cell. Instead of forty-six, I felt ninety.

The cell door finally opened, and a guard escorted me to a room unlike any I'd ever seen. It was all white—floor, walls, ceiling—with a white table and two chairs, everything smooth, the corners of the room rounded.

Ozawa, the attorney who'd rescued me from Sanchen's first interrogation, entered as I sat, took the chair across from me and placed a police-tagged datascreen on the table. "Mr. Quintero, you can talk freely in here. Notice there's no mirror, no corners, nothing where a camera or mic could hide."

I looked at his eyes and didn't respond.

"Describe everything that happened. The more you tell me, the better."

If I hadn't been desperate for news of my girls, I wouldn't have said a word. "What have the police told you?"

He repeated much of what Sanchen said when he arrested Raven and me. "The phone call between your daughter and the suspected terrorist prompted the search warrant."

I doubted that. "'Suspected'. Not confirmed?"

"His dossier reflects a handful of convictions for petty crimes. Then he dropped off the grid, which they think proves he joined one of the groups. He surfaced only once before now—an attack on a storage farm in Olympia, which the detective believes he orchestrated. He wasn't caught, but his picture was. It's the only image the police have, but it

107

matched the ATM footage. Did they tell you about your company?"

"No."

"The CEO dropped the charges against you, which allowed them to get their prototype back. Oh, and I was told you're allowed a message."

He held up a disc that projected an image to my lens-screens. Nikolai appeared as if standing before me. Words formed beneath him. *By majority vote of the Board, you have been terminated. We ask that you vacate your seat as well. Your post-employment-rights packet will be delivered to your home.*

Fucking prick.

"The charges filed are multiple," Ozawa went on, "not only against you but Raven Quintero. They've threatened to arrest your younger daughter as well, but since the results on her hands were inconclusive, they probably won't.

"As for your case," he said, turning on the datascreen, "they claim you helped cover up Trever Hoyt's murder, but they haven't charged you with it, which means they don't have enough evidence. They suspect you've conspired with domestic terrorists, but they can't prove that either. So, you should be able to post bail after your arraignment. Your company's refusal to press charges helps. The obstruction and interference charges aren't enough to imprison you until trial."

"What about Raven?" I hadn't wanted to ask directly but couldn't stand it.

"Her charges are more severe. They found her phone, which strengthens their case. The D.A. plans to take her to trial. Her arraignment will be a formality."

"There has to be a way to free her."

"They have recordings of who she talked with, her roommate's testimony — they also have proof she'd researched resistance movements on her school's computer network."

I leaned forward, my stoicism cracking. "There must be *something*."

He turned off the datascreen. "Detective Sanchen has teams searching your house for evidence. If they don't find anything, we'll claim you're just a distraught father. We should be able to plea bargain —"

"Don't worry about me. We need to help Raven."

"She's been branded a terrorist. She doesn't even qualify for bail."

"She's not a terrorist."

"If they convict her, Mr. Quintero, the penalty is death."

* * *

Mina bailed me out the next morning.

We went to her office. We needed to talk but couldn't at home, and didn't even trust our cars. Her office, however, had a unique benefit: as Mayor Gein's chief of staff, her office was swept daily for bugs.

When we arrived, she handed me a change of clothes. I'd forgotten about the risk of Sanchen planting mics. Thank god she hadn't.

I changed in the bathroom, dumped my old clothes, then went to her office, where she was on the phone. "...anymore a terrorist than the mayor is. She was a National Honor Society candidate, and graduated near the top of her class...."

Mina's office was large, formal, adjacent to the mayor's corner suite — and seemed untouched by what had affected our family. Plaques adorned the walls, and pictures had been placed throughout the room. One grabbed me: a snapshot of our kids, all three of them. It'd been taken six years ago, on Adem's first birthday, four months before he died. I remembered the birthday, his face; I had every picture of him stored in my 'net. Still, I wasn't prepared to see his smile.

His death changed us. Aching rage had consumed me while Mina withdrew — except for occasional outbursts at me for failing to protect him from something I hadn't known had threatened him and couldn't defeat.

My anger eventually subsided, though not the ache. I'd wanted to ask if it had for her as well, but didn't want to pick that scab as she dove into her career, still involved with our family but not immersed. Not like before.

Behind me, she ended the call. I set down the picture.

Her face was strained. "The D.A.'s pushing forward. He wants to be mayor, and Trever's parents could make his campaign."

"What about your other contacts?" My voice was raw from the night in jail.

"I haven't been able to get anywhere. Neither has Gein. He said he'd reach out to the governor, but no one will help someone who...."

"Who what?"

"Who's recorded as saying she wants to become a terrorist." Her voice cracked. "God, you were right about our eyes."

"You believe me?"

"When Raven was arrested, she told me she used a relay phone that connected her phone to her rebel friend, and they only talked for thirty seconds. There's no way the police would've been able to link the call unless they knew the number she dialed—which they only would've seen if they'd watched through her eyes."

I didn't feel relief that they finally believed me; anxiety hit me, anxiety that we were trapped.

"No one will help us," she said. "Gein ran on a platform of stopping domestic terrorists. I made it my mission to defeat them."

"That doesn't matter now."

"Yes, it does. We can't fight the police. We don't have the pull anymore, and they'd see anything we do. Let's leak what we learned. I know who to talk to. We can blow everything wide open."

"We do that, best case we look like crackpots. Worst case, we're taken away and killed, along with whoever you tell."

"Then what do we do?"

I didn't like the answer. "I need a burner phone."

"What for?"

"Raven and Talia have to run. You have to take them."

"You want them to become fugitives? What kind of future will they have?"

"What kind of future do they have now?"

"One with options."

"I'm doomed, Mina. Don't subject them to the same fate."

"There has to be another way. We have rights—"

"Our 'rights' are nothing more than words on paper," I said, my anxiety and desperation bursting forth. "We can't show what we're doing, can't even look where we're going, or they'll stop us. You have one chance. If you don't take it, they'll also be doomed. The authorities will use you against each other. They'll sacrifice themselves for you—or each other."

She had tears. I'd done that. It cut me.

"Dray, don't make me do this."

"If you want to protect them, you have to." When she didn't respond, I said, "Don't let my sacrifice be for nothing."

* * *

Several hours later, I followed a line of people down the rickety escalator into the Wilshire/Normandie subway station, feeling out of place as Korean, Thai, and other languages pelted me, the gloom that swallowed me barely held back by banks of bioluminescent algae light fixtures. I waited for the Number 5 train eastbound, stepped onto the seventh car as instructed, and leaned against the left pole closest to the front. I didn't look back, not at that station or the next, keeping my head down as people flooded and exited the train.

As the subway started forward again, a gun pressed into my lower back.

I turned my head enough to acknowledge but not enough to see. "I need your help to free Raven."

"Can't," Jex said, his Creole voice just audible. I knew that was his identity. Outlaw. Rebel. I wondered if he wore his barn jacket. "I would if I could. You gotta believe me."

"I do." He was risking his life being here. I knew why. "Can you help my family get away?"

"What 'bout Raven?"

"I have one option."

"To get her out?"

I nodded, not wanting to think about it. "They'll need a place to hide." I almost smiled that I was giving him orders. My brain seemed to be working again.

"Whatever crazy shit you're plannin', do it quick. No one's lasted this long being watched."

My eyes moved on their own. I yanked them back down, but not before I glimpsed a tiny robot covering the camera in the corner of the car. His doing.

The next station approached. "You'll help them?" I asked.

"Not 'til you ditch the surveillance."

"How the hell do I do that?"

"Don't know." He slid something into my pocket. Tickets. "If you do, go here. Call when you arrive. You don't get away clean, you won't make it."

The train rolled to a stop.

"We can't meet again," he said as passengers exited the car. He started to follow them, but paused. "Sorry you're goin' through this. 'Least you see the light."

111

CHAPTER FIFTEEN

I exited two stations later, the afternoon sunlight striking me when I reached the surface.

Drones hovered overhead as three silver-haired men in steel-colored suits approached me in an equidistantly-triangular fashion. They were superior. Powerful. The city's cameras were their eyes, the listening towers their ears, the drones their wings. Abilities our forefathers never could have imagined.

The drones zipped past me and down into the subway. They knew I'd talked to someone, probably noticed the car's cameras had been blocked.

I approached the silver-haired bastard to my left. "I want to see your boss."

* * *

Kieran's unblinking blue-eyed gaze seemed to peel through the layers of my mind, laying bare the last remnant of hope I'd squirreled away. "A 'deal'?" he asked.

I looked away to shake the feeling. His fellow Agents hadn't taken me to the building near the San Fernando Valley, but to one in New Downtown, a window-covered high-rise on 7th Street. His corner office, which offered an impressive view from the forty-first floor, was empty except for his onyx-slabbed desk, two chairs, a comm speaker, and a generic print of an abandoned dock. "Get Raven out of jail, and I'll work for you."

"The police have her. They filed formal charges. How would I 'get' her out?"

"You're...." Connected. All-knowing. Frightening. "An Agent of the government."

"The government she wants to fight."

"Get her out, have them drop all charges, and I'll do whatever you want."

Kieran leaned back in his leather chair. "She's charged with treason."

"You have the pull, don't you?"

"I can free her," he allowed. "Or make her disappear."

"You don't have to threaten me."

"Clearly I do. You want me to break the law, when instead you should be begging me to protect you and your family."

I fought my fear and uncertainty. "Maybe you're not as influential as I thought. You didn't stop her arrest."

"You didn't give me what I asked for."

Jesus, he let her get arrested.

He leaned forward. "You give me the hoverbike technology, your research, and your unwavering loyalty. I'll own you. And I want you to help me capture the rebels, all of them, including the one you met on the train. Don't deny it. We caught a partial image. Who was he?"

"I'd be more productive making bikes—" I tried.

"You have no room to negotiate. The police found Trever and Raven's implants."

I managed to catch the gasp before it escaped my lips.

"You have to admire their tenacity," he said. "They used a military satellite to track the implants' fall and got a submersible that can reach the ocean floor. They're retrieving them now. There'll be some corrosion, but they'll be able to extract enough footage to learn the truth. Once they do, you'll become the most wanted man in the state."

I tried not to think about the approaching fates of my daughters, fates I'd tried so hard to avoid. "Can you save my family?"

"Only if you do everything I ask."

I clenched my fists. I was doing the right thing. "Deal."

* * *

Mina took my hand as we waited outside the police station, her large purse wedged between us. Talia leaned against me, her gaze locked on the side door.

I'd grabbed the snake's tail. I would have to keep him distracted, focused on me instead of his neural feeds. Somehow.

The door opened and Raven emerged, no handcuffs, no prison jumper, though Kieran held her arm. Talia, aware that he was behind Raven's release, tensed at the sight of him.

Raven hugged us, her embrace revealing the emotions she struggled to hide.

"We need to go," Kieran told me.

I wished he would give me a moment with them in private.

I rubbed Talia's back to try to ease her worry. "I'll see you later," I told them.

"I don't want you to pay for my actions," Raven said.

"You'll pay, too," Kieran assured her. "You're going to betray your friends."

Raven's expression hardened. "No."

"She wasn't part of the deal," I said.

"This isn't a debate," he said.

Mina flashed me a look. The burden I'd placed on her was huge, but we couldn't let Raven or Talia become pawns. Even if Kieran made the charges go away, we wouldn't be free.

I said to him, "We should get the bikes right now." Kept my breathing level.

"You don't dictate this."

"I know my company. They'll move them. If you want the prototypes, we need to go."

He swiveled his gaze from Raven to me, then back. "Rest up," he told her. "We're moving on your friends tonight—and you're going to help."

CHAPTER SIXTEEN

Thirty-five minutes later, I slowed the car as we approached the building of my former company. Kieran instructed me toward the gated entrance, which guarded the employee lot.

"I don't have access anymore," I told him.

He gazed off. After a moment, he said, "I've reversed it."

"You restored everything?" This close to him, I could see data flowing across his lenses.

He nodded.

This wasn't just the access level Talia had hacked. To protect our access protocols, I'd installed additional overlapping firewalls, each with quantum coding. They should've been impenetrable.

The gate scanned my face, then lifted as if I'd never been fired.

I parked, and we entered the building.

Employees moved about the lobby as if this was an ordinary day, while a tour group listened to a guide touting our achievements and guards watched from either side of the large space. I didn't know how the guards would react to my presence. It'd only been a day since I'd been fired, but they would have orders.

Kieran kept me moving. "Don't worry. We won't be disturbed." Though we maintained a distance, we crossed the guards' lines of sight, yet they didn't react.

Seconds later, we were in an elevator. I pressed the 48th floor, and we began to rise —

He suddenly pinned me against the wall. "You lied. Your family isn't going home. They're heading east...to the Cal-Tube Station?"

"I don't know," I lied as fear gripped me.

"I don't need you to flush out the rebels. Raven will do it. Talia's life will depend on it."

I tried to push him away. The elevator wall had more give.

"Where are they going?" he asked.

"Mina might be trying to calm Raven down. She was imprisoned, remember? When they were young, we'd drive them around the city to relax them."

He pressed harder against me, then backed off.

The doors opened, and he shoved me out.

Wary to make any sudden moves, I led him down the corridor of the storage level and into the side passage. I walked slowly but found it too quickly.

The container was empty.

I didn't understand. Then I did. My flight across the city had exposed their existence. "They moved them. There are other storage areas."

Kieran was already on it, his displeasure evident. He swiveled his gaze. "This way."

He led me to the end of the main corridor and faced the wall. My confusion turned to surprise as a bioscanner formed before us. I stepped forward.

"Don't bother."

Two thick clicks echoed from the other side of the fake wall, which rose to reveal a storage area I'd never known about. Cages of various sizes stretched away before us to form two corridors. But that wasn't all. Past the containers was a workstation with tables, 3D printers, robotic assistants, even a bathroom.

As we stepped under the fake wall, I spotted elevator doors to my right. By their size and location, it had to be Nikolai's private elevator, the unlabeled middle button that was a company mystery.

Kieran closed the fake wall. "My patience is thin."

Gazing through the reinforced wire cages, I found the bikes halfway down the first aisle. Although a tarp covered them, I recognized them immediately, parked next to a stack of small crates. "Here."

Kieran's connective wizardry opened the cage. Took seconds. He ripped the tarp off the closest bike and jerked his chin toward the three-seater. "Grab that and let's go."

Mina and the girls weren't at the station yet. The clock in my vision showed the bullet train to San Francisco was scheduled to leave in thirteen minutes, which meant they'd still be driving for another five to seven, depending on traffic.

I said, "The crates will have dark matter spheres, schematics, and other things we'll need."

His eyes narrowed. "Find the spheres. Ignore the rest. You have two minutes."

"Help me search." Anything to distract him.

"You're not the one to give orders."

"It'll go faster."

As he set down his bike, my gaze wandered to the next cage. I touched the wire-mesh that separated the two cages. "I need in there."

"We have what we came for."

"My things are there, including another sphere. It was the first one I did." Almost the truth.

The cage door popped open.

I left the large cage and entered the smaller one. They'd thrown everything into boxes stacked on top of — Jesus, they'd even stored my desk. I spotted the electrorod I'd created, the handle sticking out of a box in the back.

"That what you wanted?" Kieran asked, indicating the rod. He'd followed me, his breath on my neck.

"I'm not suicidal." I rifled through the box closest to me, then the next. The sphere I'd created was buried under a hologram-CAD reader, samples of cadmium and tritium, and spare robot joints that had been dumped from one of my desk drawers. Recognizing the contents, I dug deeper — testing Kieran's patience — until my fingers curled around the pulsor I'd created for Raven.

I pulled my arms out and pretended to look at the lipstick-shaped weapon with surprise. "Check this out." I held it casually, the end pointed to the side. His eyes glowed, looking unconcerned but scanning the device anyway. Before he could discern its purpose, I swiveled my wrist and jammed the trigger.

A pulse of high-static plasma slammed into him like liquefied lightning and hurled him out of the cage. He crashed into the container on the opposite side of the corridor and collapsed to the ground.

I lifted the electrorod out of the far box, flipped it on, and set it to the max setting.

Even with the blast he'd taken, Kieran began to move. He got to one knee, his limbs jerky. I exited the cage, took a large step, and swung as hard as I could, dimly aware I roared as I swung. The electricity-augmented blow lifted him off his feet and slammed him against the mesh-lined cage. He crumpled.

"That was for Raven."

I hoped the electricity had fried every circuit in his sick head, though I doubted it.

I used binding wire to tie him and a second wire to pin his wrists to the cage wall, aware that whoever was watching my feed witnessed my actions and would send Agents after me. I checked the time. My family should be on the train now. Gone.

I sighed. I'd done it.

Mina and I hadn't discussed what would happen if I managed to get away from Kieran. I didn't know where the rebels would hide her and the girls. I assumed it'd be in the mountainous regions north of San Francisco; it's where I heard they had bases, though I didn't know for sure. If I made it out of the city—if Kieran's men didn't find me—I'd take an indirect route to the area and try to make contact.

I needed to leave. But I was damned if I'd let Nikolai develop my bikes.

Back in the smaller cage, I slipped on my datarings, searched the boxes for my ion blade, and found the other pulsor beside it. I swiped both items and returned to the bikes' cage. The orange-gray blade of my knife sliced through the smaller bike's underbelly, the edges hardening as the severed shield dropped to the ground.

I thrust my hand into the cavity and unlatched the sphere from its cradle. It popped free, and I set it on one of the crates. I freed the sphere from the larger bike as well. A quick search of the crates yielded one more.

I took all four to the work area, picking up the one from my office along the way. Nikolai could make others, but if I was lucky, all of our current dark matter inventory would be tied up in fusion reactor projects, forcing his bike team to wait for the next collector ship to return to Earth.

A pneumatic vice was bolted to one of the worktables. It wouldn't crush the spheres, as it didn't exert any more force than the amount needed to hold an object in place, but it would help.

I set the spheres on the table, stuck the one I'd created in the vice, and grabbed a handheld harmonic-saw. It was chrome-plated, had infinite speed, and was name-branded. Nothing but the best here. While the circular blade was sharp, it was enhanced by focused soundwaves that emitted along its edge, which would slice through the double-walled aluminum like tissue.

I turned on the blade and cut into the sphere. As soon as the blade pierced its skin, there was a pop, and the saw kicked back. With the dark matter released, the vice tightened, flattening the now-empty shell.

I wasn't surprised by the kick. While dark matter itself wasn't volatile, it reacted to whatever was exerted against it. The argon gas I'd used to compress it to six times its normal density dampened the matter's reaction to the blade's assault. But even so, it'd been enough to snap the saw backwards.

Resetting the vice, I removed the crushed aluminum and set another sphere in its maw. The vice tightened, I stepped back, touched the blade to the sphere, and triggered the device.

An explosion threw me across the workspace.

I slammed into the side of a cage and tumbled to the floor. My ears rang so loudly I didn't hear the vice slam shut, didn't realize I still held onto the saw. Along with the ringing in my head, I felt a searing pain in my foot. The saw's circular blade stuck out of my shoe. It had broken off of the saw, the device now a hunk of metal. The blade had pierced my skin an inch or so from my pinky toe, its momentum taking it halfway up my foot before it stopped. I didn't have to look to know it'd taken bone. Blood already soaked my sock.

The sphere shouldn't have blown like that. Nikolai must've used something other than argon to compress the dark matter, which had exploded along with the gas. Did he know the bikes were bombs? It was a miracle I was in one piece. The worktable smoked, the vice scorched.

A medkit hung on the wall behind the table, California-required, apparently even in shady secret workspaces. My body's shock both helped and hurt, shielding me from most of the pain but interfering with my movements. I crawled to the table, careful not to let my foot or the blade touch anything. When I reached it, the medkit was high enough I was forced to stand. I put my weight on my good foot long enough to unhook the plastic box from the wall, then settled on the floor.

The kit contained gauze, ointments, sealers, and other supplies. Setting out what I thought I needed, I took a breath and yanked out the blade, which sent a surge of heat through my body. Breathing quickly, I untied my shoe, my broken bones shifting as I pulled my foot free.

Blood coated my sock and dripped on the floor. My hand trembling, I removed the sock, tossed it aside, and sprayed my foot with antiseptic, cracked the pain vial and injected it into the side of my foot, then cleaned the area as best I could.

When I pulled the cinchwrap out of the medkit, I spotted two large vials underneath. I recognized them from when Dr. Nystrom had used them on Raven: nanobots. The instruction sheet wedged between the vials told me which one held the 'bots and which held the synthetic stem cells they used to regrow bone and tissue. I unplugged the 'bot vial from its charging station, the other from its cooling cradle, and injected both into the frayed gap that had been connected tissue moments earlier. By the time I emptied both vials, I was trembling.

Almost done.

I sprayed the hell out of my wound with the sealing foam, then spun the cinchwrap around my foot. Clenching my teeth, I triggered the wrap, groaning when the micro-motors imbedded in the wrap tightened to seal the wound.

As I wiped sweat from my neck, my face stiff from what I suspected was a flash burn, I heard a faint commotion. People were on the other side of the fake wall, trying to get in.

I forced myself to stand and tested my right foot. It hurt, but the cinchwrap enabled me to put weight on it. After I got my foot back into my torn shoe, I limped into the corridor and heard a whizzing noise, which then stopped. Shit. The biosensor had lowered, the reader on this side of the fake wall appearing in tandem with the one on the outside.

I limped faster.

My fingers enclosed on my remaining pulsor as the wall unlocked. It began to rise, but I was too far away.

I had one shot.

I stopped, lifted the lipstick-sized weapon, and fired. The plasma lit the cages in churning light as it arced down the corridor, over Kieran's prone body, toward the rising wall, and clipped the bottom edge of the reader on my side, which turned greenish-white as energy surged through it.

The wall froze, leaving a six-inch gap between it and the floor.

I ducked into the cage that held my desk so they wouldn't see me, though I heard them shouting. As I pressed against my desk, my phone rang. I couldn't believe the ID that flashed in my vision. "Mina?" I answered.

"We can't get inside the station."

"You were supposed to be" — halfway to San Francisco — "gone."

"They're guarding the entrances. Another train is leaving in fourteen minutes, but we can't get in."

My efforts were for nothing if they didn't get away. I searched for inspiration.

The cage I'd tied Kieran to contained boxes labeled "Fireflies". Son of a bitch. Nikolai was supposed to have destroyed them. Glass globes the size of softballs, Fireflies had been envisioned to replace lamps in people's homes. They were like stemless lightbulbs that emitted a bright glow with a single touch, the light generated from chemicals inside reacting to each other.

But they did more than that. If they were dropped, the chemicals inside exploded.

"We're at a coffee shop across the street," Mina said.

The guards on the other side of the fake wall began to bang on it, what sounded like metal on metal.

"You have to get inside," I told her. "Warrants are out, maybe for all of us."

"Police are surrounding the station."

The banging grew louder, and a crack appeared in the wall.

"I'll call you back," I said.

I grabbed an empty satchel from my desk, pulled out my ion blade, and limped back to the work area. The two remaining spheres had rolled against the wall near the work table, a dozen feet apart. I put both in my satchel, hurried back down the corridor — the crack widening, the banging louder — and veered to the cage that held the Fireflies. I sliced open the cage with my blade, ducked inside, and grabbed the nearest box.

As the wall cracked more, I filled my satchel with globes, six of them, each one lighting when I touched it, their light illuminating the dark matter spheres under them. I used padding from the boxes to cushion them, then went back to the bikes' cage. Dropping under the smaller bike, I retrieved one of the spheres and secured it inside the bike's belly.

A crashhammer popped through the fake wall. They'd broken through.

I slung the satchel across my body, climbed onto the bike, and activated it. As it lifted into the air, I steered into the corridor.

The hole in the fake wall widened. I glimpsed armed men behind the crude opening.

I flew away from them, to the work area, and hurtled a Firefly at the building's exterior wall. The explosion destroyed the worktable, but the outer wall was barely marred. It'd take dozens of Fireflies to break through to the outside.

The hole in the fake wall grew big enough for the guards to climb through.

Desperate, I considered attacking but remembered Nikolai's elevator. I flew back down the corridor past the hole, slowed, and grabbed another Firefly. Rearing back, I threw it at the seam.

The doors blew into the elevator shaft and fell, banging and scraping as they tumbled forty-eight floors. I didn't see a cable in the shaft, so I knew my way out.

I glided to the elevator shaft, hovered just inside the opening, and dropped another lit Firefly into the darkness. Without waiting, I swiveled the bike down and triggered the jets, concentrating on staying centered inside the shaft as floor after floor flew past me. Up ahead — beneath me — the Firefly struck the ground floor and exploded, blowing the doors into the lobby.

The bike's tiny front jets flared as I slowed sharply, my shoulders straining to keep me on the bike. I leveled out, then exited the elevator and flew across the lobby as former coworkers and visitors scattered, toward a deserted corner where I threw a fourth globe at a section of windows. The Firefly sailed toward the dark-matter-collecting spaceship hologram that hovered before me and was swallowed. A second later, the windows shattered.

Surging forward, I flew through the fake image, through the opening I'd created, and out of the building.

*　*　*

The Cal-Tube Station came into view minutes later, its thrusting, four-story rooftop distinguishable from the surrounding cityscape. Even from a quarter-mile away, lights from the shops were visible throughout the multi-city-block station, including a grand, open-air restaurant on the second floor — as were the cops who ringed the building, stationed every hundred feet.

I called Mina. "Be ready," I shouted over the wind.

I dropped in low, spotted the coffee shop as I came in at an angle, and slowed in front of the two cops who guarded the front entrance. "Anyone looking for me?" I yelled.

They reached for their weapons.

I flew off at quarter speed so they'd think they could catch me and tilted the bike in case they decided to shoot. I continued around the side of the building, drawing more attention, then veered across one of the parking lots, but slowed as if I was having engine trouble.

Out of the corner of my eye, I saw Mina and the girls run across the street and onto the large promenade that led to the station.

I started toward the city when someone shouted. The cop closest to them had spotted them. Before he could give chase, I pulled out a Firefly — one of only two left — and threw it, checking myself at the last second and angling it to the side. The globe exploded far enough away that it didn't hurt anyone, although it made the cop and others stumble.

"Can't catch me," I bellowed as I flew low across the lot.

The men ran after me, even the guy who'd spotted my family.

Pleased, I thumbed the accelerator, then paused. It was too easy for a reason.

Shit.

There was no time. Their train would leave any second.

I gunned the jets and banked in a circle back to the station, its front face coming around toward me. I angled for its weakness: the open-air restaurant.

Its patrons scattered as I arched over them and flew into the hologram-thick, multitrack station. Commuter trains utilized the secondary tracks, but the two main ones were for the mag-rails, the ultraspeed trains that ran direct to San Francisco via dedicated tunnels. A flicker of silver drew my attention. An Agent was in the terminal, blocking my family from getting to the train.

I plunged toward them and aimed for the Agent.

He dove to the ground right before I hit him. I flew over his prone body, then up and around as Mina, Raven, and Talia raced for the curved-sided cars.

The Agent got up and started after them. I came at him again but had to swerve as he spun with inhuman speed and shot at me, the first bullet just missing my head. Then he continued after them.

They ducked into the last car. The next moment the train began to move, but he didn't slow, gaining speed as he angled toward it. The train accelerated, each car disappearing into the tunnel quicker than the one before. He leapt for the side door of their car, grabbed onto a handle next to the door, and held on as the car plunged into the tunnel.

The roar from the tunnel grew louder as the train accelerated. In seconds, it'd reach over 400 mph.

I straightened the hoverbike, leaned over the handlebars, hit max thrust, and swooped down into the tunnel.

Sounds assaulted me—the electromagnetic warble of the train's engines and the howl of the air it displaced—and wind buffeted me, churned by the train as it increased speed. I could barely see, the only light coming from the window in the last car's rear door. I gained on the train and flew close, not slowing until I got within feet of the rear door, although as soon as I did, the train widened the distance as it continued to gain speed.

The door opened, the light almost blinding until Mina, Raven, and Talia crowded in the doorway.

Not letting myself think about what I was about to do, I yelled at them to stand back—though they couldn't hear me—hit the button to unlock the leg couplings, and set my feet, my right one flaring. I bent all the way over the handlebars and maxed the accelerator again.

The bike surged forward, my last, desperate gasp.

Just as the nose was about to ram into the car, I wrenched the handlebars. The bike went perpendicular to the train, the start of a deadly spin.

And as Mina and the girls dove out of the way, I leapt.

I shot over the blurred tracks, my body slightly askew, the wind dropping as I reached the train. For the briefest of moments, I sailed into the car, my arms stretched forward, giving me a sliver of hope. Then my momentum failed.

I landed on the floor of the train car as an explosion shook the tunnel behind me—and my body went backwards, the wind pulling me, the train outracing my momentum. Fear roared through my mind as I clawed at the synth carpet but couldn't grab hold, the satchel flapping against my back. My legs were sucked out of the door, then my waist —

Mina grabbed my wrists, Raven an arm. Together they pulled me back, and Talia fell on me as soon as they pulled me inside.

Fire-retardant foam filled the doorframe and sealed the opening. The cabin equalized, but the air pulled at the foam, stretching it as it hardened.

Talia sagged above me. "You're late."

I trembled as I lay there, the emotions that assaulted me — terror that I'd repressed, amazement, and a touch of chagrin — eased by my family's presence.

A *crack* came from the front of the cabin.

Mina sat up. "He's trying to get in."

When I could stand, they led me to the side door where the Agent hung onto the handle, his knuckles visible. As we neared, he pulled himself forward and punched at the window. Even with the lack of leverage — and the G Forces buffeting him — his blow lengthened the fracture in the glass.

I inspected the wall next to the door, pulled out my knife, and ignited the ion blade. Slicing through the inner wall's shell and padding, I exposed the screw heads that held the handle in place. I thinned the blade to minimize the damage, then after a moment of hesitation, cut off one of the heads. The other immediately ripped away, sending the Agent to his death.

Mina hugged me. They all did. He hadn't been a man anymore. Not really, with his augmented strength and multiple implants. He'd become a machine.

I swallowed the bile in my throat and held them tight.

CHAPTER SEVENTEEN

I didn't hug them for long. "Everyone OK?"

They nodded, eyes big. Except for Mina. "What'd you do to your foot?"

"Long story."

She sat me down and removed the cinchwrap.

"See what happens when you try to ditch us?" she joked when she saw the damage, though she paled. She retrieved the small medkit in the car's bathroom and rewrapped my foot.

"Why isn't anyone else here?" I asked. The car was big enough to seat at least forty, the padded benches at different angles as if this was a club lounge instead of a mode of transportation.

"They scuttled to the next car when silver dude started banging on the glass," Talia said.

We had caught a break that the train actually left L.A. — either the Agent had been too confident he could stop them or unable to override the train's software in time — but it didn't mean we'd escaped.

I grabbed a gauze pad and directed Raven to turn around. When I lifted the back of her shirt, I spotted it immediately — what looked like a blackhead pimple between her shoulder blades. With my ion blade still at its thinnest setting, I made a tiny incision and dug it out.

Her complaint about the cut turned to surprise. "What's that?"

I dropped it on the floor. "Tracking device. Insurance in case they can't find us through our feeds, probably implanted while they processed your arrest."

As Mina gasped, Talia stomped on it.

I sealed Raven's cut with glue from the medkit, then limped over to one of the car's ad displays, which turned into a real-time map when I approached. We were already over halfway to San Francisco. "We can't stay."

"In the car?" Raven asked.

"On the train. Kieran will be waiting for us. Hell, every cop in the state will be there."

"We can't just leave," Mina said.

"We were supposed to leave L.A. quietly. That wasn't quiet. I have an idea, but you might not like it."

"Which means I won't."

I indicated the foam that sealed the rear door. "We need to trigger enough of that to stop the train. At least our car. In fact, it'd be better if ours was the only one."

"Did you get a concussion?"

I caught her hand as she reached for my head. "It'll be a rough stop, but it's our only chance. Otherwise, we'll walk into a firing squad." I was tired of these no-choice decisions but hid my annoyance from them. I lifted my satchel instead, thankful the last Firefly hadn't shattered when I'd leapt onto the train. "If we're lucky, this will do it."

With the girls' help, I cut one of the benches free and wedged it into the open space between the two cars, which had wind guards around its edges. "This'll start the fire," I said over the noise as I held up the Firefly. "The smoke from the padding will trigger the sensors."

Talia's eyes glistened with excitement. "Do you have more of those?"

"Shouldn't we get closer to the city?" Mina asked from the doorway.

I shook my head. "We're already slowing down. Besides, the more mountain cover we have, the harder it'll be to spot us."

Raven smiled. "You're thinking like a rebel."

As they braced themselves inside the cabin, I picked up the Firefly, which was nearly too hot to handle, held it over the exposed belly of the bench, and sliced it open with my blade. The chemicals poured out and caught fire as they pooled in the unprotected padding, smoke rising fast and thick. I ducked inside and closed the door to block the smoke, which quickly filled the tiny area.

An alarm blared, then a second, followed by hisses as foam erupted outside our car, the sound nearly drowning out a series of clangs as the couplings along the trainline strained due to the foam expanding under the wheels and slowing down our car. The change in speed was so abrupt I was thrown forward and nearly busted my nose against the door.

Then the car tilted.

I scrambled for something to hold onto as the car rolled, Mina and the girls crying out as the foam lifted us off the tracks and our car uncoupled from the train. I managed to grab the back of a bench as the car landed on its side, which triggered a symphony of cracks and metallic groans.

The car bounced off one side of the tunnel, hit the other, then slid to a stop.

Silence settled around us.

"Everyone OK?" I asked as I picked myself up.

Mina nodded as she worked her shoulder, and Raven said she was fine. Talia giggled. "Best day ever."

Hardened foam covered the windows. We were sealed in.

Flaring my blade, I cut through the tail-shaped foam that had sealed the rear exit. When it fell away, we found white trails stretching into the darkness.

I climbed down onto the foam and reached for them.

CHAPTER EIGHTEEN

Twenty minutes later, I shoved open the access door to reveal the world outside the tunnel.

Light jabbed our eyes as we stepped onto a hillside covered with scrub grass. Other than the door behind us, there was no evidence of man's influence in the hills around us. The air was different, the smell of asphalt and exhaust absent. Almost made me believe we were free.

Raven pulled out a burner phone and started to dial.

"Wait until we're safe," I said.

"When will that be?" Mina asked. She had a point. As soon as we stepped out of the tunnel, I became worried about Kieran watching through our eyes, finding a landmark that would pinpoint us. I wanted to tell them not to look at anything that might reveal our location, but I might as well tell them not to breathe for an hour.

Raven made the call, listened, then hung up. "Downtown San Francisco."

"Did they give you an address?"

She nodded.

"Over here," Talia called from a ridgeline twenty yards away.

She pointed to a farmhouse well past its prime. An old truck, a '28 or '29, was parked under a tree away from the house. We angled toward the truck, using the trees to mask our approach. The doors were locked, but a quick slice of my blade remedied that. Less than thirty seconds later, I touched the correct wires together, and the gasoline engine turned over.

* * *

I only drove far enough away so we could switch without the truck's owners stopping us. Now, lying in the bed as Mina drove, I stared at the azure sky. The ride was rough, but Raven and I didn't complain. Of any of us, we didn't have a right.

"I think she's going to hurt herself," Raven said.

She meant Talia, who chattered nonstop inside the cab. The truck's rear window was open so we could communicate with each other.

I would've smiled at Raven but didn't want whoever was watching to see her. "Don't look at any landmarks." I propped myself up so Mina and Talia could hear me, and kept my gaze skyward. "Don't look at any signs or landmarks." As soon as the authorities discovered we weren't in the tunnels, they'd tap our feeds to find us—if they weren't already monitoring them. We had minutes, if that. Their software only needed one or two images to pinpoint us. And we were going toward the city, not away from it.

When Raven spoke again, her voice was resigned. "I need to turn myself in."

"You do that, they'll use you to make us surrender. We're all criminals now. Besides, there's no way I'd let you get arrested. Again."

San Francisco rose in the distance, and I altered my gaze. In a single glimpse I'd spotted Highcity, the towering skyscrapers connected by suspended, massive platforms that contained communal parks, restaurants, and shops. From this distance, each joined pair looked like large Hs, the massive platforms stretching above the city's fog level, landmarks that would betray us.

The bed of the truck jabbed our backs as it rattled.

"I'm sorry for screwing up," Raven said. "I shouldn't have called Jex. After Kieran attacked me, I wanted to hear his voice. I didn't think about looking at the number."

I pulled her to me, frustrated that I couldn't look at her.

* * *

Raven's instructions took us to a deserted elementary school, John Muir on Oak and Webster. I wondered if she'd gotten the address wrong. It was a big school, over half a city block, but that didn't explain why we had been directed there.

Mina parked a few spots from the entrance. The building appeared dark, the schoolyear two or three weeks away. If this wasn't our destination, we were screwed. We were all staring at the building.

We walked to the front door, not talking, not looking at the palm trees or street or grand-arched entranceway. I took a breath, reached for the handle, and sighed as it opened. I ushered them inside and shut the door behind us.

The front area was deserted—a couple of kids' drawings on the wall but little else. Hallways led in both directions, and a stairwell rose to other floors.

"Which way?" Mina asked.

"They didn't say," Raven said.

I noticed my feed was blocked, which didn't help my anxiety, although it meant I could look at them. Their strain and apprehension were noticeable; all three were dirty from the train tunnel. I signaled to the left, which led deeper into the complex.

We passed room after room, each one dark. I tried a few doors, but they were locked. I led us down an adjoining hallway, deeper still, the sunlight unable to reach as far.

I sensed a presence the instant before a distorted voice spoke. "Don't turn around." A gun cocked. "Don't move."

"We don't mean any harm," Mina said.

The person scoffed, the sound alien-like. "What part of 'get away clean' did ya not get?"

Raven slapped a hand over her eyes in an exaggerated fashion, spun, and threw herself at whoever was behind us. "I missed you."

I started to turn but was told not to. "Keep your eyes closed. There. Now you can open 'em. Wait, let me…." I felt a knit cap placed on my head, pulled down over my implant. The voice spoke again, this time not distorted. "It's safe now."

The Creole accent from my mystery contact, the one who'd given me the tickets. Jex.

He wore a barn jacket I recognized immediately. "You *were* at the hospital when Raven was there."

She gave him a look I didn't like. He was about her age, lanky except for a pair of broad shoulders. He was handsome but not overly so, what passed for rugged nowadays, with curly brown hair peeking out from under a hoodie.

"Why'd you hide your voice?" she asked him.

"You don't know the level of scrutiny y'all have. I activated the school's suppression, but it might not be enough. You're the most wanted people on the planet." He saw Mina adjust her cap, the same cap we all wore. "Don't take it off. It blocks your signals. Wire's been woven through 'em, blocks everythin' that comes in or out."

"So, I'm wearing a tin hat?" Talia asked.

"Each cap has a phased array with cross-woven nanowires...but yeah." He turned to me. "If you weren't wanted so much, I wouldn't be here. You don't follow instructions again, you're on your own."

Without waiting for a replay, he started off, holding Raven's hand; the rest of us followed. When he glanced back, he frowned at me. "What's wrong with your leg?"

"I sliced my foot."

"You seal it?"

"Wrapped it."

"You're leaving a trail. DNA's like a beacon to 'em. Where'd you hide the hoverbike? I saw videos of you flying over L.A."

"Crashed it."

He shook his head. "Better an' better."

He took us to a loading area, where a delivery van waited. Inside was a large crate. "Get 'n there. When we reach the docks, we'll load you onto the ship. It'll be a short ride."

"Where are you taking us?" I asked. "Not to Free Isle. It's the first place they'll look."

"That's why we're sneakin' you in."

Talia smiled. "Jam."

CHAPTER NINETEEN

Cramped, troubled, and wary, I caught a glimpse of our destination through one of the camouflaged airholes in our crate.

As we followed the coastline inside the Bay, the tops of the Golden Gate visible to the left, a manmade island floated into view. It was bigger than I'd expected; 280 partially-submerged, waterproofed shipping containers, each forty feet long by eight feet wide, had been welded together to make a square grid topped with buildings. Some of the buildings reached three stories, and there were even what looked like two hangars nestled in the island's interior, everything made of metal or printed parts, rust streaks the island's only accent.

I didn't like the idea of my family staying there, and not just because it looked like a steampunk construction project gone wrong. It'd been built in the night, without approval from any authority, as a haven for criminals, refugees — the desperate and hardened.

Not a place for Mina or the girls.

Even its location was a source of contention, anchored a quarter-mile from the shore to land owned by a local church, the pastor brought up on charges multiple times but never convicted. I suspected it wasn't so much from the protections his vocation enjoyed as much as the ruler of Free Isle keeping his inhabitants in line.

We neared the island, which had boats moored to its edges. Some appeared abandoned, while others were being offloaded, men and women moving pallets of food, printing material, and other supplies. We took the only empty spot along the island's south side and bumped against the dented metal until dock hands secured us.

The airtight container we pressed against was about eighty-percent submerged, which indicated how much had been built on top of the floating structure — and how many people lived here.

The place would be free of the surveillance that blanketed San

Francisco, but its people were still a danger. This whole place was dangerous. Yet I was unable to stop our crate from being transported to one of the small warehouses past the docking area. Unable to stop any of this.

Yelling erupted as we were set down. Someone threw open the crate's lid to reveal the inside of the warehouse: unmarked boxes stacked behind us, stained drums grouped to one side, armed men before us. Two guards in stained street clothes hauled us out and ordered us to our knees.

"They've got clearance," Jex shouted. "It was arranged."

We crouched instead of kneeled, not sure who we should listen to.

The guards raised their machine guns at us. I pulled Talia and Raven behind me to shield them. At the same time, Jex aimed his gun at the guards. "Drop 'em."

Motorized footsteps approached.

A woman with short hair and a scar across her neck appeared, heavily armed. I thought she had robotic legs but realized they weren't attached to her body. They were attached to a seat she sat on and steered, the 3120 Mobiler, one of my company's products. An insignia covered her left breast, a crest with images of a machine gun, a white lily, a crown, and a lion. "Arrangements can be broken. You know that."

Jex didn't lower his gun. "Your boss ain't stupid."

"Tie 'em up and mask 'em."

Ignoring Jex, her men tied our wrists and threw cloth masks over our heads that hung straight to defeat facial-recognition software. Once they secured us, they forced us to follow her out of the warehouse.

Peering through the eyeholes in my mask, I saw people of all ages and types busy along the docks—moving supplies, bartering with vendors, or embroiled in other dockside activities. Most were dirty but not all, some clean and well dressed. Others wore the same crest emblem as the legless woman, although theirs were smaller.

All moved aside when she approached.

We passed mechanic shops, a blacksmith, chainmail stores, and kiosks that sold temporary phones, screeners, and what I suspected were signal blockers, hologram covers, and other illegal items. We passed two large, two-story buildings with gated entrances, shadowed alleys, and what appeared to be a defense outpost next to an open area with a basketball hoop, the area no larger than a bedroom.

The place smelled of metal and saltwater, with a faint chemical residue.

She led us to a three-story building. Unlike the rest of the complex, which was a mix of 3D printing and scavenger parts, the building was one composite, what looked like stone but wasn't, situated a step apart from the other structures, the back side jutting out over the water, four columns framing the entrance.

The double doors opened as we neared. The inside was sparse, the walls metal, with a short hallway that led to what appeared to be a throne room. A muscular man with a large belly sat on a raised, ornate seat listening to a group of people before him. The way his shirt laid, I suspected he wore a vest.

The room was forty by fifty feet, an extravagance of space, but other than the hallway we'd taken, the only exit appeared to be a door in one corner. Even among the holograms and video displays that served as ornamentation, the room was cold. And not at the water's edge, as I would've expected, though I heard waves lapping nearby. Warning signs indicating an electrical generator decorated the back wall, which didn't make sense, especially considering the building also served as the man's home. A generator that big would not only be noisy, it'd generate carbon monoxide that could spread throughout the floors.

The woman on my company's walker faced us. "I present Sie Ehkhert, Mayor of Free Isle and future president of our free land."

I knew about him like I knew about the Founding Fathers—on the periphery of my awareness. He was responsible for Free Isle's creation, and had previously been convicted of both white-collar crimes and more violent offenses.

I tensed as he descended toward us.

"We seek asylum," Raven said.

He smiled at her as if aware of her beauty hidden behind her mask. "No. You're here to fuck my shit up."

"That's not true—"

"I've heard a lot about you, Raven Quintero." Ehkhert's eyes traveled her body before he turned to me. "Dray Quintero. I've heard even more about you. Part of the 'Gang of Five,' is it? You're known for more than that now. Dragged your wife and younger daughter into this, I see."

I flinched but didn't respond, aware we were at his mercy.

"Your names are everywhere. As are your faces. The U.S. learns you're here, it'll attack us." He came closer, his expression sly. "I heard you ripped out your kid's implant. Ruthless."

"You heard wrong," I said.

His smile showed he didn't believe me. "You killed an Agent. Big no-no. They're offering a lot of cash for you, enough that even your best friend would turn on you."

Jex pushed his way past the guards. "Their stay was arranged."

Ignoring him, Ehkhert told me, "I'm going to make this a legitimate nation. Why should I risk that for you?"

The men he'd been listening to when we arrived hadn't moved. My eyes went from them to his guards. They all had implants—and none were covered. "You're already at risk, and you don't even know it."

"You mean their 'nets? They're for show, in case mainlanders drop by. Pay me to stay, or I'll have Salinda here throw your asses into the Bay."

The robotic-legged woman stepped forward. I suspected she was his head guard, and who knew what else.

"We already paid," Jex said, his hand near his pistol but not on it.

"That's before they developed such high prices on their heads."

Mina held out her engagement and wedding rings, appraised to over eighty thousand. "These enough?"

"Untethered dogecoins only. How many you have?"

"None," I said, Mina nodding in agreement.

Raven spoke up. "Fifty."

Ehkhert smiled. "That means you have at least a hundred. I can be reasonable for one as beautiful as you. Twenty per person."

"That's too much."

"Then don't pay for everyone. Whoever you don't like, we'll cast out."

I stepped in to argue but was out of my league. "Sixty for all of us," she said.

"You and your father are enemies of the state."

"They're early-generation 'coins. No certification issues."

He leered at her. "I like you."

Two men entered. "A price was already agreed to," said the taller of the two, a light-skinned African-American. The other, a Caucasian with high cheekbones, deep-set green eyes, and fat lips, rested a hand on the massive gun at his hip. I suspected it wasn't his only weapon.

"Your 'guests' have too much heat. If The Agency —"

"I understand, Sie. Forty more. That's reasonable."

As the taller man negotiated with Ehkhert, I felt a weight in my stomach. The cryptocurrency they paid bound me to them. They were rebels, hunted men. I worried about what they'd expect in return. The price crept up until Ehkhert agreed.

As we started for the exit, he called out, "Unplug them, or the deal's off."

Outside, the two men faced us. "I'm Hale Whittock," the taller one said, shaking our hands, "leader of those who fight for freedom. This is my second-in-command."

"Cole," the man said. He didn't offer the rest of his name, or his hand. He was broader than Whittock, his voice rough, his face nicked with scars, some of which had faded. I realized that wasn't true. The scars could identify him, so he had tried to erase them — whether via surgeries, nanobots, or gene therapy, I didn't know.

"You must be Raven," Whittock said. He kissed the back of her hand. "Thank you for getting your family here. And you must be her mother, Mina."

"What did Ehkhert mean?" I asked. "If he was referring to our implants, Raven was hurt when —"

"We know." He turned to Jex. "Can you show these ladies to their quarters? I'm sure they want to relax after their journey."

"I'll stay," Raven said.

Whittock gently pulled her aside, close to me. "I'm worried about your sister. There aren't many children here, and those who are have had a hard life. I don't want Talia to see how destitute they are until she gets acclimated. Can you make sure she doesn't?"

Her eyes scanned me. I could tell she hoped for a reaction, probably my buy-in to her dreams of fighting the government. After a moment she left, staying close to Jex as he led them away.

Whittock motioned to me. "Come."

While Cole was scarred, Whittock's face was unblemished, a lithe man with a commanding presence. He had different colored eyes, one tan and the other dark, like a blown pupil. I wondered if the pupil was from an issue with his lens. "About the mayor —" I started.

"Your implant is a danger. The caps we gave you help, but they're temporary. If one slips, The Agency will find you, and we'll all suffer."

They steered me down a side passage, which didn't run straight like the road that led to the mayor's. None of the routes were large.

"Is everyone here part of your rebellion?" I asked.

"No. Some are criminals, a few are victims. Most are just trying to survive, which Ehkhert likes. He doesn't trust anyone who doesn't have something to lose. You have much to lose, don't you?" When I didn't answer, he went on. "We're fighting a war, Dray, one we want you to join."

As we approached one of the hangar-like buildings, Cole stopped. "Not this one."

"It's a better vantage point."

He stormed inside, flashing a view of a high-ceilinged training area, and barked orders as the door closed behind him.

"He doesn't want you to see our facilities until you've committed," Whittock said. "Along with this building, we have a full lab. I won't show that, though, until you're one of us."

Understanding washed over me. "You didn't want Raven. You were trying to get to me."

He gave a slight nod. "We've been watching you for some time. We were wary to contact you due to your wife's position, but when we learned of Raven's desire to join us, we thought she could be a conduit."

"Not a good way to establish trust." Raven would be crushed.

Cole reappeared, still disgruntled. "It's clear."

"Please," Whittock said, motioning me forward.

I had no interest in hearing their pitch, not after he'd used Raven, but I wasn't in a position to refuse him. Yet.

We entered the training facility. Mats, raised sparring platforms, and weights were situated throughout the space, with a simulation area and a firing range in the back. An open doorway led to barracks.

They directed me to a set of stairs that extended to the roof, which didn't help my worsening limp. When we reached the top, Whittock stepped onto the corrugated rooftop and waved for me to join him.

Something was wrong.

It was late afternoon, not a cloud in the sky, yet it was as if I wore dirty sunglasses. San Francisco looked dull, layered in smog. I couldn't even see Oakland.

Whittock saw me struggle. "Nothing's wrong with your eyesight. In fact, you're seeing for the first time. Really seeing, without their lies. Our lenses shield us from the truth by augmenting our world. Cleaning our view of it. Our country's efforts the past fifty years to ween ourselves of fossil fuels haven't been enough. Only a portion of the world uses electric cars, only a fraction of our needs is met by wind and solar—"

"That's not what I've read in dozens of reports."

"*Government* reports. Even your reactor doesn't provide all the power Los Angeles needs. And now the inevitable has happened: our planet is running out of oil. We should have ten years ago. World leaders couldn't face the chaos that would cause, so they've allowed oil companies to mix in additives to extend the remaining amount. Those additives are toxic. We've gotten used to breathing them, but they're killing us. Washington tries to blame the increased respiratory problems on diseases they've made up, but it's all lies."

I recalled my mother, coughing so hard she couldn't catch a breath, drowning in her own fluids when I was nineteen. If Whittock was telling the truth, the government had killed her. Their technology, their Agency guard dogs, had covered their crime.

I felt an old rage awaken. I'd done everything to save her— hounding doctors, researching treatments—but it hadn't been enough. A cavity had opened in me when she died. Rage filled it—similar to the rage I felt when Adem died—along with despair and pain. It took me a long time to let go, succeeding only after I swore to make the world a better place. To make up for not saving her.

I'd been fooled.

"The government's gone too far," Whittock said. "They took a basic tenet and warped it to stay in power: if you control what people see, you control what they think. We're going to correct that. We're going to take our country back."

I barely remembered our trip down the stairs. This was much greater than altered videos and fake news stories. The government had committed crimes against their citizenry, leading to the death of my mother and countless others.

Rage burned anew. My efforts had been for nothing. Who else would suffer? Raven? Talia?

We reached the exit, where Whittock faced me. "We want you to join our fight."

I wanted justice for my mother…but there had to be a better way, one that wouldn't jeopardize Mina or the girls, who were all that mattered in this plastic, toxic world. "No."

"You saw the smog. It's killing everyone, including your daughters. People need to see the truth." He paused. "If you join, we'll replace your implants with ones that are untraceable. All of yours. But only if you're with us."

"We just need ours removed. That's it."

"You can't exist without an implant. You need replacements, and they don't come cheap."

"We can pay," I said, thinking of Raven's funds.

"They're for our fighters. No one else."

"Talia's a young girl, not some fighter. None of us are."

Cole said, "A girl can get into places no one—"

"Join us," Whittock said, interrupting him, "and we'll give you and your family implants with access codes that change a dozen times a day. Agents wouldn't be able to track you long-term. You might show up on a scan, but you would become a nobody again within two hours. A ghost."

I'd caught Cole's comment. "I'm not risking their lives."

Whittock touched my arm. "I know what happened with Raven. Our scientist is confident he can replace her 'net without any damage. He's removed dozens. You can all have yours removed and get out of the chains that bind you."

"A fleet of bikes doesn't come cheap, either. I'll make bikes for you in exchange for new implants."

"You all have to join. Or leave."

I couldn't sell their futures like that. I only had one other choice. I removed the dark matter sphere from my satchel and explained what it was. "This in exchange for my family's protection."

Whittock smiled. "I wondered what you were carrying. I'll take it, but all it does is cover your protection while you're here. If you want any kind of chance, any kind of future, you all have to join. We're at war, Dray. It's time to choose sides."

"I'll join—I want to," I lied, "and Raven wants to, but Mina and Talia don't have to. It's asking too much."

"They'd both be assets," Cole said.

Whittock agreed. "Talia's an excellent hacker, and your wife has inner knowledge of L.A.'s power base. The point is, we need everyone we can get. If you want Talia to have a life, it'll be with us."

They took me to a one-story building where they'd stationed my family. "You have until morning to decide," Cole told me.

A giggle came from inside the metal structure—Talia, followed by a playful yelp from Raven.

"Give me a couple of days. Please."

"One night. Keep your cap on, even when you sleep. Tell your brats to do the same."

"Forgive my commander," Whittock said, "but he is correct. If any of you slip, it will jeopardize us all."

* * *

I entered the living quarters.

The front part contained a couple of cushioned chairs and an outdated vidscreen, along with two doors that led to bedrooms. Mina, Raven, and Talia sat at an oversized table in the back, near the kitchenette. Jex was with them.

He stood when I walked in. It was clear he sought my approval, but I'd learned the truth about why he'd recruited Raven.

My family was smiling, although Mina's was forced. I could relate. Before all of this, having my family together would have made me happy. Now, all I could think about was how to protect them.

"What do you think?" Raven asked as I took off my mask, careful to keep my cap in place. "Aren't the Founding Fathers inspiring?"

"They weren't what I expected."

Jex fidgeted under my gaze. "I was just tellin' 'em why many live here, tryin' to escape the lives they'd had—"

"Which means they could make a lot of money turning us in. You could, too."

"The rebels won't harm us," Raven said. "They're fighting for us. That's why I'm going to help. I'll make you proud."

"I'm already proud," I said, but she didn't seem to hear me.

"Did you see the flowers he brought?" They were 3D printed, a small bouquet of yellows and reds.

"You have the resources for something so frivolous?" I asked him.

"I'll go, sir." He nodded to my wife. "Thank you for the hospitality."

Raven stood. "I'll go with you. To talk about tomorrow." She steered him out, her hands on his waist.

"You can't pick who she likes," Mina said when they left. "Is that what's bothering you? You should give him a chance."

I sat in the chair Jex had vacated. "It's not him. Well, not just him."

Talia asked, "Do these dumb caps really hide us?"

"Yes, but they're not a solution. We can get our implants replaced tomorrow — but we have to join the rebels."

"No," Mina said.

"What choice do we have?" I asked, my body heavy from the weight of what was before us. "We won't last a day on our own. But the second we see our chance, we'll leave this place."

"You want me to become something I've fought to eradicate."

"Replacing our implants is the only way we'll survive."

Talia asked, "Can I keep my old one as a souvenir?"

"No," we both said at the same time.

"What about Raven?" Mina asked. "Her skull's still healing."

"Whittock assured me they can do it without harming her." When Mina didn't say anything, I added, "We can't wear these caps forever."

"I'll do it," Talia said. "It'll make me anonymous."

Raven came in, shut the door, and took off her mask. Her lipstick was smeared, which soured my mood even more.

"Go to bed, both of you," I said.

After they went to their room, I found Mina staring off, her expression reminiscent of when we lost Adem. I took her hand to pull her out of her thoughts.

"They're asking us to surrender a piece of ourselves," she said.

"I don't want to. I'll lose years' worth of knowledge." That I accessed continually at work, a separate memory bank that was precise in its recall. "If you have a better idea, tell me. I don't know what the rebels really want with us, but we have to get these things out."

She pulled her hand from my grasp. "If it's the only way to save Raven and Talia, I'll do it. But Dray, don't trust anyone."

CHAPTER TWENTY

Fog coated Free Isle, blocking the morning sun while magnifying the unfamiliar sounds of the floating settlement.

I limped slightly as my family and I followed Jex through the mist, across the fake island to a two-story structure not far from the rebels' training facility. Mina fidgeted as we neared. I reached out, but she didn't respond to my silent touch.

We entered the building, stepping into a room dominated by a tent made of thick cloth. As we removed our masks, I took in the rest of the room. Storage cabinets lined the walls, their glass doors revealing scanners, a surgical laser my company made, a bioweld, and other items. The back of the room contained a quick-cycle plasma blaster, five times the cost of a machine gun but ten times more powerful.

A giant of a man came in and removed his mask. "Hidey-hello," he said, grinning. He had sharp features, his protruding chin softened by a bushy goatee. Another time and place, I would've taken him for an NBA small forward. He snatched my hand. "The only and greatest. So good to meets, my man. Big fan. I'm Garrelson. Garly for short."

"I'm—"

"I know who you are." He introduced himself to Mina and the girls. "You're all joining our ride? Sublime." He gestured at Jex. "Did he explain to keep your masks after we do this? People here wear 'em for various reasons, so you won't stick out, but you shouldn't group together, like, when you're outside."

We nodded obediently.

"Did anyone's cap come off during the night? Anyone?" His pointed finger traced us. When we shook our heads, he smiled. "Nom'! OK, let's hit it. I've done this bunchos of times. If we had the digits to spare, I'd swing you to my lab to show how they're secured."

"Why do you need a lab?" Mina nearly snapped.

Talia asked, "Can I see it?"

For a moment, he stared at us like he'd been startled awake. "Uh, I dabble in things." To Talia, he said, "Maybe, squirt, if your dad's simpatico."

Before Talia could start pleading with me, Mina said, "This doesn't feel right."

"It's OK, we're part of the team," Raven said.

"We're good eggs," Garly said. "Some are uptight, but overall we're rad."

Mina shook her head at me, more agitated.

"I'll watch everything he does," I told her.

"I'll go first," Raven said. "You'll see it's safe."

Mina grabbed her. "You can't. She can't. Her skull can't take it." Garly tried to calm her as she said, "She could *die*."

This wasn't like her. She had circles under her eyes I hadn't noticed.

"I'm up on what happened," he said. "I'm not gonna take hers out, just the guts. It'll not only spare her brain bits, it'll keep her sack intact. We'll keep the casing in situ — just swap the innards, then she'll be ready to function."

"That'd be a good trick," I said, reluctantly impressed.

"I was hoping you'd help."

Mina looked at us as if we were mad.

"What's it gonna be like, after?" Talia asked. "I won't be able to communicate with my friends —"

"There're still ways to connect," Garly said. "A nice note, for example."

She exhaled sharply.

He pulled aside the tent's flap for Raven and me to enter. "You can watch everything that goes down," he told Mina and Talia, gesturing toward a holoscreen in the corner that showed the tent's interior.

As I'd glimpsed on the holoscreen, the tent contained a collapsible, waist-high bed and a cart that held forceps, two unmarked boxes, some gauze, and wires that were attached to thumb-controlled handles.

"Hop up," he told Raven. She got herself situated as he sealed the tent and took a spot next to the cart. "Your noggin's the trickiest, so it's good we're taking a whirls on it first. You can take off your cap." He noticed our reactions as he removed a device from one of the boxes, what looked like an old-fashioned, electronic hand-mixer. "The tent blocks all signals. You're safe in here."

I felt unsettled when she took off her cap but kept quiet. She was anxious enough. We all were.

She laid on her side, implant-side up. Garly placed the hand-mixer-like device against her skin, the ring that jutted out from its base encircling her implant. "Hold her so she doesn't jostle. This'll cut away the casing like opening a can of beans, but I gotta press down so it can scoodle under the lip. Ready-o?"

I held her head as he pushed down and triggered the device, which I suspected he'd made. As she started to quiver, he lifted away the device.

"Done."

I let go, and she grabbed her temple in pain.

"Sorry 'bout the burns, chi," he said. "Figured do it fast-like." He explained that lasers powerful enough to cut through the metal casing—and give her second-degree burns—lined the inside of the ring. He got her to roll over and tilt her head. When she did, the insides of her neural net fell out onto the table.

I heard Talia's voice. "Gross."

Raven rolled back, and he dabbed ointment on her reddening skin.

"Are you cutting out all of our implants?" I asked.

"Just hers. The rest I pop like they're designed, something the publico doesn't know. It takes two to finagle, so I'll need your assist."

As he scooped up the pieces of her implant, my breath caught. Kieran had slipped a GPS tracker into Raven's implant. How close had he been when we met up with Jex? Did he know we were here?

Garly severed her implant's battery and used the circular device to slice apart the tracker, the lasers carving it into tiny pieces.

"What's wrong?" Raven asked, watching my face.

He flicked me a look.

I forced a smile. "Nothing."

He opened the other box to reveal four implants, each sterilized and sealed. He picked up the nearest one, took it out of its wrapper, and removed the casing. I could see the interior hardware had been modified. It didn't contain any memory sticks, and the broadcasting unit was different. His eyes sharpened as he stared at me, as if he could read my thoughts. His voice came slower. Gauging. "Modded these myself. They work the same but don't have a hard-coded, steadylink

145

ID. Instead, the ID changes digits periodic-like so they can't track you for long. Also ditched the memory drives. Gotta remember things on your own now."

I hoped to deflect his suspicion. "What about our video feeds? Did you cut them?"

"Couldn't. You'd stick out. Means you needs to be super careful looking at each other. Their recognition programs will find you quick. If you gotta look, wear your caps. Or masks."

I knew why the rebels didn't want us to have long-term memory. If we were caught, our sticks could be used to find them. I didn't like that we'd still broadcast what we saw. Though I respected the logic, my stress level remained high.

He installed the modified implant parts in Raven's head, lining up the posts with the lead connectors that extended into her brain.

"How are you going to seal that?" I asked him. "If you weld it, it'll be obvious her implant was tampered with." And cause her tremendous pain.

He pointed out three thin metal protrusions that extended down from the broadcast end. "These hook to the outer ring. The 'nets are supposed to be permanent, but these are in case one is defective. We'll use the same hooks to secure her new innards." As he removed the hooks that were part of the casing of Raven's previous implant, he said, "I didn't want to try to remove her 'plant by popping these out 'cause I could've jostled her ring. Her noggin's still fragilio."

I was stunned. I'd never expected there would be a way to unhook implants. I flashed to the night Trever died, my guilt soothed by the fact I'd had to rip Raven's out.

Garly lined up the hooks of the new implant with the three slits in the outer casing and slid the hardware into Raven's skull. When it was fully imbedded, the hooks popped into place, securing the illegal tech.

Raven sat up cautiously, then stood. Seconds later, we emerged from the tent, Raven careful to avert her gaze. "Well?" I asked. "How do you feel?"

"Access is good, although the interface is off," she said, her voice business-like, which I'd rarely heard.

"That's 'cause it doesn't have your personal settings," Garly said.

Talia chuckled. "You have hat head."

"We all do," I said.

Eyes widening, Talia reached up to yank off her cap. Mina stopped her before either of us could move, pinning her head to her stomach.

Garly asked, "Who's next?"

We all said Talia, who fought Mina's grasp to get to the tent. She laid on her side on the bed and wiggled with excitement.

Garly gave me one of the handled wires. "Remember those hooks? We'll use these to shove them outta their slots, so we can pull out the 'plant." The wire, a sixteen gauge, would have to go under the skin. My admiration of him grudgingly increased.

With a quick scan, he was able to locate the three notches. "I'll do the two on my side. Ready-o?"

I nodded.

Using a thumb-joystick on top of the handle, I steered the wire under Talia's implant and slid it down the side of the ring to where the hook stuck out from under the casing's edge to catch the ring. I shifted the wire to push the hook in—and she jerked with a squeal. A spot of blood appeared along the edge of her implant where she'd pulled away from my wire.

I gently cupped her shoulder. "You OK?"

"It felt icky."

"We're almost done. Don't move."

Garly got his two. I repositioned my wire, wincing every time I moved it, and pushed.

"OK, pop it out," he said. Both of his hands were occupied, one holding each wire, so I slipped a fingernail under the edge of her implant and it came out, leads and all.

"Sick," Talia whispered, her eyes locked on the glistening leads as Garly set her implant in a sterilized bowl and picked up a new one.

"Ready-o?" he asked.

She gasped as she stared at the leads dangling from the modified implant.

"They just look scary. We all have 'em. They're good tentacles."

She warily laid her head back down. He slid the new implant into her skull and locked it in place.

I was next.

He recruited Mina to help. Her nerves took a different focus as she snaked her wire into my head. The sensation wasn't a pleasant one, almost painful, but after a few moments, it was over. I watched Garly take the implant I'd had since my sixteenth birthday and drop it in a tray.

The new one reacted the same, maybe faster, but even though the readouts were identical, there was a slight hollowness. Settings were different, nothing was in the right spot. I couldn't bring myself to confirm there was no memory drive.

After he and I replaced Mina's implant, I helped her out of the tent. "Congrats, everyone," he said. "You're now outlaws of Uncle Sam."

Cole and Whittock entered after we put on our caps, looking pleased. Garly gave our old implants to Cole wrapped in the same material as our caps.

"What're you going to do with them?" I asked.

"Wipe them, disinfect them, modify them, then put them in someone else."

Mina, who'd been staring to the side, looked frantic. "Wait, I want mine back."

She started toward Cole, but I stepped between them. "Mina, it's OK."

"No, it's not. I need it."

She tried to get around me, but Whittock blocked her as well. Before either of us could speak, Garly said, "Don't feel bad. Some people depend too much on their hook-ups. You don't know 'til they're gone."

Her eyes raked us. "It's not that. I need that information. It's important. Let me download what I have—"

"That's a no-go."

"Too risky," Whittock agreed.

She seemed inconsolable until Jex said, "I can pull the data." He glanced at Whittock. "It shouldn't take long. I'll put everything on a shielded datadisc. Nothing will get out."

"No," Cole said. "As soon as she accesses it, it'll give her away."

"I can remove her profile settings and install some safeguards."

She put her hands on his chest. "You'll do that?"

"Yeah. Give me a day or so."

As Mina thanked him, Raven gave him a big smile.

Cole scowled at him before focusing on me. "Time to get started."

* * *

Talia bounded out of the building ahead of us, the edges of her cloth mask flapping as she ran. Even though she still had to wear a cap to look at us, and a mask when she went outside, she was free of the implant codes that had ID'd her. We all were. Yet Cole's words tempered my enthusiasm.

He, Whittock, and Garly turned to the left and paused for me to follow. The fog had burned off, though the air was still cool. A chugging sound rumbled at my feet as I started after them.

Behind me, Raven said to Talia. "Keep an eye on Mom."

"Where are you going?" When Raven indicated me and the rebels, Talia muttered, "We all joined."

Raven approached us with a swagger to her step.

Cole stopped her. "Go with them."

"You recruited me to fight, not hang out with my family."

"We didn't want you. We wanted him." Cole pointed at me.

Her eyes, the only part visible, grew big. "But—"

"You killed your boyfriend and called Daddy for help. Dray not only has skills we need, he covered up your mess."

"That's enough," I said.

Jex stepped between them. "Yeah, that's enough."

Cole got in his face. "You forget your rank, soldier." As Jex stepped back, Cole told Raven, "We would've rejected you if it wasn't for your father. Trever's parents provide a key component used in neural nets. We were going to use that connection to learn how to disable the cameras in our eyes, but you killed him."

She turned to Jex. "Why didn't you tell me?"

"He didn't know," Cole said. "He's just a grunt—who needs to report to his commander for reassignment."

Now I was stunned. I'd thought Jex was a key person. Maybe not a leader like Whittock and Cole, but still important.

Jex left one way, and she went the other.

I went almost nose-to-nose with Cole. "Don't ever talk to her that way again."

"She needed a lesson."

"So do you. Push me, and you get nothing."

He smiled. "That's how you want it."

"Gentlemen, please," Whittock said.

We walked in silence toward the training facility, me seething and Cole smug. We passed a couple of patrols, though few people wandered this area; this part of the island appeared off-limits.

We stopped at a one-story building not far from the rebels' hangar. Garly's lab.

I didn't know what the place had been previously — a doctor's office or something — although I was too pissed to care. Robot assistants, printed machinery, late-model fabricators, and repurposed tools littered the room, including lathes and other high-torque equipment fashioned out of stolen metal parts.

I removed my mask as Garly closed the door behind us. "My digs, your digs," he said. "I'll give you a key — "

Whittock said, "That's not necessary. You'll be with him at all times."

"If you want the bike, I need the dark matter I gave you," I said.

"We also need weapons. Work with Garrelson to put some things together. You only have a week, so they don't have to be pretty."

"What's in a week?"

"We'll give details later." When they trusted me more, he didn't add. "Just know it'll be a coordinated attack using all of our resources, which means we need everything you can give us, including your bike."

He and Cole walked out.

Garly seemed nervous to be alone with me. "Whatever you wanna change, move, I'm gig. So excited you joined the team. You're a genius, know that? A certified genius."

"Not actually certified — "

"I saw a movie when I was a runt, one of those alien flicks where the leader was so smart, so...," he made a mind-blowing gesture, "I didn't think it was real. Yet here you are. Can't believe how you use dark matter like it's your bitch."

"Uh, thanks."

"So just you, or did all Five make that magic?"

I could hear the capital "F." "Initially, all of us. It was a long time ago."

Garly pulled out my dark matter sphere. "You could slap a few of these babies to a spaceship and with a good shove send it to orbit."

"Or blow something up. An assault is a bad idea. Even if you have hundreds of soldiers, you'll be outnumbered."

"With your help, we won't lose."

He showed me what he'd been working on: a pulse canon, a magnet relay, a harmonic rifle — "Can't get the settings right" — and timer-controlled, wallet-sized bombs that adhered to anything.

"I'd be impressed," I said, "except my children are on this floating platform, and you're showing me things that could sink it."

"Then you're really not gonna like these."

He revealed barrels of portable explosives hidden under one of the tables. I started to pace. Whatever they were planning would be a bloodbath.

"You're limping."

When I told him why, he had me take off my shoe. Using a scanner, he checked the nanobots' remaining life, then injected more.

I couldn't stop myself. "A huge battle isn't going to change anything except shortening your lifespans."

"That's why you're here, to help us."

"Best thing I should do is help you escape the country."

The humor left his face. "Only thing keeping your hands unbound is your know-how." He stood. "Show me how to activate your sphere."

CHAPTER TWENTY-ONE

It was late by the time I left Garly's lab.

San Francisco glistened in the darkness, its high-rises like glowing spikes, the H buildings connected by dashes of brilliant light.

At least the Isle's streets were empty. Kieran would have to hunt for us by other means.

The air didn't smell toxic as I made my way across the island, which meant I'd grown used to it. That was one of mankind's blind spots: its sense of smell. Mom had suffered because of it, her and thousands of others. I'd tried to make up for my father's absence, protecting her when her trucker boyfriend attacked her, but he hadn't been the only threat.

I hadn't stood a chance.

"You shouldn't be out alone." Ehkhert's head guard, Salinda. Her robotic legs reflected the faint light.

"Heading to bed," I said.

"I'll escort you." Her footsteps were like the slow churning of a recycling machine as it reduced its intake into tiny pieces. "What were you doing working so late?" she asked.

"I'm not at liberty to say."

Crunch.

Crunch.

"Mayor Ehkhert is shielding your family. That doesn't come cheap."

"That's being handled," I said.

"The Founding Fathers? They haven't paid a dime for you. Maybe they plan to pay another way. The mayor took a shining to your daughters."

I stopped, as did she. "Tell him to stay away from them."

"What did you give Whittock?"

She was asking about the sphere. I didn't answer.

She started to walk away. "You don't think we'll discover why they wanted you so much? The mayor won't like being shut out."

* * *

I reached our living quarters, which I hoped was one place on this floating barge that didn't feel perilous.

Mina sat at the table, her eyes unfocused. "Where are the girls?" I asked.

She didn't look up. "In their room."

I waved a hand in front of her face, my encounter with Salinda cutting my patience.

She continued to stare off. "You ever considered my feelings? I worked for the government, and now I'm supposed to attack it."

"No one expects you to fight."

"Yes, they do."

"We're in this together. I'll protect you and the girls to my dying breath."

"Nice sentiment, but don't be patronizing."

I felt a flash of anger but tried to contain it. "I'm not." I glanced toward the bedrooms. "How's Raven?"

"She's humiliated. I tried talking to her."

"Did you warn them not to log onto any sites?"

"They're smart. We all are."

I didn't like this side of her. "I know you're smart."

"You didn't give me a chance to find another way."

I waited for her to look at me, but she didn't. I didn't either — didn't restate my case, didn't argue. It would only lead to a fight.

With a knock, I opened the door to the girls' room. Raven was propped in bed, her body tense, a neural transmitter coupled onto her implant, which streamed content directly to her hardware. I said her name, then louder. She focused on me, then averted her gaze.

I gently pulled the transmitter away, severing her connection. "How are you?"

Her eyes glistened. "At least my guilt's gone. I felt bad about dragging everyone into this, but I wasn't the one they wanted."

Nothing in my parental experience had prepared me for this. I sat on the edge of the bed. "What're you watching?"

"Training videos. Got them from the barracks commander."

"You're not still thinking of becoming a soldier."

"I belong here. I'll prove it." She had a bite to her voice.

"I don't want you to put yourself in danger, you or...." I looked around. "Where's Talia?"

"Probably the other room."

I got up and checked the entire place, but she wasn't there. I rushed back into Raven's room, my panic rising. "She left."

"She couldn't have." She held up Talia's mask.

Shit. "Stay here. If she comes back, don't let her leave."

I considered whether to tell Mina. She'd become distant since we came here. Telling her that Talia was missing could send her over the edge. She continued to stare off, clenching what I realized was her cap.

Without a word, I donned my cap and mask and left.

The fog hadn't rolled in yet. It was still out by the Golden Gate, but it was coming. I searched the streets around our quarters, then did a bigger loop. The area contained bars, repair shops, narrow markets, and tiny storefronts scattered among various homes, most of the windows dark.

I passed a bar that was still open and went inside. A handful of patrons sat at the metal bar, the three small tables ignored, the rough men quieting when I entered. Satisfied she wasn't there — the place too small to contain other rooms — I left. Most of the other businesses were closed, except for a stand that sold cooked meats. The man didn't respond at first when I asked if he'd seen a girl pass by, but finally shook his head.

I wanted to yell at him but continued on, my pace faster.

A homeless family with twin boys and a baby, the newborn hanging from the mother's arm, wouldn't tell me anything until I gave them cash. They didn't see anything, either.

Jex approached from a side street. "Hey."

"Did Raven call you?" I asked, my voice cold.

"Yeah, and I told her squad. We're all out lookin'."

"I don't want your help. You used Raven to get to me."

"I'm sorry —"

"If you hadn't pursued her, we wouldn't be in this mess."

"She wanted to be here. All I did was get between her and Trever —"

"You did more than that. You acted like a big shot."

"I never lied 'bout that. You assumed."

I took a breath to lash out at him, but realized I was wasting precious time. "You want to help? Search another area. It's a big island. Ship. Whatever the hell this is."

I turned onto the next street to get away from him. I fumed for a few moments, but reigned in my emotions to try to figure out where she had gone. She did this for a reason. It hadn't been malicious—she probably didn't realize she'd created a panic—but something had drawn her out. At least I hoped it was something, instead of her just wanting adventure.

I wasn't far from our flimsy-metal-constructed home. I started forward to make another loop, but paused. Our "street" didn't lie in a straight line. Few did. The buildings varied in height, angled this way and that to create alcoves, some at depths of up to twenty feet. But something was off about the layout to my right. I frowned—and saw Talia in a deep alcove, thin and pale in the moonlight.

Before I could call her name, she disappeared. I dashed to the alcove, but it was empty. Frowning, I stepped back. The alcove should've extended deeper, given the spacing between buildings. I reached out to touch the back wall, and my hand went through it. I stepped forward, into what would've been the wall—

And walked through a holoscreen.

Talia clapped. "I knew you'd wonk it out." She stood in an alley that angled around a corner and out of sight.

"Dammit, Talia, you scared the hell outta me. You could've gotten hurt."

Her smile faded. "I didn't mean to—"

"What're you doing out here?"

"Raven warbled on and on about how 'great' her friends are, how 'great' it is to be here, so I wanted to 'load it for myself."

I dropped to my knees and hugged her.

"I heard you talking to Jex. Don't hate him," she said, her voice raspy as I squeezed harder than I meant to. "He's got the swoons for Raven. And he's funny-like."

My panic faded, but I was still shaky as I let go. "How'd you find this place?"

"I scoped the thickness of the building. Like you tell us, glean what's not right. There're lotso alleys all over this place. It's like a treasure hunt, only the treasure's the path. Wanna see? I don't think it's planned 'cause they're all random-like."

"You could've gotten hurt. Or taken."

"Wanna know what I found?"

I held out her mask. "Don't ever go out without this again."

She exhaled sharply and took it. "Wanna know *why* these are hidden?"

"That's not for you to worry about."

Before I could stop her, she darted around the bend. I found her down the next alley leaning against one of the buildings and tugging on something. I couldn't see much in the darkness, but the ground was gritty under my shoes, and when I touched the walls, my fingertips came away coated with grime. A pencil-thin beam of light cut across the alley as whatever she'd tugged on came away—a wire that had been tacked to the wall. She held the end of it, carefully pointing it away: a camera, which had been positioned in the hole she'd exposed. At her urging, I stepped to the tiny hole and found myself staring into a family room furnished with mismatched, printed furniture. Mesh covered the hole, painted the same shade as the walls.

"The mayor watches people," Talia whispered. "It's him, right? He and crazy robot lady?"

When I nodded, she replaced the camera, cutting off the light.

As my eyes readjusted to the darkness, I saw more wires attached to buildings on either side of the alley, located in spots on the first, second, and even third floors. Every inch of this place was under his surveillance. The cameras were hardwired so no sensors would pick them up, and mesh probably covered every lens to shield them from discovery.

"Did anyone see you back here?"

She shook her head. "I don't think people come back here. There's footprints, but they're dusty-like. We can re-checks tomorrow."

I pulled her toward the alcove entrance, growing more paranoid. I didn't think Whittock knew about the alleys. I doubted any of the rebels did.

"The alleys don't squiggle all throughs the island," she said. "There's gaps. But we can motor around lots without—"

"You can't be back here. It's too dangerous." I squatted to her eye level. "If the mayor or one of his guards finds you, he'll do something bad. Does he have cameras guarding the alley?"

"No."

"That you know of. You could get in trouble."

"I'm zippy fast. No one would catch me."

"This isn't a game."

Her face wrinkled as she seemed to fight warring emotions. "I don't wanna be a robot."

"Who called you a robot?"

"I don't want to be steered around like one. I wanna be my own me. Be remembered for something magnifico and unique. I don't know whats, though. What if I never find it?"

"You *are* unique. You know how your teacher wanted you to pick a spirit animal? I think you're a lioness."

A grin fought through her wrinkled face. "A lioness?"

I nodded. I noticed she wore her cap. "You're strong and fierce — and smart. You remembered it," pointing at her head.

"Makes me look badass."

I could read her face. "It feels different, doesn't it? Mine feels weird, too." The new implant had magnified her fears. I couldn't fight them. Weeks ago, I would've tried, thinking I could counsel her through. That was then.

"Close your eyes," I told her. When she did, I leaned close. "Listen to the creaking of the island. Feel the air over your skin. Those other senses are a part of you, too. So…when you're back here, use them."

She gasped.

"Don't be in the alleys during peak times, and make sure the coast is clear before you go in or come out. Deal?"

Her hug said it all.

Chapter Twenty-Two

Early the next morning, I entered the rebels' hangar and removed my mask.

Six men and women sparred on raised platforms, the sounds of padded blows and strained grunts filling the air as the rebel soldiers fought each other. In the back, two armed men fired silenced guns at stationary targets. The room smelled faintly of sweat and gunpowder.

The sparring soldiers, all capped, paused to stare at me. Jex was one of them, his gaze lingering before he turned away.

I approached a ten-foot-diameter platform near the back, where Raven fought an imaginary foe, dressed in black like the others. A device covered her implant, what I recognized as a holo-simulator. By the way she moved, I realized the simulator projected her adversary onto her lenses, while a spinal energizer secured around her neck sent pain signals when she was "hit", making her battle seem real to her. As I approached, she blocked a simulated blow, then fell to a knee.

I unclipped the energizer, which was damp with her sweat. She stood and removed the simulator, but didn't speak when she glanced at me.

"They put you up to this?" I asked.

She shook her head and reached for the energizer as she averted her gaze. Unlike me, she wasn't wearing a cap.

"Your mother said you moved out." Mina had woken me. Raven had left before sunrise.

She took the energizer and turned away. "I belong here."

"We need to stay together. The Agency is going to come down hard on these people."

"I stand with them."

"You didn't with Talia. You let her down." She reattached the energizer. "A soldier makes sure their squad's accounted for."

"She's not part of my squad."

Cole approached. "You here to train?" he asked me.

"How about you protect my daughter, instead?" I lowered my voice but couldn't keep out the heat. "Ehkhert's head guard made a threat about them."

"All the more reason they should know how to fight. You, too. You do know how, don't you?"

I sensed the trap too late. It'd already been sprung. The soldiers watched us, their matches abandoned. "I do when I need to."

Cole's grin turned wolfish. "Show me."

"You need me in the lab, not here. "

"You think you're better." He stepped onto the elevated sparring mat and waved Raven off. "Prove it."

I stepped onto the mat, hoping to defuse the situation. Before I could, he came at me, and I ducked his blow. I could've left the mat, but that would mean I lost—and this had been coming.

I swung at his head. Not only did I miss, Cole nailed my arm after he avoided my swing. I jumped back, my arm tingling where he'd hit me. My foot sent a twinge of pain.

Cole came at me again.

I shuffled to the side, not wanting him to notice my limp, and threw two quick jabs. None connected.

"You broadcast your punches. Don't cock back," he said. "Watch."

Before I could react, he punched me in the face, knocking me down. I got up and blocked a jab I'd anticipated, but two more shots drove me down again. My jaw throbbed. My ear rang.

He didn't even seem winded. "There's no way you'd defeat an Agent. They're not only highly trained, they're augmented."

He was right. He was a skilled fighter, almost too fast for me, but Kieran was worse.

Cole squatted beside me and dropped his voice. "You know Raven and Jex are fucking, don't you?"

I got up and lunged, fully aware I was playing into his hands but still doing it, throwing shots, both missing, only managing to connect with his shoulder as my momentum took me past him.

"Make your punches count," he said. "The only thing that did was piss me off."

He came fast and hit me three times, splitting my lip and knocking

159

me to the mat.

"Come on, Dad," Raven said, wearing a cap so she could watch. The other soldiers stood near her, focused on our fight.

I got to my hands and knees, and Cole kicked me.

"Don't give your opponent time to react," he said.

I held my stomach. "Showing off to them?"

"Teaching them. And you. Your whole family is marked, but you can't even protect yourself. You might not report to me yet, but you're a soldier now. My soldier."

One of the mayor's guards rushed inside. "Agents are here."

The rebels went for their weapons, a long-haired soldier retrieving a scoped rifle from the back.

"Where are your masks?" Cole asked Raven and me. Angry and embarrassed about the match, I dug into my pocket while she ran across the large room to get hers. Seconds later, we joined him at the door, caps and masks in place. "You," he said to Jex, who'd lingered behind. "With us."

We hurried through the thinning streets, my limp worsening as we ran, the few people still out either ducking into buildings or running the same direction we were, weapons in hand.

We slowed as we approached the main gate on the opposite side of the island. The area wasn't large, a space half a container's length square, meant as a formal entry point for tourists or dignitaries or whoever didn't have to sneak onto this dreadful place. There was even an archway, as if the island was some sort of amusement park.

A crowd ten or twelve deep — most masked like us — blocked the entry point. We joined them, hiding behind the others as they faced the Agents. Jex donned a mask of his own and stopped beside us.

Kieran's voice boomed. "Make sure they're not here."

"This is a sovereign nation," Mayor Ehkhert said. "You have no jurisdiction." He, Salinda, and three of his guards were visible past the crowd. Kieran and two other Agents stood before them, their silver hair shiny in the muted sunlight. A government-marked powerboat was tied to the island's edge behind them, also shiny.

"Politicians have tolerated your defiance, but I don't," Kieran said. "You have no sovereignty."

They started forward.

"I'm meeting Senator Dixon next week," Ehkhert announced,

stopping them. "You want to cross her? Destroy the capital she's built? My citizens have influence over the mainland, fifty thousand votes that could make or break her next election. She and I are going to discuss Free Isle becoming a U.S. province. Step one more foot and you'll create an international incident."

"Harboring fugitives *is* an incident."

Cole leaned close to Raven and me. "Uncover your implants but keep your faces hidden. They find the smallest clue you're here, we're screwed."

"We know they're in San Francisco," Kieran continued, as I lifted my cap enough to unblock my implant. Weather information and news headlines appeared at the corners of my vision. "This is the most logical place they'd go."

Ehkhert called to the crowd. "Anyone seen his fugitives?"

I tensed. One word was all it would take.

Men with the mayor's insignia, scattered among those who'd gathered, straightened, a sign of his unspoken warning.

No one answered.

Ehkhert smiled. "See? I can ask around the mainland if you'd like, find out where they are."

Kieran ignored him, his eyes glowing orange as he scanned the crowd. I suspected he was comparing heat signatures with signals to find anyone who didn't match up.

"Now we'll find out whether Garly knows his stuff," Cole murmured.

Kieran seemed to lock onto us. I didn't know what codes I broadcasted, if they revealed an anomaly. They could be someone's who lived on the other side of the planet, or not associated with anyone at all.

Raven shifted beside me. I almost reached out to her but didn't. I hoped Mina and Talia had stayed away.

Kieran finally moved on, scanning the rest of the people, while his partners focused on the buildings nearby.

"This place is filled with criminals," he declared.

Ehkhert didn't flinch. "Have a safe journey back to the mainland."

Kieran stepped over the line Ehkhert had drawn and stopped an inch from his face. "If you're hiding them, I'll send this place to the bottom of the Bay."

* * *

As the Agents left, Whittock appeared from out of the slowly-dispersing crowd. "How quickly can you get us off this island?" he asked Cole.

"Just personnel, twenty minutes. You want Garly's lab and his toys," he said, flicking a thumb in my direction, "I'll need two days. Maybe three."

"You have until tomorrow night."

A shallow-cheeked guard came up. "He wants to see you."

We followed the man to a nearby tackle and knife shop. Ehkhert and Salinda entered behind us, Ehkhert yelling at the store owner to get out.

"I knew I shouldn't have let you stay on my island," he said to me.

Whittock held up his hands. "Sie, we'll get out of your hair."

"And leave me with this mess? You're not going anywhere until I get what's mine." He faced me again. "I know what you're building. I want it."

I'd put together blueprints so Garly would know what materials we needed to construct the hoverbike. Ehkhert must've watched.

"We're not giving you a damn thing," Cole said.

Ehkhert poked his chest. "The only reason I didn't turn you in was because of his tech. Don't even think about running. You're not getting off this island unless I let you."

* * *

After the run-in with the mayor, I had to make sure Mina and Talia were safe. When I entered our living quarters, Mina was pacing the living room.

I removed my mask, making sure my cap stayed in place, as Raven closed the front door. "Where's Talia?"

"What happened to your face?" Mina asked. She touched my cheek where Cole had hit me, which still throbbed.

"Long story."

Talia appeared from her bedroom, a pack over her shoulder, her eyes gleaming. "Black-shirts barged in and held us."

"Rebel soldiers," Mina explained to me. "Two of them. They forced us to different rooms and had us take off our caps, but wouldn't say why."

"Kieran came here looking for us," I told them.

"I knew something was poppin'," Talia said. "Those stiffs wouldn't say squatzers. Kieran whack you?"

"You both need to stay here."

"I thought I'd, uh…," she said, hoping I'd get the hint. She wanted to explore the alleys, possibly snoop to see if she could find any intel.

"From now on, neither of you can leave without an escort," Raven said.

"We're prisoners?" Mina asked.

"No, Mom. Don't worry. Whittock has a plan. Once we execute it, The Agency will forget about our family."

Talia said, "Can I help?"

"Too dangerous," I said. "Everyone here knows we're wanted. They could turn us in. All of you need to stay here."

"I'm part of the rebels now," Raven said.

I snapped at her. "Family is more important. The four of us need to run the first chance we get. We can't depend on anyone except each other. Hear me?"

Talia nodded, but Raven looked away.

"Let me talk to the mayor," Mina said.

"I don't want you near that guy," I said.

"I've dealt with men like him. He may not have been elected, but he craves power like every other politician."

"He's nothing like them."

"I can't just sit here."

There was a knock on the door. We donned masks, even Talia with an eyeroll, and I opened it.

Jex stepped inside. "Garly sent me to get you," he said to me as he glanced at Raven.

Mina rushed over. "How are my files? Have you downloaded them?"

"N-not yet," he said with a worried look. "But I'll do it quick."

"Today."

"Yes. I mean, unless the commander has me—"

"Would you like to come for dinner tonight? We'd love to have you."

"Dinner?" I asked, confused.

She seemed manic, her gaze unfocused. "Yes, like before all of this started, the whole family."

163

His eyes darted to Raven, me, Raven. "Sure."

"No," Raven said.

"Mina, let's not—" I started, but she ignored me.

"Come at eight," she told Jex. "Bring my files. All of them."

He looked less certain. "OK."

Not happy she encouraged his interest in Raven, concerned about her—and our family's safety—and angry that I was being summoned away from them, I put on my mask and left.

Whether it was my attitude or seeing Kieran again, the city seemed ominous.

Jex caught up to me. "I can assist you at the lab."

"You need to do as you promised. The last person you want to disappoint is Raven's mother." I realized I was encouraging him, too. "Won't matter. She won't forgive you."

We skirted a food market, chicken and cuts of meat hanging from hooks while tubs of fruit lent splashes of color to the metal and printed landscape.

"Freshman year in high school, m' dad told Mom and me about the implants," Jex said in a quiet voice. "He wrote a chunk o' the software, directin' the computer systems that wrote some of the code. Hadn't been his idea. He was followin' orders. He was military, didn't know the score 'til it was too late, but he saw how the implants tricked everyone. So, he told us."

"Where are they now?"

"Dead. Men raided our house and shot 'em. I managed to get away, runnin' 'til I thought I'd collapse. Dad gave me a hat like the cap you're sportin', which gave me a chance. When I took it off a month later, I got a message from him, timed to send out if he didn't reset it. I don't know how long he'd had it runnin', always rememberin' to skootch forward the time 'til he was killed. The message told me how to duck bein' detected and how to contact the rebellion. That was four years ago."

I did the math. "You're eighteen?"

He nodded.

We reached Garly's lab. I was still angry, but his loss tampered it. "I'm sorry to hear about your parents. I really am. But if you think we're going to become your new family, you're fooling yourself."

CHAPTER TWENTY-THREE

Nine hours later, I hooked my dark matter sphere into the cradle underneath the bike and stood back. It was complete — at least, the gravity negation mechanism was. The bike itself was just a framework, recycled metal rods we'd cut and welded together to create the basic structure. But it would be sufficient for our needs.

Instead of satisfaction, I felt unease.

"Want me to spin it?" Garly asked. We'd pushed everything against the walls to clear a space in the middle of the lab, but even so, there was barely enough room for the bike, which was eight-and-a-half feet long and seven wide.

"I'll do it. You don't want to run the risk I created a bomb, do you?"

We'd printed the driver's seat, so it was the finished version, but the handlebar was just a bent pipe, welded to the steering column. It had taken almost three hours to get right, though, as it had to operate on a three-dimensional axis. We hadn't added the back jets, either. I wanted to make sure the damn thing flew first.

"I know you didn't," Garly said with a look of disappointment as I climbed on. He squeezed himself into a corner of the room.

I settled my weight on the seat and felt it depress. Then I kicked on the fans, which we'd taken from a medium-sized drone and attached to the bike's four corners. As papers swirled around the room, I lifted off the ground.

Garly thrust a fist into the air and yelled.

My eyes raked the wall behind him. The mayor's secret camera was there somewhere. I wondered if he would wait for us to print a body cover before he claimed his prize. Frowning, I landed and climbed off.

"A fleet of these will be a megaforce," Garly said.

I took advantage of his distraction to reach for my ion blade, but he

165

looked back before I could grab it. "We need more dark matter."

"Already leaps ahead. There's a locale in Utah that's got a spatial ton. Been there before?"

"No," I said, surprised. Our competitors had launched their own collection efforts, but I hadn't realized they'd already started bringing inventory back to Earth.

"No sweats. We'll scoop up all the dark matter you need."

Cole burst in. "Come with me." To Garly, he said, "Rub down every surface he touched. Then hide."

"Oh god," Garly said.

Cole grabbed my arm as I threw on my mask, and yanked me outside. What looked like a black cloud headed toward us across the late-afternoon sky. I slowed, not sure what it was. It wasn't natural. An alarm rang throughout the island.

"Move," Cole barked.

We ran out of the rebels' area toward my living quarters. As we cut down one of the main roads, people rushed past and doors slammed.

Before we neared my temporary home, Cole abruptly angled down a cross street that led in a different direction. "This way."

"What about my family?" I asked, my anxiety rising.

"They're meeting us."

The cloud became more defined as it descended. It wasn't a cloud. It was a swarm of hunter-drones.

We ducked into a mechanical area, rusted walls forming three sides, a fence that had formed the fourth wall kicked aside. One of Cole's soldiers wrestled with a manhole-sized hatch set in the top of the shipping container at our feet. A second hatch was visible the next shipping container over; pipes angled out of both containers and through oil-streaked pumps. With our help, the soldier lifted the hatch to reveal the container's interior, which was nearly filled with water.

"Get in," Cole said.

Four masked people ran up, a man leading two women and a child. I recognized them: Jex with Mina, Raven, and Talia.

"What's that smell?" Talia asked.

Countless buzzing grew overhead. The swarm grew closer, blocking the sunlight.

Cole pointed to the far hatch, then the one by our feet, talking fast. "That's the septic pod for the island. This is a water reserve tank."

He held out straws. "You need to submerse yourselves. One of those things spots you, it's over."

"What are they?" Raven asked.

"No time." He handed her a straw and pushed her toward the hatch.

She resisted, not that I blamed her. There was no ladder, nothing we could hold onto as far as I could tell.

The soldier took a straw, jumped in, and disappeared as he swam toward the back. Whittock appeared, took a straw as well, and seeing us hesitate, slid into the water after him.

Talia snatched a straw and sat on the lip, then dropped in.

I turned to Mina. "Go."

She looked at Cole with terror.

"I'm going to lose men because of you," he told her. "They're wanted, too. Get in. Don't let anything show above the surface, and don't move until we get you."

"We can just wear our masks," Raven tried.

"They cut through them. They scan fingerprints, run DNA samples on the fly. There's no time."

As the buzzing of thousands of tiny hunter-drones grew louder, Mina climbed in, as did Raven. I went last, taking the final straw before dropping through the hatch.

The water that enveloped me was warm in pockets, heated from the machines stationed inside the adjacent containers. Cole closed the hatch as I surfaced, casting us into darkness.

I heard him lock the hatch, then his footsteps as he ran off.

Talia grabbed at me. "I'm scared," she whispered.

I was, too. "I'll hold your hand."

Mina and Raven huddled close. We treaded water, unable to touch bottom. I could touch the top, though, which was a foot overhead.

Thin streams of light filtered down from overhead, the largest coming from the rim of the hatch where the soldier must've had to force the cover loose. Other than my family, the only things I could make out were the water, hatch, and our corner of the container.

"How can we stay underwater?" Raven asked. "I can't breathe with this little tube."

"Hold onto the wall." I slipped between her and Mina, pulling Talia with me, and touched the side of the container. "There's a handhold."

Mina and Raven joined me as the buzzing became thunderous. The light darkened, and metal taps sounded overhead as the drones landed, a few at first, then so many it sounded like rain. As the taps ended, the chittering began.

I signaled to Mina and the girls, took off my mask, and started to slide underwater, angling the straw in my mouth upwards. Talia mimicked me, and we went under. Raven followed, as did Mina moments later.

When the water settled, I saw the streams of light flicker as the drones searched every inch of the island. There were shouts, booms, and high-pitched scraping—the sounds distorted by the water—as a battle raged over our heads. The light from the rim dimmed.

A glow formed, thin and orange, and my breath caught. The glow intensified, the metal hatch melting from a drone's laser as it cut a six-inch hole. Bits of steel dripped into the water near us, the bright bits of liquefied steel fading as they sank, followed by a larger splash as the six-inch hunk of metal dropped into the water and plunged to the bottom.

Talia squeezed my hand tighter.

The light returned, brighter than before because of the hole, and flickered as one drone entered the container, then a second, then a third. The first drone launched itself and hovered over the water, while the other two crawled along the ceiling, their metal dagger-claws enabling them to adhere to surfaces. They looked like something out of a kid's nightmare, with insect-like joints, a cutting-laser tail, and an array of sensors, along with both wide-angle and spot-lens cameras.

The two crawlers split up. One headed toward us while the other scurried across the roof toward the far end of the container where Whittock and the soldier hid. We clung to a narrow ledge that ran along the inner wall of the container just below the water's surface. My arm was tired from holding my body in place, but adrenaline gripped me as the crawler stepped from the ceiling to our wall.

Raven shifted beside me. I put my free hand on her, not taking my eyes from the hunting machine.

The flying drone made a systematic sweep toward us. As the tiny robot neared my straw, I held my breath, unsure whether its sensors could pick up something that minute. It could scan DNA, so it might be able to pick up our breaths.

The drone flew over me, paused, then flew back and hovered, drawn either by the remnant of my breath or Talia's. The crawler approached the water's edge inches from Raven's submerged hand. It lifted a metal leg and tapped the wall, then dropped lower.

She pushed away from the wall, but Mina grabbed her and held her still.

More drones crawled into the container and took flight, three of them moving over us, their cameras trained on the water. We were unmasked. Their software would read our faces, would compensate for the distortion from the water.

The skittering overhead suddenly grew louder and transitioned into buzzing. I tensed, expecting more to fly in. Instead, the flying drones in our container returned to the hatch, transformed back to crawling bug-machines, and climbed out. The one that had crawled near us followed moments later, collapsing itself to get through the hole.

Raven fought free of Mina's grasp, broke the water's surface, and took a ragged breath.

Past her, I caught a flicker. It was the last drone, the one that had crawled toward the far end of the container. Drawn by Raven's appearance, it scampered toward her.

I surged upward, grabbed her head as I crested, and dunked her. I feared it was too late, that we'd been spotted, filmed, warships coming—

Talia shoved off me, using my shoulders as a springboard. There was a splash as she landed back in the water. I searched for the drone but couldn't find it. Something exploded in the distance, the detonation vibrating the container.

Raven surfaced again, coughing. Talia also appeared. "Help," she said, gripping something wrapped in her cap.

I reached for her hands, aware that she was uncovered, and grabbed the cap, which I realized she'd used to snatch the drone. "Close your eyes," I said as I squeezed, twisting my hands to crack open the machine's shell. They were probably water resistant, maybe even waterproof, but only if they were intact.

The shell splintered, and the drone shorted out.

* * *

Whittock and his soldier joined us as we waited to be let out of

169

the tank. Raven coughed sporadically, and Talia wore her cap again—which had a small tear from the hunter drone—but no one spoke. We were too drained.

When Cole finally opened the hatch, he pulled Talia and Mina out, then Raven. The hole that had been cut into the tank's hatch had cooled, the melted edges dark.

As I got out, I could see the devastation even in this back area. Walls had fresh holes where drones had burrowed. Along the side street there were crushed drones, and farther down a kid smashing what I suspected was a dead one. People emerged cautiously, looking violated.

We weren't much better. Raven was shaky and pale, and Mina looked like she was on her last thread. Talia was in the best shape, smiling as Cole steered us, along with Whittock and the soldier, into a nearby building that housed controls for the septic system.

Closing the door, Cole grinned. "We took their best shot and survived...although not without casualties."

"How bad?" Whittock asked.

"One of our men was taken, ID'd by the drones."

Raven straightened. "Jex?" she asked, her voice raw.

"No. Tonek." When Raven gave him a blank look, he added, "Your squad mate."

"What happened to him?" Talia asked.

"The drones found him during their search and carried him off."

Mina looked at me with revulsion. "Is this our life now? Being hunted and dragged away by drones?"

I reached for her, but she swatted my hands away. "We survived," I said.

"I'm not losing another child."

"Your wellbeing is our greatest concern," Whittock said. "We're family now."

Mina scoffed. "You're no family."

I stepped between them. "We heard an explosion."

"One of our men drove off in a boat filled with explosives to lure the drones away," Cole said. "When they blanketed the boat, he detonated it."

"The driver?" Whittock asked.

"He's OK, but he'll be picked up. He has his story ready. The

Agency is converging on the spot, but it hurt them. We took out virtually every drone."

I frowned. "How did he lure them away?"

Whittock glanced at Mina. "I'll explain when there's more time. We're moving out tonight, while the Agents dredge the Bay. Every boat here will be gone by morning. We will be, too."

"Kieran has something more dangerous than what they just sent," I said. I told them about his new technology, the mosquito-sized drones he planned to employ. "Their monitoring capabilities are more advanced than the things that attacked us, their sensors able to penetrate metal, concrete, whatever we try to hide behind, taking every bit of real-time data and cross-matching it with digital records. Our modified implants won't protect us. Hell, The Agency might find us faster because of them, when our codes switch but we don't. We won't know they've found us until it's too late."

Garly burst in, with Jex a step behind. "We've been duked."

Whittock frowned at the lanky scientist. "What do you mean?"

"Jacked. Robbed. I went back to my lab after the critter storm, and everything's gone: weapons, explosives...." He looked at me. "Your hoverbike."

"Ehkhert," I said. "He used the attack as cover." With his cameras, he'd know where everyone was.

We were already moving but not to the lab, carving a path through the devastation, past crowds heading to ships and teenagers scavenging abandoned stalls. The rear of the island, the mayor's stronghold, had fewer burrowed holes, less destruction. His men patrolled the brightly-lit area, in particular a building with reinforced-steel walls and rapid-fire cannons attached to the corners that could mow down entire armies. Ehkhert stood in front of the structure, legs wide, arms crossed. Waiting for us.

"You overstepped your bounds," Whittock said.

The mayor's guards, four of them, aimed their weapons at us. I hooked Talia's arm and pulled her behind me. Mina grabbed Raven and did the same.

"'Overstepped'?" Ehkhert asked. "I just lost citizens. I lost street cred. I'm owed."

"You have no right."

"This is my island. Everything in it's mine: the flying contraption, your weapons, your goddamn balls. You still owe me money. Pay me what you promised right now, or I'll have you thrown over the side."

More of his men appeared, all heavily armed.

Whittock held up his hands, then slowly began to type, his datarings flickering in the late afternoon light. Seconds later, he lowered them. "Done."

Ehkhert angled his head to the side, the fingers of one hand moving as he checked his bank account. Satisfied, he said, "I'd stay away from dark streets if I were you. You're not too popular at the moment."

We retreated a block away, out of sight from Ehkhert and his men. "Tell the captain to ready his ship," Whittock told Cole and Jex. "We leave in an hour."

Mina looked at Jex in desperation. "I have your files," he assured her. "The upload'll only take a few minutes."

They left, taking Talia with them.

"What about my hoverbike?" I asked. "If that gets in the wrong hands—"

"It's in the building they're guarding. We won't be able to sneak up on it, but we can take them," Cole said.

"You're going to steal it back?"

Whittock nodded. "It's key to our plans."

"And we need our weapons," Cole added. "Sunset's in twenty minutes. We'll strike as soon as it's dark, then we'll ship off. By morning, we'll be safely at our base."

CHAPTER TWENTY-FOUR

Raven and I returned to our living quarters to pack our meager possessions.

We found Mina scanning information only she could see, her hands out before her, Jex beside her. "Where're the rest of them? There were more files." She wasn't wearing her cap, but she wasn't looking at us. She detached the downloader from her implant and thrust it at him. "Where are they?"

"Everything's there. I didn't even scrib them, just copied every data file there was." He looked like he wanted to be anywhere else.

"Some are missing."

I turned Raven around so neither of us faced her. "Pull your cap down."

"Dray, they're not there. It didn't work. You promised."

I turned back. Her cap covered her implant. "What files are you looking for?"

She hesitated, then turned on the young rebel. "They're in subfolders. All of the ones in the third subfolder are tied together. They're corrupted — or you missed something. I can't open them."

He held the downloader to his implant, although his movements were slow, as if he already knew the answer. "You need the program that uses 'em." He looked even more uncomfortable.

Talia asked, "Can you patch it?"

"She needs to download the program to use the data." He turned back to Mina. "But you can't. The implant won't let you, 'cause some programs track you. It's for your own safety."

She looked frantic. Then her eyes narrowed. "I need my old implant back. Tell Mr. Whittock. He might resist, but—"

"Your implants were destroyed. That's how we drew away those drones. We put your 'plants in a boat, uncovered 'em, and drove across

173

the Bay. That lured the drones, and when they swarmed the boat, Cole blew it."

I felt sick. A life's worth of information—pictures of our son, our girls, years of research—destroyed.

"How could you?" she asked.

"I'd already downloaded your files—"

"Get out," she yelled.

He stood but hesitated, which prompted her to yell again, then a third time when he paused at the door. He left, clearly crushed.

I helped her to one of the chairs. "I want to go home," she said.

"We're leaving here."

"Not with *them*. We can go back, the way it was."

"Fine, we won't go with them. We'll go on our own—"

Raven spoke up. "I'm going with them. I joined their cause. We all did."

"You're doing no such thing," Mina snapped. "They're criminals and liars—"

"It's my life."

"You're my daughter."

I stepped between them. "Raven, we don't have time for this."

"Where's Talia?" Mina asked.

Shit. The door was open. She hated when any of us fought.

I knew where she'd gone. "You two work this out."

The sky was dark, the sun's rays faint overhead. A heavily-pierced butcher, wheeling meat stacked in a wheelbarrow with his wife and child in tow, passed but didn't look at me, their faces strained. I spotted a few other people, but they didn't seem to notice me as I made my way to the nearest hidden alley. Making sure no one was watching, I approached the holoscreen, which perfectly matched the shade and tone of the walls to either side, and stepped through it.

Talia squatted in the narrow alleyway with her arms wrapped around her knees. It reminded me of when she hid in her bedroom closet when she was four or five, curled among her shoes and discarded stuffed animals.

I sat beside her. "Bring up bad memories?"

She nodded, her eyes downcast. Although her cap had a tear from the swarm attack, it still covered her implant.

"Remember what I've told you? It doesn't mean we don't love each other." Mina had done virtually all the yelling back then—the times she talked to me in the months after Adem's death. Tonight must've been an ugly reminder.

"I'm still not big enough to help." She meant big enough to stop us.

"You're a lioness, remember? They never feel bad about wanting to protect their pride."

She rested her head on my shoulder—a whisper of a moment that broke my heart every time I remembered it—then straightened. "I wanna skedaddle to somewheres we can do what we want."

"Know what? So do I." I stood. "Come on, my lioness."

She gripped my hand and yanked herself up.

When we entered our living quarters, I announced, "We're leaving, the four of us. We'll pay one of the boat captains to take us out of here."

Raven pushed past, a pack on her shoulder, and headed for the door.

"Didn't you hear me?" I asked, preparing for the fight to come.

Before it did, Mina spoke in a serene voice. "Everyone stay here. I don't want you to get hurt."

Raven and Talia started talking, but I cut them off. "Why? What did you do?"

"It'll be like it was. He promised."

Outside, projectiles slammed into the island. *Chug. Chug. Chug.*

"What did you do?"

"I'm fixing what you did." Gunfire laced her words. "You took everything from me."

Raven looked outside and paled. "Ships are bombing the island."

Mina didn't flinch at the gunfire, at the screams. "Stay inside. You'll be safe."

"Tell me," I said.

Her hands trembled but not from fear. "I called them. Kieran will let us have our old lives back." She held out her hand as if giving benediction. Or salvation. "He'll even give you another chance."

Chapter Twenty-Five

My mind wanted to retreat, label Mina's words unreal, but I didn't have the luxury of denial. The Agency was coming. "You'd trust Kieran?" I asked her. "After what he did to Raven?"

"He apologized, said he'd accept punishment for it."

"He lied. And you betrayed us."

"You betrayed Adem. I'm getting him back."

Hearing our son's name was like a blade to my heart. "He's—"

"You took him from me."

Talia's voice cut through my confusion. "Dad?"

I forced my gaze from Mina. Raven and Talia looked so young. They shouldn't be exposed to atrocities like this.

I had to get them off this island. "We're leaving," I told them. "*Now*."

"No," Mina cried. She lunged for me. "They'll get hurt."

I did something I never thought I'd do. I pushed her away. When I turned back, my gaze dropped to Talia. The hidden alleys. "Can you get us to the docks?" When she nodded, I said, "Go."

She ran out.

"Watch after her—and keep up," I said to Raven. I threw an arm out to stop Mina from getting past me.

"They can't leave," she said as Raven disappeared.

I couldn't let Mina follow. She was too dangerous. She wasn't wearing her cap. I should've noticed.

I shoved her into our bedroom, so shocked and disgusted that she would turn on us like this, would betray us—me—like this, I pushed her harder than I intended, then slammed the door and broke off the doorknob. It was flimsy, as were the walls, the door, this whole damn structure. Kieran's men would shred it all.

I ran outside and nearly collided with Jex. "Where's Raven?" he shouted. "There's—"

"I know. Follow me." I didn't know if I should let him, but we would need help getting off this deathtrap. I also needed to sort out the emotions that warred inside me, but there was no time. I pulled him past others rushing by, each one a pair of eyes that could pinpoint us, to the hidden alley as an alarm sounded somewhere, and drug him through. He yipped as he stumbled through the holoscreen, then jerked from my grasp. He scanned the alley, face slack.

"Keep up," I warned him. Raven and Talia were waiting for us. I waved at Talia. "Go."

She flashed a grin before racing off, so fast I feared we'd lose her, the alley darker than the fading indigo sky. Gunfire stuttered to the right and from somewhere far behind as we chased after her, the one behind doubling in intensity. Talia cut right, then left, paused to make sure we were following, then raced off again.

The alley jerked in spots, curling toward the right, then abruptly ended, opening onto a narrow street. She waited for us by a holoscreen. As we joined her, a rebel ran past, his silenced machine gun at the ready, the weapon antiquated compared to The Agency's arsenal.

"We should find our squad," Jex whispered to Raven.

I gripped his arm. "You wanna be with us or them?"

His eyes flickered to her. "With you."

"They can help," Raven told me.

"Come on," Talia whispered, the joy in her voice as clear as her fear. She darted across the street and disappeared into a shadow-draped recess, her arm reappearing briefly to wave us forward.

Jex drew his pistol. "I'll cover you."

Raven nodded with a resigned expression.

I spotted a cluster of Agency soldiers as we ran across the open pathway, blocks away but too close, what looked like a battle past them. I didn't pause as I rejoined Talia on the other side, passing through another holoscreen.

At least one of them saw us. Gunfire strafed the pathway, a few bullets piercing our hidden alley. Raven dove at Talia and pulled her down before she could get hit. I dove as well, snagging Jex's arm and yanking him down.

The soldiers ran past, four of them. On the hunt.

"Thanks," Jex grunted when the coast was clear.

I forced myself to relax my grip. I'd never been shot at before. It was something I never wanted to experience again.

Talia crawled out from under Raven. "You think Mom's OK?"

"I'm sure she's fine," I forced out.

"She could be hurt."

"We need to get you to safety," Raven said with a pained expression. "Mom would want us to."

Gunfire erupted somewhere up ahead, with sounds of death and pain.

I stood. "Where's your boat?" I asked Jex.

"South dock. Spot twenty-three."

"Know where that is?" I asked Talia.

She nodded solemnly then took off, leading us through the maze of alleys as the gunfire continued. After a couple of minutes, she took a sharp right and raced between lower buildings, the smell of the Bay growing stronger. She slowed as we approached a holoscreen. "Past this, we run," she told us.

Two long buildings stretched away to either side of where we stood, past stacks of crates and drums, the buildings dark in the fading light and distorted by the holoscreen's projected image we hid behind. Between the buildings was the ocean. Something was wrong, though. Streaks of light chopped the waters.

Multiple explosions shook the island. As the smell of smoke and melted plastic reached us, I pressed my head through the screen and focused on the Bay. The angled lights illuminated an intercostal vessel bobbing at an angle, taking on water, along with two fishing boats, still tied to the dock, which issued smoke. I followed the lights back to their source, and found overlapping police and coast guard boats in either direction.

The island was surrounded.

Other boats were past the line of government vessels. It appeared they'd tried to get away but had been caught. Men in military uniforms swarmed the boats I saw.

The holoscreen buzzed as Jex joined me.

"Which one's yours?"

"Shit. The one that's sinkin'."

A secondary explosion, this time from the rebels' area, caused him to stumble forward. I hauled him back behind the screen as a column of smoke rose past the rebels' training building. As far as I could tell, all of the boats had either left Free Isle or been damaged.

"Tell me you've got a backup," I said.

"Whittock just arranged one boat."

"What are our options?" Raven asked.

"We can hide 'til they clear out."

I remembered Kieran's threat. "This place won't be floating much longer." Then it hit me. "The hoverbike. Raven and Talia can use it to escape."

"That'd be dangerous—" Jex started.

"They'll fly low, head across the Bay, while we distract everyone." It wouldn't go fast, but it was their best chance.

"No, Dad," Raven said.

"You need to get Talia out of here."

"We'd be able to snag our weapons," Jex pointed out.

I faced Talia. "Can you find the mayor's armory? It's a building covered in steel plates and has guns on the outside."

"I think so."

She took a deep breath and sprinted down the crooked alley, taking us back to the junction before heading east. There was a cascade of footsteps, though I didn't know if they came from Agents as they advanced, Ehkhert's men trying to drive them back, or innocents scrambling for survival.

We passed openings in the alley, catching images of people flickering past. I wanted to grab them, but the risk was too great. When we approached the east side of the island, Talia slowed. The air reeked of smoke. Holes riddled the buildings around us.

I took the lead and held out a hand to keep her behind me, making sure we all wore our caps, as I didn't want to give that silver-haired bastard an edge.

There was an angle to the ground. The waterproofed shipping container we stood on, maybe more, had been damaged. Leaking. We continued past the growing puddle and found the end blocked by a ten-foot metal panel.

I looked back at Talia, confused.

She pointed to the wall beside me. "This is where you said."

I realized she was pointing at the rear of Ehkhert's armory. Like the front, it was covered in steel plates. An unmarked door was the only break in the steel—that and a wired camera.

I smiled at her. "Good job."

If I had my ion blade, I'd cut a hole in the wall big enough to climb through. Instead, I stood back and motioned for Raven's gun.

"Wait," Jex said. He squatted in front of the door. The lock was an old-style tumbler, which he conquered in seconds. He stood, Raven raised her pistol in case of an ambush, and he opened the door.

We entered the building, which had metal shelving against every wall, with a freestanding group in the middle of the room. Virtually every shelf contained weapons, ammunition, and explosives. The rebels' arms were clustered on shelves on the far side of the room, toward the front. My skeleton hoverbike was in the corner nearest them, wedged between the shelving and the group in the middle of the room.

"Load up," I whispered.

Jex stepped past a cluster of unmarked crates and grabbed machine guns. Raven and Talia hurried past him to the rebels' weapons, while I approached the hoverbike. It appeared unharmed, so my plan would work. The girls could fly it to safety.

They'd need cover, distractions, the bigger the better.

I searched among the items taken from Garly's lab—the 3D handheld printers, chemical emulators, and aeroserators—for the satchel I'd brought from my office, spotting it seconds later. As I hooked it over my shoulder, my eyes rested on the timer-bombs Garly had shown me, which were stacked on a nearby shelf. I put two in my satchel, followed by two more, then spotted my ion blade and grabbed that, too.

Talia was unsure what to do, so Raven had her collect ammunition, pairing them with machine guns and pistols she selected. I snatched a machine gun myself as Jex rifled through the weapons and stuffed various ones into a bag he'd found.

Returning to the bike, I pulled it out of the corner toward the door. The batteries were fully charged.

"We'll launch out front," I said. "The alley's not wide enough."

Before I could say more, the front door opened and a silver-haired Agent walked in. I couldn't move—didn't have time—as the Agent pulled his gun. There was no place to hide. Before we could take two steps, he'd shoot us down.

"They're in here," he yelled to whoever else was outside.

He lifted his pistol, aimed at me—

A shot from the side nearly took his head off. It was Raven, standing five feet away. The Agent collapsed and she dropped her pistol, her face horrified.

With the Agent down, I saw twenty or so SWAT-like men out front in vests with Agency logos. Two more silver-haired Agents were with them.

They raised their weapons.

I lunged for the door and slammed it closed as pulsefire erupted, the energy pulses denting the reinforced door. I locked it, then noticed a red button. It was brutal, but they left me no choice. Closing my eyes, I slapped the button, and the rapid-fire cannons outside whined as they activated. Thunderous fire erupted from both sides of the building, laced with cries of pain, sounds that ripped through me. Good or evil, those were human lives.

I'd become a killer.

The carnage would draw more government forces. This place would be inundated. I opened my eyes. There was no way the girls could use the bike now.

A shrieking sound cut through the gunfire, and something exploded against the building, silencing one of the cannons.

"Go," I yelled at them.

Raven picked up the pistol she'd thrown and grabbed Talia, who had paled from the sounds outside. I lifted the bike's edge, triggered my blade, and sliced the sphere from its cradle. Jamming the sphere into my satchel, I followed the girls out the back door. Jex brought up the rear, machine gun in one hand and a bag of weapons in the other.

Talia paused at the first intersection and looked at me for direction, her eyes huge.

"The mayor's house," I said. "He'd have an escape of some kind." If nothing else, he'd have guards. Fortifications. Something.

Behind us, a blast took out the other cannon.

Talia took off as fast as she could. We followed, the narrow alley seemingly tighter than before. To either side and behind us were shouts. Footsteps. We ran faster.

She cut down a new alley, past two and three-story buildings, gunfire erupting behind us. No one was visible, but flashes from pulse rifles illuminated the grimy metal walls as we ducked past, the orange-tinted projectiles powerful enough to drop a 250-pound man.

Talia took another passageway, then slowed and looked at me anxiously. She'd done it. We'd reached the main road that led to the mayor's residence.

She stopped before the holoscreen that hid us, the screen set three feet back from the street. Light spilled onto the roadway as if it was any other evening, the area's hodgepodge of lampposts making the area bright as day. I couldn't see much of the actual street from where I stood, as the screen was too far back. All I could see was a narrow section of road and an unmarked building across from us.

I smelled it first—spent gunpowder; cooled plasma; melted steel; charred flesh.

Motioning for the others to stay, I stepped through the holoscreen and peered around the corner to see the rest of the street. Bodies laid in both directions, and buildings were pockmarked from gunfire. Worst of all was the mayor's residence. It had been struck by an explosive of some kind; remains laid scattered across and down the roadway, some pieces bigger than the hoverbike, a couple impaled into the sides of buildings. Some portion of the house remained, but I couldn't tell how much from where I stood. Thin smoke hovered over the street, and pools of water stood in pockets where containers had been damaged.

The lamplights half-blinding me after our run through the dark alley, the only movement I saw came from the end of the street, where the Bay was just visible. Boats floated to either side of the mayor's demolished residence, a few listing, most tied to the coast guard and policeboats that barricaded the island.

Our chances had run out.

"Is it clear?" Jex asked, leaning close.

Sounds grew in the alley behind us. Footsteps. The clink of weapons.

I signaled to the girls. "Go."

Jex led them into the roadway, though they slowed when they saw the devastation and death. I pulled a bomb out of my bag, hit the timer—which was preset to twenty seconds—and stuck it to the side of the building just inside the alley, down low.

As the time started down, I grabbed Talia's hand. "Let's move."

We started toward the Bay, Raven and Jex with their weapons

high. I'd never felt so exposed.

We jogged past the bodies and debris. I could tell Talia was scared by how hard she gripped my free hand and how closely she stayed beside me. This would scar her for years. I wanted to hurt Kieran and his Agency for traumatizing her like this.

"Stop or you're dead," a voice shouted behind us—an Agent, wounded, gun steady as he aimed at us. We had no cover, the closest debris big enough to use as a shield two body-lengths away. Footsteps grew louder from the alley.

The timer reached zero.

The explosion sheared the building and took out the Agent, throwing him like a discarded toy into the building on the far side of the street. We ducked, although the building sheared by the blast shielded us. Smoke and grit ballooned outwards, temporarily blinding us, and bits of debris pelted us.

When the smoke cleared, the building laid at an angle, the sheared end resting below street level. A container, maybe more, had been damaged.

Jex ran to the fallen Agent. I turned Talia away and covered her ears before the shot came. She didn't fight or make a sound, although her eyes were wide.

Straightening, I followed her gaze and saw the mayor—what was left of him. Ehkhert's killers had propped up his body near where his front door had been, a warning for anyone who resisted.

Raven saw it as well. "His getaway is still here, isn't it?"

"I don't know."

Jex joined us. "The bomb sealed part of the alley, but not all of it," he said. "Whoever survived the blast will be able to get through."

Our best chance was whatever Ehkhert had set up as his getaway. If it was still there.

We headed for his residence.

Shouts and periodic gunfire came from different points on the island, but I couldn't see where. All that was visible ahead of us were the remains of Ehkhert's building, the blocked Bay, and a sliver of Oakland in the distance. Behind us, the street narrowed as it cut deeper into the island and angled out of sight.

As we approached the wrecked mayoral residence, I slowed. The buildings to either side were the last. Once we stepped past them, we'd be exposed to the north and south, as open space occupied the island's entire eastern edge. I barely blinked as I scanned the area, tense for the slightest movement.

Beside me, Jex stiffened. "What is that?" he drawled, indicating the residence.

It hadn't been completely destroyed.

Ehkhert's throne room, where we'd first met the mayor, had been laid low, littered with debris, its walls shredded — except for the one in the back. The one that had indicated a generator.

Wreckage stuck up high enough that I couldn't see it fully, but I could see it well enough. A rectangular building jutted out from the island, thick, taller than me. Too big for what a generator would need.

On an island where every inch was a premium, Ehkhert's lie was revealed.

"Son of a bitch. The generator's fake," I said.

"You shittin' me?"

"That could be our way out."

"There's a door," Raven said.

She was right. A narrow door had cracked open, possibly due to the explosion that had leveled the building. Ehkhert must've had the fake generator structure reinforced. Otherwise, it would've collapsed from whatever took out the rest of the building, though the structure listed to one side, the shipping container under it weakened. The opened door could've meant someone else had already taken Ehkhert's getaway — or was waiting for us. But we didn't have any other options.

I hurried forward, my pace quickening — and gunfire erupted.

CHAPTER TWENTY-SIX

Bullets and pulse fire whizzed close, the sound deafening, and punched into the wreckage around me.

I froze.

Jex yanked me behind a pile of crumpled support beams and debris that had been part of the building's exterior wall, although the remains lay a few yards from where the rest of the building stood. I'd been so distracted by the fake generator that I'd stepped into the open without checking the area, becoming visible along the length of the island's edge — and had nearly paid for it.

Slugs triggered puffs of dust in the debris, puffs that could become plumes of blood if I didn't get my head out of my ass.

Jex and Raven took positions to either side of the devastated exterior wall and prepared to return fire. The pulse fire came from the edge to our right, what was vaguely south. The open space along this edge of the island was about twenty feet wide, whether for offloading of goods or as some sort of public space, I didn't know. It sounded as if gunfire came from multiple spots.

We had to get us off this damn island.

A brief lull settled, so I stuck my head over the barrier. Even in the fading twilight, I saw our enemies. Ten men, maybe more. All armed. And a gleam of silver hair.

I ducked back down. I wondered if the machine guns and timer-bombs we'd stolen would be enough.

"Come on," Talia called. She darted out from behind our protective cover toward a collapsed section of building just inside the mayoral residence. I stood as she ran and brought up my pistol, spotting four Agency soldiers nearby, two to the left and the other two in different spots to the right. I fired at them, but was more focused on running to Talia.

Lurching out into the open, nothing around me, I fired again and ran. I reached the cover and dropped beside her.

I was vaguely aware of footsteps far to the left. They grew louder, but were faint compared to the blood in my ears.

She gave a worried grin. "Ready?"

The generator waited thirty feet away.

Two piles of debris, large enough to serve as cover, were spaced along our path, the first one five feet away. Neither pile rose very high, both about Talia's height in the middle, but the second one was long, made up of a pile of broken wall, a collapsed dresser on its side, and rubble. Unfortunately, the last dozen feet to the door was exposed. We'd be exposed.

As she crouched to run, gunfire pierced the air. I pulled her back. The gunfire was different. It came from the north — our uncovered side.

We were trapped, pinned down from two sides.

I covered her body with mine and aimed my gun toward the new threat. Two men in black gear moved in coordinated fashion toward us. I tightened my finger on the trigger but paused. The gear looked familiar. The men aimed their weapons past us.

These weren't government forces. They were Cole's men.

Their machine guns blocked their faces as they shot at our attackers. More gunfire came from behind them. The first two rebels took positions near the front of Ehkhert's residence. As they exchanged fire with the Agency's forces, the other three, two women and a man, moved forward. They took out a soldier, then two more.

Raven and Jex launched themselves across the open expanse toward Talia and me. I wanted to shout at them to stay back, but they joined us before I could.

Gunfire escalated on both sides, bullets chewing up the debris. The rebels maneuvered past us. I didn't understand.

One of the lead rebels lowered his machine gun — Cole. Farther back, Whittock was with the two women, coming closer. I wondered why they were here. Where the others were. Should be four more at least, plus Garly.

The closest was twenty feet away, creeping past us, using the terrain as we had.

"We should join 'em," Jex said.

"Us or them, remember?" I said.

"Knew you'd say that," he muttered. He waved to the rebels, one of whom continued past us. Then I understood. They were trying to draw fire away, provide cover.

Cole signaled to us. He wanted us to retreat.

The level of gunfire dropped, but footsteps grew. More Agency soldiers were joining the fight.

I checked my satchel. The three timer-bombs and the dark matter sphere were still there, but they weren't enough. I didn't think Whitlock and his team would be, either. Our only option was Ehkhert's escape.

I signaled to the girls. "The generator. Go."

Talia darted across the open space, my heart thudding with each of her small footsteps as she revealed herself to the rebels. Two steps, three, four. I was already moving, launching myself from behind the mound of debris, Raven a step behind me. She fired as we ran the half-dozen feet to the next barrier.

Talia slid as she dropped behind the beams and rubble, safe, and I nearly barreled into her as Raven and I joined her. Jex came next, firing a few shots blindly as he ran toward us. He landed ungracefully, the bag of weapons weighing him down.

Bullets carved at our barrier, at the spot where Jex had been right before he joined us. The rebels returned fire.

One last section of cover, twelve feet at least. Seemed like miles.

I looked behind me just in time to see it. Whittock stood to advance—and was shot.

"No," Jex yelled.

The blast threw Whittock backwards, and he crumpled to the ground. Raven gasped. The rebels stopped shooting, stunned by Whittock's fall.

I needed to balance things, keep them moving.

I removed one of my bombs and shortened the timer to five seconds, figuring to throw the explosive at the soldiers to screen us so we could get away. I didn't like hurting anyone, but they were trying to kill us.

Maybe fiddling with the device was why I missed it. Or just didn't suspect it, even though I should have. They had no humanity.

Mina's voice cut across the battlefield. "Raven. Talia."

She sounded calm, only the slightest fear and worry. Calmer than I could understand, although it took me a second to recognize the emotion.

Took me too long to realize what would happen.

Talia, my lioness, my fearless, impulsive daughter, reacted before I could. "Mom!" She dashed out from behind the mound of debris, lulled by the cessation of gunfire, driven by her love.

I lunged for her and snagged her arm at the last second, stopping her from getting away. She was already past our shield, visible, smiling, probably making eye contact with Mina.

I yanked her back. A shot rang out as I pulled her behind the debris. She was already falling, the bullet twisting her, and I roared in anguish. Blood sprayed the area. Her blood. I caught her before she could hit the container-floor, my last act of cushioning her from the harsh world.

"*Talia*," Raven shrieked. She collapsed beside us and put her hands over the hole in Talia's chest as if she could keep her with us.

I cradled Talia's head, wanting to sob, to help her, to soak up these last seconds. I was faintly aware of Jex firing above us at whoever was with Mina, of Mina crying Talia's name. None of that mattered. I stroked her hair, inadvertently pulling off her cap. My lioness.

She hadn't experienced enough life to learn how people disappointed each other. Betrayed each other. Not until it was too late.

The light in Talia's eyes faded. "Daddy?"

Then it went out.

Raven sobbed as Talia's body stilled, her tears sprinkling Talia's favorite shirt, a souvenir from Yosemite.

I held her to me. I don't know how long I crouched there. Seconds, hours. Time lost meaning.

Jex put his lips to my ear. "We don't move, they'll get us."

His voice was raw. I didn't even trust mine.

He pushed. "We gotta go *now*."

I became aware of my surroundings. Gunfire rattled from both directions. I glanced to the west. Cole and his men fought a group I couldn't see. Another rebel was down. Cole directed his remaining two fighters to split up, to clear a path.

In the other direction, gunfire interrupted Mina's wails.

"Go with Jex," I told Raven. She looked at me, not comprehending. "The generator. It's your way out."

She clenched my arm. "You're coming, too."

I'd have to leave Talia, I almost said. But that was foolish. Talia was gone. I knew this numb feeling, from after Adem died. If I let it take hold, it'd paralyze me.

Jex hovered too close, as if he was prepared to pick me up and carry me.

I nodded. "I'll cover you."

They crawled to the edge of the debris as I gazed at Talia, continuing to stroke her hair. If it wasn't for Raven, I didn't know if I'd stop.

I had to.

I carefully lowered Talia's head to the ground, then kissed her forehead, and with an effort removed my hands. Her cap lay nearby, as did my machine gun. I swiped both, set the machine gun to my shoulder, which brought feeling back to my body, and rose.

Illuminated by lamp posts, Kieran stood a block away, in the middle of the open space that ran along the island's edge. A dozen or more of his men were to either side of him, along with three other Agents partly hidden in the shadows. The men were crouched from Jex's earlier gunfire, but Kieran stood tall, thirty feet from me. He used Mina as a shield, an arm around her waist, easily holding her as she struggled to get free. When she saw me, she strained harder, bending forward to try to break his grasp, to reach Talia.

Exposing him.

I aimed and fired.

The bullet clipped the side of his head, sparking as it hit metal. The two collapsed as they were thrown back, and I opened fire on the others.

Men dove to either side. I'd hit one at least. The rest hid.

"Dad," Raven shouted.

She was in the fake generator's doorway, gun in hand. She fired at Kieran's group to give me cover, her face anxious.

I wanted to hurt him and every one of his men. But this wasn't the time or place.

I ran to Raven. We ducked into the building and shut the door. Gunfire peppered it, making it crack.

The fake generator room held a small powerboat in a pool of water. Jex was already at the wheel. When I looked at him, he pointed to a red button by the door and turned the engine over. As the boat roared to life, I hit the button, and the wall facing the open water separated into thin slats that rose up into the ceiling, revealing the Bay.

An explosion rocked the building, followed by metallic groans as the structure tilted. Water poured into the pool, lifting up the boat. "Hurry," Jex yelled as Raven and I climbed in.

As soon as we were aboard, he launched us into the dark night.

We shot out of the room, the sudden expanse around us shocking, and across the water. Two coast guard ships blocked our path, nearly crisscrossed in front of us. Jex wrenched the wheel, steering us between and past them before they could react, then angled toward the San Francisco shoreline, while behind us smoke rose from the listing Free Isle and the boats that surrounded it.

I faced forward, holding Raven as she broke into sobs, the roar of the engine and heartbeat-like splash of waves punctuating her wails.

The wind snatched my tears as Jex drove us away.

CHAPTER TWENTY-SEVEN

The moonless night claimed us as we raced away from Free Isle, the lights from San Francisco too weak to reach us.

Jex steered south, following the shoreline but staying far enough out that we seemed to be driving blind. Not that I knew where to go or what to do, my dream exhaled by Talia's final breath.

The waves didn't have shape. They rolled and surged without warning or reason.

Jex slowed, then angled toward the light-dotted peninsula. I wanted to ask, to figure out a next step, but didn't. Couldn't.

I realized my foot was throbbing. I'd reinjured it at some point. I'd cut it off if it would bring her back.

Minutes later, the ship's bow glided up onto a patch of sand. We'd pulled into an inlet approximately three miles south of downtown. Across from us was a larger beach, some trees, possibly a park.

"Come on," he whispered. "We're too exposed on water."

I climbed off somehow, as did Raven.

He handed me his bag of weapons, then reversed the boat. We watched in silence as he aimed it toward the opposite side of the Bay, gunned it, then ran and jumped off the back of the boat, nearly tripping at the last second. By the time he reached shore, the boat was gone.

Raven helped him out of the water. "Shit, that's cold," he said. "Let's go."

He led us down an uneven road, past a warehouse-type building streaked with graffiti and holopaint. We had weapons, but Jex was the only one who had his raised, aiming at every shadow we passed. I held Talia's cap in my other hand, my fingers clenched tight.

A brick building loomed ahead, easily a hundred years old, abandoned like the rest of the area. A fence topped with razor wire ran to our right.

I hadn't even realized Jex had gone ahead until he reappeared. "We have to scoot faster."

I shook my head. "I can't."

"They're gonna follow our tracks—"

"In the morning." Raven looked as gutted as I felt. "We'll stay there."

Jex wavered as he eyed the brick building; he clearly wanted to please me but also protect us.

I tried the door. It was locked, so I pulled out my ion blade. He stopped me before I could fry the lock and used his tools to get us in.

I let him steer us past the peeled linoleum and up the stairs, its printed banisters warped with age. My brain struggled to retain even the simplest of details. Water stains. Earthquake damage. We stopped on what was probably the top floor. Rooms were empty, dusty. Suited me.

Raven stumbled into one of the rooms and slid to the floor, her back against the wall and her head in her hands. I joined her, my arm around her shoulders. Jex joined later and sat by the open doorway, his weapon across his lap. We all kept our caps on.

They talked. I didn't catch it all.

"If I hadn't joined, Talia would still be alive," Raven whispered.

Just hearing Talia's name thickened the fog in my mind.

Another snippet. "You knew they didn't want me—"

"I wanted you." His eyes darted to me, then away, embarrassed I'd heard.

I forced myself to speak. "You didn't do this," I told Raven. "Mina did."

"Why?" Her face was open, shattered, no pretense, nothing but loss and confusion.

"I know," Jex said. A tick of the head. "'Think I do. The data I copied for her, the biggest chunk, were InMemorium files. It's a program for loved ones who've passed, recreates them so they seem like they're still 'round. It links to the company's site, which takes the datafiles you got of whoever's gone and…projects the person…onto your lenses.…"

Memories connected, a pattern I'd ignored. Mina distracted. Mina seeming to talk to someone else at odd times, starting a few months after Adem's death. She'd abruptly become happier, no longer yelling at me or accusing both of us of failing him. I hadn't pushed because I'd feared she was having an affair.

"I hoped you knew," Jex said.

"How old was he, in her...?"

"Seven or eight."

She'd been so excited when her doctor told us we were having a boy. She'd hoped her father would live long enough to hold his grandson, play catch with him, teach him things. He never had a son of his own, just Mina and her sister. He loved his girls but always wanted a boy, to pass along things his father had shown him.

He'd lived long enough for Adem's birth. And his death.

"She'd have'ta start over, but it wouldn't be the same. The software sticks in random variables to mimic life, which alters the personality that develops," Jex said. "But she couldn't even do that. The implant Garly gave her blocks software like InMemorium because it tracks back to the user, takes locations to blend the construct with the real world. And records it."

"I had no idea she created an avatar of him," I said.

She must not have realized she'd lose him again, blocked from accessing the software and losing the files she'd created. To her, I'd murdered him. But that didn't justify her betrayal. She'd jeopardized us for a hologram. She knew he wasn't real, knew the price we'd pay, yet she'd still called Kieran.

Raven curled against me, thinner than I'd realized, and eventually fell asleep. Her cries would've cut me except I was numb, the same feeling I had when I'd lifted Adem's casket, Mina's father on the other side. The sunlight angling into the church had suggested a heavenly Father, but there wasn't, just a mortal one desperate to remember the sound of his son's voice—and understand how he could've failed him so completely.

Neither Mina nor I had realized the danger when it happened. He'd scratched himself, walking and crawling around our friends' yard as our kids played together and we enjoyed their wine. We hadn't worried about the cut. Third-child syndrome.

I told myself even if we'd cleaned the wound, rushed him to the hospital that night instead of after he became sick, it was too late. The strain of hantavirus that took his life three weeks later—carried by rodents that no longer had a habitat of their own—had entrenched itself in his system before we'd finished our glasses of Malbec.

My grief never left, but it had faded, hastened by the needs of my daughters.

I'd nearly given up on Mina rejoining our family, but she did on Talia's first day of kindergarten. I'd planned to take her, but Mina came out of the bedroom dressed, almost herself — distracted, a little frantic at first, but present again.

She even went back to work, diving into her new boss's campaign. I'd figured her being detached was how she coped, possibly locking away the memories too painful to relive.

Instead, she decided to deceive herself.

My mind recalled Talia's last moments, her eyes — which sparkled when she mocked my music collection, which had drooped halfway through the midnight movie premier of *The Thundergals Return* — closing for the last time.

Her cap smelled of her.

My efforts, not only to make the world better but to bring Adem back in my own way, the robots and glider and encouraging her and Raven to be bold like I assumed he would've been, hadn't been enough. If I'd been less driven, less focused on growing the company and making products, would I have stopped Mina from making the choices she'd made? Would I have discovered she'd resurrected our son? I hadn't been aware Kieran had reached out to her and played on her vulnerability. Yet he had. He must've. How else would she have known how to contact him?

Along with the grief that weighed on me, I was furious. This time I had a target for my anger. Kieran. The Agency. The whole damn system.

I found myself staring out the open window. It was morning. Maybe I'd slept. The cut of sky was bright, so bright I missed it at first: a flickering along the edges of the window. Red and blue flashing lights.

Cops.

I was alone in the empty room.

A steady buzzing sound grew louder as I approached the window. When I looked outside, it took a moment to register what I saw. Four police-drones hovered a dozen feet or so beneath the window, spread out in a square, bathed in the lights of a police car parked near the front door.

I retrieved my machine gun, propped it on the window ledge,

and lined up my shot, then fired. I took down the first drone, which burst apart, then the second, each more satisfying than the last. The last two angled away. The first I got right as it started to move, clipping it enough to make it corkscrew as it fell to the ground, but the last darted almost out of range. I managed to hit it at the last second, my finger squeezing the trigger, the stream of noise from my gun comforting. The drone spun, smacked into the side of the building, and plummeted.

As soon as I released the trigger, a male voice spoke. "Don't move."

The man pressed a gun against my back and took my machine gun, then wrapped a segmented object around my left wrist. Self-locking handcuffs. He wrenched my arm behind me, then the other — the cuffs snaked around my right wrist and wrapped tight — and turned me to face him. A cop, mid-thirties. His eyes cataloged me, alerting my enemies.

"A lot of people want to talk to you."

He pulled me out of the room and down the stairs. No way could I claim mistaken identity. I had explosives and a dark matter sphere in the pack strapped across my chest.

We stepped outside, and I saw Raven in the back of the cruiser. Captured. My heart began to pound. She was as good as dead. I was going to lose her, too.

The cop pushed me toward his car.

I heard a *thunk*, then the cop's grip loosened and he collapsed. I turned to find Jex standing over the man's body, holding his machine gun like a club.

He swiveled me around. "Squat down." When I did, he lifted the cop's hand to touch my cuffs, which uncoiled. "Help me with him."

Together, we lifted the cop.

"Knocked out his par'ner while you went gun happy. Get all the drones?"

I nodded.

The cop didn't wake as we jostled him. Jex touched the officer's fingers to the door handle, unlocking the car to free Raven. Another touch removed her cuffs. "Let's put him in the trunk," he said.

"Why not leave him?" I asked.

"Car won't start without 'im."

"Where are we going?" Raven asked.

"Away from here. This place'll be crawlin' in minutes."

After we dumped the cop in the trunk, I reached for his pistol.

"Don't bother," Jex said. "It's coded to him. Doesn't fire for anybody else."

We piled into the car, Jex in the front and us in the back.

"What about your bag of weapons?" I asked. My mind was starting to work again.

"No time," he said, his voice reproachful. He put the car in gear and floored it.

I hugged Raven. "You OK?"

"I'm so mad that cop caught me." Her expression softened as she held up a lump of familiar-looking material. "I used Talia's cap to take out one of his drones, but the propellers tore it."

There must've been more than the four I shot down. The cap had been torn into large strips.

"It's OK. She'd understand."

Jex pulled over, opened the car's navigation system, and selected a police station in Palo Alto. Before he hit "go," he opened his door, initiated the program, then got in the back with us, using his coat to prevent the rear door from latching when he pulled it toward him—and slid a metal disk into the resulting gap. The disk completed the connection, fooling the car's system into thinking the door was closed, and the car started off.

Sirens grew in the distance. Cops coming for us.

"What's the plan?" I asked.

"Be ready to bail."

Three blocks later, we reached a stop sign, he opened the door—snatching the metal disk before it fell to the ground—and we got out. When he closed the door, the cruiser continued on its way to the far-off station.

"They'll have seen us get out," Raven said. Cop cars were layered in cameras.

"There's a camera over there, too," I said with a nod toward a light post.

"You two gonna wait 'til they come?" Jex asked.

He ducked onto the side street and walked away, his head down, his machine gun hidden in his coat. We followed, my satchel just covering my machine gun.

The streets became cleaner, the structures better maintained as we wove our way inland and north. The warehouses we passed became office and retail buildings, which quickly succumbed to residential neighborhoods with townhomes, trees, and planter boxes.

Jex finally paused, stopping in a secluded spot near a corner shop that hadn't yet opened for the day, although someone moved around inside. Farther down, a woman in gray slacks and a cream blouse exited a townhouse and drove off in one of the cars parked along the street. She seemed nice enough—professional, law-abiding. One glance from her, though, could've condemned us.

Jex pulled out his phone.

"What're you doing?" I asked.

"Calling Cole."

"No. We're staying away from them."

CHAPTER TWENTY-EIGHT

I could tell Jex wanted to yell at me, even though doing so would attract attention. "Are you nuts?" he said, his voice strained. "My group is the best chance we have."

"We need to keep moving," Raven said as she eyed the townhouses around us.

"If they're even still alive, they're being hunted," I said. "I'm not risking it—and I'm not fighting their war. I need to protect Raven."

"Dray, please—" he started, but I cut him off.

"She's all I have left."

Raven took my arm. "They can help."

"I can't lose you."

She didn't turn away from my gaze. Didn't judge.

The thought came too quickly to stop: what would've happened if she'd succeeded in running away with Trever? What would our lives have been like? I would've remained clueless—about Mina, about the implants—but Talia would've still been alive.

Jex put away his phone, his face tight with sorrow and frustration. "We need a ride."

I indicated the cars parked along the street. "Take one of these."

"We do that, the cops'll track us down even faster."

"We can't stay here," she said.

"We'll hook up with a friend of mine. She'll help," Jex said.

"'She'?"

"A friend. Mainly of…well, mine too. We should change our appearance."

None of us had grabbed extra clothes, and we weren't about to go shopping. "Lose the barn jacket," I told him.

He turned it inside out and wrapped it around his machine gun. "Ditch your caps. If we get caught, the gov'ment will learn how we block our nets."

"Without them, we *will* get caught."

He started to remove his, but Raven stopped him. "Keep yours. We'll take ours off. Dad, don't look at me." She rearranged her hair to hang in front of her face.

I hoped it'd be enough to avoid tripping their facial software. I turned away and took off my cap, which I knew she did as well. I felt a slight panic as information appeared on my display. I'd reconnected with the world.

Shielding his face, Jex took our caps, tossed them in a trashcan, and motioned for us to follow. My satchel thumped against my stomach as I jogged after them.

I tried to scan everywhere at once as we headed northeast. There could be eyes anywhere — looking out a window, driving by unexpectedly — and cameras on every corner. We stuck out. Didn't belong here.

A man in a tight suit crossed our path. I pulled Raven behind me, but he didn't look our way. As he approached a blue BMW sedan, Jex lunged forward and grabbed him before any of us could react. Raven and I stopped, unsure what to do as Jex pinned him against the car and whispered in his ear. The man unlocked the doors, and Jex gestured us into the back without facing us.

I wondered if Raven was fine with this. I wasn't, not that I had a choice.

After the man got into the front seat, Jex climbed in beside me. Forced into the middle, I slumped down as much as I could and put my hands over my face.

"Drive," Jex told the guy. "North. Avoid the interstate."

I was part of a carjacking. But was it wrong compared to what others had done to us? Or was that just an excuse?

Jex gave the driver quick directions without saying the final destination.

The BMW we rode in was being tracked — all cars were, actually. Our only hope was to get away and out of the vehicle before the authorities located us in the flow of the morning commute, although it wouldn't take them long. They'd scan the movements of every car that left the area, comparing historical data to find any that acted out of the ordinary.

We'd probably already tripped The Agency's computers.

The buildings grew taller, the traffic heavier, the city waking to a new day of lies. With land so valuable, high-rise complexes had taken over much of the area, some gleaming and others utilitarian boxes.

With a bark, Jex had the man drive into an alley. The driver did, his breathing louder as he drove farther away from the busy street, from witnesses, from safety. "Stop." The guy did, and Jex waved us out. Following us, he said, "The dude we're meeting hates strangers, so you better motor."

The driver sped off.

Jex smiled at us. "Cool. We're close." He continued down the alley.

"That was dangerous," I said.

"He's fine, just a little late for work."

"He'll turn us in."

"This part of town, he won't tell. He'll think we're connected."

"Connected to who?"

He led us out of the alley, and I jerked to a stop. Across the street was the red, ornate entrance to Chinatown.

I'd been worried about where I looked, but now I worried about everyone else. This was one of the most popular tourist spots on the coast. "No way," I said.

"My friend will help—" Jex started.

"Dad's right," Raven said. "This is too risky."

"She can hook us up with Cole and the others when we—you know, wanna call 'em. Besides, this is a great place to hide. You can't cover your face, though. Look normal."

I started to argue, but he turned away and took off his cap. Shit. Raven pulled her hair across her face and started after him. I stayed close, unable to look at her but desperate to protect her.

It was early in the day, yet the sidewalks were already crowded. We crossed the street toward the entrance. I tried not to glance at the drivers as I passed in front of them. They were cameras too, as were their cars, the traffic lights, security cameras, and ad displays—each one tracking, each one to betray us as Mina had.

I was barely aware of passing under the ornate gate into Chinatown, torn between fear and grief, my hand aching to hold Talia's one more time.

Chinese men and women passed us, a few tourists as well, each one implanted. Throughout the West Coast — and most of the country — people were a wide variety of nationalities. Many were mixed races, mixed heritages, the blending of languages and cultures and customs a part of everyday life. But I was struck by how many people here were Chinese. I remembered an article about how the residents here tried to block all other nationalities from living in Chinatown. The reality was striking.

I hid my head to try to keep a low profile. I realized I was limping, my foot maybe permanently off. I struggled to walk straight, to keep the grimace from my face. Look normal. In front of me, Raven pulled her gun and held it behind her leg.

The place smelled of fresh paint. The signs around us, all in Chinese, added to my disorientation.

Someone bumped me. I started to turn — and jerked my head back as I continued forward, hunching my shoulders. Someone else brushed past. The sidewalk grew crowded as it angled up the hill. No way to run if trouble came.

Raven stopped for a second due to the throng, only for a second before starting again. It made me look up, though, into the eyes of an older Chinese woman with pinned-back hair. She saw my face as she passed. All of it. Software would find me. Us.

I surged forward, aggravating my limp, ducked in front of Raven, and grabbed Jex's arm to steer them into an alley. "We can't stay here."

Jex put on his cap and faced us. "We're safer than you —"

"This is suicide."

Raven agreed. "There are so many people."

"It's OK. Locals don't want Uncle Sam knowin' their business, so they installed those," he said, pointing up. Mesh stretched across the top of the alley, along with the street we'd just left, the one on the far side — everywhere I could see — attached to the edges of rooftops and supported by strips of metal that arched over the streets, the metal ribs spaced forty feet apart.

"It's to keep out drones. The Chinese think this place is part of their country. Got their own rules, own heavies — and don't want no one watchin'. The cops try. Since they can't use their drones, they keep sprayin' the area to try to track what goes on. But the Chinese paint over the suckers." He pointed at the wall behind me. It was nondescript, a textured, freshly-painted, orange wall. "We don't have cameras to worry 'bout! You don't see it?"

Jex was flighty, and had let us believe he was more important than he really was, but he didn't strike me as delusional. I looked again.

Tiny bumps, clusters of them, like a rash, pockmarked the wall behind me. They weren't abnormalities, though. Each bump was a microcam that could be disbursed like an aerosol and stuck to whatever it touched. They coated the wall. I suspected other buildings were just as bad. Everything was painted. The dragon-twisted streetlamps glistened with green paint; fire escapes had paint that had dried mid-drip.

"The mesh covers every street?" Raven asked. When he nodded, she asked, "Who are these 'heavies' you mentioned?"

"Triad. Act as their cops, but more brutal."

I indicated a row of paper lanterns that hung over the street. "They're not just for decoration, are they?"

"Nope. The Chinese know the tech that's out there. Built most of it. That's why I came here, see? It's a safe haven."

"But everyone's a walking camera," Raven said.

Jex paused. "Most aren't payin' attention to us, though."

"Those men up the street are. They're watching everyone."

"We stick out," I added, as Jex glanced to see who she referred to, two black-clad men at the next intersection.

"None of these shops can have cameras," he said. "Those guys are the equivalent, watchin' peeps to deter theft."

"They serve the same purpose for The Agency. Kieran can monitor the whole area by tapping into them." When Jex couldn't answer, I said, "Raven and I are leaving. We just need you to steal a car for us. I won't ask for anything else." He started to protest, but I cut him off. "No more arguing."

He suddenly ducked into the flow of traffic and walked away, deeper into Chinatown.

"Jex," Raven hissed.

"Son of a bitch," I said as he disappeared. I pulled her to me without looking at her. "Let's go."

She slipped her arm around my waist and rested her head against my shoulder so her hair would mask her face. With a deep breath, we left the alley, Raven's gun behind her back, and started up the busy sidewalk toward the ornate entrance. We made it a block before Jex ran up to us, cap still on his head. He dug into a shopping bag and pulled out a floppy hat and sunglasses. "Tried but true."

"We're not staying," I said as Raven donned the hat and glasses. We needed out of the country. If we could find a boat, we could take it to Canada, disappear into the wilds up north.

Jex handed me a cap and bug-eyed sunglasses. "If it doesn't pan, we'll go wherever you want."

"No."

"She's close. Real close."

This wasn't safe. Yet, as I eyed Chinatown's entranceway, which grew packed with tourists, I didn't know what was safe anymore — and we sure as hell couldn't stand around arguing. "You have one shot."

He led the way.

We followed close. I kept my head down, my shoulders slumped. The disguises didn't feel adequate. They weren't, with decades of facial recognition software and surveillance tech working against us.

Jex took us down one block and up another, then down a side street which was nearly deserted. "This way," he whispered.

We entered a narrow alley. Rusted panels of corrugated metal had been bolted into the old-brick buildings overhead to form a crude roof. The relief from being hidden by the disjointed roof was replaced by anxiety that I couldn't see much around us. Couldn't tell if anyone was watching.

Paths branched off the alley in irregular intervals. Jex took the second one on the left, which snaked between boarded-up buildings to an apartment-type structure that blocked the end. Without a word, he took us down a set of stairs that hugged the building's foundation to a basement door. While the stairwell hid us from view, it also trapped us. Black spots on either side of the door were remote lasers, able to flood the stairwell. The concrete behind us, which lined the stairwell, was scarred with thin lines.

Jex seemed at ease as he knocked, but I pulled out my machine gun.

Another knock, a whispered codeword, and the door opened, the interior dark, the barrel of the machine gun in the Chinese kid's hand darker. He wasn't much older than Talia had been, but he'd lived harder, his body lean, his gaze cold, his handling of his gun second nature.

I lowered mine. When I did, the boy's gaze shifted to Jex and warmed. "Back so soon? Why the dumb hat?"

Jex pulled off his cap. "She around?"

He gestured to us. "Who are they?"

"Friends. Can we come in?"

"You know the rules." He waved his gun at my pack and Jex's wrapped machine gun, his eyes on my trigger finger.

"It's cool," Jex told us. He handed over his weapon.

I didn't want to relinquish my gun or the dark matter sphere. They were the only leverage we had.

The boy eased to the side. The remote lasers gleamed at me, his machine gun pointed at my head. We reluctantly handed everything over, including Raven's pistol.

Only then did he let us inside.

We stepped into a large basement area with a painted concrete floor and bare walls. The ceiling was low, a metal grid fashioned in a geometric, repeating pattern nailed into the floor joists above us. The room contained tables loaded with small sculptures and jewelry boxes. The sculptures looked fragile, like twisting string frozen in movement, mathematical computations brought to life. Most of the gift boxes were empty, but they wouldn't be for long as 3D printers stacked four deep fashioned the sculptures, while other machines created intricate, ringed necklaces, dexterous metal fingers weaving them into creation.

Jex walked to the far basement wall and pressed on it. A three-foot wide section swung back, a fake door made to look exactly like the poured-concrete wall. I heard more printers running.

"Tianshi!" he called out.

The boy hooked our possessions under his arm, aimed his machine gun at us again, then hurried after Jex.

"You're not due for a week," a woman said from the hidden room.

Raven followed the boy and I followed her, though I paused at the entrance. Lasers lined the inner edge, ready to incinerate everything on the other side, which was as big as the front room.

A woman in her twenties, of medium height with hair buzzed on the sides and iridescent on top, stood near a table of military gear and pointed a pulse box at Jex. The weapon was powerful enough to fry everything in the room, us included. "What're you doing here—and who are they?"

I stepped in front of Raven, although the pulse box made the gesture pointless, and we both shielded our faces.

She frowned. "So, you know. How bad you wanted?" Unlike the boy, she had an accent. When we didn't answer, she indicated the metal grid, which covered the ceiling in this room as well. "Blocks signal. No one can see you."

I hadn't noticed my readouts were gone. The grid was designed to interfere with specific wavelength bands, what I realized was an expanded version of the design that had been woven into the caps we'd worn. I was relieved to be able to look at Raven. Her grief and anxiety were evident, but even so, it was a balm to gaze at her.

"We need your help," Jex told the woman.

"You tell her about the implants?" I asked him, nodding toward the ceiling.

"Nah, she already knew." He grinned at her. "What do ya say?"

"You endanger Shon-ye."

Jex faced the boy. "Not tryin' to endanger you. We didn't have anywhere else to turn."

When I took in the room, I understood her hostility. Tables held government-grade sensors, camoshields, and medical equipment. Specialty printers in the back made shield pods, detonator-rings, and battle-drone chasses, while buckets closer to us were full of cube processor chips, datastream encryptors, and holo devices. Shelving to the side and behind her contained ID printers, pharmaceuticals, muscle enhancers, jars of stem-grown parts—eyes, teeth, fingers—and mass cubes with neural-net interfaces.

"What's your name?" Raven asked her.

"Tianshi." To Jex, she said, "Don't say she's pregnant. Won't help."

"I'm not—" Raven protested.

"You followed?"

Jex said, "No. We gotta keep movin', though, to stay ahead of the feds."

Tianshi put down her weapon. "Your people know you're here?"

"We're tryin' to get back to 'em." He glanced at us. "Tianshi is our supplier. She gets us—"

"Not their business."

She waved Shon-ye over. At her direction, the boy placed our possessions on the table. A shelf behind her held a row of boxes labeled

Plastibots. I flashed Jex a look, and he grinned. He didn't realize my expression wasn't a good one.

"Where did you get all this?" I asked.

She watched Shon-ye unveil our weapons and unzip my pack.

"She skims things off shipments," Jex answered for her. "It's not really illegal. Shippers don't report all they bring in."

I pointed at the mass cubes. "Those are banned in over a hundred countries, including this one." They were designed to download a lifetime's worth of a person's memory, the claim being the person could live forever by copying their brains. It was a lie. The cubes held a recording of a life, but not the spirit that lived it.

"I don't sell," she said. "I rent. People come every few weeks to upload new memories." She smirked. "Those who look up old ones regret it. Our brain never accurate. Cracks their minds."

"You take advantage of their hopes."

"I don't force them." She rested a hand on the pulse box.

"Is he your brother?" Raven asked, indicating Shon-ye. When Tianshi nodded, Raven dropped her gaze, though I caught her sadness, which stirred my own.

Shon-ye pulled everything out of our packs. He held up my datarings.

Tianshi's eyes darted to me. "Yours? Top of the line, four-axis aptitude, five-mile broadcast." She reappraised me, then focused on the contents of my bag. She held up my dark matter sphere. "What's this?"

"Failed tech," Jex said. "Tianshi, we need help sneaking away —"

"Not getting involved."

Raven lifted her head. "But you've helped the rebels."

"To support Shon-ye and myself."

Jex leaned on one of the tables, then stood as it nearly tipped. "Don't you wanna fight the Agents? Really fight them? You know what they do to us."

"You put us at risk. These two," she pointed at Raven and me, "are responsible for dead Agents. All over the news."

Jex slapped a datastack on the table, followed by some crumpled bit cards, untraceable currency. "All of this. Right now. Whatdaya say?"

"What're you doing?" I asked.

"Bargaining. Don't block my flow." He set down a semi-clear rock as well, which Shon-ye snatched up. I suspected it was an uncut diamond.

Tianshi shook her head. "Not enough to hide you."

I stepped forward. "You have major stuff here—"

"You threaten me, I give you to the Triad. Besides, I don't sell weapons, just things rebels could get elsewhere."

I needed leverage. "What do they give that you risk Shon-ye's life for?"

"My business, not yours."

I knew what they gave. Implants.

"I get it," I said. "The rebels are a means to an end. You're helping people from China who are here illegally." Their government had cracked down on freedoms over the past decade, the worst oppression in three generations.

Tianshi waved her hand. "The ID machines? Just a license here or there, nothing to get puffed up about."

"You give them new looks, new identities. I see the drugs, the joint enhancers, so those who weren't mobile can walk. You hide their injuries, alter their faces, even their teeth. They'd leave Chinatown so changed Agents wouldn't even notice them. This part of your arrangement with the Triad?"

She didn't respond.

I pointed at the plastibots. "Plastic surgery nanobots. We want them, too. All three of us."

Raven looked confused. "What for?"

"Alter our looks, get out of here without notice."

"You want to change our *faces*?"

"If they make me better lookin', I'm in," Jex said, which triggered an elbow from Raven.

I stepped toward Tianshi. "We need new identities, not only our looks but credit cards, passports, licenses. I saw the printers you have. They're government quality—"

She jabbed a finger in my face. "Don't threaten me."

"I'm not. I'm asking for help, which isn't easy for me to do."

"Don't care. Get out."

Raven spoke up. "Agents killed my sister. She was around your brother's age." Tianshi looked away but didn't comment. "You

207

would've liked her—probably better than any of us. Help us like you would've helped her."

When Tianshi didn't speak, I asked, "How much do you want for the plastibots?"

"Not selling them, sob story or no." She paused. "Sorry about your sister. But no."

"We'll trade all of our currencies," Jex said.

"Leave. Now."

CHAPTER TWENTY-NINE

We hurried back through the covered alleyway, thin shafts of light slipping between the metal sheets overhead as we moved. "Take us the fastest way out of here," I told Jex.

He hooked his jacket-wrapped machine gun under his arm and picked up the pace, a pack he'd swiped on the way out slung over one shoulder. I'd hidden my machine gun, which was shorter than his, in my satchel. I figured we'd head to the docks and sneak or bribe our way onto the first ship we could find. We needed out of the country.

As we reached the street, he abruptly stopped. Footsteps. Coming fast.

I reached for Raven, but he pulled her to him and hid her face as a cluster of armed, black-clad men ran past. Triad. He continued to hold her after they disappeared until she pulled away.

"We should snag new disguises," he said.

"Smart," she said, almost reluctantly.

"No, he's not," I said without looking at her. "His plan didn't work."

He joined the foot traffic. I donned my sunglasses and followed, as did Raven, her hair pulled across her face.

Two more Triad barreled past.

As I tugged my hat down, I glanced across the street. A woman caught my attention—young, harried, struggling not to drop a cake as she negotiated the angled street, a birthday bag swinging from her elbow.

The memory came too quickly to stop.

A few months after Adem's death, I asked Mina out to dinner. She agreed, more elated than I'd seen her since his funeral. I didn't realize the date, not until I saw her expression of hurt and incredulity at the restaurant. She'd thought the occasion was to celebrate his birthday, which was the next day. I'd intended it to be a romantic dinner, to rekindle our marriage.

Like most husbands, I'd learned to agree with my wife regardless of the circumstances. Not that time. "Why would I tear open something we can't seem to close?" I asked.

She left the restaurant.

The following year, I wanted to say something, show I'd remembered, but she didn't come home the night of his birthday until after midnight. From then on, she marked the date by herself. It hurt me, but she usually came home buoyant, so I didn't interfere.

I didn't know she'd started pretending Adem was alive.

Jex pulled me from my memory by yanking me behind a parked van. He and Raven looked anxious. "Cops. Three cars' worth."

I peered around the edge of the van. We were less than a block from Chinatown's boundary, five or six storefronts from the end. The police cruisers blocked the eastern boundary. The cops had set up roadblocks—for pedestrians as well as cars.

We retreated down the street and ducked around the nearest corner.

"We should go that way," Jex said, pointing north. Which meant crossing the street in full view of the police.

"Chinatown is narrow. This way will be quicker," Raven said, pulling him west.

He resisted. "It could be blocked." He was thinking the same thing I was: the roadblock we'd encountered wouldn't be the only one. The land sloped down to the east, which meant we could see roadblocks in that direction. We couldn't see anything the other way.

"I'll go first," I said. "Anything happens to me, use the distraction to get away."

Raven's eyes widened. "No, I need to protect you—"

I walked into the open before she could stop me.

People filled the sidewalks, many unsure of which direction to go. Voices rose from the roadblock as some tried to force their way past the cops. I cut through the blocked traffic, my foot flaring from when Jex had jerked me behind the van. I expected cops to start shouting at me.

I reached the north curb, passed a realtor's office, and stopped just past the edge of the building, out of sight from the roadblock. Raven and Jex joined me, arm in arm, Jex using his body to block hers from view. She glared at me.

"This way's parallel to the border," he said. "First clear exit we find, we should snag it."

Each street we passed heading north was blocked, cars bunched together, horns blowing. Crowds formed on the sidewalks as the police scanned everyone who tried to get through. I didn't know what their scanners were searching for, exactly, but it had to be linked to us.

We neared the northern border, but it was also blocked, so we ducked east onto a side street and found ourselves on Columbus, a four-lane thoroughfare with street parking on both sides that angled across the northeastern tip of Chinatown, topped with mesh like the rest of the area and decorated with three rows of paper lanterns.

Columbus was open; cars were leaving the area.

We turned left and nearly ran up the sidewalk toward the border, where Chinese-labeled shops ended and English-signed establishments began.

Three police cruisers appeared and pulled across traffic ahead of us to form another blockade. Doors opened, and patrolmen launched irregularly-shaped projectiles at the cars that drove past. The robotic projectiles descended on the cars, adhered to their trunks, and shorted out their electrical systems, while metal spikes dropped into the roadway to stop the disabled vehicles. Other cruisers blocked the street farther down, sealing off that border as well.

Raven, Jex, and I ducked into the doorway of a noodle place, the windows half-covered by holograms of rotating bowls. More police cruisers arrived, along with a modified truck. As soon as it stopped, the truck's rear cover opened, and monitor drones rose into the air.

"Now what?" Raven asked.

I unzipped my bag to get my machine gun. "Fight our way out. We have to move fast. The whole area will be surrounded."

"Not a good play," Jex said.

"No choice." I had to protect Raven. "Stay close. We just need to punch a hole through. Once we get past, we run."

They readied their weapons, their expressions a mix of uncertainty and grim acceptance. When they were ready, I led the way, my gun pressed against my leg.

The sky began to darken as the police drones flew overhead, most already under the mesh that was supposed to keep them out, while up ahead, five cruisers now blocked the street, eight or so cops crouched in defensive positions behind their cars.

I kept close to the shops as I jogged toward them.

A trio of motors above us suddenly revved up, then bolts of electricity erupted from the paper lanterns and pierced the drones, frying their circuits. Virtually every drone fell to the ground, destroyed by the electrostatic dischargers the lanterns had hidden.

We ducked under the awning of a supply shop as the drones fell around us.

The sounds of the drones shattering were joined by gunshots that made us press against the wall. Triad-clad men, two dozen yards behind us, fired high-powered rifles to take out the drones that had survived the dischargers.

The cops opened fire.

I pulled Raven into the store. The man behind the front counter, who I assumed was the owner, flinched when he saw our weapons.

Jex closed the door behind us. "There a way outta here?"

The owner didn't answer.

The gunfire outside intensified. As bullets cut the air, car windows shattered and people yelled. Tracer fire from both sides lit the block.

The front part of the store contained scarves, clothes, doll faces, and two display cases of watches and jewelry. Tourist crap. Past a divider, though, the store held media cubes, processor skins, and music synthboxes, along with trays filled with parts and wires. A door at the rear led to what I hoped was an exit.

Black-clad men flashed past the storefront windows—a dozen, maybe more. The proprietor's eyes flicked from us to them. The gunfire spread out.

"Come on," Jex said. He and Raven headed for the rear. I followed. Then I heard his voice.

"Concentrate fire. Don't stop advancing."

Kieran. He sounded a few buildings away, but his voice cut me. I could tell Raven heard him, too. Her pain cut me as well.

As she turned away, I spotted a pulse drill. If I removed a regulator and jacked up the power, I'd turn it into a pulse gun. I picked it up. The rage that surged through me filled my hollowness.

Jex grasped my arm. "We can't let 'em box us—"

"To have a chance, we need more than a couple of guns." I picked up a covalent-cutter and turned it on, its beam almost a vibrating absence of light. "This excites at the molecular level, disrupting the properties that hold atoms together. If you hold it to a material long enough, it starts a chain reaction that causes the material to disintegrate. That includes a person's body." I was amazed it was here. They were only found in heavy manufacturing facilities, used to cut the hardest of metals.

Raven blinked. "What else can we get?"

"Split up. Find recon drones we can use—"

"Don't have 'em, remember? Or cameras," Jex said.

"Right. Keep an eye on the door. Raven, grab a 3D printer with plastic, silicone, and metal material kits. And one of those electrostatic dischargers, if you can find it."

As they hurried off, I grabbed a three-dimensional helix grower, which fused with modified DNA to create virtually any shape, building objects stronger than 3D printers. I also grabbed wires, a scattering of motherboards, and liquid data-memory capsules.

Jex hurried over. "The Triad's holdin' back Kieran's group, but The Agency's SWAT teams just pulled up."

"Tell Raven we're checking out."

I went to the counter, where the owner seemed mystified by our shopping spree. Raven joined me, adding the printer and amplifier to our purchases.

As the man bagged everything, Jex said, "How 'bout a robotic dog? For protection-like?"

I shook my head, but noticed a toy-sized, remote-control car, an older model that didn't sync with an implant. "Grab the car, though."

Jex scrambled for it.

"Is this how it is to shop with me?" Raven asked. I nodded. She mouthed "Sorry" as he gave the car to the owner. She handed over a credit card.

I leaned close. "Whose card is that?"

"Trever's. He got it when we were going to run away."

The transaction went through.

Outside, men began to shout orders, followed by a roar of gunfire from Kieran's side. The sudden change made me realize our error. They'd been alerted to our transaction. Read the name on the card.

They knew where we were.

"Move. Now," I said. Jex and I grabbed the bags, and we ran for the rear exit.

The gunfire intensified.

Raven opened the exit door, and we hurried out the back as Kieran's men crashed through the entrance. We were in an alley, dirty but brightly lit. Jex led the way, first to the left, then right into an adjoining alley as the men shouted at us to stop, Raven freeing her machine gun as we ran. We angled toward another turn as they appeared behind us and opened fire. A bullet zipped just past my head, while others pinged off the wall ahead of us.

Raven returned fire.

We made the corner, Raven catching up as we ran, but the alley we entered was too long; it stretched for three blocks to a distant street, empty except for a dumpster twenty yards ahead to the left and another farther down to the right. Occasional doors dotted the alley, back entrances for the buildings to either side of us, but they were too far away to matter. Fire escapes crowded either side, but the ladders were out of reach.

We had seconds before our pursuers reached us.

I stopped, pulled my machine gun from my satchel, and faced the alley we'd left. Men appeared, Kieran and three SWAT men, all heavily armed. I fired before they could react and managed to hit two, but the third ducked back in time. Kieran dove past the entrance to our alley, too fast to nail.

"Come on," Jex yelled. He and Raven had hidden behind the first dumpster.

I wanted them to keep going, get to safety. My words would fall on deaf ears.

Raven laid cover fire as I ran to them. When I made it behind the dumpster, she hugged me, then reloaded her machine gun as Jex crouched near the edge, prepared to fight. It was a surreal moment.

The government forces opened fire.

The dumpster didn't completely protect us. A few-inch gap existed at our feet, as the dumpster rested on wheels that held it off the ground. It and the other dumpster were the only cover, though. The alley continued for at least fifty yards before ending at what looked like a side street. We'd never reach it.

More footsteps grew from Kieran's direction.

"I tell you how badass you are?" Jex asked Raven as she prepared to shoot back.

I rose over the top of the dumpster to open fire, and spotted Kieran. His head was pink from regenerated skin where I'd shot him the day before. He wasn't hurt enough, though.

I opened fire. He and his team ducked back behind the buildings. They took turns shooting at us, but I focused on Kieran, aiming for his head whenever he peered out. I missed, but my gunfire made him jerk back.

Beside me, Jex took out a SWAT member, and Raven took out another. More arrived, though, along with another silver-haired Agent. Kieran reappeared, and I fired again, this time catching him in the shoulder.

I wanted to yell, the thrill savage and hot.

A door burst open across the alley behind us, just past the other dumpster. Triad men poured out, six of them, and used the dumpster as a shield as they shot at the invaders. The door behind them remained open. Gunfire intensified on both sides.

I needed to get Raven out of there.

I pulled her down behind the dumpster. "Face the Triad as we move and hold your hands up so they don't shoot us."

She nodded in understanding. I shouldered my weapon and had Jex do the same. On my count, he and I pulled our dumpster away from the wall, our bags dangling from our shoulders, and angled it across the alley toward the Chinese.

Kieran and his men increased their attack.

Bullets pinged off the dumpster as we hauled it, bumping and shifting, across the alley. We made it to the Triad soldiers, who held their fire, but when we crashed our dumpster into theirs, our front left side hit first, and the impact caused the dumpster to turn, the front end swinging out. Jex, Raven, and I strained to arrest its momentum, then pushed the front-end back to make our dumpster flush with the Triad's.

As soon as we did, the defenders went around us to continue their fight.

I pulled Raven toward the open door. Jex hesitated, then followed while Kieran yelled at his men to stop us.

We ran through the door into a dash-and-go food place, passing a small display case filled with meats and fish, the employee behind the counter barely reacting as we dashed past.

We made it to the store's entrance and nearly collided with other armed locals. More were outside, most in Triad clothing but not all. Many rushed past us into the store, while others raced to the end of the block to flank Kieran's team.

Sirens grew in the distance, audible among the gunfire and shouts.

We hurried to the end of the block, away from the battle, took the corner, and Jex slowed us to a fast walk. The streets were heavy with people, many fleeing the gunfire, but almost as many running toward it. We passed a camera-supply store and a small market when gunshots erupted behind us. Kieran was half a block away, along with two Agents and four SWAT soldiers.

We ran. People around us ran as well, many crying out. Kieran's group ignored everyone else as they chased us. When I glanced over my shoulder, I saw him shoot a man who stood in his path without breaking stride.

Beside me, Jex opened fire. I grabbed Raven and pulled her behind a newsstand as Kieran's team scattered. Jex yelled at us to follow him and took off across the road, still firing. We raced after him as the gunshots drew more Triad members, who engaged The Agency forces.

We took the corner but weren't safe. Kieran could see us through every person we passed. "Find somewhere to hide," I told Jex. "Away from everyone."

We ran for two blocks, avoided a cluster of Triad that raced past, then ducked into an empty alley and sprinted down to where it intersected with a longer one. When we entered the new alley, I paused. "Wait." I crouched beside a stack of crates and opened one of the bags. "Jex, do you have the discharger?"

He pulled it out. "You see more drones?"

I flipped the tabs to remove its cover. "No. We need different protection." To Raven, I asked, "You have your tool kit?"

She pulled out the small kit I'd given her for her fifteenth birthday and handed it over. As Jex watched, I modified the electrostatic discharger. She helped, able to anticipate what I needed from a lifetime of assisting me on projects.

"You're really good at that," he told her.

She shot him a look, then ignored him as she and I lowered the electrical charge output and changed its frequency. The grid in Tianshi's basement had clued me into the wavelength I needed to target. "It'll only give us a few seconds worth, but it might be enough," I said as I latched the cover into place.

Raven actually almost smiled. "To blind the Agents."

"Right." I stood, the loaf-sized device in hand, and cautiously returned to the alley we'd left. I couldn't let a single person see me. I waved Raven and Jex back, then triggered the discharger and rolled it like a bowling ball down the alley toward the street we had left. Not waiting for it to trigger, we ran down the longer alley away from the discharger, toward what I hoped was a clear escape.

A strange sound, like a throaty buzz, sounded behind us. My display pixelated, the time and temp I kept in the corner breaking into pieces before winking out—which meant everyone's implants were affected, their feeds knocked out in a two to three block radius. People cried out, adding to the cacophony of sounds that flooded the streets.

We hurried to the end of the alley and paused to make sure it was clear. Storefront signs awaited us, along with a group of four Triad men patrolling a block away. It was as good as it was going to get.

I stepped out of the alley in time to see vehicles approach—SWAT vans, two of them. They stopped a block up the street and heavily-armed troops began to pour out.

Raven, Jex, and I retreated into the alley as the Triad men ran toward the vans.

"What now?" she asked.

They were sweaty. So was I. My foot throbbed. "Find another way, before the discharger quits. We don't have much time."

Jex looked up. "I got a better idea."

Chapter Thirty

Before I could ask Jex what his idea was, he jogged to a nearby fire escape, which was close to the street—too close. The SWAT team was a block away.

"We have to go," Raven said to me in a quiet voice.

He waved up at the ladder. "Give me a hand."

I opened my mouth to argue when my feed started to flicker. Systems were coming back online. Raven was right. We had to go. But without the cover from the discharger, we didn't stand a chance. Every person would become a threat, every moment a risk.

Against my better judgment, I went to him, cupped my hands, and lifted him up.

He grabbed the bottom of the ladder and pulled it down, the sound broadcasting our intentions as it rattled. I wanted to bolt, but he was already climbing, although he stopped at the first landing and looked down expectantly, a bag of supplies pinned between his body and the railing, his stuffed pack hooked across his back. Raven motioned for him to come down, but I realized that wasn't why he'd stopped.

I grabbed the ladder to keep it from springing back up. As soon as I did, he crossed the landing and climbed the first set of stairs. At the second landing, he paused, made a weird ducking motion, then climbed the stairs to the top floor. He peered in the window, then crouched beside it.

This was too dangerous. The SWAT teams were fanning out, their staccato speech and coordinated footsteps growing louder. The end of the alley was less than thirty feet away. I raised my machine gun and faced the street, though I leaned against the ladder to keep it in place.

A sound made me look up. Jex had opened the window and climbed through. He waved at us to join him.

I didn't like this, but we couldn't stay on the street. I motioned to

Raven without looking at her.

"I'm going to strangle him," she muttered as she began to climb. I followed, each step increasing our exposure, bags hooked over my shoulder, one hand on my gun, the other on the ladder.

The SWAT team sounded closer.

I made it to the landing and stepped off. Raven was already on the stairs.

I nearly let go of the ladder, remembering at the last second that it was spring-loaded, and guided it as silently as I could up its track. When it was up, I took the stairs to the second landing, stumbling as I scanned the street instead of watching where I stepped.

At the landing, I remembered Jex's strange ducking motion. I had to pass an open window. I could see a galley kitchen, wood table in the dining area, a couch and teleprojector past that. A pot boiled on the stove, the steam pinning me. I couldn't tell if someone was in the kitchen or not. A shadow shifted. One person was there, maybe more.

I was alone on the fire escape. Raven had disappeared.

Even if I ducked under the window, I could be seen. Besides, I'd have to stand in order to climb the stairs to the third level.

Below, the clicks of the SWAT team's radios reached me, the throbbing of their plasma weapons.

The shadow in the kitchen shifted. Risking it, I lunged past the window, grabbed the railing, and hauled myself up the metal stairs, bags swinging. My heart pounding, I reached the top landing, where the window Jex had used stood open.

I dove inside, spun, and closed the window.

The apartment was empty: scratched hardwood floors, a cheap light fixture dangling over a deserted dining area, and a galley kitchen with forty-year-old appliances.

"You climbed really well," I heard Jex say from another room.

"You almost got us caught," Raven said.

"I saved us."

I followed a short hallway past a bathroom to the apartment's lone bedroom, where they huddled by a window that faced the street.

A roar grew as I approached. I thought I felt a tremor, although it could've been my imagination. The window looked dirty, the street beyond gray. As I got closer, however, I saw that it wasn't dirt. Smoke from gunpowder darkened the view of the battle that erupted below — the roar was unleashed gunfire from both sides. I spotted three Agents, two at the forward edge with the third, Kieran, to the side, directing a group of riot-clad officers. They had superior firepower and organization, but the Triad were organized as well. Lethal. And they were on their home turf. As we watched, they cut off a contingent of SWAT forces, slaughtered them, and descended on the Agents.

We couldn't go out. Not in that.

The first Agent went down. The second almost made it back to the government's main line before also falling under the Triad's assault.

I wasn't sure how long I sat there. As Raven watched the battle and Jex periodically checked the windows and front door, I recalled what we'd done, the decisions we'd made, cataloging the times we'd made wrong moves. This wasn't inevitable. We could've escaped. Or could we? The monitoring devices and software, the layers of surveillance and communication and law enforcement agencies, Kieran's fixation with us, might've been too much regardless of what we did.

It was inevitable now.

The front door wasn't enough to protect us. Neither were our weapons. We could've been seen. Most likely had. Fooling ourselves to think otherwise would only hasten our end.

I got up, retrieved the bags we'd carried from the supply shop, and opened the accordion doors to the bedroom's closet. The narrow space was empty, but had what I wanted: an overhead light.

I turned on the naked bulb, sat under it, removed the items we'd purchased from the store, and got to work.

* * *

"What're you making?" Raven asked sometime later, her voice soft.

I finished connecting the motherboard. "A screen shield. When the field's activated — after I complete the emitter — the wave frequency generated should absorb pulse blasts." Not the kinetic energy, but at least the electrical.

I wondered if I'd printed it big enough.

"Can I help?"

I avoided looking directly at her but could see the edge of her face. "You know how to program the helix grower?"

She shook her head, so I explained how to use it. Before I finished, she said, "I'm sorry, Dad."

"For what?"

"Using Trever's card. I didn't think they knew about it."

Jex spoke up. I hadn't been aware he was nearby. "Hey, it's OK."

"He's right," I said.

She shifted away so I no longer saw even the sliver of her. "No, it's not."

She wasn't the type to obsess about mistakes she'd made. At least, she hadn't been. I should've said more. Should've reassured her. Mina had been the communicator, the motivator. But she wasn't a part of us anymore. I couldn't contemplate her fate. Where she was. What was happening to her. She'd chosen her path.

Jex picked up the scanner, now a pulse gun. "This is sizzle. Whoever's on duty should have it. We need to pull shifts, guard the door at all times," he said in response to my questioning look. "They take us by surprise, we're dead."

"I'll do first shift," Raven said.

"No, I will. Link with your pops."

I handed her the covalent-cutter, which was lethal up close, but she shook her head, her hair in front of her face.

"You keep it. I want you safe."

"This isn't up for discussion," I said.

Jex started for the living room. "Any other weapons you can make, we'll need it."

"No matter how many I create, we'll still be outgunned."

Raven straightened. "I have makeup and can modify our clothes. We can sneak out of here."

I looked at Jex. "You want to tell her?"

He grimaced. "Scannin' software checks bone structure and spacin' of the eyes, nose, and mouth. Makeup doesn't change any of that."

She went into the other room, taking a spot near what sounded like the front door. Now wasn't the time to sulk, but I couldn't find the words to comfort her. Jex stayed in the bedroom with me to give her space.

I set aside the shield, not in the mood for defense. I was tempted to fashion a weapon out of the sphere, but the dark matter was too precious. I didn't know when or if I'd ever get more.

Eyeing the timer-bombs, I removed the remote-controlled toy car I'd had Jex grab and started the helix grower. As its spindles wisped in a circle, I measured the car's body and keyed the dimensions into the grower, then did the same with a bomb. The grower adjusted and continued to build.

I kept everything close in case we needed to run.

The grower finished, its spindles retracted to reveal a double-sided bracket. I removed it from the grower, attached the larger side to the car, and secured a bomb inside the smaller side. The bomb could adhere to the car's plastic hood, but the bracket would keep it in place. Better to think of that than what I might use this for. I removed the bomb, made sure its timer was off, then put both it and the car in the bottom of my satchel.

I checked the rest of my supplies to determine the best way to use them when Jex called me over. He was by the window, his face anxious. "I didn't see him 'til just now."

Kieran faced the building to the right of ours, a four-story structure on the other side of the alley. Dead bodies littered the street behind him. His handiwork. He'd been working his way up the street toward us.

An explosion ripped the silence as ordinance tore away the building's entrance and Kieran's men rushed inside. The Triad responded by attacking them, darting past our building to get to him and his team. His men fought back and he reappeared, taking down three Chinese on his own. The last one he shot in the shoulder to disarm him, then shot him four more times, purposefully missing vital organs to give him a slow, painful death.

Another Agent appeared, along with more men.

"We need to go," I said. They'd use scanners, drones, brute force — everything at their disposal to check every inch of the place.

Kieran and his men approached our building. "Guard the alley in case they're in here," he told his team.

I hurried to the closet as Jex ran to get Raven. There was a crash as the cops entered our building. I scooped up my stuff, turned off the bulb, and joined Raven and Jex in the living room. Footsteps filled the stairs.

"Think we can get to the roof in time?" I asked Jex.

"Even if no one's guardin' the fire escape, their satellites will be watchin'. We'll be spotted." He grabbed his machine gun. "What weapons you got?"

I pulled out a timer-bomb.

Raven seized my arm. "No. Come with me. You, too," she said to Jex.

She led us to the bathroom as crashes, screams, and gunfire filled the lower levels. She pulled out an implant-blocking cap and jammed it on my head. Talia's. It had been shredded but was now mended; a section was just raw metal, the woven wires scraping the back of my neck as the cap strained to fit my head.

"How — ?" I started.

She silenced me and waved at Jex to put his on.

He dug through his pack as Kieran's men climbed the stairs to our floor, while doors farther below crashed open. She searched her own pack, motioning toward the bathtub with her head as if she wanted me to climb in. I hesitated, unsure. She removed a fragment of a cap, the missing piece of Talia's.

Jex yanked out his cap, and Raven nearly pushed me into the tub.

Someone pounded on our door.

She climbed in after me, laid on top of me, and placed the fragment on the opposite side of her exposed head like a tiny blanket. Our cheeks touching, she slid her thin fingers under my cap, her fingernails scraping my scalp, and pressed the material against her implant, our neural nets only an inch or so apart.

With her free hand, she waved Jex into the tub, who wedged alongside us.

We held our breaths as the pounding came again — then went silent.

The chill of the cast-iron tub seeped into me while Raven's and Jex's bodies warmed me. I couldn't see them, her hair covering my face, but I could feel them. Raven trembled, whether from fear or adrenaline I wasn't sure.

The silence extended.

My breath was short, and I couldn't unclench my fists. Then a voice shouted — and footsteps retreated. We didn't move until the only sounds we heard were sobs and muted voices from elsewhere in the building.

Jex sat up. "What happened?"

I pulled away so I could see her. "You saved us. You knew they'd track our feeds."

"Luckily, they don't know we can block them," she said, then added, "The tub was to mask our body heat."

She'd guessed The Agency scanned for neural net signals to find anyone hiding. If they searched for heat signatures as well, Kieran at least suspected we could block our feeds. Still, it worked—and she'd used the torn piece to make sure her feed didn't emit through her brain and out the other side, which could've been picked up. "That was smart, using Talia's cap."

"I wove mesh into it in the design of Tianshi's ceiling to fill the tear." She gave me a crooked smile. "I stole some of your wire. Sorry."

She hadn't been sulking. She'd been preparing.

I smiled. "You did good."

CHAPTER THIRTY-ONE

The war raged, as it had for hours, mostly on our street. Of course. Kieran knew we were close.

The 3D printer churned as it molded the shape I'd estimated. Imprinters sloshed through the liquid, the machine muffling the sounds of battle outside — but not the blows from the next room. Grunts punctuated fists striking flesh as feet shuffled. Blows struck in quick succession, paused, then came again.

Raven and Jex were sparring. Honing skills, releasing aggression, I wasn't sure which.

The material rose from the liquid into two mounds of pink material. They looked like slugs. I took them out of the tray. True to my instructions, they felt like rubber — were as close as I could get outside of a rubber plant. But they were too big.

The sounds of battle seemed louder.

I went to the window and risked a glance. The Agency and Triad forces had shifted, but didn't appear to be any closer. I wasn't sure if that was good or bad.

I retreated from the window and reached for my ion blade. Adjusting the output so the particles streamed razor-tight, I angled the blade along the edge of the first rubber insert, put it against my face, then made another curved cut.

As I trimmed the insert's length, I heard a thump. I bolted to the next room, flicking the knife to its longest setting. "Raven?"

She stood over Jex in a fighter's stance. "That was him."

He stood, a little wobbly. "Good hit. You're gettin' quicker."

The blade in my hand seemed inadequate, the rubber slugs foolish. I put both on the sill by the fire escape.

We had our implants covered, Jex and me wearing the caps while Raven had wrapped a piece of cloth around her head to hold the fragment in place.

"Ready for more?" she asked.

The two fought, though they connected without putting their full weight into their throws, attacking in ways I didn't expect.

Raven stepped back and lowered her fists. "It's quiet."

We went to the bedroom and looked outside.

The fighting had stopped, the two sides withdrawn. Bodies lay scattered along the street as far as we could see in the afternoon light, most solitary but a few clumped together. Wheeled robots moved about, although for reconnaissance or to search for survivors, I didn't know. They were the only movement.

"Should we leave?" she asked.

I hesitated. "Where's Kieran?"

A crew of locals appeared and spread out. Some cleaned the area, moving bodies and collecting weapons, while others installed some sort of porta-shields, stronger than concrete barricades.

"They're gettin' ready for another round," Jex said, his voice grim.

"Teach me to fight," I said to him. "I want to learn—not be beat down like Cole did, but actually learn."

Raven spread her arms. "You saw me knock him down, right?"

"It was a great shot." I turned back to Jex. "Well?"

"He doesn't need to teach you. Kieran won't get close enough to touch you."

"I need to know how to fight."

Jex looked perplexed. "Fam'lies really do argue?"

She removed her sparring gloves and dropped them at my feet. By her expression, I could tell I'd insulted her. Before I could apologize, she grabbed her pack, went to the bathroom, and slammed the door.

"You're not helping yourself," I told him. I could've said the same thing to myself.

The shower turned on, the sound filling the empty apartment.

Jex took me to the other room, showed me how to get into a fighting stance, then paused. "Sorry I drug her into this. If I hadn't done it, someone else would've."

His earnest face was too young for this life. I felt a pang of sadness. I had to let Raven go though I didn't want to, let her follow her own path.

When he got into his stance, I noticed he wore his datarings.

"Won't you damage those?"

"Lead with your knuckles, not the middle of your fist." He showed me what he meant, then taught me a half-dozen moves and countermoves.

"How will I know which one to use?"

"Practice. It'll come to ya. Main thing is play to your strengths."

"You mean I'm better off making things."

He shrugged. "If that's your strength."

I motioned for him to come at me. He did, getting in shots before I could react. I was thinking too much. I had to—my muscles didn't have the knowledge they needed. We circled each other and went again.

I grew sore but didn't complain as we sparred. I managed to improve my reaction time and even got a shot in, stepping into his throw and throwing a forearm to his throat a little harder than I meant. I snatched his arm as he was thrown back. "You OK?"

He nodded.

Raven had entered the room. I didn't know how long she'd been there. I wanted to say something to her, but the words jumbled. My mind was on fighting, not making amends.

Jex saved me. "He shouldn't get his ass kicked next time." He looked back at me. "Cole isn't a bad dude, just intense."

"Do you think he's intense?" I asked her.

She looked hurt. She gave a half shrug and went into the bedroom. I knew to go after her, but Jex went before I could. They talked briefly, then quieted. I paced. This was the first time I didn't feel connected to her. Everything had become heightened.

Jex poked his head in. "I checked an ol' chatboard we use. Cole's alive. There's a procedure to connect—"

"No."

He pursed his lips. "Fine. C'mere then."

He led me to the bedroom window. The street was quiet, three armed Triad the only people visible. They stood at the far intersection, guarding the area.

"Coast is clear." He picked up his jacket. "I'll snag us some food."

"You're not leaving," Raven said.

"I don't go, it may be days 'fore we eat." When he saw the look on her face, he said, "Locals ignore me, and Agents…well, I got experience avoidin' those silver-headed pricks."

227

"Their men are all over the place. Kieran won't stop—"

"We have to eat."

Her voice dropped to a whisper. "I can't lose anyone else."

He went to his pack and pulled out a media rod. "Here. Watch some TV."

I frowned. "Where did you get that?"

"Tianshi's."

I couldn't believe he had one. The base was two feet wide—some models were much bigger—with speakers imbedded in it. He plugged it in and turned it on. A rectangular screen rose from the base and began to broadcast a historical fiction drama. He lowered the volume, saw that neither of us were interested, and turned it off. "Jus' an idea."

Raven was right. Kieran would be back. They'd search every building. This time, they'd break into every apartment, abandoned or not. "We should leave Chinatown," I said.

"Tonight, after it gets dark. So long's they don't start fightin' again, we'll have a chance."

If it was safe enough for him to go out there, it should be safe enough for all of us. One moved quicker than three, stood out less, but we couldn't stay here. I opened my mouth to argue, but saw his expression. What he was planning was riskier than he let on.

He went to leave.

I retrieved the pulse drill I'd modified into a gun and caught him at the door. "It packs a punch," I said as I handed it to him. "Be careful."

He thanked me and left.

I considered trying to talk to Raven but didn't. Instead, I took the rubber pieces I'd made, went to the bathroom, and inserted them in my cheeks. The inserts puffed my cheeks but didn't change my looks. Tasted like shit, too. They wouldn't fool the software in the least.

I knew she was upset about him, about me. Mina wasn't around anymore to parent her, to say the perfect thing.

A sound came from the bedroom. Raven had turned on the TV.

I heard her flipping channels. She stopped, and Nikolai's voice floated toward me. "...no longer the visionary we knew. We've fired him and categorically condemn his actions." I tossed the inserts in the toilet and started for the bedroom. "Dray, surrender before anyone else gets hurt."

He was staring at the camera, his sincerity false, probably

encouraged by our company's lawyers.

"Change the channel," I told Raven.

The next station broadcasted an interview Senator Patricia Dixon gave inside a synthetic-paneled banquet hall, the caption under her name identifying it as part of the McCovey Cove Convention Center. "…not aware of any problems in Chinatown."

"Authorities have cordoned off the area," the reporter said.

"If there are tensions, I'm confident our law enforcement will handle matters—"

Raven muted the broadcast. "She's clueless."

She left the bedroom, and I unmuted the TV. The senator didn't say much more, and didn't comment on Free Isle or Mayor Ehkhert when the reporter asked. After the interview, the news program didn't mention Chinatown any further. None of the other channels talked about it at all, at least not that I found.

I returned to the main room where Raven practiced various moves. She paused. "Anything?"

"No."

She seemed bothered. I held out the lipstick-sized weapon I'd developed back in my office, which I'd recharged. "Keep this at all times. You never know."

She pocketed it before she continued, swinging at the air harder than before.

I wanted to give her space, but I needed to reach out to her. "What're those moves?"

"Jujitsu."

"Will you teach me?"

She avoided my gaze as she nodded. Other than explaining what a move was supposed to do—block an attacker, break a hold—she didn't talk. I mimicked her moves, hoping to bond with her. Her eyes flickered to me at one point. I gave an encouraging smile but didn't press.

We continued, until I asked, "Can we spar?"

She was fast, though she backed off after the first few strikes. "It's OK," I told her. "Don't slow down."

I launched quick jabs to force her speed back up. She threw a palm against my chest, making contact, then swiveled and brought up an elbow I barely blocked in time.

Her moves became aggressive, angry. Two more blows came fast, both connecting.

"Hey, wait—" I said.

"Why?" she spat. She threw an elbow I somehow managed to block. "Why didn't you protect Talia?" Nailed my ribs. "Why didn't you stop Mom?"

"I tried—"

"Did you know she'd betray us?" She struck my face, though I jerked back when she swung, which lessened the blow.

"No."

"Why should I believe you? You didn't depend on me. You act like I'm helpless."

"I'm trying to protect you."

She punched me in the sternum. "You didn't protect Talia."

"Don't hate your mother. She never got over your brother's death."

"Talia's dead because of her."

"Raven—"

She continued to lash out. Her blows stung, but I'd take whatever she threw.

"Your mom," I said between strikes, "she was always fragile."

"Stop." She threw a punch. "Stop taking her side." Her chop at my neck was weak; tears coated her cheeks.

"I'm not. I'm...." Trying to salvage your memory of her.

Raven dropped her fists, her face creased with grief. "I miss Talia so much."

My voice broke. "So do I."

I reached for her, but she pulled away.

After she composed herself, she began to practice Jujitsu again, facing away from me. I understood her anger, deserved it to a degree. I'd been angry as well—at myself, at Mina, and at Raven, ever since she'd lied to me. As she swung at imaginary foes, I remembered her tearful confession in the shower.

Our anger didn't do us any good. It only risked us failing. I wanted to tell her that, but a tear had opened between us. I didn't know to heal it.

Jex burst into the apartment. "You need to see something."

CHAPTER THIRTY-TWO

Rebel caps and sunglasses were our only defense as we angled over one street and down another, the avenues empty except for a few locals who walked as quickly as we did in various directions. I hoped whatever Jex wanted to show us was worth the risk. One look at our faces would be our undoing.

Talia would've loved the thrill. The thought wrenched yet warmed me in a weird way.

Jex steered us through a nondescript door into a four-story apartment building and up three flights of stairs to a window that looked onto the street below.

The drone-blocking mesh was attached to the building's roof one floor above us. Held up by metal ribs, the mesh stretched away to the left across Chinatown but ended a block to the right, dipping toward the police blockade that awaited us like a large, cloth awning. Past the line of police cars, the old Transamerica Building stood in the distance, barely visible through the mesh and smog.

Jex pointed toward a tree-accented public square diagonally across the street. "See what they're doin'?"

I didn't catch it at first, as the balcony from the pagoda-topped building next door blocked part of my view. Then I did. An Agent stood guard along one edge of the square, a second on the opposite, and two government vehicles occupied the space in the middle, one a modified van and the other a trailer with an angled sphere on the roof: a covered communications array. Cables ran between the vehicles and down into a manhole.

"What're they doing?" Raven asked.

I wasn't sure at first. Then Kieran exited the trailer, and I knew. He headed toward the van, where a stack of oversized, suitcase-like containers stood off to one side. They'd be heavily padded, filled with

231

tiny drones.

"They're setting up a command center for Kieran's new monitoring system," I said. "He must've had it shipped here. Once those drones are up, they'll blanket every inch of this place."

Raven frowned. "Won't the Triad block them from entering?"

"These are too small to stop."

"A few baby drones won't find us," Jex said.

I described the system Kieran had shown me, how they layered together. "Our fake implants will be abnormalities, profiles they can't match."

"Can we disable them?" Raven asked. "Give their software a virus?"

"They'd use a closed system."

"They have to communicate with the base, though. That could be a vulnerability."

Jex agreed, and they threw out ideas on how to tap into the network. As they talked, the enormity of the threat—to us, to others—hit me. The kids' ideas wouldn't work. Once we were caught, The Agency would dismantle Chinatown in retaliation for its inhabitants' resistance. Actually, the government would dismantle it whether we were caught or not.

I looked at Raven. "We caused this. We brought Kieran here. We need to fix it."

* * *

Tianshi opened the door herself this time, her eyes narrowed. "Go away."

"We need to talk," Jex said, crowded next to me and Raven in the stairwell to Tianshi's basement entrance.

She aimed a pulse gun at him. "I'll cook you."

"You have bigger problems than us," I said.

She searched my face, then waved us inside and closed the door. "So talk."

I told her about the command center and Kieran's technology.

"Your war, not mine."

"You think they'll go away after this? You're especially vulnerable. When they see people's feeds cut off down here, they'll swarm this place."

She hesitated.

I noticed her brother wasn't there. "Shon-ye's fighting with the others, isn't he?"

"Your fault, all of this. I should shoot you, end this myself." She raised her gun.

Jex stepped between us, but I pulled him back. "We'll take out their mobile center."

Raven and Jex were surprised. "Three of us against at least three Agents?" she asked.

"That's a terrible idea," he said.

I ignored them. "After we take it out, Shon-ye won't have to fight. In exchange, you give us the plastibots."

"They're not for you," Tianshi said.

"What will The Agency's surveillance do to your business? Your neighborhood?" I watched as she mentally ran through her options. "I want to protect my daughter. The 'bots are our only chance to get away."

Her face puckered. "Fine, but you pay. They're not cheap."

"We'll need IDs, too."

We transferred all the cryptocurrency we owned.

"I need one more thing," I said. "A sniper rifle."

Chapter Thirty-Three

As we left Tianshi's, Jex said to me, "Ya got a plan. Please tell me ya do."

"The start of one."

He nodded toward the sniper rifle, which she'd wrapped in synth paper. "What the hell are you gonna do with that?"

"Can you get Raven back to where you showed us the square?"

He nodded.

Even though Raven was still standoffish, she said, "I don't want you to risk yourself."

"If we succeed, we might create enough chaos to get out of here." She didn't look convinced. "Besides, people need to be woken up."

That got a ghost of a smile.

Jex grimaced. "There's no way I'd normally agree to some half-cooked plan, but I love you, Raven, so I guess we'll all die together."

Her face went slack. "You tell me that *now*?"

* * *

We gathered our things from the empty apartment. Regardless of what happened, we weren't coming back.

Twenty minutes later, I walked past the pagoda-topped building. I hadn't figured out every angle, but there was no time. Kieran's drones would take flight any second.

I crossed the street and approached the square. Instead of families and tourists, The Agency's vehicles dominated the public space. Even so, a handful of old people sat in spots around the square, seemingly ignoring the intruders, although two clusters of young men, probably Triad, hovered at the fringes, watching the Agents. The Agent nearest me was aware of them; they took most of his attention.

It's what I was betting on, although when I stepped from Clay Street onto the square, his focus switched to me. He stood twenty yards ahead, positioned to intercept threads from this angle. Another Agent guarded the far end.

As I walked toward the first Agent, I kept my hands visible, though I used one to scratch my head to partially block my face. I wore sunglasses and had stuffed the horrible-tasting inserts in my cheeks, but he would see through my disguise. I wanted to use my other arm as well, but I needed to keep it where it was. Jex's barn jacket was snug, but its pockets were big.

I altered my step so I'd pass the Agent out of arms' reach. I needed him to look away, just for a moment. He didn't, though, and I strode past. I imagined him scanning me. No time.

Pulling out the Free Isle mask Raven had kept, I slipped it over my face, spun, and aimed my engineered pulse gun at the Agent. The man, younger than Kieran but taller, froze, then coiled. He'd attack the moment I became distracted.

"Tell whoever's in the trailer to come out," I said.

He tilted his head as someone behind me started to run: the Agent on the far side of the square, heading for us. "We'll match your voice," the near one said. "Analysis is running now."

"They have three seconds to get out."

The trailer door opened and Kieran emerged. "Quintero," he yelled. He leapt to the ground, followed by a second Agent.

Jesus, there were four of them.

The Agent from the far side of the square passed Kieran, running faster.

"Stop," Jex cried. He'd approached from the side street, his machine gun aimed at Kieran's head. The three Agents paused—including the one who had been running, who slid to a halt—then tensed to strike.

Before they could, I said, "We have a sharpshooter."

They followed my gaze. Raven was in the window near the pagoda-topped building, her face obscured by the rifle scope she peered through.

"Step back," Jex said. He needed to move quicker. Even with Raven, we wouldn't be able to contain them for long.

Kieran moved away from the trailer, as did the Agent who'd followed him out, although the Agent only moved a few feet.

I started to warn Jex, but it was too late. He pulled out a timer-bomb and tossed it toward the trailer's open doorway, but the second

Agent swatted it away. The bomb, which wouldn't activate until it made contact with metal, clattered to the concrete-covered ground.

Kieran and the Agent from the far side of the square started for me. The one I'd trained my pulse gun on launched himself at me, hands outstretched. I pulled the trigger, the nearly point-blank blast driving him to the concrete.

Kieran and his companion were two dozen yards away, coming fast.

Over my shoulder, Raven fired, but not at them. Jex had been losing his fight with the Agent by the trailer. When she fired, the Agent sagged, and Jex kicked the bomb into the trailer. It hit the far wall and started to drop, but then the bomb's magnet pulled it towards the metal racks that held liquicore processors, adhered to them—and its timer activated.

He started to run. So did I.

As we scrambled, the Agent Jex had fought lunged into the trailer to try to reach the bomb.

I barely got two steps before it exploded. Light dazed me, noise deafened me—and the concussive wave threw me. I flew out of the square, lifted by the explosion, and nearly sailed all the way across the street. When I landed, debris pelted me and larger chunks crashed into the pavement around me. Ignoring the twinges of pain, I stood.

The trailer was gone. So was the Agent who'd dove inside. The blast had also sheared the van in half, its insides crushed from the explosion.

Jex, Kieran, and the third Agent were down. So was everyone else in the square.

Jex got up first, somehow in one piece. I ran for him as cops swarmed in from the barricade and entered the square. My foot flaring, I grabbed his arm and hauled him back the way I'd come, away from the devastation, while Raven fired shots over our heads to keep the cops at bay. They returned fire, which forced her to duck. Jex and I reached the apartment building where I'd stationed her.

I glanced back at the square as Kieran got to his feet. Bloodied and bruised, he started after us. Gained speed.

I followed Jex inside and shut the door. "Get Raven and get out like we planned."

He bounded up the stairs.

As Kieran raced toward the building, I pulled out my ion blade. Using the flat side, I began to melt the metal frame to seal the door, steering the liquefying metal across the gap before it rehardened, then liquefying another section.

I'd only sealed a few inches when he crashed into the door so hard it flew open. I rocketed backwards, the blade sailing from my hand, and landed a few feet away.

As I got up, he grabbed me and heaved me across the narrow foyer. I slammed into the far wall, taking out a stand with discarded magazines as I fell to the ground. My blade was almost in reach. Fighting through the pain, I lunged for it.

Kieran reached it first. He brought his foot down and destroyed the device.

I jerked back. Before I could stand, he picked me up and threw me again. I crashed near the door. He walked toward me, a satisfied smile on his face.

My blade gone, I searched Jex's coat for anything I could use. My fingers wrapped around a short tube. It was the covalent-cutter I'd bought for Raven—she must've given it to Jex.

Kieran lifted me to my feet.

I flicked the cutter on, brought my arm up, and sliced his bicep, the device hitting bone. He let go with a shout, and I sliced his other arm at the wrist, severing tendons. He stumbled back, but I wasn't done. I stepped forward and jammed the cutter into his shoulder. In seconds, the chain reaction would begin.

He swiveled quicker than I could react and knocked me away. The cutter bounced as it hit the far wall and fell to the scuffed floor.

I went for the stairs and took them as fast as I could. My foot had healed during our stay in the apartment but had set wrong, and being thrown out of the square and tossed around by Kieran had aggravated it.

He started after me, his steps loud in the stairwell but slower than mine.

Using the railing, I pulled myself to the second floor, then the third. I stepped into the hallway. To my dismay, Jex and Raven ran toward me. They hadn't gotten away.

"Are you OK?" she asked. She'd abandoned her rifle but had a pistol. Our bags were slung over her shoulder.

"No time," I managed. There was only one way out, and Kieran was closer than I'd hoped. I took one of the bags. "Come on."

I led them to the roof, the route we'd planned, up the stairs, and through the rooftop door. I hurried toward the building to the west and bounded over the two-foot-tall lip of the roof that separated the two identical structures. The rooftop door ahead offered a way out. Past it, mesh extended in every direction like a shroud, connecting this rooftop to the ones across the street.

We ran to the door, which we'd propped open earlier, but someone had removed the stick of wood. The door was closed, which meant we were trapped, as neither this door nor the one we'd exited had outside handles. We couldn't open it—and couldn't go back.

I steered Raven and Jex to the far edge of the building. Below us, Grant Avenue was visible; I could make out Triad men running toward the Square.

I pointed to the building on the other side of the street. "That's our way out."

"No fuckin' way," Jex said.

"You see the metal supports?" I pointed to the ribs, which I wished were closer together.

"They're like fish bones, prob'ly as flimsy."

Raven nodded when I looked at her and approached the ledge.

"Babe, don't," he said.

I took her hand. "We'll go one at a time. Take the first step. You'll see."

Squeezing my fingers, she extended her foot as Jex groaned with worry and walked onto the mesh. She sank a few inches, but the mesh held. With a glance behind us, she let go of my hand and took another step. She continued forward, a breeze lifting her hair, the support arches wobbling, although she continued to sink as she proceeded, the mesh straining under her weight. By the time she reached the center, her head was nearly level with our feet. She dropped to her knees, as the rest of her journey was uphill, and with her bag dragging under her, crawled to the far side.

As she climbed off of the mesh, I pushed Jex forward. "Move."

The stairwell door we'd used opened, and Kieran staggered onto the roof.

"Yep, I'm moving," Jex said.

He walked onto the mesh, nearly fell, and took a number of quick steps to stay upright. The mesh stretched greater than before, and he dropped lower than Raven had. As he hurried forward, the metal supports curled toward him, shaking with every footfall.

Kieran reached the divider between the two buildings, holding the wrist I'd cut. As I watched, the bloody fingers moved, healing somehow—or I hadn't hurt him as badly as I'd thought. His other arm was bloody too, but functional. And he was coming, silver hair bright in the sunlight.

Jex was a few feet from the far side, the mesh stretched to such a degree it appeared solid, a black slope he clawed at. Raven reached down and grabbed one of his hands. Kieran's footsteps grew louder. Faster. I stepped onto the ledge.

Jex reached the far side and hauled himself onto the building's roof. As soon as he stepped off, I saw it: the mesh sagged, weakened from their journeys. I didn't think it would take my weight.

I ran along the edge of the building, away from Kieran. Away from the weakened section. His footsteps changed as he angled toward me.

I passed one of the metal supports, thin ribs that did look like fishbone, then stopped. No choice. I was heavier than Jex. Not fat, but thicker. It would hold me or wouldn't.

With Kieran's ragged breath growing loud, I stepped onto the mesh. I sank, the material becoming opaque at my feet, and I dropped too much. The mesh couldn't hold me. I worried it'd fail completely. I shot a glance at Raven.

My drop slowed, then stopped.

I was thirty feet in the air. People ran under me as the battle for Chinatown renewed, and red paper lanterns swayed gently, both barely visible past the stretched material.

Forcing my eyes up, I took a step, then another. Pain spiked my damaged foot, nearly causing me to tumble, the mesh pressing against the offset bone.

"Stop," Raven yelled.

I did. She held her pistol high, but she wasn't aiming at me. Kieran had reached the ledge, the black-bladed cutter in his hand.

He looked at me. "Dray. I deserved what you did at your office. I get it. Let's start over, find common ground. Mina misses you. Both of you. Don't you want to see her?"

I continued forward, the mesh straining.

"Don't make me do this," he said.

"Don't move," Raven shouted.

I went faster, my ears straining for her shout, for gunfire, for any indication he made good on his threat. The street moved slowly under me, the stabbing pain in my foot making me sweat. Jex waited at the far side, hand outstretched, while Raven remained focused on Kieran.

I got within fifteen feet. Ten. And that's when Raven cried out. "No."

She fired. I lunged.

My damaged foot betrayed me, robbing me of the strength I needed. I landed five feet short of the building. The mesh tore behind me as the damage spread.

"What's happening?" Kieran asked.

From his tone, I could tell he didn't understand. He hadn't just cut the mesh. He'd started the chain reaction.

I dug at the slick surface, clawing forward as the material sagged. I got two feet closer before I started to slide backwards.

"Get him," Kieran called out.

Jex's canvas bag swung down and hit my arm.

I reached for it, a last, desperate grab, and hooked the edge as the mesh disintegrated under me. With the mesh gone, I swung forward, nothing beneath me but the street, and smacked into the side of the building. The impact jarred my grip, but I managed to hold on.

Jex and Raven pulled me up, both straining. When I reached the ledge, I hauled myself onto the roof with their help.

Raven hugged me, the barrel of her pistol warm against my shoulder. When she let go, I looked back across the street. The mesh was gone; in the distance, the chain reaction consumed the last remnants.

Kieran appeared relieved that I'd made it. He raised his blood-covered hands when Raven aimed at him, then dropped to the rooftop, the ledge providing just enough cover to shield him.

She tensed but didn't fire. I gently pulled her away.

She helped me to the rooftop stairwell, as my limp had worsened. Unlike the other roof, we could get into this one. We ducked inside and headed to the street below.

CHAPTER THIRTY-FOUR

I knocked on Tianshi's door loud enough to be heard amidst the sounds of battle and mayhem that had spread across Chinatown. The skirmish we'd initiated had morphed into a major assault. Agency forces and police attacked from the south and west, while Triad squads fought from what seemed to be every alley and rooftop.

The door opened, and we hurried inside. "We held up our end," I said.

"No, you haven't," Tianshi said. "Shon-ye isn't back."

"After we leave, they will, too." She didn't look convinced. "I have a way to end this once and for all."

Raven gave me a quizzical look.

Tianshi frowned. "Don't buy promises."

"We did what we said we'd do," Jex said. "And paid you."

She sighed. "Fine. Your choice."

Tianshi led us to the back room and waved at chairs she'd set out. As we sat, she pulled down the white-and-pink boxes that contained the plastibots. They looked innocuous, yet held our hope. She opened three of them and began to remove mini-tubes, gauze pads, and bottles of pills. Flickering her gaze at us, she stopped before removing anything else.

Opening one of the mini-tubes, she dabbed topical cream on my face, which became numb. She nodded at my reaction. "Disinfects skin, too." She used a tube on each of us. When she finished, she said, "We wait."

"We need IDs as well, cards, everything," I reminded her.

She nodded, went to the first box—the one meant for me—and lifted a handheld computer, which had wires attached to something inside the box, possibly to whatever she'd kept hidden.

"Will this be permanent?" Raven asked.

"Of course," Tianshi said.

I read the emotions that gripped my daughter: anguish and uncertainty, panic and fear.

"Whatever happens, you'll always be you," I told her. "If there was any other way, I'd choose that instead."

"Your face isn't your best part," Jex said. "Your heart is."

I wasn't sure if she heard us, too absorbed by the fact that her looks would change. She didn't get up from her chair, though, didn't pull away when Jex took her hand.

The battle outside grew louder.

I looked at Tianshi. "Inject me."

"Your face isn't numb enough."

I suspected as much. "No time."

She removed a cylinder from the box, the one attached to the wires. It was the size of a tall beaker, probably 400 milliliters in volume, filled with what might've been mistaken for hand soap. But I knew why the liquid was shimmery: it was from the hundreds of thousands of nanobots. Tianshi aimed the handheld computer at me and took a picture, then with a series of adjustments, programmed the microscopic robots.

The last thing she pulled out was an oval-shaped contraption with needles sticking out of one side at the top, bottom, along the edges, and in the protrusions that jutted toward the center of the oval.

I tensed. I knew what it had to be for.

"What the...?" Raven asked.

"Look away," Tianshi told her. She attached the cylinder to the oval device, then pinned my head to the chair's headrest. With one hand on my throat, her fingers gripping the back of my jaw, she settled the device over my face and pushed it home. Needles jabbed me along my forehead, brow, cheekbones, and jawline, many of the needles hitting bone.

The cylinder began to drain as the nanobots filled the oval device. The next moment, I felt the thick liquid seep under my skin. Burning. Foreign. The liquid spread, and the 'bots went to work. They tore through skin and built bone, adding to my cheekbones and chiseling down my jawline. I knew Raven was beside me, but I couldn't help crying out in pain. More 'bots slid down the inside of my nasal passages and up my forehead to sculpt the inside of my nose. A sharp ache shot through my forehead as they narrowed my skull. It was only a fraction of an inch, but it was what I imagined getting hit with an axe might've felt like.

The pain stopped and I lurched forward, nearly falling out of my chair.

My breath raspy, I blinked a few times to clear my vision. Tianshi had set my eyes closer together. I hoped I'd adjust quickly. We didn't have time.

Raven put her hands on my shoulders. "You OK?" I suspected she was terrified — she'd leapt from her chair to help me — but the numbing agent had slackened her face.

"How do I look?"

Her eyes took me in. "Why don't you look more different?"

"It's enough to fool software," Tianshi said as she filled the next oval-shaped device. "More would've been unnecessary." She waved Raven to her chair.

"Dad? I can't do this."

Tianshi touched her arm. "You won't change as much. Besides, he didn't wait. Face wasn't numb. Yours is."

She pushed Raven into the chair and pressed the device to her face. I watched the cylinder empty. Raven moaned but didn't cry out. The numbing worked. Seconds later, she opened her eyes. "I didn't like that." Her cheeks had been widened, as had her forehead. She still looked attractive, just in a different way. More refined. Slightly older. I wondered how Jex would react.

As Tianshi worked on him, I checked my face in the mirror. I could see the effects: the slightly narrowed forehead, the thinned jaw, the slightly raised cheeks. I was still me, to a degree. My skin had been tightened, too, probably to highlight the changes.

When I came back, Jex was recovering — he almost looked dashing now, god forbid — as Tianshi loaded our images into her system. "You'll delete the files when you're done, right?" I asked.

She looked at me with contempt. "Of course." She selected what she wanted from a menu, and the government-quality printer cycled up.

"I also want access badges."

When I told her where to, her contempt shifted to something else. "Why?"

243

"You have the format, don't you? Can you add us to their database?"

"I'd have to key the badges to match your implants."

I glanced at Jex, who was assuring Raven about her appearance. "How often do our implants switch codes?"

"'Bout every two hours." He checked his watch. "If I'm right, we got thirty minutes."

Tianshi scanned our implants and printed the badges I'd asked for.

I grabbed my bag. "We need to go." To Tianshi, I said, "You should leave, too."

"I thought you were taking away the danger."

"I am."

* * *

When we left Tianshi's, I told Jex to go north. He led us out of the covered area and onto the scorched and pockmarked streets. We kept out of sight as much as possible, using abandoned vehicles and bullet-scarred buildings as cover as we snaked toward the northern edge of Chinatown. Around us, gunshots and cries came from the battle we'd initiated, some faint, others near. We passed damaged shops and dark apartments, every door busted. Other streets appeared untouched, though they were no less dangerous.

The battle bothered me. I'd wanted to stop the fighting, not trigger it.

We reached the farthest checkpoint. People trying to escape the quarantine filled the street, the large crowd scrutinized by a squad of armed national guardsmen stationed in front of and on top of two green-painted dump trucks that blocked the intersection, which created a checkpoint each person had to pass through.

I leaned toward Raven and Jex. "Go ahead of me. Act like a tourist couple." She nodded and hooked her arm through his, her other hand in her bag as they disappeared into the crowd.

I slipped on my sunglasses and waited a full minute before I started after them. I elbowed my way past people, taking a few shots myself, and once stumbling when someone stepped on my bad foot. I shoved forward, my satchel hooked over my shoulder, the bag the only thing that might be recognizable. I'd left Jex's coat at Tianshi's. If she was smart, she would burn it.

We'd also left the sniper rifle.

My face still sore, I neared the barricade. Though it was wide enough for three people to pass through at once, the guardsmen only allowed one at a time, stopping each person to scan and interrogate them.

I found myself a few feet from Jex and Raven. As I approached, she was pulled aside by one of the guards, his hand on the butt of his pistol as he detained her. Jex was waved past, a guard on top of the dump truck not directly pointing his rifle at him but not pointing it away, either. The guard who'd grabbed Raven held up a miniscreen to her face.

I shuffled past her. If I made even the slightest move toward her, we'd both be captured or worse, though I paid more attention on her than what I was doing.

One of the guards stopped me. "You're not a local."

"I got trapped when all this started." I almost said more, but remembered I hadn't altered my voice.

His eyes narrowed. "Take off your glasses."

No choice. I did. Jesus, he stared right at me.

"What were you doing in Chinatown?"

"Visiting my girlfriend." I couldn't look away. His gaze dropped to my wedding ring. I forced a shrug. "You know how it is."

He frowned, an image of my prior face probably showing on his lenses, reflecting a slightly different guy they'd been directed to find. I feared he'd see through my alterations or decide my looks were too similar to their quarry. They knew about plastibots. I should've changed my hair, worn something in my shoes to appear taller.

He aimed his miniscreen's camera at me. I nearly swung at him. He scanned my face at different angles, then ran the images against the software.

No matter the computing speed, it still seemed to take forever.

"Go on," he said.

I waited until he turned to the next person escaping Chinatown before I hurried off, wincing as I tried to mask my limp. I didn't see Raven or Jex anywhere. I couldn't stop, though, or I'd arouse suspicion.

Across the street, I heard her whisper, "Over here." They were in the doorway to a pharmacy. I hugged her tight.

When I let go, they were both smiling. "Beauts," Jex said. "Now's our chance. Let's call Cole and rally with the others."

"And fight back," Raven added.

"No. I'm ending this," I said. "We're going to Senator Dixon and surrender to her if we have to. She can warn Congress, cut off The Agency's power and dismantle it." She was young, different than her predecessor. She'd been elected on a ticket of change, answering the mood of the state, and while she hadn't done anything remarkable so far, if things went my way, she would.

Raven frowned. "You really think she can stop them?"

"That she'll even listen?" Jex asked.

"We don't have the strength to stop The Agency, not without a much bigger gun," I said. "Congress is the biggest there is."

By a shift in his gaze, I could tell Jex had accessed something online, probably the senator's schedule. "She bolts t'night. She's at a fundraiser right now."

"At the new convention center."

"That's why you wanted those badges," Raven said.

I nodded.

Jex said, "We'd need to plan this out, set up diversions, disguises —"

"There's no time," I said. "It's worth the risk. She can take down The Agency."

"If she refuses to help us, they'll know our new faces," Raven said.

"It's our only chance."

"It's batshit crazy is what it is. We won't get past her guards," Jex said. He looked at Raven and took a breath. "OK, I'm in. I have a move we could use."

Her smile dropped when she turned back to me. "Jex and I will do this. You stay safe."

"I'm involved, too." I saw the fear in her eyes. "This isn't a good life for you. Or anyone. It's time to change that."

CHAPTER THIRTY-FIVE

We took a taxi to the McCovey Cove Convention Center. Exposing ourselves to the driver and the cab's internal cameras was a risk, but we had to reach the senator before she left San Francisco.

One of the H-shaped, Highcity complexes straddled the water inlet that connected to McCovey Cove. Two thick skyscrapers, each over ninety stories tall, rose on either side of the inlet, connected by a platform as wide as the skyscrapers and almost as long as a football field. The platform was suspended by massive cables that arced from anchor points on both buildings, which allowed the horizontal platform to sway during earthquakes.

We approached the center, which abutted the inlet next to the south tower. The convention center was three stories tall and windowless, with the obligatory cameras on the corners.

Keeping my head down, I steered Raven and Jex around the side. Jex had downloaded the diagram of the place, so he knew where we needed to go.

Before we reached the rear alley that led to the employee entrance, I stopped at a dumpster. "Can't go armed," I whispered.

They clutched their weapons—Jex's machine gun barely hidden inside his duffel bag, and Raven's pistol close to her side.

"There will be scanners," I said.

"I'm likin' this less and less," he murmured, reluctantly pulling his hand out of his bag.

They dropped their firepower into the dumpster. I set my bag in as well. It still held the dark matter sphere; other than Raven, it was the last connection to my previous life. My fingers were stiff as I let go.

As we approached the alley, Jex scratched his arm nervously until I shook my head at him. We reached the corner and stopped.

"Wait a few seconds, then come," I whispered.

After they agreed, I stepped around the corner, trying to seem like a haggard employee as Jex had suggested. Three guards blocked the entrance, one to either side of the open doors, a third inside the foyer behind bullet-and-blast proof glass. They weren't normal guards. They had multiple implants, almost as many as Kieran did, although they weren't Agents and their hair was jet-black—secret service or private security, maybe even ex-Agents.

I forced myself to quicken my pace as they watched me approach. When I neared, the one to my left held up a hand. "Name?"

I gave the fake one Tianshi had assigned me. The guard accessed the center's database while the second one—taller, with a deep frown-line—tensed. Raven and Jex had appeared.

This was the moment of truth: whether my implant's codes still matched my badge.

The second guard aimed his weapon at Raven and Jex as his frown deepened.

"We work here," Jex said. "Check the list."

The first guard focused on me. "You're not scheduled for another five hours."

According to their system, I was a janitor on the night crew. "I'm picking up extra shifts." I tried to sound convincing, but my voice wavered, which threatened to fuck everything up.

The second guard pushed Raven and Jex against the wall. His weapon wasn't aimed at their heads, but he seemed agitated. If either flinched, I feared what would happen. With his free hand, he searched them and removed something from Raven's pocket. It was the other lipstick-sized pulsor I'd made. "What the hell is this?"

"Don't point it at me," she said. "It's a gag lighter, but when I tried it, it sent a weird surge. I meant to throw it away."

I could tell she wanted to say more. Jex visibly tensed, as if he was about to attack. If we tried to fight our way inside, we'd lose.

"Can I go?" I asked, hoping to distract everyone. "I'm late."

My guard nodded.

I entered the building. The guard inside the booth watched me, but I paused anyway in case an attack broke out. The other guard finally waved Raven and Jex through.

Past the booth was a camera-lined hallway that led to the employee locker rooms.

Raven was quiet until we reached the locker rooms. "Sorry, nearly blew it," she said in a low voice before she stepped through a screen to the women's side.

Inside the men's room, Jex searched the stacks of clothes for waiter uniforms and tossed me a shirt, slacks, and coat. We changed into the outfits, the material adjusting to match our body measurements.

When I was done, I opened an empty locker. "Keep whatever's important."

"Like a weapon?" he grumbled.

I pocketed my datarings. I still had Talia's mended cap. Relieved the guards hadn't guessed its real purpose—the woven mesh too fine to trigger their sensors—I stuck it in my pocket as well, thinking it could help convince the senator, and shoved my clothes into the locker.

Raven joined us outside the locker rooms in an outfit similar to ours.

Jex steered us through the wide, sterile hallways, past various halls and convention areas, to the banquet hall that housed the senator's event. A final guard blocked our path, his black hair gleaming in the fluorescents. He tensed when we appeared, his weapon at the ready, only marginally relaxing when his eyes flashed with information. He'd been told to expect us. If we'd delayed, he would've come after us. He still would, once our codes changed. Either way, we only had seconds.

He motioned for us to remain quiet and opened the door to the banquet hall.

Senator Dixon's amplified voice filled the darkened hall as we entered. We were near the back. A row of cameras against the rear wall gazed over a sea of black-clothed tables to the stage at the far end, each table filled with formally-dressed men and women that were little more than shapes outlined by the light from the stage at the far end of the room. The senator hunched over a wide podium, bathed in lights, the podium too low for her. Large media screens hovered to either side, stereo images of her face as she spoke.

"...the need for greater control of our future is our best hope of achieving that dream," she told the audience.

As my eyes adjusted, I found guards spaced throughout the hall, watching the crowd—and us. Two more blocked the stage. I couldn't draw attention to myself, not when we were so close.

Jex and Raven stepped past me, the white of their shirts catching the reflected light from the stage.

Needing to get closer, I picked up an empty server's tray from a nearby stand.

"...working with my fellow senators, we will ensure that the next hundred years are better than the last...."

I picked up an empty plate at the first table and proceeded to the next. Another plate, and I moved forward again, this time three tables. A serving dish joined my disguise, then a dessert dish from another table.

Raven and Jex followed my lead. She picked up plates and set them on a tray he carried. They were three tables to my left, nearly level with me.

I ignored the senator's words, too focused on the problem before me. I didn't know how to get past her guards, who were similar to the ones at the employee entrance. Four tables stood between her and us. We might be able to reach the front, but if we stepped past the first row of tables, we'd become a threat. They would grab us. If that happened, we'd lose our one chance.

I was close enough to see her clearly. She wore a violet pantsuit, expertly tailored but wrinkled. Off in some way. My vision flickered. In that moment, Senator Dixon's face disappeared. In her place was a stooped, older woman with a glowing headband. My vision flickered again, and Dixon's face returned.

I froze.

I didn't know what I'd seen, what it meant. I glanced at Raven and Jex. They'd stopped as well.

The senator continued her speech, her voice filling the hall as if nothing had happened.

A dark premonition gripped me. The implant—it had to be. I pulled out Talia's cap, the one I'd meant to have the senator put on, and pressed it against my implant, cutting off all data streams. As if a switch had been flipped, Senator Dixon's face disappeared to reveal the old woman hidden behind the mirage. She wore Dixon's dress, spoke with her voice—a disc covered her throat—but she wasn't Dixon. Her glowing headband was visible, as was another band, the second one draped around her shoulders like an oversized necklace. She also wore a dot on either cheek. The senator's posture made sense: she wasn't stooped because of the podium. It was due to age. And she wasn't just any old woman. She was Senator Bobina Smithy, the woman who'd supposedly retired instead of losing the last election, whose seat Dixon had won.

Smithy hadn't stepped down. She'd taken a different persona, one projected by the implants.

She and others — The Agency, the government — weren't using the implants to hide damage to the environment. They were using them to stay in power.

Chapter Thirty-Six

I needed to move from my spot near the stage, to act natural, but I was too stunned. The lies were greater than we'd realized, the threat beyond our ability to fight.

Raven looked horrified. She'd taken my cue and used the piece from Talia's cap to discover the truth. She handed the cloth to Jex, who jerked in surprise when he covered his implant.

I spotted a pair of kitchen doors past him — a way out. I headed for them. Raven did the same, flashing me a warning look. I already knew. We'd attracted attention.

She and Jex reached the kitchen first, and the door swung closed behind them.

Out of the corner of my eye, I saw a guard angling toward me. The senator continued to speak, but her words were lies. I was a fool to think she'd help us.

We needed to get away.

I reached the door and entered the bright kitchen, metal counters that connected to a dishwashing apparatus to the right, cooking and prep area directly ahead and to the left. Kitchen staff, clustered between a row of stoves and the serving area, barely registered our appearance.

I only took three steps before the door opened again and the guard charged inside. I spun — and spotted Jex and Raven hiding on either side of the door. Jex tackled the guard, slamming him into the dishwashing machine, and punched him repeatedly to take him down, but the guard remained on his feet as he fought back. Before I could put my tray down to fight, Raven swiped the serving dish I'd picked up and launched herself at the guard.

The door opened again as I set down my tray, and a second guard appeared. Metal water pitchers were clustered next to the dishwasher. I grabbed one, stepped forward, swung it — water arching across the room — at the guard, and bashed the pitcher into the side of his head. He fell, arms flopping like a broken toy.

Raven's guard fell as well, the serving dish shattered at her feet.

The kitchen grew quiet, the staff eyeing us.

"Come on," I said as Raven pulled Jex free of the guard, who'd taken him down with him.

Jex swiped the guard's pistol and straightened. "This way."

We ran through the kitchen, past a fleet of walk-in coolers, and into a back hallway. "We need our bags," I huffed as we ran.

"They could catch us," Raven said.

"No choice." I needed the dark matter sphere. It would be key to the coming war.

"I knew this was a bad idea," Jex said. He steered us down an adjoining hallway and into a massive storage room. Exhibit materials, supplies, and equipment filled the dim, cavernous space. We ran straight ahead, past crates, strangely-shaped mounds, stacked boxes, and clusters of lighting mounts.

Footfalls echoed behind us — guards. Coming fast.

We ran faster, my foot hurting, the still-active nanobots in my system unable to completely heal the poorly-set bones.

We burst from the stacks, and skidded to a stop. Doors were spaced along the wall before us. I panted as Jex swiveled his head. I could almost see the map he'd downloaded reflected in his lenses.

He pointed to the left. "That one."

Taking the lead, I threw open the doors and was momentarily blinded by sunlight. When my eyes adjusted, Jex was already across the alleyway and reaching into the dumpster. Seconds later, bags in hand, we ran out of the alley.

The city's skyscrapers stretched toward the clear sky, the nearest one only a few blocks away, the area's density promising anonymity but threatening revelation. Cars appeared out of the city mass and cut into the parking lot from two directions heading toward us. I just caught a flash, but the silver hair of one of the drivers was unmistakable.

Raven pointed at the sky. "Drones." Three of them.

The Agents were the bigger problem. Kieran drove the lead car, I was sure of it. He and the other vehicles blocked our path to the heart of the city. To the right was the Bay, a dead-end. That only left one choice. "Come on."

We went left, and ran like never before.

Images and feelings flashed: Raven in front of me, hair streaming. Parked cars a blur. Throat ragged, my bag hitting me. Cars' augmented engines audible. Kieran's men closing in.

We passed the edge of the conference complex. The land next to it was a large public space with manicured grass and cut-stone walkways that led to the H shaped building. Raven took the lead, veering across the space, past people oblivious to our fight, and toward the glass-walled entrance.

Tires screeched behind us as we charged up the stairs to the doors.

The lobby was bright and airy, which made our dash more obvious. A bank of elevators, fifteen or so, stood on the far side. Raven rushed to the nearest open one, Jex and I only steps behind, and we dove inside. She jabbed the control screen, selecting the suspended platform level labeled "SunCity" that connected to the other tower…

Shouts reached us across the lobby. Kieran and his team were here.

…and the elevator doors closed.

I leaned against the wall as we rose and tried to catch my breath. Jex did as well, letting his bulky sack thump to the floor.

"It can't be the *entire* government," Raven said. "There are checks and balances, oversight, two political parties opposed to each other."

"They can look like anyone," he said. "Elections don't matter. Wrong cat wins, he'd be swapped out."

"Jex is right," I said. "They must have consolidated their power years ago, after the neural nets went wide. If someone didn't conform, they were probably eliminated."

"Why would any politico resist? They'd be set for life."

"Did you and the other rebels know there was a goddamn coup?"

He shook his head. "Thought Agents were the problem."

"The whole country's been hijacked," Raven said. "Do you think governors are in on it, too? Mayors? Mom's old boss?"

"Maybe," I said as the elevator rose. The numbers didn't pass quickly enough.

"The implants weren't to help us. They're to manipulate and control us."

I agreed. "No one could object if they didn't know what happened."

"That's sick," Jex said. "We haveta pull down the curtain."

I glanced at the elevator's readout. Kieran would follow us, would know what floor we chose. We were outgunned and outmanned. I looked at Raven, taking her in as the elevator slowed.

The digital screen with the floor numbers flickered and winked out. Jex lunged for the doors as the elevator stopped. "They'll send us back down."

The three of us forced the doors open, which triggered a safety mechanism that prevented the car from moving, then the outer ones, which were four feet higher. We'd stopped between floors.

After we crawled up and out of the elevator, we hurried to the stairwell and climbed the last two flights to SunCity. We stepped from the stairwell into a crowded antechamber filled with kiosks and seating areas.

The far wall of the antechamber was gone, replaced by a fifty-foot-wide entranceway that revealed SunCity beyond, the sunlight-filled, suspended structure that stretched away from the tower. The massive cables arched down and cradled the public space as it extended over the McCovey Cove slip to the sister tower, the cables from this angle like gargantuan spider legs.

SunCity was too damn big. It was a town in the sky with restaurants, shops, parks with trees thirty feet high, and open areas for concerts and communal events. Glass walls lined both sides of the structure, protection against a fatal fall.

Two Agency drones rose up over the side of the structure. Dozens of people roamed the area, oblivious to the drones—and the danger that was coming.

Raven and Jex hurried onto the suspended level, but I paused. A rolled-up gate lined the entranceway to SunCity.

I only had seconds before Agents arrived.

A woman cried out as I ran to where the wall ended and the entranceway began. Jex had pulled his machine gun from his bag. He fired at one of the drones. It took a couple of tries, but he shot it down.

People ran for cover, most swarming past me for the elevators.

When I reached the wall, I found a control panel and the emergency switch. I hit the red button, and the gate began to descend as an alarm blared. The remaining people, the ones hiding on the platform, scrambled toward the entranceway as the gate dropped. I ducked under it and onto the suspended structure, then backpaddled away from the building. The gate was thick. Sturdy.

I hoped it'd be enough.

Elevator doors opened, and Agents cut through the mob toward us. Most slowed as the gate descended, but Kieran ran faster. The gate was halfway down, three-quarters —

He dove under it before it closed and thickened, designed so whatever natural calamity that prompted its closure didn't send shrapnel into the building.

Kieran stood. Behind him, Agents crowded the closed gate, the gaps too small to stick their fingers through.

Raven took my arm. "Come on."

I wanted to inflict as much pain on him as he'd inflicted on us. Then maybe we'd be even.

"Go," I told her and Jex. "I'll meet up."

"You're coming, too," she said as he handed me a pistol.

I looked at him. "Get her out of here."

Jex pulled her away, ignoring her objections, which grew more frantic as he dragged her toward the opposite tower.

"You can't win," Kieran said. "Besides, all I have to do is catch her, and I'll get both of you."

"You have to go through me first."

There was no cover, the closest building a restaurant forty feet away that had a large outside seating area with metal furniture. There wasn't even cloud cover; sunlight beat down from a clear sky to warm the mezzanine. San Francisco wasn't visible from where I stood, just the sister tower and other H towers in the distance, the mass of downtown skyscrapers sticking up past the glass wall on the far side.

"You act as if what we've done is wrong, Dray. This isn't like the old shows you watch. The world's changed. Join us. Your skills will help us help others."

There was a gunshot behind me. Jex had taken down the other drone with his pistol, which had followed them to the sister tower. As I watched, he pulled Raven inside the building.

Kieran frowned, displeased. I backed away.

"You think you can escape this?" he asked. "We're linked, you and I."

"There's no 'link'. You killed my daughter."

"You killed one of my men." He stepped forward, and I raised Jex's pistol, which made Kieran pause. "You've sacrificed. I have, too.

I didn't want the surgeries, the intrusions. I had to. I've seen things I'll never forget."

"Stay back. This is your last chance."

"No, Dray. It's yours."

When I didn't respond, he threw a small disk at me and charged. I pulled the trigger again and again. The disk warped my vision, seeming to pull light toward it as it dropped toward my feet, which made me miss. As it fell away, Kieran spun me around, which caused my next two shots to shatter a section of glass wall in front of one of the massive steel cables attached to the platform. Before I could break free, he punched me hard enough to drive me to the ground. I fired again, the bullet glancing off his ribs and making him stumble back.

Fighting through my pain, I got up and lifted my gun, but he hit my wrist and knocked it from my grasp. As my pistol skipped away, he swung at me, but I ducked under and punched him in the ribs as hard as I could, then swiveled as Raven had taught me.

He struck before I could, hitting me so hard I went flying. I just managed to cover my head before I crashed into one of the metal tables, my fall knocking a couple of chairs out of the way.

He'd thrown me over twenty feet.

To my right, the gate blocking the entranceway groaned as the other Agents raised it a few inches.

My body throbbed as Kieran approached. If I didn't get up, it'd be over. My bag was nearby; it'd fallen from my shoulder and landed a few feet away.

Kieran grabbed one of the chairs I'd knocked aside. I stood, grabbed one as well, and brought it up to fight back. He swung his chair, the blow so strong it ripped mine out of my hands.

I was doing this wrong. I needed to play to my strengths. As I thought this, I dropped down—causing Kieran to miss me as he swung his chair a second time—and punched him in the side of the knee as hard as I could. For all his enhanced strength, the angle and pressure point took his feet out from under him. He fell to the ground.

I only had one chance to keep him down. I lunged for my bag, caught the strap, and swung it at his head. The bag hit with a metallic sound, and he collapsed.

I got up and hooked my bag across my body, then reached for a metal chair. As I did, a strident sound came from the gate. Agents had forced it higher. The gap they'd created was almost big enough for them to crawl through.

I turned back to Kieran and found him standing over me, nose broken, blood coating his left temple. Before I could react, he ripped the chair from my grasp, lifted me off my feet, pivoted, and heaved. I arched through the air, over the rest of the tables and chairs, toward the section of wall I'd destroyed.

I was going over the edge.

CHAPTER THIRTY-SEVEN

Unable to stop my flight, I sailed over SunCity's edge, the city of San Francisco — the old ballpark, the buildings, the Bay, and the bridge to Oakland — visible fifty stories below. The telephone-pole-thick, spider-leg-like suspension cable was the only thing in my path. I reached out, desperate to catch it.

I smacked into the corded metal cable at an angle and strained to hold on as my momentum swung me to the side. My legs came around, nothing under me but the dark water of the inlet far below, which was bracketed by walkways and the convention center and apartment buildings, the other H tower close but too far away. My momentum tried to tear me away as the world tilted, my fingers slipping, and then my body swung back towards the platform. I hooked my legs around the cable and held on as I slid down it, the metal scraping my hands.

I dropped below the edge of the suspended promenade.

The two-hundred-foot-long structure was five feet high, consisting of a surface level followed by a grid of metal and carbon fiber, the suspension cable attached to the bottom of the grid via a wide, metal coupling.

I landed inside the V between the cable and the structure, my bad foot wedged in the junction where they were bolted together.

I heard Kieran knock a table out of the way as he headed toward where I'd landed. The city swayed beneath me, the metal coupling the only thing between me and it. Wind battered me as if trying to push me off.

My hands shaking, I unhooked my satchel and opened it. The timer-bombs were on top, both of them, along with the pistol I'd stolen earlier.

I grabbed the Glock and raised up to look over the top of the platform.

The other Agents had joined Kieran, their guns drawn. Kieran was the first to see me. He lifted his gun, but I fired first, clipping his shoulder. The others dropped to the ground.

An Agent to the side shot at me, causing me to duck. As I cringed, more opened fire. I shot back, though I kept my head down as I blindly pulled the trigger twice more. I didn't have many bullets left, maybe four or five. As soon as I was out, they would kill me.

Kieran yelled at the others to move back. He wanted to finish this himself.

I dropped the pistol in my satchel and reached for a timer-bomb. When I removed it, I saw what was underneath: my dark matter sphere. It was dented. It must have struck Kieran's head when I hit him with the bag. It had lasted so long, had stayed with me, my hope for the future.

The Agents fired more shots, bullets pinging off the cable above me.

Remembering when I'd cut into one of the spheres with the harmonic saw, I had an idea.

The ramifications of what I considered ran through my head. The suspension cable arched up and out, connected to the far side of the sister tower and resting inside a support arch that added tension. Didn't matter. Even if I didn't make it, I'd take him out once and for all.

I let go of the cable, which had gouged my hands with rust and grime, grabbed the dented sphere in one hand, and extracted a timer-bomb from my satchel with the other. Using the bomb's adhesive properties, I attached it to the dark matter sphere where it had been dented.

The city wavered far below.

Pushing my body against the side of the structure, I keyed the bomb for seven seconds. I wished I'd said the things I wanted to say to Raven.

It wasn't her fault. I was proud of her.

I allowed myself to think of Talia, remembering her inquisitive face and mischievous smile, and of Mina, though I no longer felt love for her, only contempt and sadness.

I started the timer. *Seven.* Dropped it in my satchel. *Six.* Took the strap — *five* — swung the bag out over the city — *four* — and slung it over the top of the platform. *Three.* It sailed toward where Kieran hopefully was. *Two.* I hugged the cable as tight as I could — *one* — and closed my eyes.

A roar of sound, light, heat, and pressure slammed into me, threw me, the explosion stronger than I'd imagined. I flew out and away, the blast assaulting my ears. I felt myself shoved away, falling —

Then I tilted, there was a jerk, and I shot upwards.

I risked a glance behind me. A forty-foot hole had been carved out of the suspended platform where my cable had been attached. I caught a glimmer of trees knocked down, the restaurant destroyed — and Kieran. He clung to the side of the hole, one arm askew, his leg at an unnatural angle, thrown from the initial site of the blast.

I didn't catch whether he was alive or not as my cable, now free, flung me upwards, thousands of pounds of pressure set loose and launching me like a slingshot. The buildings angled and dropped away as I arced through the air, bits of the structure attached to the metal coupling I clung to breaking free. The cable was shredded above me, gouged from the blast. I plateaued, higher than the top of Heaven Tower's buildings.

Then I started to fall.

The support arch swiveled with the cable as I flew. I sailed out and down, faster, the buildings below growing larger. There was a sudden jerk, and I nearly lost my grip as the cable caught momentarily in the support arch. I hung on, the cable arrested, but then I continued to fall as the cable broke free of the arch, my momentum pulling me downward. My speed grew again as I plummeted toward the city.

I shot past a cluster of apartment buildings toward a street lined with townhomes.

The cable reached its limit, slowing my fall but stretching, the ground approaching, the townhomes growing larger, rooftop furniture and planter boxes becoming visible.

I dropped past the edge of a townhome, toward the street, slowed, then stopped a few feet above the street. Before I could react, the cable lifted me up. My weight pulled me backward, and I smacked against the side of the townhome as I rose. The impact paused my upward flight for a flicker of a second.

I had no choice. I let go.

I fell toward the small patch of yard as the dented metal coupling zipped up and out of sight, catching the top of the townhome and ripping away a chunk of bricks as it disappeared. I dropped a dozen feet, hit the ground hard, and rolled to the side to try to absorb the impact. My foot screamed, my body throbbed, and my head spun from the journey I'd just taken.

I didn't think I'd ever like heights again.

I needed to move. Whether Kieran had survived or not, his employer wouldn't stop. Drones would look for my body. Agents would cordon off the area.

I stood with difficulty. Nothing was broken as far as I could tell, although my foot was on fire. I started forward, limping, and reached the sidewalk. Someone had to have seen me land, though I didn't see anyone. Then I did: five people, grouped at an intersection two blocks over, drawn out by the explosion, staring up at the destruction—and over at me.

I hobbled down the street in the opposite direction. I needed to get away and find Raven.

I reached the end of the block, not sure which way to go. Spotting the top of Heaven Tower past the apartment buildings, I started the other way.

A car approached, gunning past stop signs. I searched for a place to hide, but it was too late. They'd spotted me.

The driver hit the brakes. "Dad!"

Astonished she'd found me, I stopped as Raven lunged out of the driver's seat. She ran over and hugged me, squeezing my ribs, which were sore. Everything was sore. Didn't matter. I held her.

Her voice was thick with panic. "I hoped you were on that cable. I don't know how you did it." She hugged me tighter.

Jex got out as well. "No fuckin' way."

"Are you hurt?" She pulled back to inspect me. "God, don't ever do that again."

"I'll try not to," I said.

Jex looked at me as if I was a ghost.

"I can't believe it, either," I told him. "Thanks for pulling her out of there."

"He's gonna pay for it," she said. I started for the car. "You're hurt."

"I'm fine," I lied.

She angled me to the backseat. "You drive," she said to Jex. Within seconds, he was behind the wheel, and we were in the back. "You need a doctor."

"There's no time."

"He's right," Jex said as he drove us down the townhome-lined streets.

"You don't get a say," she snarled. She turned back to me. "Please?"

My body throbbed, my forearm bled from a cut I didn't remember, and it felt like there were metal spikes in my foot. "We can't risk it."

She looked like she wanted to argue. Instead, she turned to Jex. "Pull over. I'll drive."

She climbed into the front seat as he went around the car, and nearly drove off before he could get in. As she accelerated, he turned to me. "We good now?"

"I owe you one, but we're not 'good'. You lied to her."

"Not lettin' that go, are ya?"

"I told him if he ever drags me off again, we're done," she said.

Tensions were so high, the air seemed to thrum.

"We have to work together, all of us," I said. "Can we do that?"

After a moment, Raven took a breath and nodded. He did as well. "Where should we go?" she asked, her voice slightly calmer.

"Can't go back to Chinatown," he said. "See the smoke? I bet it's crawlin' with Agents."

When I looked out the rear window, I caught the smoke in the distance. Helicopters hovered over the area, and at various spots ahead of us. I suspected they were stationed throughout the city. "We need to leave town."

"Drive straight along the Bay," he said. "We'll follow it—"

"No, there's only one road that way. If they block it, we'll be trapped."

Raven turned right at the next intersection instead. This path gave more options, but we quickly encountered traffic. She was forced to stop at a light. When she did, Jex just sat there, not bothering to hide from the traffic cam.

"Jex, cover your face," I said.

"We changed our looks."

"Which we revealed at the senator's banquet." We even still wore our waiter outfits.

He shielded his face. "Shit."

The light turned green. Raven accelerated, cut around a minivan, and took the curved onramp onto 280. Jex and I hid our faces with our hands as she drove down the interstate.

She glanced at me in the rearview mirror. "If we go to a hospital, we can reprogram your nanobots, get new identities—and get you medicine."

"Too dangerous."

"If Agents show up, we can lose them. Hospitals are mazes."

Jex said, "If we can alter our faces again, we'd disappear."

He was trying to get on her good side. "No," I said.

She gave me a pleading look. "I have to make sure you're OK."

"Protecting you is more important. Take the next exit. We're too exposed."

She switched lanes.

"The Agency's probably pieced together where I landed, the car we're in," I said. "We should dump it, get another."

"God, I hate this feeling," she whispered as she slid down in her seat and picked up speed.

"We need to contact Cole," Jex said.

"No," I said. If we rejoined the rebels, Raven would want to fight. After what we'd discovered, the prospect terrified me. "We need to get the hell out of here."

Raven exited at Junipero Serra Boulevard, and we entered Daly City. I stiffened. Junipero was a wide street with too many cameras.

Before I could say anything, she turned onto a side street, away from the cameras, and drove past colorful, two-story homes.

"The Agency will destroy Chinatown," Jex said, straining to see the still-visible smoke. "I hope Tianshi's OK."

He wasn't as self-centered as I'd thought—the opposite, in fact. He and Raven were fighting for the right things. "What's the government's plan, long-term?" I asked. "They can't lie forever."

"They'll increase their surveillance," she said, "starting with those tiny drones. Our country will become even more of a prison. The worst part is everything seems normal on the surface."

Jex frowned. "What about the refugee camps, the increased fighting?"

"I mean for most people. They go about their lives, unaware they're breathing toxins and being lied to. By the time they find out what's happening, it'll be too late."

We needed to tell the rebels, figure out a plan, though I was torn with keeping Raven safe. "Keep going south. Get us out of the city. Don't stop unless you absolutely have to."

She turned at the next intersection onto a four-lane road. Cameras blanketed the area—at the fast-food restaurants, on the hologram billboards, and around the apartment buildings and other dwellings to either side of us. She must've recognized the danger, for she took the first left into an older neighborhood.

I felt strangely naked without a weapon. I searched my pockets, but all I had were my datarings and Talia's cap. Everything else I'd lost. I slipped on my datarings. They weren't weapons, though, so I searched Raven's bag, which she'd placed behind her seat. Her gun was inside, but it only had three bullets.

I handed it to her. "Keep this on you."

The bag also contained Jex's knit cap and the fragment of Talia's. There should've been three caps, not one. I kept thinking Mina and Talia were with us, that they were nearby or were going to meet us somewhere. For a moment, I understood the allure of the InMemorium software Mina had used—but I could never lie to myself like that.

Raven turned onto a wider street to continue south, and we started down a long hill.

"Dad," she said, her voice tight.

Brake lights filled our windshield; over two dozen cars were stopped in front of us. Police cruisers blocked an intersection six hundred feet ahead, and forced each vehicle into one of three makeshift lanes. I saw the lead vehicle in each lane being inspected, the cars' passengers forced to get out. Cops were scanning their faces, running their IDs.

I knew the purpose of the roadblock.

It was to find us.

Chapter Thirty-Eight

The roadblock before us wouldn't be the only one in the city. The government would have a line of them across the San Francisco Peninsula to cut off our escape.

"What do we do?" Raven asked as she stopped behind the car in front of us. Others stacked up behind us, extending the line.

Parked vehicles dotted the street, while houses—many sharing a wall—sloped down the hill on either side. The damn houses looked ancient, but they hemmed us in.

"Turn 'round," Jex said.

"We'd be spotted."

I leaned forward. "Up ahead. There's a cross street."

Our anxiety increased as we inched closer. If we could get off Hillside—the road we were on—we'd have a chance. If not, we were finished.

We approached the intersection, but a police cruiser blocked Price Street.

"Shit," Raven whispered. She pulled out her gun.

Jex put his hand on hers. "We shoot 'em, they'll know where we are."

We crawled through the intersection, past the cop, our faces hidden. Military helicopters hovered low over the checkpoint—which meant there weren't any drones.

I sat up. "We have a chance."

"Don't be playin' with me," he said.

"They can't fly drones with helicopters so close. We get off this street, we might be able to get away."

"There's nowhere to park," she said.

She was right. "Put the car in autodrive. Send it home, wherever that is." As Jex pulled up the car's nav system, I said, "When we get out, you two go up the street and I'll go the other way."

"We stay together."

"No. We stick out more." And I could be a distraction if our enemies spotted us. "We'll meet behind these buildings, get to the next street, and look for a way past the checkpoint."

"My bag's in the trunk," Jex said.

"Leave it."

"I've got weapons—"

"Can't risk it."

Raven eyed the rearview mirror. "The driver behind us looks distracted."

I risked a glance. The guy stared off, probably watching a show as he waited in line, his car on autopilot. "Let's go."

They got out, as did I. We closed the doors and stepped to the sidewalk in front of a two-building apartment complex, though Raven had to pull Jex with her, away from the trunk. She waved back at our car as if someone was still inside—which I thought was brilliant—then steered him up the street. I turned the opposite way but dropped to a knee and retied my shoe. As I did, I strained to hear sirens, shouts, anything. Raven and Jex angled across the driveway in front of the apartment building to the right, reached the gap between it and the house next door, and slipped through it.

I stood and started down the hill. My limp was worse, my foot stiff, as were most of my muscles. I kept my head down. Cameras were on me, attracted by my movement. If they captured even a partial of my face, they'd ID me. A line of sweat traced my spine.

I angled toward the far side of the apartment building and picked up my pace as soon as I was out of sight, jogging as well as I could to the back, where a solid, eight-foot fence blocked our escape.

Raven and Jex waited for me near a minivan. As I neared, Raven climbed onto the minivan—bumper, hood, roof—then leapt over the fence and disappeared. Jex helped me onto the minivan. I got up to the roof, saw Raven on the other side encouraging me, and leapt. I landed ungracefully, my body flaring as I tumbled in the overgrown grass. I picked myself up as Jex landed beside me.

Grumbling under my breath at his athleticism, and lack of mine, I followed them to the far side of the fenced yard. "You can hotwire any car, right?" I asked him.

"We need one parked on the street." He nodded at the houses across from us. Cameras were attached to most of them, ready to capture our images if we entered their properties.

Raven opened the gate and hid her pistol behind her back. "Let's get farther away."

We hurried to Castle. A police cruiser to the left blocked access to Hillside, so we went right. We cut across the road, moving at a diagonal away from the cop, the move risky but necessary. As we did, a woman walking her dog glanced in our direction.

"You think she'll call the cops?" Raven asked me after we turned the corner onto 2nd Avenue, which had been gentrified with a newer apartment building on one side, in contrast to the old homes on the other.

"Doesn't matter. We appeared in her line of sight. It's all Kieran needs."

Jex approached one of the cars parked on the street but paused. I heard it, too. Sirens. Multiple ones, from both directions.

We started to run.

I saw a storm drain up ahead. "Wait," I called, pointing to it.

"Seriously?" Raven asked.

Amidst the growing sirens, I caught the sound of a helicopter accelerating. I dropped on top of the concrete square beside the storm drain and dug my fingers into the notch of the thick manhole cover. As I lifted it, Jex squatted beside me to help; in seconds, we had the cover propped vertically on the edge of the opening.

The drain was eleven feet deep, the bottom angled downward to direct rainwater—which had increased in frequency and amount the past decade—to connecting drainage pipes. Rebar bent into loops created a crude ladder down the shaft.

The helicopter grew closer, as did the sirens.

I perched on the rim, grabbed the top rung of the ladder, and quickly descended to the bottom, where fiber optic and water-optic cables tied in thick bands stretched from one connecting pipe to the next. Raven climbed down toward me, while above her, Jex twisted his body into the drain and started down, dropping the lid into place — and casting us into near darkness—as the sirens grew louder, the sounds echoing in the concrete-lined space. I removed the cap I'd taken from her bag and handed it over, along with the one I'd carried. Raven and Jex put them on while I held the fragment from Talia's cap to my implant, using a free finger and my other hand to block my ears.

The sirens stopped.

Car doors slammed, and men shouted as they spread out. The helicopter flew past, then Kieran's voice cut through the noise. "They get away, I'm taking it out on every one of you." Whoever's vision we had crossed—probably the dog walker's—must not have shown us climbing into the drain. But he knew we were close.

We couldn't see anything other than a thin bar of sky through the narrow drain opening overhead, but I could tell he was near the manhole cover. I was tempted to take Raven's gun, climb the ladder, and end this—but it would mean the end of us as well.

He grew silent, which was worrisome. We had heated the manhole cover with our body heat when we moved it. Only by a fraction of a degree, but some sensors could pick it up. I didn't know how sensitive the ones on his brow were, but if even the tiniest amount registered, it would draw his gaze down, where he would spot our heat in the drain.

Even if he didn't, we couldn't stay.

The drainage pipes at the bottom of the shaft were four feet in diameter. Like the street above, the pipes stretched away to the north and south, the darkness punctured by shafts of sunlight from other storm drains in the distance, the cables following the pipe.

The cops' shouts continued, their voices sharp.

Careful to keep the cap fragment against my implant, I entered the south pipe. Any sound we made would be magnified, so I avoided the walls as much as possible—which was difficult given the width of my shoulders—and half-crawled toward the next drain area. Raven and Jex followed.

After the near-total darkness of the pipe, the light from the next storm drain made me squint. I wanted to stretch my back but didn't slow, ducking into the next pipe instead. When we reached the third storm drain, the noise from a passing helicopter masked our sounds, which allowed us to move faster.

The next storm drain was longer than the others, narrow but over a dozen feet long. It connected to a larger pipe—although it wasn't large enough to stand in—which cut through the storm drain from the northeast to the southwest and lit in the same manner as the others. The fiber and water-optic cables curved into the northeast portion of this new pipe and disappeared into the dark.

We entered the larger pipe, traversed it northeast for two blocks, then paused inside a larger storm drain. Voices echoed from above, punctuated by the slamming of car doors and trunk lids, the sunlight that angled into the drain tinged with flickering red and blue light.

Raven tensed as the truth hit me: we were directly under the checkpoint. The culvert we'd entered followed Market Street and traced the blockade The Agency had set up. The massive effort to capture us — the police and sensors, helicopters and scanners — was right over our heads. If we were caught, no one would know what happened to us — rebels, Nikolai, the world. We'd be wiped away.

I deserved it, as I'd turned my back on everyone except my family. But Raven didn't. If anything, she deserved recognition, a medal, the thanks of those oblivious to the charade of their lives.

Jex tugged at me to go back the way we'd come. I resisted. We needed to get past the blockade.

The civil engineers would've used the land's natural design to direct rainwater when they installed these tunnels, but they wouldn't have depended on just one path. They would've designed this system to handle hurricane-level rainfall, no matter how improbable the event.

I proceeded into the next tunnel, which ran under Hillside Boulevard. Raven and Jex hesitated, then followed. We moved quietly, passing bits of trash and a couple of decomposed rodents. As we passed a shaft topped by a manhole cover in what I guessed was the middle of the street, there were shouts and the sounds of stunsticks charging. My pace slowed. Those people didn't know why they'd been stopped, didn't know they were no longer free, their digital lives tracked and monitored in every way, and their physical ones betrayed by their own eyes.

They were being harassed because of us.

They remained blind because of us.

Raven put a hand on my shoulder, and I continued forward, my footsteps heavy.

A drainpipe appeared to our right. I steered her and Jex inside and led them under Market Street. We stayed in the pipe until the noise and lights from the roadblock faded, took a smaller pipe that angled away from Hillside, down a side street, then stopped in one of the storm drains. As I strained to listen for threats above, Jex stretched and popped his back. I frowned at him, then climbed the ladder to peer through the drain opening. I could see a gray Nissan sedan parked close by, and the edge of a small house, but nothing else. The street was silent, as if the manhunt had been a figment of my imagination. It seemed safe, but Kieran could be right above me, waiting for us to appear.

Raven and Jex watched from below, their altered faces catching the edge of the sunlight.

No longer bothering to cover my implant, I climbed the last few rungs of the rebar ladder, took a deep breath, and lifted the manhole cover. Sunlight poured in. Fresh air. I stuck my head out. No cops, no Agents. The street appeared empty, though someone could be watching or just glance outside — a retired person, a kid, someone working from home. It only took one.

I climbed out.

Raven started up as I scanned the street again. We were too visible.

She joined me, followed by Jex. I grabbed the manhole cover to hide our tracks. He reached to help, but I shook my head. "Steal the car." I quietly dropped the manhole cover into place and stood.

They were already in the Nissan, which started as I ducked into the back.

"Where to?" he asked as he sped onto Hillside Boulevard and headed away from the checkpoint.

"We need to join up with your friends," I said.

Raven turned in her seat, her eyes hopeful. "Really?"

"We're fighting the same fight." A fight I'd resisted long enough. Holding the cloth to my implant, I gazed at her face. I hoped the rebels were strong enough to keep her safe. I glanced at Jex. "Call Cole."

He patted his pockets. "Oh shit. You have a phone, either of ya?"

We shook our heads. "I got rid of mine in Chinatown, so they couldn't track us," Raven said.

"Mine was in my bag. Dammit. I *knew* I should've grabbed it."

I grimaced. Mine had been in my satchel. "You know his number?"

He nodded as he took off his cap, a slight glow appearing in his eyes, which I caught in the rearview mirror. "Made us memorize it. OK, I found a place to snag a phone."

Burner phones couldn't be bought from a machine. State law. We'd have to interact with a salesperson.

"I can't believe you left it," she said.

His voice grew heated. "Wasn't my choice —"

I interrupted. "Sooner we call, the better."

She glanced out the side mirror at the chaos behind us, the lights from the roadblock reflected in her face. "I know."

Minutes later, Jex cut across traffic and angled into an empty lot. With a slam of the door, he got out, crossed the side street to a cinderblock building smaller than a house, and disappeared around the front. There was only a modest sign to indicate it was a retail store.

In the passenger seat, Raven crossed her arms in annoyance. By their attitudes, whatever had gone down before they found me lingered.

Mina would've known what to say.

Thinking of her didn't help. I didn't know how to face my failure of not seeing the danger, of not stopping her.

Cars passed, occupied by people living lives they thought were their own.

The weight of unspoken words settled on my shoulders. Now that Raven and I were alone, I had a chance to talk to her, tell her things she should know. It was obvious she felt responsible for me, her overprotectiveness a way to make up for everything that had happened. I wasn't sure how to convince her she was wrong. My strength was engineering, not reassurance.

A person meandered along the opposite side of the street, his fingers flickering, connected to a virtual world instead of this one. A bus passed between us, cutting off my view of him. The bus's windows reflected the store Jex had entered, a plain storefront with bars over two small windows and a single-entry door. Just before the bus disappeared, I caught an additional reflected object that had been hidden from our view: a police car, parked on the opposite side of the burner store.

CHAPTER THIRTY-NINE

I jerked forward, nearly drawing level with Raven in the front seat. The bus was gone, but I knew what I'd seen. "Jex is in trouble."

"What? Where?"

"The store. There's a cop inside, maybe two. Their car is on the far side of the building." The police must've decided to stake places we might go. A store like this probably sold contraband on the side, along with the burner phones they advertised.

"We have to save him."

We only had seconds before whoever was inside alerted their precinct—and The Agency. I snatched Jex's cap, which he'd left on the seat. We got out and darted across the street toward the rear of the building. I couldn't see any cameras, but that didn't mean they weren't any.

A ten-year-old, self-driving Ford sedan was parked in the gravel behind the building, the front bumper feet from the back door, which had been propped open, possibly to let in a cross breeze.

I heard someone speaking inside the store. The cop.

Donning Jex's cap, I risked a glance inside, saw display cases on the far side of the store, a few aisles, the front door, the police officer — and Jex, on his knees, hands behind his head.

The cop seemed to be alone.

He stood between us and the front door, surely to keep an eye on both entrances, though his back was partially toward us. Then I realized there was a third person, behind a counter I couldn't see other than its glass front—possibly a clerk. Jex said something to the person and slid a few inches toward the counter, which caused the cop to turn away from us.

A hallway branched off a few feet from our position, between us and the retail area of the store. It was our best option, though I didn't know where it led or how big it was.

With the cop still facing away, I stepped into the doorway and then into the building, trying to watch him and where I was going at the same time. I took three steps and ducked into the side hallway.

It was small, no more than a dozen feet long, its wood-paneled walls sprinkled with papers—old calendars, OSHA notices, and store advertisements—with two clipboards hanging on bent nails. A bathroom was located on one side, a storage closet on the other. Stacks of unmarked boxes filled the far end.

Raven joined me, moving quietly, her gun in her hand. I didn't want a firefight. Enough people had been hurt. Besides, she only had three bullets.

Silently opening the closet door, I found a row of shelves stacked with small boxes and cleaning products. Nothing to threaten the cop with.

I needed to draw him away from Jex.

I steered Raven into the bathroom, mimed for her to stay, and gently shut the door. Then I grabbed a pen that was hooked to one of the clipboards and slipped into the storage closet, which had just enough room. Pressing my back against the plastic shelves, I closed the door most of the way and tossed the pen through the gap I'd left.

It hit the floor.

The cop's voice jumped. "Who's there?"

Seconds later, a shadow entered the hallway. I tensed, ready to lunge—but it wasn't the cop. It was Jex, his hands still behind his head. The cop used him as a shield, pushing him forward. From the cop's stance, I suspected his gun was pressed into Jex's back.

Jex seemed to stare at me through the inch-wide gap. If he knew where I was, so would the cop.

The cop pinned him against the wall next to my hideout. He held him in place, then focused on the closet door, his gun pointed at me as it came closer. I realized he was going to open the door with the barrel. My only chance was to duck under when he opened the door and lunge at him, but I didn't have enough room to crouch.

His gun reached the door's edge.

"Hey," Raven called out. "There's no toilet paper."

The cop spun at the sound, aiming his gun at the bathroom. He took his hand from Jex's back, grabbed the bathroom door handle—

and Jex struck, throwing himself backwards and slamming the cop into the wall. The bathroom door swung open as the cop's arm was shoved forward, exposing Raven.

I sprang from the closet.

I was vaguely aware of her sitting on the toilet, but my eyes were locked on the cop's gun. As he brought it around to shoot Jex, I grabbed it and slammed into both of them. We fell to the floor, my hands wrapped around the barrel. I tried to stay on top as both men rolled under me.

Jex spread his legs to anchor himself as the cop struggled to get free, unable to, though we weren't in a position to do anything other than pin him. I held onto his gun, determined not to let go even though I was at a bad angle, the side of my head pressed into the wall. I jerked the weapon upwards, away from everyone, and tried to wrestle it away.

Raven dropped on top of me and snaked an arm between Jex and the cop, who shouted at us to get off. With a wrench, he knocked me back. Raven and I tumbled off the pile, but I maintained my grip on his gun, my hands sweaty, my knees hitting the floor near his outstretched arm. With our weight gone, he was able to push Jex off with his free hand, but Raven gave a chop to his neck. I hyperextended his arm and punched the back of his elbow. He cried out but kept hold of his gun, until she slammed his head into the paneled wall.

He slumped.

I yanked the gun free and aimed it at the officer, but he didn't move. Keeping the gun on him, I checked the back of his head while Raven unlocked Jex's cuffs. No blood. She hadn't hurt the man too badly. His bodycam was unplugged, which she must've done during the fight.

"Everything OK?" someone called out.

Shit.

I got to my feet and entered the store proper. A clerk with gray hair parted to one side stood behind the counter, his eyes wide. Scars in the shape of tribal art graced his arms.

I aimed the pistol at him.

He raised his hands. "I didn't see anything."

I motioned with the pistol, taking advantage of his assumption it would work for me. "Look down."

He dropped his gaze, placing his hands on the glass counter, symbols of dead societies angled down. "I didn't memorize your face. We're cool."

Raven and Jex appeared from the back. Jex walked past me to grab a burner phone.

"Where's the cop?" I asked.

"Cuffed and stuffed in the bathroom," he said, smiling.

Raven wasn't. "Let's get it and go."

The clerk's head jerked up when he heard her voice. "What —?"

I shoved the pistol at him. "Don't look at her."

Frowning, he lowered his gaze.

The store felt like a cage. "Come on," I told Jex.

He set a burner phone on the counter and wiggled a tube at me. "For your foot."

Biomaterial. I didn't think it'd help, but I stuck out my leg anyway. What I really needed was to rebreak the damn bones. He jabbed the needle through my shoe and dumped the contents.

The clerk glanced at us. "You're freedom fighters, aren't you? I am, too. Well, I want to be. I can help."

Even though he was a decade older than me, he seemed innocent. I'd forgotten that still existed. Or maybe everyone living a normal life seemed that way now. "No," I said.

"You're running. Take my car."

"What's in it for you?" Raven asked.

"I don't need to explain, and you don't have time." The way he spoke, it wasn't innocence. He had a quiet nobility.

"You'll get thrown in jail."

"I have no problem making the sacrifice. We don't help each other, we don't deserve to be here."

The way he carried himself, what he offered, scratched at my skepticism.

He held out his hand to Jex. "Give me your keys. I'll hide your car." When Jex did, the clerk said, "You should get going."

"The police will chase you," Raven said. "They might hurt you."

"I've had worse. Go. I need to lock up."

* * *

Jex drove, though Raven reached over to steer while he pried open the hard-plastic packaging to get to the burner phone. He dropped the plastic in his lap, turned on the phone, and retook command of the

276

steering wheel. Raven rested her hand on his thigh as he dialed Cole's number before she pulled away.

I looked out the back window. A dot in the sky grew bigger and coalesced into a government helicopter. A second came from the west, both zeroing in on our last location. That clerk wouldn't last long. I wondered how long we would.

Jex spoke a passcode, waited, then said, "Sir, callin' for extract... yes, we've survived so far...thank ya, sir."

I wasn't thrilled to rejoin the rebels, even though it had been my suggestion.

He grew quiet, nodded, then hung up.

"What'd he say?" Raven asked, though she didn't look at him. She'd taken her cap off, as had I.

Jex let go of the steering wheel to snap the phone in half. "Gave me directions. It should take 'bout a half-hour."

In a kind voice, she said, "You should trust me."

It took him a block to cave. "We're goin' to Foster City. South of here. I can give ya the address."

"That's OK." Her hand returned to his thigh.

"You're right, I should trust you. So, to tell the truth...I'm not a year older than you. I'm a year younger."

She pulled her hand away.

He shifted, clearly struggling to find the right words. Before he could, she whacked his stomach. "No more lies. Ever."

"Yes, ma'am."

Across the bottom of my vision public announcements appeared, about us. They listed our names and descriptions, along with a warning that we were armed.

Jex sped up. He'd seen it, too.

We slid low in our seats, Raven using her hair to hide her face, Jex using his cap, me using the car itself. The neighborhoods passed in a blur, half shielded by the car door. "Stay down," he warned as police lights brushed our vehicle.

When we passed Millbrae Avenue, I spotted cop cars—and a line of trucks—approaching from the west. They were going to form another checkpoint. If we'd been slower, we would've been trapped.

I ducked lower. Jex accelerated.

A few blocks later, I peered out. We'd entered a mixed-use area with a hodgepodge of businesses, warehouses, and homes, the gleam of downtown's skyscrapers far to the north, leaving only the pitted and the stained.

Every mile should've given me relief, but we remained in mortal danger. Maybe always would be.

He turned onto a wide boulevard. In the distance, a bridge rose. It'd be guarded, blocked.

Raven saw it, too. "Tell me we're not going that way."

"No," he said. He took a right and accelerated, the bridge disappearing behind us as he followed a curved road that descended into a neighborhood of townhomes, the buildings undulating to either side, identical structures with basement-level garage doors and steep front stoops. They had either been abandoned or condemned, even though they only looked about twenty years old. The buildings were a strange bluish-gray, as were the sidewalks and driveways, the grass a slightly different shade.

An industrial byproduct had rendered the area uninhabitable.

One of the garage doors stood open. Jex pulled into the garage— and my feeds winked out.

He killed the engine, and a heavy silence settled. When I exited the car, I noticed an eighteen-inch-cube-sized device affixed to the ceiling. I wondered if that was what had blocked my feed.

He led us through a door into the dark basement, empty even of rodents, and across to an exit into the backyard. A deck, thicker than it needed to be, jutted over us.

He shut the sliding-glass door and raised his hands. My back stiffened. We weren't alone.

I had no weapon, nothing. I pulled Raven behind me. "Jex."

"Wait."

An electronic clicking sound emitted to our left.

He dropped his hands. "This way."

My implants flickered back online as we followed.

The overhead structure extended for three houses, one deck seamlessly connected to the next before ending at a walkway that ran between two of the homes. Jex pressed against the wall, then motioned for us to follow as he walked under a makeshift cover, no more than three feet wide, that stretched to the next deck. Film arched overhead, some sort of augmented photo paper that shielded us from satellites.

My tension didn't ease when we reached the next deck. We were outside in a strange area. If Kieran found us, there'd be no way to protect Raven.

We reached the end of the townhomes. Instead of continuing past them into the open, Jex led us into the basement of the last house, where a tunnel had been dug into the floor. We climbed down and followed it underneath the ghost town, globe lights illuminating when we neared. We continued for five minutes, maybe ten.

Stairs had been carved into the end of the tunnel. I followed him up the steps, Raven behind me. We ascended into an empty basement, then up another set of stairs to a dust-layered kitchen—where Cole waited.

His expression hardened when we appeared. "Arms out."

Jex held out his arms to either side. Raven and I followed suit, and Cole ran a scanner over us. "Is it smart to be here?" I asked as he pulled Raven's gun—our only weapon, as I'd left the cop's pistol at the shop—and set it on the island. "You don't know how deep this all goes."

"Oh, I know."

He scanned me a second time. I was too aware of the last time he'd been this close. Past him, a sniper rifle leaned against the island. He'd watched us since we'd stepped out of the first townhome. I suspected he had someone else watching us now.

Satisfied, he stepped back. "Nice faces. I admit, I didn't believe you'd survived this long. Thought you'd been turned. Must've beat some sense into you."

Jex said, "It's good to see ya, sir. We're ready to skeet and shoot."

Cole frowned at him. "You ignored orders. Why didn't you contact me sooner?"

"The orders didn't fit."

"Remember your place."

"Where's the rest of the squad?" Raven asked.

"You two and Bhungen are all that's left. The rest paid the price for your family's visit."

I told myself not to let him bait me.

He led us into the living room, where blue-gray dust coated the front window.

"What is this place?" she asked.

"A failed attempt to create a second Silicon Valley after the

279

computer companies moved to Omaha. They managed to sell a few units, luring people with cheap rent on tech space, but when the battery factory opened west of here, the whole place grew toxic."

"So, this as a safehouse?"

"Drop-off location. Scouting robots make sure the area's secure before we use it. This'll be the last time, though. Agents will be crawling all over this place within a day."

His tone bothered me. It was condescending. "We discovered the truth about Congress," I said.

"Don't get cocky that you worked it out. You're not out of the woods yet." He led us to an attached garage where an unmarked van waited.

"How did you survive Free Isle?"

"I'm a fighter. You're lucky I came for you. You cost me most of my squad."

"Did Whittock make you?"

"He's dead."

I'd feared that was the case. "So, you're the leader now?"

"They chose someone else. Besides, I'm not a leader. I'm a commander." He looked at Raven, who'd gone quiet. "You're not still mad, are you? I'm sure you'll show your worth."

Jex stepped between them. "She already has. She's a big reason why we survived."

"Stop sticking up for her."

"We made it by bein' a team."

"You think you've 'made it'? The national guard's blocked every highway and bridge, cops have checkpoints in a line across the peninsula, and search 'bots are scouring the woods in case you tried to run on foot, all with overlapping drone, helicopter, and satellite surveillance to find you. They're even installing DNA scanners. I've never seen them move so many assets to capture one person."

"Three," Jex corrected, but was ignored.

"The scanners are the biggest threat. You can alter your faces but not your DNA. You come near one, they'll ID you."

He opened the van's rear doors and felt along the inside corner. There was a click, and the metal floor angled up to reveal a compartment just big enough to fit the three of us. He could see by our expressions we'd guessed his plan.

"You really think this will work?" I asked.

"It's sealed and lined with sensor blockers. They shouldn't detect you, or your body heat, though if they scan repeatedly, enough anomalies will appear that'll alert them." He touched the side of the van. Words and graphics formed for a laundry service. "I'll change it to a recycling company after we get past the checkpoint. If we get past."

We'd be completely in his hands. I didn't think he'd deceive us, but we'd cost him soldiers — and he'd lied to us before. It made me wonder where his group had obtained the implants they gave us, whether it'd been from battle, black market, or betrayal. We didn't have a choice. Not with him, nor our mode of transportation. But I did have a say.

"I'll do it. I'll join your cause. But only if you keep Raven safe. Agree, and I'll make whatever you want — weapons, the bike, anything."

She was shocked. "What? No. I'm going to fight."

Cole laughed. "'Safe'? I thought you learned. Nowhere is safe."

"Then get her as far from here as possible. Canada. Central America."

"She can take care of herself."

I couldn't look at her. "I won't let anything happen to her."

"Like your other girl? It won't bring her back." When I didn't respond, he said, "Stop carrying the guilt. It makes you weak. We need everyone for what we're planning."

"Not Raven."

"You don't make that choice. We're attacking tomorrow night."

That caught us by surprise. "That's still on?" I asked.

He pulled out a datacast and projected a satellite image of the Pacific coastline onto the garage ceiling. "These are our targets." Circles appeared around tiny dots that lined the shoreline, clustered primarily alongside the major U.S. cities. "The desalinization plants. It's where they broadcast their lies. The Agency's focused on San Fran looking for you, so our teams will hit the plants in L.A., San Diego, Portland, and Seattle. We'll hit here too, using drones we've developed, though they'll probably get shot down. Even if that happens, this is an opportunity we can't pass up. Almost everyone on the West Coast will see the truth."

"What about everywhere else?"

"If the truth doesn't spread, we'll hit the East Coast, then the Gulf, area after area until it can't be contained."

"We should find where they broadcast from. They'd have a central spot hardwired to their broadcast antennas to avoid interference. If we figure out the location—"

"Even if we did, the place would be fortified with their most lethal defenses. We'd be slaughtered. The plants are the only way. We'll knock them out simultaneously using every soldier we have. Including you."

"Not Raven," I said. "She stays out of it."

She took my arm. "I want to help."

I avoided looking at her. "It's my price."

She crawled into the hidden space, rejecting me. Jex hesitated, as if wanting to say something, then followed her. Cole waved at me to get in. He didn't say he agreed but didn't have to. I'd won.

Jex maneuvered Raven to take the middle of the carpet-lined space and laid down to her left. I crawled in and laid to her right. She didn't look at me, turning her back and clinging to him instead, but I could feel her fury.

Cole shut the trap floor, sealing us in and cutting our feeds.

Within seconds, we started to move. I had no sense of the route he took, what was going to happen, whether we'd make it through. The carpet and layers of material that had been installed to block our signals and heat signatures muffled much of the road noise. We could've talked if we wanted.

No one said a word.

I thought about Cole's statement. Talia had been stronger than me, more open, more fearless. Better suited for the life we now lived. I felt like I'd taken the spot meant for her. If I let go of the guilt, I'd be letting go of her.

The van slowed, then stopped. We'd reached the bridge. We heard voices, then the driver's door slammed. Raven tensed beside me.

The voices encircled our vehicle. Cole responded, his words muffled.

This was taking too long.

The rear doors opened. I caught parts of sentences, the government forces that guarded the bridge demanding information on the fictional company Cole worked for, the deliveries he claimed to be making. They could check his story, discover it was fake.

The voices grew quiet.

We should've gone a different route.

Seconds later, the rear doors closed and Cole climbed back into the driver's seat. All three of us exhaled, though as we started forward, my relief was tempered. We were being taken toward a destination I didn't know, led by a man I didn't trust.

CHAPTER FORTY

Twenty minutes later, bright light pierced the secret compartment as Cole lifted the van's false bottom. "Get out."

Raven climbed out first, not looking at me. Jex followed. As I stepped onto the asphalt, my feeds came back online.

Cole had driven us to a parking lot inside a large park, the manicured land stretching away from us toward Oakland, which rose to the west. We must've driven straight through the city after we crossed the Bay. To the east, a thick forest pressed against the lot, the only opening a dirt road that disappeared into the forest's depths.

Three other vehicles occupied the parking lot, later-model Jeep transports, hardier and bigger than SUVs. The name of a tour agency adorned their sides, but I knew that was a cover, just as I knew the vehicles had holographic camouflage, heat-signature masking, noise suppression, and other gear.

A half-dozen men and women in forest gear loaded containers into two of the three transports — weapons and supplies. We'd coordinated with a resupply run. The third vehicle was for the troops — and us. Rebel guards had spread out, three of them, focused primarily to the west, while the others loaded the two Jeeps.

Alerts flashed along the bottom-third of my vision. They listed all three of us, with post-plastibot pictures of our faces. The warnings offered $2,000,000 rewards.

A rebel in civilian clothes climbed behind the wheel of Cole's van and drove off. I watched the van, unsure I'd made the right choice, as the driver followed the road, which curved in an arc along the edge of the large meadow to the exit.

"We'll go as soon as they finish," Cole told me.

There were still at least twenty containers and a dozen long boxes to load. "I'll help."

"You'll get in the way." He smirked when I fidgeted. "I saw it. Two mil's pretty tempting."

Raven seemed as anxious as I was. She and Jex stood off to the side in a heated discussion. I was surprised at how much he seemed to be standing up to her.

"Once we reach base, you won't have time to worry," Cole said. "You'll be too busy getting my squads ready for the assault, ninety-six men and women. They have weapons but need explosives, shields, and any gadgets you can put together. You better be up for it."

One of the scars he'd tried to erase ran from his ear to his jaw. It was mostly gone, but in the afternoon light, it was noticeable. "Why aren't you the leader? I don't buy that you didn't want it."

He lost a little of his attitude. "An innocent died because of me, a pregnant woman. Why didn't you take control of your 'Gang of Five'?"

"I don't crave the spotlight."

"You played a big part, though, right? Or was that marketing bullshit?"

"I made their theories reality." Most of them. "Why do you ask?"

"Making sure this was worth it. I'm not convinced."

"Put me on your assault team. I'll show you."

He indicated my foot. "You're injured."

"The bone needs to be rebroken. We do that now, I'll be ready by tomorrow night."

He smiled and started away. "When we reach base, I'll break it myself."

The first transport vehicle started up and took the dirt road into the woods. The remaining supplies were less, no more than a half-dozen long boxes and almost as many containers.

Raven was alone. She'd approached the transport vehicle but didn't climb in, taking in the scene—and me—instead. We'd been through too much to have tension between us. Her mix of Mina's need to protect others and my rebellious nature had taken us to a place I never would've expected. Yet it had opened my eyes to the truth.

The second Jeep started up and drove off. Only a couple of long containers remained, which would go in the back of our vehicle.

I'd talk to Raven after we got to the rebels' camp, before the assault. We had a lot to air out.

Cole's team filed into the transport. He waved me over as Jex followed Raven into the vehicle, motioning toward the last containers.

As I headed toward him, I heard it. Drones. And something else.

I scanned the skies to the west — and almost didn't believe my eyes. Hoverbikes. Three of them. Coming fast.

The drivers had silver hair.

Cole saw them, too.

He ran to the transport calling my name, but there was only one way to protect her. "Get Raven out of here," I shouted.

"We can—"

"They'll outrun you. Go! Keep your promise."

Raven tried to climb over Jex to get out of the transport. I shook my head, and Cole pushed her back as he climbed in.

"*Dad*," she yelled.

The first hoverbike ripped over our heads while the other two arced to either side. Across the park, two cop cars and a government sedan entered the grounds, along with a military-transport vehicle and a truck with an array of weapons that jutted from its roof.

Four drones came at us.

"Go," I shouted one more time. Without looking back, I ran to the containers. Inside the first I found high-powered machine guns; the second held grenades, C-4, and other explosives.

Raven yelled again, her cry swallowed by the roar of the Jeep's engine as it drove into the forest.

I grabbed a machine gun, extra clips, and five grenades, shoving the clips and grenades into a sack that was in the second container. I needed to distract the Agents, give her and the others time to get away.

Hooking the sack over my shoulder, I ran toward the invaders. I didn't know how they had hoverbikes — they shouldn't exist. The only one that did was the two-seater I'd left in Nikolai's secret storage area. These were one-seaters.

The first hoverbike came back around. I lifted my machine gun but froze when I saw Kieran's face, his damaged arm encased in a black sleeve. My anger surged, and I fired a short burst but missed as he flew past.

He wasn't the only danger.

Quickly gauging The Agency forces, I started running toward the military trucks, which had ignored the curved road and drove directly across the park grounds toward me, the weapons truck decelerating.

The land was mostly level, though there were small hills to my right and a creek bed nearby to my left. Clusters of trees dotted the manicured lawn, some shading picnic tables and grill pits.

Gunfire erupted above and behind me. Kieran. I swiveled and returned fire as he flew past, but missed him.

The four drones banked toward me. At the same time, a hoverbike swooped around from the opposite direction. I fired at the silver-haired driver, then jerked back as gunfire from my left nearly hit me. Kieran, coming in for the kill, slowing to line up his shot.

I was trapped. I aimed at him, though I knew I was an easy target. Shots erupted —

But they weren't aimed at me. Bullets pinged off Kieran's bike, then off the second hoverbike's hull. Cole stood forty feet away as he fired at the Agents, a machine gun in his hand and a camouflaged pack on his back.

I watched, stunned, as he shot down the second hoverbike, the Agent disappearing in a flash of fire as the fuel tank exploded, then I lifted my gun and fired at Kieran. He banked as he flew past me, but I hit him in what looked like the upper back. He jerked as he sailed over the forest and angled out of sight among the trees. Seconds later, I heard a crash.

I nodded at Cole as he jogged toward me, glad to see him.

There was one more bike out there. The hoverbikes could be made better, more responsive. I'd redesign them so a rider could manually cut and reestablish gravity at a moment's notice to create quick stops, make them harder to hit.

A strange whine pierced my ears.

Cole rushed forward and tackled me, sending us over the edge of the creek bed and into the water. Doused and confused, I sat up as the whine became a high, throbbing sound, the noise laced with cracks and crashes, and the creek rose around us, water droplets shaking in the air before falling when the sound stopped.

Kieran's forces had used a sonic cannon on us.

Half-deaf from the blast, I crawled to the top of the creek bed. The cannon jutted out from the side of the weapons truck, which was approximately fifty yards away. Everything from it to the forest behind us had been flattened: grass, trees, even a picnic table.

Gunfire raked the ground in front of me as the last hoverbike flew past. The drones circled overhead like vultures.

Cole and I scrambled out of the creek bed and ran to where a cluster of four thick trees had been knocked over by the sonic blast and laid on top of each other. The hoverbike driver took another pass, shooting at us, and we returned fire before ducking behind our makeshift shield.

"What the hell were you thinking?" Cole demanded.

"They would've caught us."

More gunfire came from the other side of the shield. "When this is over, I might shoot you myself."

The sonic cannon revved up and unleashed a blast that slammed into our shield. The energy lifted the trunks and shoved them toward us, the wood splintering from the assault, but the trunks managed to stay intact. I doubted they would survive another assault.

Cole jabbed a finger at the hoverbike as it came around again. "You see why you're so important?"

"We need to destroy it so they don't reverse-engineer them."

"Take out your company then. Where do you think they came from? Hell, who do you think footed your R&D?"

A disturbing thought had plagued me about how the government maintained their lies. If what Cole said was true, then my thought was true as well.

More bullets pelted the ground around us, only they didn't just come from the hoverbike. The drones had joined the attack. Cole and I shot back, using the trunks as cover, but we were pinned down.

He squatted. "Cover me."

I fired at the drones, the hoverbike already past, as he removed a box from his pack and set it on the ground. When he flipped open the lid, small, black metal objects bristling with protrusions shot into the air. They were "pit bulls", which I'd heard of but never seen before. They expanded in a cloud, then swarmed over the military-grade drones and destroyed them. When they finished, they fell to the ground, expended, the disintegrated remains of the drones pelting the grass around them.

Cole donned his pack. "We blinded them for a second, so use it. I'll deal with the soldiers. You handle everything else."

"Everything else?"

"This was your plan, Einstein."

He ran to the left, leapt over a narrow section of the creek bed, and angled toward the far side of the troop transport, which had parked away from the cannon and was disgorging men.

The sonic cannon revved up again, only instead of aiming for him, it went for our shield. I ran away from the trunks, my foot sending spikes of pain. Before I got more than a few steps, the cannon fired, the blast reducing the trunks to splinters. I stayed on my feet, having avoided the blast radius, but another danger approached: the two police cruisers and an Agency vehicle, racing along the park's main road toward me, engines straining, The Agency vehicle in the lead.

I unhooked my sack, pulled out a grenade, yanked the pin, and heaved.

The grenade hit the ground a dozen yards from the lead car, bounced, then landed by the sedan's front right tire and exploded, the blast and the car's momentum throwing The Agency vehicle up and to the right. It landed on top of the nearest cruiser. The driver of the other cop car swerved and crashed into a nearby tree.

Gunfire alerted me to Cole's assault. In seconds, half the soldiers dropped, the rest forced to use the transport as cover.

Overhead, the remaining hoverbike slowed as the driver surveyed the scene. He and I made eye contact before he took off and swooped over the cannon. I knew what he was going to do before he started to curve back around. He was reorienting himself, aiming for the forest.

Raven.

I brought my gun up, but he flew past before I could fire. He'd find Raven and the rebels. As he soared over the shattered remains of our makeshift shield, I had one last chance. A risk.

I turned, slinging my machine gun over my shoulder, and ran toward the cannon. As I did, I pulled out three grenades, the most I could hold in my hand, dropped my sack, and yanked their pins.

The cannon revved up.

I threw the grenades as hard as I could, but angled them toward the upper edge of the blast radius, then leapt to the side.

The cannon fired.

In a flash, I saw the grenades thrown backward by the sonic blast, the cannon launching them after the hoverbike and catching me while I was midair. A force I'd never felt before hurled me across the park, twenty yards, forty, sixty, past the parking lot, the force fading but still pushing me—

A burst of pain took me.

CHAPTER FORTY-ONE

I woke in a strange room.

It was windowless, the walls brown, a couple of generic paintings the only embellishment: mountains shrouded in fog in one and a lake that could've been anywhere in the other. The door at the far end of the room was open, though only a white wall was visible past it—what I assumed was a hallway. The floors were hardwood.

Everything had a dreamlike quality to it, like I'd been drugged.

After a few moments, my vision improved, the dreamlike edge fading. I was in a hospital bed hooked to a heart monitor. A tray containing a thermometer, bandages, and skin-patches rested on a stand pushed to the side. A small dresser stood in a far corner.

I wasn't in a hospital, though. The walls and floor were wrong, the dresser the kind found in homes, not medical centers. The bed was less sophisticated than the one Raven had been in, with only a thin sheet over me. And instead of a hospital gown, I wore the waiter outfit from the senator's banquet.

I was sore but could move. I had my wallet, still wore my datarings. My machine gun was propped against the far wall by the door.

I had to be at the rebel camp. Cole must have saved me.

Sitting up, I braced for my head to throb, but it didn't.

Without a window, I had no idea where the camp was situated. That made me unsettled, as did being alone. Where was Raven?

As if in response to my thought, I heard her in the next room talking to someone. "I'm awake," I called out, my voice weak. I guess I'd been knocked out harder than I'd thought. I checked for bruises and discovered a thick bandage around my head.

The voices grew in the other room. "Time to go, everyone," Cole said. "Our attack starts in exactly two hours."

I threw aside the sheet.

He raised his voice. "Dray, you coming?"

He must've been told my injuries weren't serious, and they weren't. I'd been knocked unconscious, but could get up. Fight. He wouldn't sympathize that I was sore as hell. "Yeah, I'm coming."

I climbed out of bed, but the feeling that something was off returned. I heard more voices outside the room, men and women preparing to leave. I stepped forward but paused. My foot felt better—from Cole's announcement, I realized I had slept an entire day, so it made sense—but there was still a twinge. The bones hadn't been reset. Why didn't he do it while I was out? I was less effective this way.

It seemed whoever fixed me had only focused on my head, which felt fine, if a little warm. My whole body felt warm. So why was I wearing a bandage? Raven and Jex knew I still had nanobots in my system. Where the hell were they, anyway?

"Raven?"

"Come on, we're leaving," she called from what sounded like the hallway.

The voices. They were off.

I closed my eyes. "Raven?"

No answer.

I shuffled my good foot forward. The floor didn't feel like hardwood.

I heard her again. "Dad, we have to go—"

Sounds of gunfire cut her off. "They found us," someone cried.

I opened my eyes. My instincts roared at me to rush forward, but I stopped myself, although the effort was so difficult it hurt. I strained to make out what was happening, but couldn't see anything other than the narrow patch of hallway.

I listened harder.

The noises sounded as if the attack came from just one targeted spot, as if I were listening to a movie broadcast in the next room. No depth. No vibrations in the floor.

A faint breeze touched my face. That shouldn't be. There weren't any windows.

My paranoia, honed by however many days we'd been on the run, fought my need to protect my daughter. I dug my fingers into my palms.

If this wasn't real, if I'd been captured by The Agency, they would've killed me — or locked me in a hole somewhere. Not put me in a fake camp somewhere, to...what? Reveal things I didn't know?

My urge to leave, to get to Raven, to understand what was going on, was so strong I continued toward the door but dropped to my knees. I didn't trust any of this.

Cautiously, I crawled forward. After a couple of feet, my hand went through the floor — and I started to pitch forward into what was empty space. I jerked back, scraping my wrist on a rough edge as I heaved my whole body backward. An edge I couldn't see.

I didn't understand.

The breeze came again. I closed my eyes and tuned into my other senses, like I'd taught Talia to do. The floor under me felt like concrete, not dirt. I thought I felt the ground sway a little.

I was on the edge of a building. There was no other explanation. I hadn't gotten away. I'd been captured. And blinded. My heart pounding, I scooted away from the edge. I stopped, though, not sure what was behind me. I didn't know what was real.

I remembered the number of suicides the last few years, especially in California. The notoriety I had from being one of the Gang of Five. The Agency wanted me to go away, to become a nonissue, to kill me — but without making me a martyr. If they made it look like I took my own life, I'd become a pathetic footnote instead of a rallying cry.

The sounds of battle continued, and Raven screamed. It all seemed to come from a speaker, set high and to the side. The realization helped me ignore the distraction, but that was the only victory. Everything I saw was fake, except for the bed and maybe the heart monitor. I'd almost been tricked into falling.

It shouldn't be, though.

The bandage.

I worked my fingers under the gauze wrapped around my head. The implant was different. The edges were thicker and rough. They'd replaced my implant and were streaming images to me, using my lenses against me. I tore off the bandages, not that it helped. I couldn't see past the image projected onto my lenses that masked what was really there.

The power my enemies wielded was stunning. No matter how smart I was or what I accomplished, no matter what weapons I carried, it wasn't enough.

I had to get off this roof, ledge, whatever I was on. Kieran was watching, I was sure of it. Would he come push me off, now that I'd discerned the truth? I crouched lower. He could be an inch from my face, and I wouldn't know it.

They wouldn't let me go free.

There had to be a camera somewhere, probably multiple ones. They would've wanted to show me alone as I walked off the ledge.

I forced myself to stand. No one was going to rescue me. No one knew where I was.

The sounds of battle—and Raven's screams—increased. Even though it was fake, it pained me to turn away.

The wall past the bed was the way out, unless I was actually on a wide ledge, and it also led to my death. I didn't think so. It made more sense to put me on a rooftop, to proclaim I'd killed Talia, tried to hurt Mina, and took my own life out of despair. Thinking of them triggered a sadness that nearly debilitated me.

I walked past the bed, approached the wall, and lifted my hands. My fingers met no resistance as they slid through the illusion, the wall seeming to swallow them. Taking a deep breath, I stepped forward, went through the wall—

My vision went white: pure, solid, every molecu-pixel that covered my lenses blasting my retinas and filling my view. I swiped the air as if I could clear it away, but nothing changed. I continued forward, hoping to escape the light I couldn't look away from, then tripped on something and fell. I landed hard, smacking both elbows and nearly my face.

The voices from the speaker grew in simulated fear and pain.

A light breeze blew over me. I had to think, but it was difficult with the relentless light blinding me. Shutting my eyes seemed to intensify the assault.

I felt grit on my palms, like concrete dust. I sniffed the ground. It smelled of freshly-cured concrete. I suspected I was on a half-built building. I could walk straight off the edge in any direction.

I didn't know if I was in Oakland or San Francisco, but it didn't matter. I had to find a stairwell—which would be unfinished, probably open to the other floors, a maze of ways I could fall—and get away from here.

With an effort I stood and stepped forward, hands splayed. I didn't even know how narrow the building was. I could fall into an empty space. I took another step, then another, each one a gamble. The breeze changed slightly, nearly imperceptibly, but I reached to my right and waved my arm. Another step, and when I waved again, my hand scraped concrete. A wall of some sort. My fears, which had been screaming at me, settled for the briefest of moments. The wall could be connected to a stairwell. I felt along it until I came to an end, then stepped forward as I held onto the edge—but there was no step.

I jerked my weight back as I gripped the wall, slipped on the raw floor, and fell to the floor, nearly tumbling into the empty space before me, the lip cutting into my thigh when I landed. With a grunt, I wrenched my body back. My wounded foot flared, my fears roared, and sweat coated my fingers as I held onto the wall.

It hadn't been a stairwell. It had been an elevator shaft.

My body trembled as I got to my hands and knees. The stairwell would be nearby—but so would other shafts.

I told myself I wasn't going to end like this. The faintest of moans came from the shaft, a warning I'd missed. With the white light blasting my vision, I crawled forward, using my hands to check the path ahead, to inspect the shafts I passed, a second one, then a third. The moaning faded, and I stopped. At first there was just a wall to my right, then a cutout. The acoustics were different.

I reached out, down, and found a step. It extended about four feet to either side, open on both ends.

Sitting on the top step, I reached out, my hands flailing, and my knuckles banged against a metal railing. I gripped it tight. With a breath that was supposed to be calming but wasn't, I used the railing to stand and started down.

My movements were slow. If there was any debris, I could trip and fall, and with my sight blocked, I wouldn't be able to catch myself. The inner part of the stairwell was open, no railing or anything.

I reached the first landing. Ten steps. I scooted across the landing, located the next railing, and continued down. Navigating the stairwell consumed my focus, tense for an obstacle or danger that would dislodge me. But underneath the focus, my anger grew. It wasn't enough that The Agency would've killed me. They would've made Raven question why I'd committed suicide, a mindfuck that would've haunted her.

They'd pay for that.

I lost count of the floors I passed. It was more than forty—maybe a lot more. I traversed the next landing and reached for the railing to continue down, but there wasn't one. I cautiously moved forward, expecting to encounter steps, but the floor remained level. I'd made it to the bottom. A part of me wanted to fall to my knees, but my anger wouldn't let me, and I still couldn't goddamn see.

I exited the stairwell and listened as I shuffled my feet. The acoustics reinforced my conclusion that I was at a construction site. The Agency would've left a way for me to get into the site—a door unlocked, a gate open—as part of the suicide story they would've spun.

The lobby had to be nearby, the front entrance past it.

I pushed forward, hands before me to search for danger. After a dozen steps, I tripped and fell into a stack of coiled electrical wire. A few feet past that, I nearly hit a column. A pipe of some sort snatched my footing. I fell again, hard.

Outside, a car passed.

I got up, the light in my eyes not only blinding me but screwing with my equilibrium. I felt nauseous. Heat began to warm my hands and face. Sunlight. I'd found the entrance.

I made it to a fence, which rattled when I grabbed it. It felt loose to my left—an opening. No one called out to me, no one stopped me. Of course. They would've been witnesses. This was the weekend, so no one was here.

My hand encountered a gap in the fence. I stepped through it and onto what I thought was a sidewalk. Without my vision, I didn't know which way to go. But I couldn't stay here.

A car passed in front of me, heading from left to right.

I turned to the right and started down the sidewalk, but resisted the urge to hold my hands out in front of me. I focused on where I stepped, alert for clues I was about to walk into an intersection.

Another car passed.

I couldn't go on like this. They would come for me. I had no resources, no weapons, no way to fight back. It was as if they'd already killed me. I just wasn't dead yet.

I smelled body odor. I slowed and lifted my hands defensively. The odor grew stronger, joined by footsteps, and someone passed me. I veered to the right to get out of the way and nearly smacked into the construction fence.

More footsteps grew behind me.

Using the fence as a guide, I walked away from whoever was approaching. He or she could be an Agent or cop—maybe even Kieran, if he'd somehow survived the park—someone who would cuff me or kill me.

A conversation drifted on the air up ahead. Two men were talking about preseason football, oblivious to my struggle.

I hurried toward them.

I stopped before I reached them and took on the slack zombie look of someone staring at content on their lenses. After a moment, their voices began to fade. I took a step forward and felt the sidewalk angle down. I was at a curb.

They were crossing the street.

Using their voices as a guide, I hastened after them, but discovered too late that my path was off. I tripped on the opposite curb, stumbled forward—

And someone grabbed me.

CHAPTER FORTY-TWO

Hands seized me. "Watch where you're going," a man said.

The panic I'd tried to restrain flared as bright as the light that blinded me. I fought free of his grasp and swung.

"What's wrong with you?" he asked.

I stumbled back, my fists raised. "What do you want?"

"For you to not fuck my shit up. You 'bout crashed into my table."

"Sorry. Didn't, uh—can you tell me where the nearest bus stop is?"

"You kiddin'? It's right there."

"I mean, is it the bus that goes to the Mission?" I asked to cover my blindness. The Mission was near Chinatown. With me captured, The Agency might have left the area. Maybe Tianshi could help me.

"The Mission? You're in L.A., man."

My face slackened again, this time from shock. I couldn't wrap my head around being back in L.A. This was worse than I'd realized. They'd brought me back to where it all started.

"What's wrong with your eyes?" His voice grew closer. "Damn, did you have a blowout? Your lenses are like headlights."

I swiveled my head away to try to avoid his gaze. He was endangering both of us.

"I heard that could happen but never believed it," he went on. "You can't see shit, can you? No wonder you were flailing. You almost plowed into my stand. I got watches, sunglasses, all kinds of good stuff for sale. You wouldn't be looking for a present for someone, would you?"

"No." I started to walk in the direction I thought the sidewalk led, lifting my arms after a couple of steps.

"The bus is comin'. You sure you don't want it?"

I stopped. "Yes. Which way…?"

"Here." He led me by the sound of his voice. When I got near, he said, "You look familiar. Wait, you're that rebel, Dray Quintero. No *way*. I looked you up."

He shouldn't have recognized me. Then it hit me. The Agency must've reversed what the plastibots did to my face. Of course. They would've wanted to stream the old me walking off that building, the one people knew.

I needed to run. Hide.

The guy sounded more fascinated than worried. "They say you're dangerous. Seem helpless to me."

"I don't want trouble."

The bus's transmission whined as the vehicle slowed.

Something brushed my hand, which startled me.

"Take this. For the bus." He pushed a currency card into my palm. "I got no love for cops."

"Thank you. Really."

I rubbed the paper card, my fingertips grazing its tiny chip. I had no idea how many credits he'd given me. Even though he'd helped me, L.A. felt dangerous. Perilous. I didn't know what part of town I was in or where to go.

Despair took hold. I had no idea how I'd get around as a blind man. I doubted I'd last a day.

The bus disturbed the air as it rolled past me and stopped, its doors opening with a hiss. Sliding a hand along its side to guide me, I found the entrance and climbed inside.

I fumbled to find the machine to deposit the currency card; when I did, it sucked the card in and kept it. A pleasant, mechanical voice welcomed me, so I turned and took a few tentative steps down the center walkway. I tried to imagine the bus's layout but didn't know how the seats were laid out or how full it was.

Risking another couple of steps, I tried to gauge whether I passed an empty seat but couldn't. I heard a few low voices, but either the bus barely had any passengers, or the others were quiet.

I held my hands before me and continued deeper. The bus started forward, which threw off my balance. I lurched, reaching blindly, and almost fell into an empty seat. I sat and closed my eyes.

My relief was fleeting. The white light screamed at me. No matter where I looked, what I did, I couldn't escape it. The only way was to remove the implant, block it maybe. My skin was tender where the implant touched the side of my head. I feared I knew why the edges were rough.

I wasn't going to go home. No point. I could only come up with one option: Sanchen. If I could convince him I wasn't a criminal, get him to listen long enough to tell him about the implants and the senator, he might help.

The bus rattled as it drove over bumps and potholes, its under-lubricated joints squeaking, punctuated by the tin shrill of brakes as it approached the next stop. This added to the other sounds that tapped at me — the murmur of people and the hum of traffic. L.A.'s buses were old, retrofitted with solar panels and software to run by themselves.

I hid my face as passengers boarded the bus. I felt a greater affinity for society than ever before. We were all blind. Only, I was aware I couldn't see. I had the urge to yell at everyone that they were being lied to. I resisted, though. It'd bring attention I couldn't afford.

My vision suddenly cleared, the white light parting. I nearly cried with joy. The bus was mostly as I had envisioned, less full than I'd feared, with only about a dozen people scattered about. I was in a seat a third of the way back, in the first forward-facing row.

I gazed at the people who got on the bus. Past a smaller, heavyset woman and a teenager with a curly mop was Kieran, impeccably dressed.

I needed to run, but the bus was already moving.

He sat in the chair perpendicular to mine. Confident. Arrogant. "I'm impressed you got this far."

Heat flashed through my body. "Too bad you didn't die in that forest." My hands curled into fists.

"It's a shame you figured out the rooftop. It would've been so much cleaner."

"I have a score to settle first."

"You know I can't let you live," he said, which caused a nearby passenger to look at us. "You've learned too much."

"There are witnesses here, not to mention the bus's camera and however many others we've passed. You'll be caught."

"By who, your detective friend? He was killed last night."

"You bastard."

I glanced at the passenger, an older man with glasses and sideburns. I wanted to warn him, warn everyone, about who Kieran was — what he was—but that would endanger them.

"They can't see me," Kieran said. "I've wiped myself from their vision. To them, you're talking to yourself in two different voices. When you're found dead, everyone will think you took your own life, the same narrative we planned."

I swung at him, hitting him in the jaw, but he blocked the second shot and twisted my arm nearly to the breaking point. He stood and dragged me toward the door as the bus pulled over. I couldn't break his grip.

He pulled me off the bus. We stepped onto a sidewalk between two stucco buildings. Palm trees arched along the street, and more trees lined a path that led between the buildings to a rear parking lot. Past the lot was the interstate, probably the 10, a chain-link fence between the highway and lot.

The bus drove off. No one looked out the windows at us.

The area appeared deserted, but that didn't deter me. "Help," I yelled.

"Don't bother. You've been erased from existence. That's power you could never defeat. It's too bad you didn't join us. Waste of talent."

"You're going to kill me over hoverbikes?"

"It's not just the bikes. I wanted your reactor, Dray. It's the biggest achievement of the century—and it'll insure our images are never cut off. When I heard your name the night it lit, I wanted you to join us. You could've created so much more. At least we have the reactor. It'll guaranty our control for generations."

He let go, but I wanted to strangle him, not run. "Even if you kill me, there'll be others."

"You know why the promise of enhanced humans was never realized? The gene modifications, the 'designer bodies'? We kept the technology for ourselves. We truly are better than you. My employers have modified us, our children, and their own, who will eventually take their places. It'll be the smart, strong, and powerful against the rest of society. You can't stop it. Nor can your friends. You're going to die, and tonight, so will they. I know about their plans. They'll be finished by morning, just like you."

I launched myself at him, and my vision turned blinding-white. I missed him and stumbled, but as I turned back, a fist hit the side of my face, driving me to the side. Kieran grabbed me and pulled me close. I heard the snick of a knife right before pain—sickening, searing pain—erupted in my stomach. I grabbed his hand, which held a knife. He pulled it out, and I collapsed to the ground, holding the wound he'd created.

He dropped the knife at my feet. "Don't bother yelling. No one sees you."

His footsteps faded.

A panic deeper than I'd ever experienced struck me. I was alone, invisible, dying in broad daylight, the only sound the dull roar of traffic as my blood seeped through my fingers.

CHAPTER FORTY-THREE

Lying on the walkway between the two buildings, waves of heat rolled through me as I struggled to understand. Kieran didn't need me anymore. He had the hoverbikes. And with his obvious partnership with Nikolai, the fusion reactor.

I'd deluded myself. Nikolai had stolen my bike technology, and he would replicate the fusion reactor throughout the country—not to give everyone cheap, reliable energy, but to ensure the government's control.

No wonder my company had been able to secure so much dark matter.

I was as naïve as Mina. Her delusion had killed Talia. Mine was going to kill me, doom Raven, and keep everyone else imprisoned.

Thinking about Talia magnified my pain. I'd failed her. Kieran was right. I had failed both of my daughters.

I'd been blind a long time. My marriage. My company. My grief over Adem's death, which had driven me to obsess over making sure I never lost another. I'd been blind to everything else—and to my belief in authority, as if doctors, nurses, cops could fix anything. It had seemed that way when I was young, after those police officers cleaned up my mess. Since then, they could do no wrong. Or so I'd believed.

My abdomen burned. A final price to pay, my reluctance to fight my heroes—I hadn't battled the police directly, only Kieran and The Agency—leading me to my end while Raven walked into a trap.

I'd had such faith in the authorities, in the technology of this age. We all had. Except her. She'd raised her voice. Hell, the only person I'd told was the doctor who'd operated on her, and only because she'd been in the room.

Nystrom, that was her name.

My body went cold, but not from the wound.

303

Nystrom.

My mind began to race, but one thing tempered my thoughts: if I got up, I'd have to leave my beliefs behind. This wasn't just about mine. It never had been.

Cole was almost certainly dead. He wouldn't have let me get captured, which meant his agreement to keep Raven from tonight's assault wouldn't be honored. Even so, I couldn't focus on her, or I'd fail again.

I pressed against my stomach to try to staunch the blood and rose to my knees, then to my feet, the pain like ion blades deep inside of me. Holding my stomach, I started toward the sounds of the highway. I stumbled off the curb, my wound flaring as I took a few quick steps to catch my balance, then continued across the empty lot.

There was an onramp near the parking lot. A slim chance.

The whoosh of highway traffic grew louder, punctuated by an occasional combustible engine. I found the far side of the lot, then the fence. It was stable enough that it held my weight as I climbed, though my wound felt like it ripped wider as I reached upward, careful to secure each toehold in the links before I shifted my other foot.

My energy was leaving me.

I reached for the next section and found air. I'd made it to the top. I swung a leg around to climb down the other side but moved too quickly, became dizzy, and fell. I landed hard.

Calling on the last of my strength, I picked myself up. The dizziness remained, and my sense of touch dulled as I pressed my fingers to my wound.

Cars whizzed past, only feet from me. The white light from my lenses blocked everything. I wouldn't see what came at me.

I felt the gravel under my shoes as I walked forward, though I hesitated when I reached the shoulder, aware the drivers were as blind to me as I was to them.

I shuffled forward, raised a bloody hand, and stepped onto the highway.

I heard as well as felt a car shoot past in the next lane, then a second. I yelled at whoever was coming at me in my lane, even though it was pointless, my heart pounding. Brakes wailed and grew loud, heading straight for me. I vowed not to pass out, kept my fist raised.

The car stopped, and a door opened. "Holy shit, where'd you come from?" The driver sounded young.

"Help me," I said.

"You came outta nowhere." The other door opened and someone else got out. "You hurt? We didn't hit you, did we?"

A woman spoke, also young. "Here, sit." Soft hands moved me to rest against the hood of the car. Behind me, cars braked, horns honked.

"Call an ambulance," I said. My voice was feeble. "I was stabbed."

The guy got on his phone, his words rushed.

His car's anti-collision sensor had spotted me in time and braked hard enough to avoid hitting me. As I'd hoped, the sensor was independent of whatever program Kieran had used to wipe me from everyone's vision. It reacted to my presence, and once that happened, his software had to let them see me. To run their lie, they had to avoid conflicts in logic. Keeping me hidden after I triggered the car's sensor risked unwanted questions, and might have violated logic parameters that their software wouldn't be able to reconcile.

More drivers came over.

I felt an outpouring of affection and community as hands moved me gently to the curb. Reassuring words caressed me. I acted dumb when they asked about my eyes. I didn't want to endanger them any more than I already had. I held onto my stomach, the pain spreading, and kept my head down, hoping for their sake they wouldn't recognize me.

The wind picked up, and a series of whooshes grew to a roar, the wind pummeling us as metal feet touched down. It had to be an ambulance capsule, a type of hybrid helicopter-drone emergency vehicle. Luckily, Los Angeles hadn't converted to all-robotic transports like other cities had.

Men approached, lifted me onto a portable transport, and started for the capsule. "Wait," I yelled over the sound. "Where's the woman from the car?"

She took my hand. "I'm here."

"The paramedics. What color is their hair?"

"Brown, both of them. Why?"

I thanked her and let them put me in the capsule. As they strapped me in, I said, "Take me to Whittier Medical Center."

"That's farther away," one said.

"I have to go there."

* * *

When we touched down, I shielded my face, even though I was certain The Agency knew where I was. The paramedics wheeled me inside and down a hallway to a room filled with voices and the smell of antiseptic. I kept my face hidden as men and women moved about me.

"Sir, you need to let us help you," someone said.

"I need Dr. Nystrom."

"I'll take care of you. My name—"

"I insist." My voice faded at the end. I forced more out. "It has to be her."

Their voices dropped. I could imagine them huddling. I kept my eyes shut so the staff couldn't see my lenses, as they would generate more scrutiny. Hands tried to gently roll me over, but I resisted, though it caused more pain.

It was a gamble. I didn't know Nystrom other than from the time in the ICU, the one visit to her office, and the E.R. encounter. But she hadn't turned Raven in when she'd refused her implants, hadn't alerted the cops when I begged her to remove all of ours.

Finally, the person who addressed me said, "The nurse is getting her." Someone started an IV, but other than that, they left me alone. Most of the room cleared out other than what sounded like a nurse or two. I remained curled on my side.

I heard her enter. "I understand you asked for me?"

I waited until she approached my bed, then uncovered my face.

"Mr. Quintero?" she asked in surprise. "What'd they do to you?"

"We need to talk in private."

"Whatever it is—"

Heat flashed through me, the same heat that had been growing in my belly. It stole her words and control over my body. I could no longer sense, touch, or smell anything, the white light fading. I was vaguely aware I was seizing, my back arching.

Alarms blared and people shouted, but the sounds faded with the light.

* * *

The blinding light from my lenses was the first thing I noticed, followed by the steady beep from a monitor. I must have passed out. The realization snapped me awake.

"Dr. Nystrom?"

306

"I'm here," she said quietly. "Don't move. I'm finishing up."

I couldn't feel what she was doing. "How long was I out?"

"Almost an hour. You went into septic shock."

I struggled to sit up. "We need—"

"Stop." She held a hand to my chest. "I injected bacterial gel into your cavity to encapsulate the refuse that leaked from your bowels, then sutured them. Now I'm sealing your wound. You need to take it easy the next few days. You're at risk for a staph infection."

"I don't have time. None of us do." I lowered my voice. "Are we alone?"

"For now. What happened? You have ambulatory nanobots in your bloodstream, a lot of them. They're nearly worn out. And your lenses are at full power, no variation in color or intensity."

"I've become an enemy of the state. They tried to assassinate me."

She paused, whether from my statement or some other reason, I couldn't tell. "They almost succeeded. The nanobots saved you. They're programmed to respond to coagulants any time they detect them, following them to whatever injuries a person has. Your small bowel was sliced in three places. You should've been dead in minutes."

"I need my implant out."

"Mr. Quintero—"

"Raven needs my help. She's going to be captured tonight—or killed."

"It's against the law to remove it. Besides, you need to rest. Your body is already working overtime to heal from your injuries. You need a day or two at least."

"Look at what they're doing to my eyes. They're blinding me."

She was quiet.

I told her about the lies we'd been told, of how Mina had been fooled, Talia killed, Raven now with the rebels. "They killed my youngest. Don't let them take Raven, too."

"You know what you're asking?"

"I have nowhere else to turn."

I couldn't see her face; the whiteness robbed me of any ability to gauge whether she'd betray me.

I sensed more than felt her working on my abdomen, which had been numbed. "You're not going to stop, are you?" she asked.

"I can't."

She squirted something, tugged on my skin, then set instruments on a tray. After a moment, she raised the side rail on my bed, then released the brake and pushed me forward. I stayed quiet as she maneuvered me out of the room, down a corridor, and into another room. Seconds later, she parked my bed.

Only then did she speak, leaning close to my ear. "I remember what that Agent did to her." I heard her open cabinet doors and search a couple of drawers. She returned to my side. "We're in the calibration room. This device should remove your implant without damaging your ring."

She gently pushed my head to the side so my implant stuck up. Her breath caught.

"What's wrong?" I asked.

"It's welded in place."

I'd feared it ever since I'd felt the rough edges. "They would've used solder. It just needs to be reheated. It's actually a fairly-low temperature —"

"Even if I did, solder could've seeped into the ring's threads. I wouldn't be able to heat all of it."

"There has to be something you can do."

I heard more rustling, followed by a light hum. "I'm using a handheld scanner to check your skull," she explained. After a moment, she said, "Three metal rods extend from the ring into your cranium. They braced the implant in place. It'd take major surgery to even attempt to remove it."

My earlier despair returned. Kieran hadn't had to arrest me. He'd rendered me helpless with a new implant and a few keystrokes. First Talia, then Raven. Their safety was the only thing I'd wanted.

"Maybe we can hide you," Nystrom said. "We can talk to the police. I know a couple of good ones, ones we can trust."

"Even if I wanted to, their resources are linked to our enemies. We would play right into The Agency's hands."

"That's a grim assessment."

If I'd had one of the rebel's caps, I could block my feed, but I didn't; nor did I have any material to try to make one. But there could be another way.

I sat up. "We need to do something unexpected. Burn a hole in my eyes."

CHAPTER FORTY-FOUR

I couldn't see anything past the light that blanketed my vision, but I could imagine her expression.

"No," she said. "Hurting someone wasn't why I became a doctor."

I wanted to grab her arm—anxious we were wasting time, aware her eyes were broadcasting my image, and God knew how many people recorded me when I was brought in—but didn't. Couldn't. Instead, I said, "The senator is what scares me the most. Even if we expose her, force a new election, it won't be enough. The people behind this will just replace whoever's elected with one of their own. One senator couldn't have done this by herself. It had to be a group of people who started this until they'd either recruited or replaced all of Congress—and the president."

"They'd retain control." Her voice was thin.

"For generations to come. The rebels are our only chance, but they're walking into a slaughter. What time is it?"

"Six forty."

"We have two hours. Maybe less. They're attacking at nightfall."

"A part of me wishes I'd never met you."

"I took the scales from your eyes, Dr. Nystrom. Remove mine."

"Call me Anya. I don't want to be reminded I'm a doctor."

"You'll need to be fast. The Agency may already be on their way."

She didn't respond. I didn't know if I'd lost her.

She moved, her clothes rustling, and opened a drawer. When she returned, she touched my cheek. "I found a laser pen, but it was designed to cauterize. I could burn your retina. Your sight could be permanently scarred."

"I trust you."

She leaned close, her breath on my face as she sighed. "Don't move."

There was a light hum. Among the white light that consumed my vision, a brighter light appeared in my left eye, a round spot like the burning sun. It grew bigger, the edge arching in a circle, and seared away the solid-white light. My instincts shouted a warning. The spot seemed like a fire that would consume my eye and leave a trail of darkness in its path.

It stopped and, as my vision adjusted, I saw Anya through the spot that had flared. "Well?" she asked.

The hole was small and rough, not every pixel burned away, but through it I rejoined the world, which seemed dim among the intense light that continued to assault the rest of my vision. She filled most of what I could see, her blonde hair tucked over one shoulder, her forehead creased with concern. "You're beautiful," I blurted, not sure if it was my relief or her looks that made me say it.

She blushed. "I need to check your retina for damage."

"No time. We have to go."

She backed away as I slid my legs off the bed and stood. I saw the room for the first time: monitoring equipment and surgical-instrumentation machines nearby, glass-doored supply cabinets against the wall, a white-sheathed safe that I suspected contained implant devices in the corner.

Anya watched me uncertainly. "I can't leave. The next shift doesn't come until eight."

"They saw what you did. You're part of this now."

"I shouldn't have helped you."

But I knew she didn't mean it.

"You have a car?" I asked. The handheld scanner she'd used rested on a tray along with a scalpel, forceps, and the laser pen. I took the scanner, along with medical tape and two surgical caps. I didn't bother to take the scalpel. They had guns.

"Adding theft to your crimes?" she asked.

"Try not to look at me. They'll track everyone's feeds to find me."

"That's paranoid." Next to the door was a nanobot dispensary. She took an auto-syringe, motioned for me to lift my shirt, and injected me with more medical 'bots. She grabbed an extra. "Just in case."

"Grab all of 'em."

She did, putting the three full syringes in her lab coat.

We left and snuck down the hallway, away from the hustle of the

E.R. Acutely aware of how vulnerable we were, I scanned the corridor with my limited sight as we moved. She checked the corner before we stepped into the adjoining hallway and hurried to the elevator that led to the parking garage. As we waited for the elevator to arrive, I went to the nearby window.

The city spread to the north and east, most of it visible from our fourth-floor vantage point, including my old office building. Blue glass and silver trim gleamed in the late afternoon sunlight as the building twisted toward the sky.

Nikolai had been in bed with the government, maybe since the beginning.

I leaned against the side of the glass and peered as far to the east as possible. Hacienda Hill hid the fusion reactor from view, but I could see the edge of the facility where Raven had been attacked. It was basically on the opposite side of the Hill. I hadn't realized how close Hoyt Enterprises was to our reactor. I'd never looked at a map after that terrible night.

It wasn't a coincidence. I hadn't stopped to think about how the government planned to protect and extend their lies. Nikolai had selected the fusion plant's location for more than just the city's protection from a potential blast.

I had an idea where the central communication hub was that Cole had talked about.

The elevator arrived. As we descended, I explained the hub to Anya. "I bet it's located equidistant from the four treatment plants. Maybe at an angle, but still." Their broadcasts would exist in perfect synchronicity to perpetuate their lies.

"You're not going to do something stupid, are you? Remember, you were stabbed."

I remembered vividly. I also remembered how I got there. The guy at the burner store who'd sacrificed. As had the freedom fighters — and still were. Jex. Raven.

The elevator doors opened onto a parking garage.

I urged Anya to move quickly. "Which one's yours?"

Seconds later we were in her car, a white luxury coupe. I hid my face from the garage's multiple cameras as she backed out of the space and headed toward the exit, although it was probably too late. "The hub will be heavily guarded. It'd be easier to cut its power supply."

"That sounds safer," she said as she drove down the exit ramp.

"They'd anticipate that, though, bury the power lines to hide them." Just like they buried cables in the sewer drains. "The reactor itself should be shut down, but that's too risky. The fusion core is designed to burn for decades, a self-perpetuating energy source. There's only one thing to do."

I wanted to go the other way, to the desalinization plants to rescue Raven. But that would continue what I'd been doing: abandoning everyone else for her. Even taking out The Agency's drones in Chinatown had been to protect her. She was all I had left, all I cared about.

Though it pained me, I had to make the smart choice. If I did, I'd be more than the person she wanted me to be. I'd be emulating her. As she grew up, I'd seen myself in her. I hoped when she looked back on this, she'd see herself in me.

Turning to Anya, I silently apologized to Raven, even though she would've wanted me to do this. Maybe would've been proud. "We take out the hub."

"You said it's heavily guarded."

I saw as well as felt the datarings I still wore. "We're going to need muscle."

"Meaning what?"

"Meaning I know where to go."

* * *

As Anya drove toward downtown, I focused on the handheld scanner. The device was about a foot long with a thick handle attached to a wide, curved head. The handle's plastic cover felt solid, but I knew better. Digging my thumbs against what would be the weak spot if I'd designed it, I pushed—and the bioplastic cracked open.

"What are you doing?" she asked.

"Something illegal. Don't look." As I expected, the energy emitter was in the handle; the swivel head merely focused the output. Layers of material encased the emitter to shield the user from stray energy, with metal threads woven in the same pattern as the metal grid in Tiashi's ceiling.

I worked the material free and touched it to my implant. The white light winked out, and the world returned in all of its full, dangerous, vivid glory. Not just a tiny spot, but across my entire vision.

312

I could've moaned in relief. Instead, I lowered the material—letting the white light return—and tried to separate the material into two pieces using the tiny, imperfect spot of vision Anya had burned to see what I was doing. It didn't tear, so I opened Anya's glovebox. "You have scissors?"

She handed me a pair of medical scissors she had in her lab coat. "We're here."

My former office building rose before us. "Park over there."

I gathered the material, surgical caps, scissors, and tape as she pulled into an empty space fifteen yards from the building. The dock entrance was almost straight ahead, both entrance and exit open, but gated and manned. A smaller door stood ten feet from the dock entrance, a side entrance I'd thought was a waste, but that Nikolai had insisted on.

"Mr. Quintero, I don't know how much help I'll be."

"Call me Dray." I got out and she followed, though she paused to take off her lab coat and leave it in the car. She wore a dark blouse that went well with her slacks.

"Your wife really betrayed you?" she blurted as we walked toward the structure.

I nodded. "They used her delusion against her."

"She must've suffered terribly."

The sky darkened as the sun set in the distance.

We reached the unmarked side door, which had both a keypad and scanner. I didn't use my code to get in—not sure if Kieran's earlier wizardry had restored it—but stepped up to the scanner instead and briefly covered my implant to expose my retinas. A beep told me the software still recognized me as Nikolai, my earlier hack undiscovered. I was amazed he'd forgotten I wrote the security software when we constructed the building. Had he been working with the government even then?

I ushered Anya inside.

As I led her down the cinderblock hallway, I slid my datarings down my fingers to let them scan my prints, then slid them back up. The rings connected to the building's internal network, but I could only see flickers of data, the information a slight variation of the white light that blinded me.

I took the rings off and handed them to her. "I need you to use

313

these," I whispered. "They're keyed to the operating system of a new class of robots. You need to guide two of them down here."

Her whisper was louder. "Robots? Are you serious?"

"I'll walk you through it."

She gave a you're-shitting-me look as she put on the rings. I imagined the data that appeared in her vision and walked her through the access points. In a few seconds, she controlled two of the machines.

"Send them to the freight elevator."

As she sent the commands, I steered her along the hallway to the large dock area, where the overhead lights had been dimmed this time of night. Two semis were parked to the left side of the large space, and three parcel-delivery-size trucks stood in a row straight ahead, along the far side, with a forklift and pallets of materials spaced toward the back. Two guards manned the entrance booth, though with the onset of evening, they'd be relaxed.

They wouldn't be once the building's systems alerted them to my presence.

"Ready?" I whispered.

"What do I do if someone gets in the way?"

I didn't know if she meant the robots or us. Either way, the answer was the same. "Don't stop."

She gave me another look, then refocused on the robots.

I needed to keep us moving. With the overhead lights dimmed, though, I could barely see through the hole she'd made due to the light blasting my retinas. I wanted to strap the signal-blocking material to my head, but I'd look suspicious. I needed to pretend I still worked here.

I put my arm around her waist and led her into the dock area.

She kept her hands up as we walked into the open, using the feed from the robots' cameras to steer them, more focused on them than our surroundings. As for me, I strained to see in the darkness as I maneuvered her across the wide area. I had no idea if the guards noticed us but gave a wave just in case. I moved us between the first two delivery trucks to block us from the guards' view, although we couldn't hide from the cameras overhead.

Quickening my pace, I dragged her to the driver's door of the lead truck, which was emblazoned with our company logo. It was unlocked, but when I climbed in, I stopped. The rear was loaded with boxes.

I got out and led her to the second truck. It was also loaded, the boxes nearly spilling into the driver's cab. The third, though, was empty, its rear door rolled up in anticipation of being filled.

"They're in the elevator," she said.

"Send them down. Have one of them press the button for the first floor." I reached under the steering wheel and fished at the wires.

"My god, what kind of robots are these?"

She must've seen the blade that served as the robot's finger when it pressed the elevator button. "I need you to drive." Remembering how Jex had hotwired the last car we stole, I separated the wires I needed and started the engine, then straightened. "I'll take the robots. Set commands to hand-gesture."

She did, then handed over my datarings. I held on as she put the truck in gear and reversed toward the freight elevator. As she slowed, the freight doors opened to reveal the two digger robots she'd summoned. I directed them forward, off the loading ledge and toward our truck. Anya stopped and gasped when she saw the eight-foot-tall, dagger-fingered robots. Following my commands, the lead robot ducked its head and climbed into the back, its weight causing the truck to tilt. I beckoned it toward me, its hydraulics quiet as it loomed close, then waved for it to stop. After it did, I directed the second robot in behind it. After they were in, I slipped past them, grabbed the rear door, and rolled it down. "Go."

She aimed for the exit. "What do we do about the gate?"

I made it to the front in time to see the guards' casual manner turn business-like as we approached. "Gun it."

"I should've stayed at work." She floored the engine.

The guards shouted at us to stop, but Anya crashed through the exit gate, sending the arm flying, and drove out of the complex.

I gave her directions where to go, then said, "Uh, I need to get under there." She nodded, and I slid under the steering wheel, aware my back touched her leg. I found my company's GPS chip and unplugged it, then searched for the truck manufacturer's GPS box. As soon as I located it, I yanked out the wires, severing its power. I extracted myself and sat in the passenger seat.

She gave me a nervous grin, which I returned before I removed the scissors and supplies from my pocket. It took longer than normal with my limited sight. Even so, I was glad the rebels had shown me about the caps. I would've gone insane from the white light.

Using way more tape than I needed, I stuck the material to the inside of one of the blue surgical caps, put it on my head, and tied it in the back. As soon as I covered my implant with the material, the light from my lenses winked out.

Able to fully see, I quickly assembled the other cap and put it on Anya's head. "Can you access any outside content?"

She shook her head. "What did you do?"

"Blocked your connection. You don't have to worry about where you look now."

"Your eyes are normal."

"For now. I'll have to take off my cap to use the robots."

"Use them for what?"

"To end this."

CHAPTER FORTY-FIVE

The sun had set by the time we arrived at the Hoyt Enterprises facility. Raven and the other rebels would attack the desalinization plants at any moment. We had to move fast.

I was certain this was the right place. Trever might've known the truth all along: not just about his parents' involvement and the lie about the implants, but about the building on the hilltop next door.

Anya and I eyed the spot where I'd snuck into his parents' facility what felt like a lifetime ago. The hole in the ten-foot-high wall had been boarded up and sealed. We needed another way in.

The hilltop building wasn't visible from where we idled, but I knew it was there. We drove farther down the empty street, past silent houses on the right and the wall to our left, before Anya pulled over.

The wall continued in either direction, an imposing structure I knew was fortified and probably unbreachable. Which was why I'd brought the diggers.

I removed my cap, flinching as the white light burst forth, and activated the robots. Following my commands, they exited the truck, making it rock, and joined Anya and me on the side of the road. The first one bent down. I climbed up to its shoulder, a hand on its head to steady myself, covered my implant to cut off the light, and gazed over the wall.

To my left was the Hoyts' facility.

As my eyes adjusted to the darkness, I made out the cluster of buildings from that fateful night. To the right, the structure that I suspected housed the communication hub was visible. The area appeared to be abandoned, fenced off and topped with a small building that was dark. I couldn't see any antennas or broadcast dishes, but there wouldn't be. They'd rely on cables, not airwaves.

The barrier that separated the hill from Trever's family's business stood almost directly in front of me, dividing the view on the other side of the perimeter wall.

I knew where to dig. I didn't know what awaited us, though. The Agency wouldn't just depend on the absence of light to keep their secret. Objects stuck out of the ground past either corner of the dark building, what looked like small obelisks. They concerned me, but I couldn't turn back.

I climbed down. "Stay here. I don't want you to get hurt."

"What did you see?"

"Not much—which is what worries me."

Pushing my cap off my implant, I linked with the robots again and steered them to a spot along the exterior wall, then set the first one into motion. With a violence that surprised me, the robot began to dig, the sound splitting the night, churning and digging as motors whirled and blades clacked. In seconds, the digger dropped three feet into the ground. Dirt continued to fly to either side as it dug deeper, curved under the wall, then up and out the other side. When it was through, the second digger crawled through the hole and disappeared.

I covered my implant and crawled into the four-foot-wide hole, under the wall, and up the other side. As I got out, Anya appeared and motioned for me to help. I would've argued but didn't bother. When we got to our feet, we gazed up the hill to the dark building. Nothing moved, nothing changed.

Kieran would have most if not all of his resources at the desalinization plants to fight the Founding Fathers, to ensure the rebels didn't succeed. Still, I didn't trust it.

"Stay here," I told her. "If this goes south, run away and don't look back."

She nodded, and I pulled off my cap.

As my eyes adjusted to the brilliant light, I directed one of the robots to follow the fence that ran between the hub and Trever's family's facility. After a hundred feet, I rotated my left hand. The robot turned to the right in response and started up the hill.

Then I directed the one in front of me to move, sending it in a straight line for the top, and followed. I had to jog to keep up. The robot was top-heavy, but its thick legs churned, the torso bent forward, arms lifted off the ground.

Motorized sounds came from the hilltop.

As I jogged, I angled to the side and looked past the robot. Two of the obelisks at the top of the hill began to unfold: the one directly ahead, and the one that the other robot was charging toward. The obelisks rose, weapons jutting out as they unfolded, thick machine gun turrets ringed with heat-and-motion sensors — automated sentries, heavily armed.

I ducked behind my robot, and the obelisks opened fire.

Bullets lanced the air as their weapons chugged. My robot sparked as it was struck repeatedly, bullets piercing its armor and damaging its gears. The robot continued forward but jerked, the gunfire constant. We'd barely made it halfway to the top. To my left, sparks lit up the other robot as it was hit. I commanded it to drop to its hands and knees to give it a lower profile, did the same to my robot, and dropped as well.

The gunfire intensified.

Risking a glance, I spotted a third sentry, this one to the right of us, gunfire spitting from it. The obelisk sentries were stationary, but from their placement, they could defend the entire hill.

My robot stumbled from the onslaught. Its right arm hung useless, shredded. The robot couldn't crawl forward effectively. I had it stand to continue, my hand on its lower back, but with a grinding sound and whiff of hydraulic fluid, it fell to its knees, bullets sparking, and dropped forward.

I ducked behind it again, using its metal body as a shield. Bullets flew within inches of my head, the *wuup wuup* of their travel assaulting my ears. I was pinned. Couldn't move forward, couldn't retreat. I thought Anya yelled from below but probably imagined it.

There was one chance. Grasping at the idea, I steered the other robot toward me, forcing it to run as fast as it could. The sounds of gunfire to my left changed as the sentinel swiveled to chase it. I didn't dare lift my head to confirm the robot was nearing. Didn't need to. The robot bounded toward me, chased by streams of bullets. I steered it poorly in my prone and partly-blinded position, though, which caused it to miss me by twenty feet. I angled it toward me and sent a stream of commands.

The robot churned, kicking up clumps of grass, and leapt over me. When it landed, I had it reach down and grab the sparking remains of the robot I hid behind. It then straightened and charged up the hill, using the disabled robot as a shield. The sentinels fired at it from three sides, but I drove the robot onwards, not slowing. It would only last a short time from the onslaught. Already, one of the legs of the disabled robot had fallen off, severed by gunfire, the appendage rolling down the hill toward me.

I pushed the remaining robot faster. If it failed, the gunfire would turn on me — and I didn't have cover.

The robot was ten feet away. Five. Responding to my command, it leapt forward and crashed into the closest sentinel. The robot's weight and momentum knocked the motorized sentry to the ground, disabling it.

I had the robot stand, throw the torso at the sentry to the left, the robot's sensors enabling it to hit the weapon-bristling obelisk even from the forty-foot distance, then pick up the first sentry it knocked down. Using the defunct device as a shield, it ran to the other sentry and took it out as well.

Silence returned.

I let out a sigh. It wasn't over, though.

I stood and climbed to the top of the hill. In the moonlight, I inspected the digger that had survived. It was still functional, but it no longer had the strength to dig deep enough to get to the cables. I'd planned to have the robots sever every cable that snaked out of this place, to cut off the government's broadcast, but one of the robot's hands was mangled, with three of its digger claws missing. The other was functional, with only one claw damaged, but it wasn't enough. Even if I found the power cables, it'd take the robot too long to dig down and sever them.

I'd have to do this another way.

I stood next to the porch-like entryway of the building, which was about the size of a large ranch house, although it wasn't a house as far as I could tell. There weren't any windows, just a door, which was locked. One more thing for the robot to do. Using its strength, I had it break the lock. The door nearly flew off its hinges as it swung open. I tensed as the sound echoed throughout the building.

Someone approached behind me. I spun — but it was Anya. "You OK?" she whispered.

With a nod, I put my cap back on to clear my vision and faced the entrance. The building, like the hillside, appeared to be abandoned.

"Stay behind me."

We entered the broadcast hub.

The building was essentially one large room housing the equipment that stored data, disseminated it, and ensured it synched perfectly. Datatanks, each one able to store a year's worth of data generated planet-wide, were spaced in rows on either side of the main room, ten to a side. The room below us—visible as the floor consisted of metal grating—held massive servers, over twenty of them, each processing terabytes of information every second to perpetuate the government's lies. Cables and pipes dropped past them into the earth, energy drawn in from the fusion reactor and digital lies pushed out to the desalinization plants.

The metal grating enabled the heat generated by the servers to dissipate throughout the building.

An elevated platform stood on the far side of the main level with a large datascreen and a row of smaller ones, all connected to the system. Alarms flashed yellow and red on the various screens, warnings of a breach in their defenses. To the far side was a door that led to one or two other rooms. I took off my datarings, stuck them in my pockets, and headed for the raised platform.

Anya checked the back rooms as I oriented myself with the hub's system. The software was familiar, its layout, file structure, and command keys similar to the one I'd created for the national camera monitoring system. The thought that had plagued me was true: the software they used was mine.

It made sense. The government needed a dynamic communications structure to maintain its lies among the hundreds of millions of implants that moved about the country, able to handle instantaneous changes between towers and locales seamlessly and adapt in real time to rapid transit, interferences that arose, data that conflicted with their images, and any other issues. This system could do that, I knew, because I'd designed the core structure, which they'd modified to their needs. The realization sickened and appalled me—but steeled my resolve as I navigated the massive network.

Anya returned. "There's a storage room and bedroom suite in back." She joined me on the raised platform. "What do you want to do? Shut it all down?"

I was tempted. This system had been woven into the very fabric of our lives. Shutting it down would expose the truth—but it carried risks.

"I have something else in mind. First I need to turn off the goddamn program that's blinding me." I pulled up diagnostic programs and searched for what I needed, aware that Raven could be fighting for her life at this very moment.

"How are you even going to find yourself?" she asked.

The screen showed a scrawling mass of "users," every person in the city, with data going in and out. I pointed at the levels. "With this cap on, I'm not sending out any data, even though the data being sent to me is high—and constant. We find that combination, we find me."

"If someone's output is zero, wouldn't that mean they're sleeping?"

"They'd still broadcast. It'd be different, though, a baseline that would indicate there wasn't a connection issue." I glanced at her. "It's how engineers think."

I scrolled faster. I had to be quick. It was the only way to help Raven, to give her a chance.

A voice cut through the room. "You don't quit."

Kieran.

He stood in the doorway, a weapon of oppression and death. Tingling heat ran from my head to my toes, for he'd caught me actively rebelling, committing treason. All of my actions could've been explained as me protecting my family or trying to survive—until I broke into this place.

I should've barred the door. But even if I had, even with his damaged arm in a black sleeve, he would've been able to get inside.

My heart pounded as I looked for a weapon.

"I watched you steal those robots," he said. "Clever. You not only defeated our defenses, but faster than I thought possible. You would've made a good Agent."

He sounded like he reluctantly admired me. Didn't matter. He wouldn't let me live.

Off to the side, near the closest datatank, was a section of piping. I bolted out of my chair and scooped it up, but it wasn't even metal. I should've taken one of Anya's scalpels.

"You're being shortsighted, Dray. My employer has been more effective than any police force in history."

"You didn't do this for the greater good."

"We've stopped crime."

"At the expense of people's freedom."

He moved toward me, though he paused when I lifted the pipe like a baseball bat. "We've also stopped terrorism."

"Terrorism is still a threat."

"We let you think that. It focuses the public, gives them something to worry about. The domestic groups have been troublesome, but they'll be gone soon. Just like you."

Jesus, had The Agency let the last few terrorist attacks happen? Did they cause them?

I raised the pipe higher and ran at him across the grated floor.

He brought up his good arm, but I went low, aiming for his knee, the right one this time. The blow knocked the leg out from under him. I spun, brought the pipe around as I stood, and connected with the edge of his jaw as he fell to the ground.

The blow drove him into the grate.

I raised the pipe over my head and brought it down hard.

The pipe struck the grate. He'd rolled out of the way before I could hit him and was already on his feet. I swung the pipe upward, the tip arcing toward his head. At the last possible second, he twisted out of the way. Before I could pull the pipe back, he snatched the end—and squeezed.

The plastic crumpled.

I tried to jerk the pipe free, but he ripped it from my grasp. I stepped back as he came at me, bigger, faster, and stronger than I could ever be. I dropped and punched his left knee, the one I'd injured before. Instead of buckling him, the blow nearly shattered my hand. It was like punching an engine block. He'd had it reinforced.

He backhanded me, nearly knocking me to the ground. I crawled backwards to get some distance, but he followed. "You failed, Dray. Failed your daughters and failed your mission."

"You have no right to talk about them," I said, shaking with rage and exhaustion, afraid he was right, that I hadn't done enough to save Raven, just like I hadn't done enough to save Talia or Adem.

Kieran smiled, and I knew I was doing this wrong. Cole would've taken a different approach.

"You seem worried," I said with bravado. "Afraid you're going to get demoted? Unplugged from all of your—"

He picked me up. "I had such devious plans for you, but to hell with them."

He held me by one arm and cocked his other back to punch me. I was quicker, with a jab to his brow. It wasn't strong—I didn't have the leverage—but I hit him where the sensor had been woven into his brow. He flinched from the pain, and I hacked at the arm that held me.

He let go.

I stumbled when I hit the grate, managed to stay on my feet, but before I could attack, he ripped the surgical cap from my head, removing the material that blocked the signal to my implant. My lenses turned bright white.

"I could've ended this before it began," he said. "All I had to do was watch your damn feed the night of the reactor, but I didn't even think to tune in."

Before I could adjust my vision to see out of the hole Anya had made, he punched my stab wound. The blow rippled through me. It felt like my stitches ripped open.

He picked me up by the neck.

"Don't like the light, huh?" he asked. "How about a different view?"

The white light disappeared, replaced by nighttime, a moving vision. I was looking through someone else's eyes. I glimpsed a pistol in their hand. Shots were fired. There was a dock, buildings, a smattering of return fire. Bodies lay on the ground, three of them, dressed in black.

I couldn't hear the battle, but I did hear Anya curse from the console.

"The slaughter's already begun," Kieran said. "Raven and the rebels are surrounded. You get to watch them die."

I struggled in his grasp, fighting with every ounce of strength, but only managed to snatch a quick breath before he cut off my airway again.

A woman dashed across the broadcasted vision. I wanted to shout a warning, though of course she couldn't hear me. I couldn't help them. I forced myself to ignore the vision and focused on the tiny hole Anya had burned into my lens. I could see her past Kieran's shoulder, hunched over the data screen.

I punched at his arm, but it was like iron, so I kicked him in the groin as hard as I could. His grip lessened, but only for an instant. As

I gasped air, he threw me down, pinned me to the grated floor, and repositioned his hand around my throat. I fought but couldn't budge him. I reached for his eyes but my arms weren't long enough, my fingertips just grazing his face.

I was trapped.

Chapter Forty-Six

Kieran was quiet as he strangled me, his breath rapid for the first time.

I thought my vision darkened but couldn't tell, not with the scene playing on my lenses. I had seconds. A strange ringing grew in my ears, and my fingers began to tingle.

I stopped struggling. He had the strength and the angle. His legs pressed against me as he sensed the end.

That's when I felt them—almost didn't, had forgotten them. My datarings.

I tried to get to them, but Kieran's legs were pinned to my sides. I didn't have the strength to move him. Desperate, I twisted my body and managed to jam my right hand into my front right pocket. Touching my ring, I pulled it out quickly, trying to get it on my finger—

It slipped from my grasp.

The sound was dull. Maybe it was my ears. It bounced, a muted *clink* as it hit the grate. I saw it hit a second time, then slip through the opening and disappear, falling to the floor below.

A readout appeared in my vision on top of the night battle, which was now punctuated with flashes of gunfire, as the dataring's movement was registered as a command. The robot responded, its gears straining as it stood.

Kieran shifted above me as he turned to the door, distracted by the noise. I got a rush of air as he eased up on my neck, and when he turned, he created a gap for my left hand.

I shoved my fingertips into my left pocket, hooked my remaining ring, and worked it onto my middle finger.

He felt me move and looked down, frowning as I removed my hand from my pocket. Before he could put it together, I thrust my arm to the side. My dataring, which was also still synched with the robot, responded. My last hope crashed through the doorway, taking the doorframe and part of the wall with it. It ran forward, coming for us.

For him.

Kieran stiffened. I steered the digger robot toward us and flicked the command to launch. Wires sparking, the robot surged forward, its clawed hands thrust forward, and flashed above me as it crashed into Kieran. They flew past, an engineered boot nearly taking out my chin as the robot crashed to the ground atop Kieran.

I got to my feet.

The scene he'd been broadcasting suddenly winked out. My normal vision returned as if I still had my cap on, although I also had the readout from the robot.

Anya smiled at me. She'd done it.

Kieran scrambled toward me. He'd gotten out from under the robot—I'd been distracted by being able to see again—and had a knife in his hand, similar to the one he'd stabbed me with. I dove to the side, causing him to miss, got to my knees, and commanded the robot to get up. It swiped at Kieran, its blades catching his side. Another command and metal arms wrapped around him, then threw him down. A final command made the robot drop on top of him, capturing him.

Kieran squirmed helplessly as I approached. "I'll kill Raven," he roared. "I'll kill them all."

I had the robot pin his head down with his primary implant—the same one everyone had—facing up. I tapped the implant's curved-metal end. "I bet all of your fancy upgrades run through this." I picked up his knife, which he'd dropped. "Don't move. You know how these things are. Wrong angle, and I could splinter your skull."

I squatted over him, worked the knife under his implant's edge, and pulled. The implant lifted slightly and he roared, but it stayed in place.

"For Raven," I said, and yanked with all of my strength.

His implant popped out of his head, bounced off the robot, and wedged between two slats in the grated floor.

To Anya, I said, "You have those nanobots?"

She tossed one of the syringes she'd taken.

I unscrewed the needle, turned the syringe over, and squeezed the contents into the hole in his head where his implant had been. "Within a day or so, it'll be like you never had a neural net," I told him. "You'll be nothing."

Kieran shouted but couldn't get free, couldn't wipe away the milky liquid I poured into his indentation, the thousands of tiny medical nanobots that got to work. His face turned red, coated with sweat, and he began to hyperventilate. Seconds later, he passed out.

CHAPTER FORTY-SEVEN

With Kieran neutered and unconscious, I went to Anya and hugged her. "How'd you clear my vision?"

"Once I found you, I saw the interference and traced the links to the program that was flooding your lenses. Well, there were two or three other programs running, so I had to do a little trial and error to find which one was The Agency's feed. But don't worry, I turned the others back on."

"Did you see how the signal is picked up from the eyes and where it goes?"

"Yeah. It wasn't that different from searching for anomalies in biodata. You were an anomaly." She smiled. "A good one."

She had a great smile. I grinned in response.

She swiveled back to the control panel. "I'll try to find Raven so you can warn her. You think there's still time?"

"I have another idea. I need a mirror—and I need you to broadcast my feed."

"There's a bathroom next to the bedroom," she said, clearly mystified. "It has a mirror."

"Good. We'll need to broadcast across all spectrums." I pulled up the program she would need and explained what I wanted to do.

She got to work. "OK, I can lock out anyone from interfering once you start," she said as I headed for the bathroom. "The other part will be trickier."

I glanced back. "You can do it."

She put on her cap and gave another smile.

In the bathroom, I stuck a mic to my shirt and faced the mirror. As I'd suspected, my face was battered and bruised but back to normal. Yet there were lines I didn't have before, a result of the heartache and strain and fear of these last few weeks. My family had disintegrated, the lies and discoveries, the risks and betrayals and struggle that led to this day—and to one desperate chance, for that's what this moment was.

I couldn't reach across the city to protect Raven. Not physically. This was the only way. But this was for more than just her. I couldn't let others remain unaware of what we'd learned. They deserved a chance. I hated public speaking, yet here I was. Talia would've loved this. I imagined her beside me, bobbing in excitement. I tried to channel her spirit.

Taking a deep breath, I closed my eyes. Anya gave the signal, and I opened them. My face appeared in my vision. In everyone's.

"Hello," I said. "My name is Dray Quintero."

Across all of Los Angeles, possibly the entire West Coast, everyone saw what I did: my face reflected in the mirror. I'd directed Anya to go small at first, half a person's vision.

"I'm talking to you, with closed-caption for those who aren't able to hear me, because what I have to tell you is important enough for everyone to hear.

"You're being lied to. All of you.

"This isn't a dream or hallucination. For those of you driving or in a position where you could get injured, pull over. Stop what you're doing. You'll need to focus on what I'm about to tell you.

"Your world is a sham. You see how you can't get past my broadcast? I've blinded you—but you've been blinded for years. You just didn't know it."

I knew my face was growing larger in their vision.

"You are seeing me as a result of the cameras in my eyes, which the government installed without my knowledge or consent." I turned my gaze away from the mirror and took in the room, so they could tell I spoke the truth. "They did the same to you. They've taken your freedom. We all thought our implants were to help. They're not. They're to track you.

"To fool you.

"The lenses in our eyes have tiny cameras attached to them which rest in our blind spots. The medical profession was led to believe they were to maintain our perfect vision, but the cameras are to watch us, record us, and enable those in power to manipulate us. They can see everything we do: the things we do when we're alone, what we read and write about, what we desire. Crime is down and access is available without lifting a finger, but it comes with a price. Our freedom."

I tapped the sink, my signal for Anya.

Images began to appear in my lenses, which meant they started to appear in everyone's: a view of someone at home, their male feet up, looking at a fireplace. A second image at a restaurant, the curly-blonde-haired woman across from the viewer clearly stunned, the restaurant nearly frozen behind her. A third of water spraying against a woman's hands as they pressed against a tiled wall.

"Who did this to us?" I asked. "Our leaders: the president, Congress, maybe even our governors and mayors. The men and women who enforce their lies have silver hair."

As I talked, more and more feeds crowded in, covering around my eyes and across my cheeks, the feeds growing smaller to make room for others: kids playing, couples clutching each other, soldiers and businessmen and others unmoving, their lives upended. The images formed a checkered pattern as they filled in my face.

"Those with silver hair are your enemies. The police know about this lie as well. Don't trust them. Why do you think they're able to solve virtually every crime committed? They've watched criminals in the act from their own eyes—just like they watch you."

In a corner I spotted Raven, through what was probably Jex's eyes. She was staring at him in shock and wonder. I thought I recognized where they were: Santa Monica pier, its cacophony of lights darkened this time of night, the pier close to one of the desalinization plants.

"Our leaders have hijacked our country. They won't release their hold. We have to make them," I said, my gaze flickering to the tiny view of her.

She and the other images faded, leaving just my face for all to see.

"Make your future. Fight for it. Take back your country. Take back your life.

"Take what's yours."

Acknowledgements

The creation of *The Price of Safety* was a journey filled with twists and more than a few surprises. While the journey was mostly solo, I couldn't have reached the end without the help of many wonderful, caring, and generous people (a couple of whom are a little twisted themselves).

I want to thank my wife Janelle for encouraging me to take classes at the University of Iowa's Summer Writing Program, for your unwavering support, for your insightful and helpful notes, and for kissing me first. Thank you to Dad and Debby, and to my sister Lisa Rine, for reading my stories and always finding something kind to say. To my nephew Daniel Rine for being the first to see the potential in this story. I love you all very much.

To my other Beta readers: Sarah Greenwell, Nancy Broudo, Rene Alvarez, and Todd Bradel. Thank you for braving the first draft and your feedback. To Jen Brody for your edits, to Tiffany Hawk for your enthusiasm and great suggestions with the first chapter, and to YiShun Lai, Roz Ray, Rachael Warecki, and the other amazing people at Red House Writers for your comments. Also to Cheryl Bostrom and Jackson Smith for your notes and support.

I particularly want to thank my writing brother Robert Kerbeck for your constant support, keen insight, and fantastic notes.

A huge thank you to Adam Rocke for introducing me to World Castle Publishing, for your generosity, and for your stellular guidance. To Dorothy Mason for *The Price of Safety*'s incredible cover. You are truly gifted. To Karen Fuller, Maxine Bringenberg, and everyone at World Castle Publishing, thank you for believing in this story and for your support.

Lastly, I thank you, dear Reader, for taking a chance with a new writer. I truly hope you enjoyed *The Price of Safety* and will continue with me on Dray's journey. The second book is well on its way.

Michael C. Bland

About the Author

Michael is a founding member and the secretary of BookPod, an invitation-only, online group of professional writers. He pens the monthly BookPod newsletter where he celebrates the success of their members, which include award-winning writers, film makers, journalists, and bestselling authors.

One of Michael's short stories, "Elizabeth", won Honorable Mention in Writer's Digest 2015 Popular Fiction Awards contest. Three of the short stories he edited have been nominated for the Pushcart Prize. Another story he edited was adapted into an award-winning film.

He also had three superhero-themed poems published on *The Daily Palette*.

Michael currently lives in Denver with his wife Janelle and their dog Nobu.

His novel, *The Price of Safety*, is the first in a planned trilogy.

CPSIA information can be obtained
at www.ICGtesting.com
Printed in the USA
LVHW110925050520
654560LV00007BA/67/J